SALVATION, BOOK 2

HAUNTED

K.C. WELLS

Title: Haunted (Salvation #2)
First Edition
Copyright © 2023 by K.C. Wells
All rights reserved.

Editor: Sue Laybourn
Cover art: Meredith Russell
Photographer: Furious Fotog
Model: Kevin R Davis
ISBN: 978-1-915861-93-1

PROLOGUE

From *Wrangled...*

Toby

I gazed at the faces around the table. Robert had made the pitch, and now it was up to them. "So, what do you think?"

Butch stroked his chin. "Let me see if I've got this right. You wanna bring a load of gay guys to Salvation, to get up to a load of kinky shit?"

Robert coughed. "Pretty much, yeah."

"But we wouldn't have to *see* the kinky shit, right? Or participate in it?"

"Absolutely not."

I grinned. "Unless you wanted to."

Butch's lips parted, and I would have given anything to know what passed through his mind right then.

Zeeb looked me in the eye. "So this means you'll stay?"

I smiled. "It does."

He mimed mopping his brow. "Well, thank fuck for that. Looks like I don't have to kill you after all."

"I like the idea," Teague announced, putting his phone on the table. He grinned.

"What are you thinking?"

He'd been on his phone as soon as Robert had shared my proposal.

"Oh, just imagining this place, with guys walking around in leather, or jocks, or nothing but boots and a leash."

I arched my eyebrows. "*Someone's* been doing some research."

He flushed.

Walt chuckled. "Wow, things sure could get interesting around here. One week per month? It'll make the rest of the month seem tame in comparison."

"So you're all with me on this?" Robert asked.

"With *us*," I amended, and he gave me a grateful smile. "With us," he echoed.

CHAPTER 1

Saturday, August 6, 2022

Butch Buchanan leaned on the fence that surrounded the paddock, yearning for a cigarette and watching the sky reveal its colors for the new day. The sun had been up maybe ten minutes or so, but the guests in the bunkhouse were still sleeping. After a week of being up before dawn, this was a luxury only afforded them the day they were due to leave Salvation.

Butch had been awake for an hour or so, early enough to catch sight of Toby Merrow and the boss trotting out on Lightning and Rusty, heading for the pasture. It had become a thing of theirs during the last three weeks, a morning ride before the sun came up, when the world was painted in twilight, hues of purple and pink that would soon give way to orange and red.

Is it only three weeks since Toby became a permanent fixture around here? Day-um.

A helluva lot had changed in such a relatively short time. For one thing, two weeks ago the cement trucks had arrived, and when they'd left, there was a flat surface that was to be the base of the new barn. A week after that, the walls had gone up, along with the joists for the upper floor. And when Monday morning arrived, so would the carpenters and plumbers, ready to work their magic. Butch marveled at the speed with which Toby and the boss had gotten the blueprints ready. He'd taken a peek. The upper floor was to be accommodation in small rooms, nothing fancy, just a sink, a toilet, and of course a bed. A large shower room would take over one corner of the floor, and that was no mean feat, getting the water system designed.

The first floor, however? That was intriguing. There was to be one main room, with smaller ones set off from it, but that wasn't the interesting part.

No, that was the drawings Toby'd had done. Sturdy beams complete with hooks, solid metal rings attached to posts, cabinets, and some benches that had provoked a lot of speculation, not to mention the drain in the middle of the concrete floor.

Why do they need a drain there?

Not that it was any of his business. Butch wasn't about to become one of the imminent guests for Salvation's new venture. Every time he thought about it, he imagined guys in leather chaps and very little else, wandering around the ranch, the air full of strange new sounds of implements connecting with bare flesh. Maybe the *crack* of a whip too, although that might have nothing to do with horses.

That part had him more than a little curious, with a spoonful of fascinated thrown in for good measure.

Butch figured the bill for all this construction would be enough to make *someone's* eyes water. He guessed that would be Toby. Then again, Toby had said it was an investment.

He's not only investing in Salvation, but in the boss too.

That was certainly paying dividends. Butch hadn't seen Robert Thorston this relaxed, this content in his own skin, for a long time—well, for five years since Kevin Porter had fallen off his horse and broken his fool neck. Kevin had been good for the boss, and as for how he'd gotten Robert in that particular state?

That had provoked a *lot* of speculation, not just on Butch's part. And now there was Toby, working his own brand of magic. Several of the hands had wondered out loud a few times just what Toby did to get Robert into that state of being, Butch included, but he soon scrubbed the thought from his mind.

I don't want to know. Like I said, it's none of my business.

But it sure was intriguing.

One thing was for certain, however. The way they gazed at each other when they thought no one was looking? The slight touches now and then?

Something was growing between them, and it appeared to be a whole lot like love, even to Butch's inexperienced eye.

Good for them.

Butch surveyed the ranch stretched out before him. Little by little, a new Salvation was emerging, nothing like the one Robert had inherited when his dad passed.

Which is a damn sight more than I'll get when my *dad goes.*

Dear Lord, when was the last time he'd thought about the old man? And he *would* be old by then, about seventy-seven by Butch's reckoning, long past the age of working his ranch. That was probably Deke's job now. Butch's younger brother had followed Dad around the ranch since he could toddle.

Butch hadn't laid eyes on any of his family for thirty-four years. And counting.

There were days when he told himself that was a good thing. He and Dad had never seen eye-to-eye. They'd busted heads ever since Butch had gotten into his teens, and he didn't suppose that relationship would've changed much.

Nothing like the relationship between the boss and *his* dad, that was for damn sure. Calvin Thorston had been one tough old bird, but he'd treated his workers well and earned their loyalty, a skill he'd clearly passed down to Robert. The boss always said Salvation was their home, and they were family.

He was easier to get along with than his dad too.

Butch patted his pocket where his pack of cigarettes were stowed, and sighed.

You know the rules. Cigarettes and hay were not a good combination. He'd have to wait until he was off the ranch. Fuck, he'd been trying to quit anyhow.

He strolled toward the barn that had been standing back when he'd arrived at Salvation in 1989, a tall, stocky nineteen-year-old misfit. A year of moving from farm to farm, ranch to ranch, working his ass off, had worked wonders for his build, but left him tired of not having a place to lay his head and space to call his own.

Going home had not been an option. Too many goddamn memories.

Calvin Thorston had offered him a home, but not until they'd had a long chat. Butch didn't blame him for that. He'd wanted to know if he was inviting trouble to come knock at his door. And he'd appeared satisfied with Butch's responses.

For the most part.

Butch couldn't tell him what he was doing on the road. He certainly didn't tell him why he'd left Wyoming. And in the end, Mr. Thorston had come to a grudging decision.

Butch was welcome to stay—he just wasn't welcome to get too interested in Mr. Thorston's daughter, Diana. Not that he'd said the latter part out loud. His glances and hard stares should have been enough to deliver that particular message, and he seemed to keep that expression for every hand under the age of twenty-five.

That was fine by Butch. He was happy to keep his distance. He wasn't about to get hauled off to jail for messing about with a girl Diana's age. Two years later, however…

But it wasn't me who was doing the chasing then, now was it? That was all on her. The same rules still applied, but by then he'd found it a little easier to ignore messages he didn't want to hear.

Ignoring Diana was an impossibility, especially when she set her sights on something—or someone. Thank God she'd waited until she was legal before making a move on him. Resisting her after she'd made that move had proved a hard enough task, and Butch was only human.

He pushed the barn door open and ambled into the dark space that smelled of feed, wood, hay, and dust. It was an odor he'd known since he was old enough to follow his dad into their own barn. The sweet smell of hay was almost like a perfume, one that had mingled with the scent of Diana's hair, her skin…

A scent that carried him back in time, rekindling pleasant, illicit memories.

One particular memory had stayed with him for thirty years.

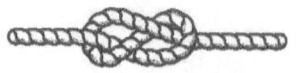

Friday, June 19, 1992

"We shouldn't be doing this," Butch murmured.

"You're right." Diana Thorston's mouth might be agreeing with him, but the way she arched her back when Butch kissed her neck, the way she scraped her fingers through the hair on the back of his head, down his nape to dig into his shoulders, said something else entirely.

He knew what she wanted. What she always wanted. The way she drew up her jeans-clad legs to grip him around his waist reinforced her intent.

"Diana…" Christ, the heat of her. A heat he knew only too well. It would have been so easy to give her what she needed—

what they both needed—but her dad had gone someplace with Robert, carrying out last-minute tasks, and they could be back at any second.

She kissed his cheek, then pressed her lips to his ear. "It's our last chance," she whispered.

The words fell like a splash of cold water on his face, cooling his desire and killing his erection.

Can't do this anymore. Especially not today.

Butch broke free of her embrace. "We need to stop this." His voice sounded even, firm, and more in control than he really felt.

Diana froze. "Why?"

Despite his inner turmoil, Butch cracked a smile. "Because you're marryin' another guy tomorrow. Remember? Orange blossom and white lace? Saying I do with your daddy standing beside you, giving you away?" He stroked her cheek, then took her left hand in his. "Wearing Newt Webster's ring on your finger?"

She sat up, removing bits of hay from her long blonde hair. "It's not too late, y'know."

"Too late for what?"

"I can still change my mind."

He gaped at her. "And what would be the alternative? Me asking your daddy for your hand in marriage? After he all but shoved Newt in front of you last year at that dance over in Billings?" He snorted. "And what if I did? Do you know what he'd do to me?"

"Fire you?"

Butch cackled. "Oh sweetheart, losing my job would be the least of my worries."

It was the fate of his balls that concerned him most.

She swallowed. "But I don't want to marry Newt."

His chest tightened at the plaintive edge to her voice, and he struggled to remain firm. "Why not? He's a good guy. He'll treat you well. He'll make you a fine husband."

Butch wasn't so sure about that last part. Newt hadn't impressed him from the start, but he was her daddy's choice, and there was no going against that. Six months after Mr. Thorston began trotting Newt in front of her every chance he got, there had been an announcement. Some ranch hands had wondered if there'd been a shotgun involved.

7

Butch knew better than to comment on that.

"Sure—and then he'll bore me to death."

Butch held his arm wide, and she snuggled up to him, her head resting against his shoulder. He pressed his lips to the top of her head. "He doesn't know about me, does he?"

Good Lord, he hoped not.

Diana tilted her head and stared up at him with wide eyes. "Are you kidding? He still thinks I'm a virgin, and *that* boat sailed about the same time Dad started mentioning his name at regular intervals." She chuckled. "I'm sure you remember your part in it. This part, as I recall." She slid her hand over his belly, heading south, but he stopped her before she reached his dick, his fingers wrapped around her wrist.

"I mean it," he said softly. Butch hadn't so much as glanced in her direction for two years, but when she reached eighteen, the brakes had come off and Diana Thorston made it clear what she wanted—well, which part of Butch's anatomy she wanted, and where. She'd waited until her dad had left the ranch before tugging him by the hand toward the barn.

At least she didn't lead me there by my cock. Butch was sure all the hands knew what was going on, and he lived in fear of someone whispering in her dad's ear. Calvin Thorston was nobody's fool. But nothing was ever said, and if he knew about the shenanigans in his barn, he never let on.

"Would you have asked him?" she murmured.

"Hmm?"

Diana peered up at him. "Would you have asked my dad if you could marry me?"

Shit.

At the age of eighteen, he'd made himself a promise to be a better person, and good people didn't tell lies.

"No, honey."

She stiffened. "Oh."

Christ, he hated being the cause of that pinched look, but this was no time for seeing the world through rose-colored spectacles. Tomorrow she'd be someone else's bride.

She needs to forget about me.

Butch trailed a finger over her soft cheek. "Don't you go pretending you're in love with me, because I think we both know that's a crock. You were itching to fuck, and I was handy." Her breathing hitched, and he nodded. "You know I'm right. Plus, there was the thrill of getting caught. I was your little rebellion. And that was fine by me. We got what we wanted. But the plain truth of the matter is this—your daddy wouldn't let you marry me."

"Because you work for him? Is that it?"

Butch squeezed her hand. "No, because you're better off without me." He let go and tilted her chin up with his fingertips. "I wouldn't be good for you, darlin'."

And wasn't that the God's honest truth?

She gazed into his eyes for the longest time, and every second tightened that fist around his heart. Her lack of a response told him plenty, however.

Diana was nobody's fool either.

Except he hadn't told her the whole truth, and he knew it.

"Will you be there tomorrow?"

He shook his head. "I can't. But you won't miss me. You'll have too much on your mind to think about me, and that's as it should be on your wedding day. I'm not gonna be around to distract you." He inclined his head toward the upper open window, from which a beam of sunlight pointed at them like an arrow, piercing the barn's semi-darkness, motes of dust dancing in it in a lazy motion. "I think they're back."

She was up on her feet in a heartbeat, and he joined her. He gave her the once over, making sure no hay lingered. Diana came up to his shoulder, nineteen and as beautiful as the June day outside. She locked her arms around his neck.

"One last kiss, then?"

He knew what she wanted, but he just couldn't.

Butch kissed her forehead. "You're gonna be happy. You wait and see." Then he patted her on the butt. "Now git."

Diana clambered down the ladder from the hay loft, walked across the straw-covered floor, and out of the door without a single backward glance.

"Butch? You in there?"

Zeeb Nolan's voice broke through, and Butch gave himself a mental shake.

"Yup."

Zeeb poked his head around the door. "What in the Sam Hill are you doin' in here? You not plannin' on working this morning?" His lazy grin was a slice of normality Butch needed right then.

"Just ruminating." Butch walked toward him.

"Ain't that what a cow does?"

He snorted. "If you're comparing me to cattle, have the decency to make me a bull at least."

Time to leave the memories behind, and get back to reality.

He paused at the door and glanced up at the hay loft.

Christ, it seems like a lifetime ago.

Butch was a different person now. His past actions had forced him to lead a better life, but not a healthy one. There was still too much guilt rolling around inside him to allow him to be happy.

He couldn't be happy, because Scott Nelson never got the chance to be happy.

Scott never got the chance to live past seventeen, and that was down to Butch.

CHAPTER 2

Butch parked the truck beside the bunkhouse and switched off the engine.

Thank God that's over for another week.

Saturdays were the fussiest kind of day, guests coming and going, and what with cleaning up after one group and getting ready for another, picking up new arrivals from Bozeman, and generally making sure they were all happy, supper time was there before he knew it. Being busy was just fine, however. He'd rather be occupied than twiddling his thumbs.

Except there was always something to do around the ranch.

Zeeb had taken the new guests indoors, and Butch was content to let him deal with them for a moment. Four this time, all keen to spend a week on horseback. The weather forecast was good, and Teague had drawn up a list of trails. Paul was ready to school the newbies—there were two of them—in how to take care of a horse, but that was all to come.

Food first.

Butch knew there'd be plenty to eat—Matt saw to that—and besides, he wanted to enjoy the scenery, the place he'd called home for the last thirty-three years.

He glanced at the empty paddock. Paul was probably in the stables, checking on the horses. Then he noticed a figure leaning on the railing, the waning sun filtering through her hair, creating a glowing halo.

He smiled to himself at the thought. *Diana ain't no angel.*

Butch strolled toward her, his feet crunching on the gravel path. She turned as he approached, her smile instantaneous.

"Hey you."

Butch rested his arms on the wooden railing. "Hey yourself. What you doing here?"

"I came to see Robert."

Butch grinned. "Well, you won't find him down here. He'll be up at the house."

Diana's cheeks pinked. "He is. But I didn't tell him I was coming, so…"

He saw the light. "Ah. He's… er… occupied."

She coughed. "That's one way of putting it. Serves me right for not calling first." Diana shook her head. "There are some things a girl does *not* need to know about her brother."

Yeah, he wasn't gonna go there either.

"Shouldn't you be at your fancy-pants ranch, looking after your new guests?"

She rolled her eyes. "It isn't that fancy. I don't know why you always say that."

"It's swankier than Salvation."

"Newt's taking care of the guests. He's better at public relations than I am."

Butch studied her for a minute. Thirty years hadn't changed her all that much, except that her long blonde hair was now short, white and wavy. She'd kept the same trim figure she'd had the day he met her. If anything, she was a little leaner, her face less full than it had been.

She was still a beautiful woman.

"Do I have something on my nose?" Sunlight and amusement danced in her eyes.

"Can I ask you something?"

Diana blinked. "Okay."

"Do you ever regret marrying him?" Then he remembered his place. Whatever their history was, he worked for her brother. "Forget I asked. None of my business."

"No, it's okay. If anyone can ask that question, it's you." She smiled. "A wise person once said marriage was like a pot of boiling water. Once you're hitched, the heat gets turned off and gradually cools. A few other things cool with it. But in marriages like mine, the water starts off cool and little by little it gets warmer, and you adjust to the changing temperature."

"And what's the temperature like now?" He smiled, resisting the urge to push a strand of hair back from her face. "As I recall, you like it hot."

Her face tightened a little. "The water heater's a bit temperamental. Occasionally it gets up to where I'm happy with it, but not as often as I'd like."

"Maybe we should talk about something else." Discussing Diana's love life—even in a roundabout way—sent a quiver through his stomach.

She arched her eyebrows. "Why, Butch Buchanan, are you embarrassed? Whatever happened to the boy who—"

He stopped her words with a finger to her lips. "Let's not go there, okay? Some things are best left in the past."

Except *some* things didn't stay there. They crept into his dreams, twisted his guts, and were always there, like a stubborn stone in his shoe that he couldn't remove.

Diana was a pleasant memory.

Scott lurked in a dark fissure of his mind.

Diana chuckled as he removed his finger. "Fair enough." She gazed at the changing sky. "Can we be serious for a minute?"

That quiver from a moment ago developed into something roiling deep in his innards. "I don't know. Can we?"

"You asked if I regretted marrying him. The answer is no."

"I'm glad to hear that." Butch had hoped she'd be happy.

"But…"

Shit, why does there always have to be a but?

"Look, like I said, this is none of my business."

The sigh that fell from her lips tore at his heart. "Maybe not, but it would help if I can talk about it." She turned her head toward him. "If you don't mind listening."

"I can do that." He shifted closer, and she leaned against his shoulder.

"Thanks, Butch." There was a pause. "You were right all those years ago. Newt's a good man. And he *has* treated me just fine. But he's had to deal with… something, and lately life has been a bit more of a struggle."

Butch had a feeling he knew where this was heading. *Looks like Newt might need a helping hand from some little blue pills.* He said nothing, waiting on her.

Another sigh, one that sounded as though it came from someplace deep. "Newt suffers from depression. There are good days and bad days, and the bad ones can get… really bad."

Oh God.

"I had no idea. I mean, he looks just fine. Well, he has every time I've seen him." He felt as if he was rambling. What the fuck did he expect someone with depression to look like?

"Newt's what they class as high-functioning."

"And that means what?"

She shrugged. "He can do what he needs to and appear okay. Except he's *not* okay, because the rest of his life is falling apart, a total shambles." Butch put his arm around her, and she tilted her face upward, her eyes warm. "Thanks. That does help, you know."

"He taking anything for it?"

She nodded. "He has his meds. Plus, he goes to therapy. I go with him too sometimes, because as he says, it affects my life too."

"It can't be an easy life."

"I hate the days when he's under a black cloud that's so thick, it's as if I can't even see him." She scowled. "I tried sharing how I felt with a friend once, over coffee. Her response? 'Can't you just tell him to pull himself together and snap out of it?'"

He snorted. "Yeah, that's really helpful." Butch knew he could be an asshole a lot of the time, but even he wasn't *that* much of an asshole. And he could be there for Diana if she needed a shoulder to lean on.

"Listen. Any time you wanna bend my ear, you know where to find me."

Her smile lit up her face, washing away any sign of the discomfort that had lurked there mere seconds ago. "Thanks, Butch. I'm sort of surprised we've never talked like this before now."

"You mean, given our history?"

She chuckled. "Ancient history, at that. Yeah, I guess so."

"You've had your life to lead, and I've had mine. And then there's the fact that you're the boss's sister."

"You're not scared of Robert, are you?"

"I wouldn't say scared, but I don't think he'd be happy about you sharing personal stuff with one of his hired hands."

She gave him a mock glare. "You're *way* more than that, and don't you forget it."

He shivered. "Whoa there. Robert might not scare me, but when *you* look at me like that…" Butch grinned. "You always were feisty."

Diana preened. "Good to know I've still got it." Her eyes

twinkled. "You know, it's not too late for you to make some woman a wonderful husband. A lot of women out there love a silver fox."

Butch laughed. "What woman would put up with me?"

"*I* would have, given the chance." Before Butch could utter a word, she held up her hand. "I know, you thought I was better off without you. But you turned out to be a rock-solid man." She grinned. "In more ways than one."

Behind them, the stable door creaked open, and Butch withdrew his arm. He didn't turn to see who approached. Diana twisted and glanced over her shoulder. "Hey Zeeb. How's it hanging?"

"About a foot off the ground, same as usual." They laughed.

It was their standard greeting, one that never failed to raise the boss's eyebrows.

Diana was something else.

Yeah, and she could've been my *something else.*

Except Butch knew better now.

Then he shoved that thought out of his mind.

Nope. That's not what I am.

There were days when Butch wasn't sure what the fuck he was anymore.

Diana's phone buzzed and she removed it from her jeans pocket. She smiled. "Looks like I'm safe to go on up to the house."

Zeeb let out an explosive snort, then quickly got himself under control. "I came out here to tell you the food is disappearing mighty fast, so if you want feeding tonight, you'd better get your ass in there."

Diana laughed. "And that's my cue to go see Robert." She patted Butch's arm. "Thanks."

"You're welcome. Anytime."

She gave a nod to Zeeb before strolling toward the sloping path that led up to the big house. Butch watched her. Diana had been a wild filly in her youth, but age had given her grace of movement.

Then he realized how quiet it had gotten. He glanced at Zeeb, to find him staring, arms folded.

"And what precisely is she thankin' you for?" Zeeb's eyes gleamed.

"None of your damn business." Butch inclined his head toward the bunkhouse. "I guess I'd better grab some supper." He walked off, following the sound of raised voices and laughter.

He loved the company of his fellow ranch hands, but sometimes he liked the peace and quiet of being alone with his thoughts.

Well, with *some* of them.

Butch hung his hat on a peg beside his bunk, then sat on the edge of the bed. The new guests seemed to have settled in fairly well: the two sisters were on the upper floor—a pair of middle-aged women excited to ride the trails—and two guys who were in with the rest of the hands. They were asleep, buried beneath thin blankets.

Walt Crosby glanced at their bunks. "They looked worn out already," he said in a low voice. "How are they gonna cope with getting up at the crack of dawn every day?"

"Well, they'll either cope, or they won't." Butch grinned. "I can have a pail of cold water ready if we need to get 'em out of bed." He gazed toward the end of the bunkhouse where Zeeb lay on the top bunk. Butch stood and strolled over to him, resting his arms on the mattress. "What were you mumbling about over supper?"

Zeeb rolled onto his side to face him. "I was sayin', I'm gonna be forty next month. Forty! Where'd the time go?"

Butch let out a low chuckle. "Yeah, the older you get, the faster the years speed by. Don't sweat it. Forty's nothing to worry about." He grinned. "Although you might come across as a little younger if you did something about that grey in your beard."

Zeeb glared at him. "Ain't nothing wrong with showin' a bit of silver. Women dig that."

"So how're you gonna celebrate?" Walt asked.

"I wanted to do something I've never done before."

Butch arched his eyebrows. "I'm almost afraid to ask."

Zeeb rolled his eyes. "I'm talking about going to a casino. I've seen 'em on TV, but I've never stepped foot in one. So I reckon I'll give it a shot."

"Then start saving," Walt commented. "Money can drip through your fingers in those places. My uncle was a gambler. Mom says he lost ten thousand dollars in one night once."

Zeeb whistled. "No shit."

"You figurin' on going to Vegas, then?" Butch inquired.

He snorted. "Hell no. I was thinking 'bout someplace closer to home. There's the Magic Diamond casino in Livingston. Or there's the Jackpot Paradise, Lucky Lil's… I was planning on drinking and playing cards till they kick me out, then spending the night in a fancy hotel. The Murray would do at a pinch. Who knows? If I win big, I might even find me some company for the night." He grinned. "You boys can come along too. Just don't expect me to share a room with any of ya."

"Can you all stop talking and go to sleep?" Paul whispered from his bunk. "It's late. Save the conversations for the morning."

He had a point.

Butch sighed. "G'night, boys. Let's be ready for a new day." He wandered back to his bunk, stripped off his clothing down to his shorts, then lay on top of the blanket. He switched on the little night light hanging above him, and folded his arms under his head, Zeeb's words dancing in his mind.

Livingston. The Murray.

Livingston had been his dirty little secret—until the day someone had uncovered it, and that had changed everything. He'd gone there for the first time when everyone had been dancing their feet off after Diana's wedding.

Butch had been in no mood to dance.

All he'd wanted was to get blind stinking drunk.

Except I got a lot more than that, didn't I?

CHAPTER 3

Saturday, June 20, 1992

By the time he'd drunk his third glass of the cheapest whiskey available, Butch knew he wouldn't be driving back to Salvation that night. Not unless he *wanted* his ass thrown in jail for DUI. He'd sleep in the truck he'd borrowed, if necessary, because he knew he couldn't afford a hotel room.

Yeah no. The boss didn't pay him *that* much.

As for not being at the ranch first thing in the morning, Sunday was generally a quiet day and his absence wouldn't be noticed, provided he didn't get back *too* late.

The bar was full, because hey, it was Saturday night after all, but the music wasn't overwhelming, thank God. Not that Butch intended on having a conversation with anyone.

The voice inside his head was doing plenty of talking.

You knew it couldn't last, right?

How long did you think you could get away with fucking the boss's daughter?

You're lucky it lasted this *long.*

You're lucky she didn't get pregnant.

You're lucky old man Thorston hasn't strung you up by your balls.

That goddamn voice sounded way more sober than Butch felt. And the one thing it *wasn't* saying?

You just lost the love of your life.

Diana was never that, and they both knew it. She might have made noises about marrying him, but that was all they were— noises with no substance, nothing but the flapping of her lips. The bare bones of their situation was this: she'd used him, he'd used her, and knowing that was all it had been between them made him feel like a total bastard.

I'm not a nice guy.

Except that notion had been driven home back in 1988. There was a reminder etched into his skin, lest he forget. And on those rare occasions since when he thought he was on the road to becoming a better person, along would come another reminder.

I am so *not a nice guy.*

There were other times too, when that inner voice got a little darker, a little too close to the truth. Times when it whispered the *real* reason he'd given Scott Nelson—and others before him—such a hard time.

And before it got *too* murky inside his head, another voice would respond, one he was more prepared to listen to.

Nope. Not gonna go there.

"Looks as though you're carrying a heavy burden there, dude."

Okay, that was freakin' weird.

He glanced to his right. The guy perched on the next bar stool was staring at him. Butch didn't know him from Adam. He was older than Butch, no more than a decade, he estimated, with a strong jawline, closely cropped, dark brown hair, and brown eyes. His plain black T-shirt was stretched tight across his broad chest, and his shoulders and upper arms were well-defined with that almost sculpted look.

Someone spends a lot of time working out.

Butch didn't need a gym. Salvation provided all the physical activity he'd ever want.

"You talkin' to me?" He did his best to keep his voice even.

The guy nodded. "Been watching you for maybe a half hour. You got the look of someone who's trying to drown his sorrows." His eyes twinkled. "You *also* don't look old enough to be downing that whiskey, but I guess the bartender knows his business."

"Not that it's any of *your* business, but I'm twenty-two." He gestured to the bartender. "He's seen my ID. Do you wanna see it too?" Butch quipped.

The dude laughed, revealing perfect white teeth. He waved a hand. "You're good."

To Butch's somewhat uncultivated ear, he sounded as though he hailed from the east coast. "You seem to be a long way from home."

And I'm a long way from sober.

Not long enough but the night was young. Everyone would still be square-dancing back at the ranch: the boss was throwing a huge party, but Butch doubted he'd be missed.

Diana certainly wouldn't miss him. She was probably too busy getting used to being Mrs. Newt Webster, not that he begrudged Diana her new life. What stung most was that he'd have to search for alternative…entertainment? Exercise?

Yeah, I ain't no nice guy.

The guy laughed. "Guilty. I live in Boston. I'll be transferring here next month, so I thought I'd check the place out."

"You got a job in Livingston?" It wasn't a huge town from the little Butch had seen of it—seven thousand people or thereabouts—and *he* was only there because no one from Salvation ever ventured into Livingston, and if he was gonna get drunk, the last thing he wanted was spectators.

"In Billings."

"What kind of job?"

The guy's cheeks flushed. "Insurance." When Butch didn't offer an opinion, he rolled his eyes. "I know, right? I can barely sit still for excitement."

Butch snorted. "Hey, it's your life, dude. Why're you being transferred?"

"Let's just say I wanted a move, and leave it at that." He nodded toward Butch's empty glass. "What'll you have? Another whiskey?"

Butch blinked. "You *have* been watchin' me, haven't ya?" He grinned. "Sure. Gotta keep the tank topped up, right?"

The guy laughed. "I think your tank is doing just fine." He signaled to the bartender. "Two whiskeys, please." When the bartender turned to grab a bottle, the guy shifted closer, nudging his stool toward Butch's. "Okay…. Who are you drinking to forget?"

"Who says I am?" Butch retorted.

"You've got this look about you." He propped his head in his hand. "So? What's her name?"

Butch sighed. "That isn't it at all."

"Then acquaint me with your tale." He aimed a hard stare at Butch. "Only, if we're going to swap stories and buy each other drinks—you *are* gonna buy me a drink, aren't you?"

"You bet." The dude was starting to grow on him.

"Well okay then. If we're doing this, at least tell me who I'm talking to."

Butch held his hand out. "Butch Buchanan."

The guy straightened and they shook. "Race Prettyman."

Butch froze. "You're shittin' me. That your real name?"

Race nodded. "The hardest part is making sure I live up to it." He cocked his head. "How'm I doing?"

Butch chuckled. "I guess you'd pass for pretty." Race had lashes that Diana would kill for, thick and long, framing his milk chocolate-brown eyes.

"My mom entered me in one of those Beautiful Baby contests when I was a kid. Back then I had thick curly hair. I look at the photos and I swear, I could've been a girl."

Butch glanced at the wide chest, the denim-encased muscled thighs. "No one could say that now," he murmured.

Their drinks arrived, and they clinked glasses.

"To a new town, and you forgetting your troubles."

Butch let out another sigh. *If only it were that easy.* Race's words came back to him. "You wasted a weekend flying all the way here just to check the place out? Is your life in Boston *that* boring?"

Race cackled. "I had my reasons. Now, why don't you tell me all about Montana? What have I been missing all my life?"

He let out a snort. "I'm the wrong guy to ask. I've been here three years, give or take, and all I've seen is Bozeman, and the ranch where I work."

Race asked a lot of questions about Salvation, and Butch was happy to provide answers. The more they talked, the more Butch liked the guy. He felt… comfortable, as though Butch had known him a damn sight longer than a few hours. Race didn't push him for details about the mystery girl who'd broken his heart, for which Butch was grateful. Only, his words became increasingly indistinct the more alcohol he drank, and by the time he'd bought a round, and Race was on his second, Butch knew he was licked.

"I think I'd better call it a night." While he could still get off his stool with some degree of dignity, instead of falling onto his ass.

"Well, what else would you call it? It *is* night out there." Race pointed to the windows. His brows knitted. "How're you getting back to that ranch?"

"'M not. Gonna sleep in the truck."

Race's scowl deepened. "Like hell you are. I'm stayin' across the street at the Murray. Why not stay there?" Before Butch could respond, Race surged ahead. "You don't need to splash out on a room. There's a couch in *my* room with your name on it. You can sleep on that. It's gotta be more comfortable than your truck, dude. An' there's this fancy shower that you *know* is gonna feel amazin' in the morning."

Lord, that was tempting. Less chance of the cops tapping on his window too.

"You sure?" Even as he said it, his booze-befuddled brain was already telling him—*way* too loudly—that Race's suggestion made perfect sense.

"Wouldn't have said it otherwise." Race tossed some bills onto the bar top.

"Then it's a deal." Butch tried to stand, but the world shifted instead and he lurched off the stool. Race grabbed his arm, and they negotiated their way out of the bar, Butch's arm slung around Race's shoulders, watching his feet that seemed to be moving independently of him.

Crossing the street was a trickier business, and they surged forward when a gap appeared in the traffic. The Murray Hotel's lobby was busy, and Race guided him to the elevators, Butch doing his best to appear inconspicuous. At least he didn't heave in the elevator. He wasn't *that* drunk.

Once they were inside the room, Butch made a beeline for the john. "Sorry. I'm gonna bust."

"You do your business, then I'll do mine," Race fired back.

His bladder emptied, Butch washed his hands and went back into the room.

Race's room wasn't small, and he hadn't lied about the shower, but one glance at the couch brought Butch to a standstill. He stood at one end of it, gazing at its length, trying to picture himself stretched out on it.

Nope. Did not compute.

"Hey dude?" he called out to the bathroom where he could hear Race taking a leak that sounded never-ending.

"Whassup?"

"As my dad used to say, 'Houston, we have a problem.'"

The toilet flushed, and Race stumbled out of the bathroom. "We do?"

Butch pointed to the couch. "There's no way I'm gonna fit on that."

Race followed his finger and scowled. "Well shit. That's dinky." He raised his head and blinked. "Dude, you won't fit on that."

"Didn't I just say that?" Butch peered at the carpet. It was thick enough to make sleeping on the floor a viable—if a little firm—option.

Race grinned. "Then you take one side of the bed, and I'll take the other. It's a king. Hell, you could build a pillow fort in the middle and we'd *still* have enough room." He arched his eyebrows. "Unless you feel funny sharing a bed with a guy?"

Butch snorted. "I ain't never shared a bed with anyone before, guy *or* girl."

"It's real easy. You strip off, get in, cover up, turn out the light, and go to sleep. You won't even know I'm there."

The bed did look way more accommodating than the carpet. "Deal."

Race rolled his eyes. "Thank fuck. I'm about ready to drop." He tugged his T-shirt over his head, and Butch had to admit, the guy had a great body. Next-to-no hair on him, not even a treasure trail. Then Race unbuttoned his jeans and shoved them to the floor before stepping out of them.

Butch knew he was staring at Race's underwear, but they had to be the skimpiest briefs ever. Not only that, the front pouch seemed to have been designed for a long dick.

And yeah, Race was *well*-endowed in that department.

Race cleared his throat. "You're staring, dude."

Butch jerked his head up. "I've worn nothing but boxer shorts since I persuaded my mom to stop buying me little boy underwear. You know the kind? Spiderman, spaceships, trains…"

Race guffawed. "Now *that* takes me back." He cupped his package. "I like these. They're a good fit."

Butch could tell that much. Then he remembered. He'd gone commando.

Race noticed his hesitation. "Something wrong?"

"I usually sleep in my shorts," he admitted. "But… I'm not wearin' any."

"Well then, tonight you sleep in the raw, Princess. It's not a big deal 'cause you'll be asleep, an' so will I, in about ten seconds."

"'Princess'?" Butch gave him the finger, and Race cackled again. That did it. Butch removed his clothing in Olympic record-breaking speed, snaked himself between the sheets, and got comfy. "Damn, this feels good."

Well, it would when the room stopped spinning.

Race slid his fingers under the waistband of his briefs and shimmied them over his hips, removing them. Butch averted his gaze, because he just knew if he didn't, he'd be caught staring again.

Looking at Race's dick would be *way* worse than staring at his briefs.

Race climbed into the bed, and Butch realized he'd been right. An ocean of mattress separated them. He closed his eyes, then immediately snapped them open. It felt as though the bed was trying to eject him.

"Whoa. I haven't drunk that much in a long time."

Four years to be exact, since he'd stolen a bottle of whiskey from his dad's liquor cabinet and drank the whole damn thing, only to throw it all back up a short time after.

"That's a date, isn't it?"

"Hmm?" Butch turned his head, and found Race pointing at the tattoo on his right arm. A trickle of ice dripped down his spine, and he told himself it was the AC.

"Roman numerals, right? I could never get my head around them." Race frowned. "What is that? Your birthday?" He grinned. "No, wait. I got it. It's your mom's so you never forget it."

He was half right.

"'S jus' a date," Butch mumbled. Except every trace of sleep had fled and he was wide awake.

Race seemed to be similarly afflicted. He lay on his back, staring at the ceiling. "You were right to call a halt to the drinking. Four's usually my limit, and we passed that an hour ago." There was a pause. "You gonna tell me now what was goin' on tonight? 'Cause *something* sure was."

Butch would rather have crawled through glass than discuss his tattoo, so the change of subject was more than welcome. He rolled onto his side to gaze at Race. "I guess you could say I needed to get my mind off of something."

"And? Did it work?"

Butch chuckled. "Nope. She's still in there."

Race grinned. "So I was right. This *was* about a girl."

He nodded. "I've known her for a while. And today, she got married."

"Obviously not to you. Were you close?"

Butch bit his lip. "Yeah, you could say that."

"How come she married someone else? Why not you? Seems to me she'd be damn lucky to have you."

Butch raised his eyebrows.

Race chuckled. "Oh, come on. You're a good-looking dude. Put it this way. *I* wouldn't kick you outta bed for eatin' crackers."

What the fuck?

Before Butch could find a suitable response, Race flushed. "Sorry. I shoot my mouth off sometimes. Tends to get me into trouble."

Butch propped his head up in one hand. "You get a lot of guys in your bed?" His heartbeat quickened, and sounding normal took real effort.

Race grinned. "A few. But I've never shared a bed with one of 'em just to sleep. You are definitely a first. I put it down to that look you had about you, as if you needed rescuing."

"So… you're gay?"

"Bi, actually." Race stilled. "Houston, do we still have a problem?"

Ice and heat vied for control of Butch's body. "I… I guess not."

Race's eyes glittered. "Dude. I am *not* about to jump on your bones, okay? Like I said, tonight is all about sleepin'." And with that, he stretched out a hand to the bedside lamp and plunged the room into initial darkness. "G'night."

It took Butch's heart a moment to return to its normal rhythm. "Night." From the sound of Race's breathing, he was already asleep.

Butch didn't shift position, but lay on his side, watching the lights from the passing cars in the street below creating patterns on the ceiling.

Well, this is a first. And certainly not how he'd expected the day to end.

Then fatigue crashed over him, and he was out like a light.

Butch had no idea of the time. Outside was quiet, so he guessed it was the early hours of the morning. He opened his eyes, wondering what had awoken him.

Something was different.

His chest was pressed up against Race's solid warm back, his arm draped across Race's waist—and his bare cock was trying to make itself a nest between Race's ass cheeks.

Butch froze, listening for any sign Race was awake.

Nope.

He wanted to move, but for the first time in his life he was wrapped around another person, and *damn*, it felt good.

Then it hit him.

He was hard.

Fuck.

He closed his eyes and explored the sensations. Race smelled of cotton sheets, a lingering scent of something spicy, and underneath it all, a musky aroma that reminded Butch of the bunkhouse. He wanted to move in case Race woke up and got the wrong idea. Butch was used to waking up with a raging case of morning wood, but if it was *him* having to deal with a hard-on up close and personal behind him? Yeah, that would be weird.

Race might think I wanted to do… something else.

But in the next breath he wanted to stay a while, to enjoy this new experience. He craned his neck to gaze at the sleeping Race— and saw his tattoo in the room's dim light.

Butch removed his arm as though contact with Race's skin had burned him. He shifted across the mattress to his own side, and rolled over.

"Hmm? Wha?" Race's drowsy voice broke the silence, and Butch did his damnedest to breathe as though he was asleep, frozen into immobility, waiting for slumber to claim Race once more. It didn't take long for his breathing to drop back into its previous pattern, and Butch relaxed.

You moved like you were scared shitless.

He couldn't deny that. He even knew what had scared the fuck out of him.

Curling around Race's naked body had felt good.

Go to sleep. You're drunk. You'll have forgotten this by morning.

Shit, he hoped so.

Butch flipped the shower off and toweled himself dry. Race was still asleep when he'd snuck out of the bed. The sun was already up, and Butch needed to get the hell out of there. He imagined there would be quite a few thick heads on the ranch that morning. They'd be too busy dealing with their own hangovers to notice his absence.

Except maybe the boss. He saw *everything*.

Butch's head was still on his shoulders and the ache had subsided after two glasses of water and the shower. He squirmed into his jeans, jumping at the light knock at the bathroom door.

"Sorry, but I need to take a piss."

Butch opened it, and Race stood there in his jeans, fly open. Butch grabbed his shirt and dove out of there, listening to Race hum a little tune while he did his business.

Okay, this was awkward as fuck.

He couldn't just leave, not after Race had been kind enough to let him stay the night, but the memory of what had passed in the night lingered. Butch knew he wasn't running from Race— he'd done nothing, for fuck's sake, except be a gentleman and sleep—but from his own reaction.

The toilet flushed, the door opened, and Race came out. "You wanna grab some breakfast? I saw a place along the street that looks good." He cocked his head. "Unless you have to run."

"Yeah, I do. But thanks for last night."

Race's eyes gleamed. "No, thank *you*." He smiled. "I didn't expect that, but it sure was nice while it lasted."

Holy fuck.

Butch was under no illusions as to what Race was referring.

"I thought you were asleep." The words came out as a croak.

"I was—until something poked me."

Aw fuck.

Then the full import of his words sank in.

"But… you didn't… and you could've…"

Race's expression lost all trace of amusement. "No, I *couldn't*," he said in a gentle tone. "Much as I would have liked to roll over and… enjoy it, there was something vital missing."

Butch caught up fast. "I'm not your type." He wasn't sure if he was relieved or disappointed.

Race laughed. "Oh baby, you are *so* my type. No, what was missing was one thing—consent. I don't take something without asking, and I don't take advantage of guys—or girls. Now, if you'd *wanted* to play? Hell, I'd have thought Christmas had come early. But that obviously wasn't the case. Your reaction told me that much." He smiled again. "You're a conundrum, Butch Buchanan, and I'd love to take a peek at what's going on inside that head of yours." He went over to the nightstand, picked up his wallet, removed a card, and held it out to Butch.

"What's this?"

Race rolled his eyes. "My number, dude. I'll be moving here next month, remember? At least I know there'll be one person I'm already acquainted with." He peered closely. "Maybe a dude who wouldn't mind meeting up for a drink, or shoot some pool?" When Butch didn't reach for the card, Race let out a sigh. "No funny business, okay? Consent, remember? But I really enjoyed talking with you last night, and I think you did too—before your, er, anatomy got other ideas." He proffered the card once more. "You don't have to give me your number if you don't want to."

Butch took the card and glanced at the number. "This looks weird."

"That's because it's the number for my cell phone." He pointed to the small black object next to his wallet. "That's it over there. The company provides it. So even though I'll be moving, you can still contact me on it." There was that keen glance again. "If you want to."

Butch thought quickly. "The only number I've got is for the ranch." And he didn't want Race calling him there. He *had* enjoyed the evening, however, and he genuinely liked Race. He stuffed the card into the back pocket of his jeans.

Race waved his hand. "That's okay. I'll leave the ball in your court." Butch shivered and Race frowned. "Hey, what's up?"

"If you've been a different kinda guy, last night could've gone in a whole different direction."

His warm eyes were kind. "I'm thirty. I've been around. I've also met too many predatory types out there. That's not me. I'm happy just to be a friend."

Butch could deal with being a friend.

"And for the record?" Race squared his broad shoulders. "If you ever want to ask questions—and I don't care how personal they get—then that's fine by me."

"What makes you think I have questions?" *And damn, just how much do you see?*

Race studied him in silence, and Butch's scalp prickled. Finally, Race nodded. "Okay. Clearly I got it wrong." His stomach growled, and when Butch's rumbled in reply, they laughed. "I think breakfast was a good idea though."

Butch couldn't argue with that. He'd rather deal with a growling stomach than think, any day. Especially thoughts that led him to—

Nope. Not gonna go there.

CHAPTER 4

Sunday, August 7, 2022

With hindsight, Toby Merrow should have seen it coming.

Everything had moved so fast: the architect's plans, consultations with building companies, carpenters, plumbers... It all pulled together in a short space of time—which it had to, if they were to be ready before the end of September—and once the ball got rolling, it picked up speed and then there was no stopping it.

Robert had seemed okay with the rapid progress—on the surface. There'd been glimpses of something brewing, but Toby had assumed if there was a problem, Robert would have *said*, for God's sake.

Toby's first mistake. He fucking *assumed*.

The previous week, Robert had been out of sorts. He was a quiet man at the best of times, and Toby was still getting to know the man he'd fallen for, so he took silence for everything being hunky dory.

Toby's second mistake. He should have gone with his gut instinct and gotten Robert to talk.

And then that morning, it had all spiraled out of control, and Robert had lost it. Well and truly lost it. So Toby had to take control, to stop this wildfire before it had a chance to burn down everything they'd built since June.

He'd stood in the living room watching Robert pacing, scraping his fingers over his scalp, rubbing the back of his neck, unable to keep still for a second.

"I think you need to calm down," Toby said quietly.

"And I don't think you've listened to a word I've said," Robert retorted. "The plumbing company just called. They said there could be a delay in getting it all done on time."

"Then we'll find another company who can deliver." Toby strove to keep things on a practical level.

"Just like that, huh? Aren't you at all concerned? After all, this is *your* brainchild, right? Why did I think we could do this? Neither of us are rich, and yet we've sunk money into this venture, and it could still go belly up."

Toby knew there had to be more to this than a delay with the plumbing. "Is that it? Or is there more?"

"You bet there's more. Doesn't it bother you that we've only got one booking so far?"

"And we've got *how* many weeks left before we open? Six, seven maybe?" Toby smiled. "To quote one of your favorite movies, 'People will come.'"

His attempt at levity sailed over Robert's head. "But this is such a risk."

"Yeah, and you've taken risks before. You turned Salvation into a dude ranch, remember?"

"Yeah, but *this*…"

Toby had heard enough. "Can I just stop you for a moment?" Robert blinked, and Toby studied him. "Now… think about what you've said, the things troubling you. Then look at how you're reacting."

He knew Robert was better than this.

Robert took a couple of deep breaths. "I'm blowing it up out of all proportion, aren't I?"

There was his Robert.

"And now you're going to hand over all that anxiety." Toby smiled. "On your knees."

Robert's eyes bulged. "Seriously? This is not the—"

"On. Your. Knees." Toby locked gazes with him, and this time Robert stilled. He sank to his knees on the rug, swallowing.

Toby gave a nod. "Hands on your thighs." He waited a moment. "Now take a deep breath, hold it for four seconds, then let it out, slowly." Robert's chest swelled, and he nodded once more. "Again. Keep doing it until I tell you to stop."

He could almost see a layer of calm settling on Robert's shoulders, easing them down. Toby left him like that for ten minutes, until he was sure Robert was once again in control of himself. Toby opened the drawer in the chunky coffee table and removed a couple of lengths of jute. He placed them on the couch, making sure Robert saw them.

He couldn't miss the moment when Robert's mind connected

the dots.

"Thank you, Sir." Robert's voice had lost all of its previous edge.

"Take off your shirt."

Robert's fingers fumbled a little as he unbuttoned the cotton shirt, shucked it off, and placed it on the coffee table. Toby set to work creating the rope harness, taking his time, twining the rope around Robert's upper body. As soon as he'd tied the first overhand knot, Robert's breathing caught and he closed his eyes.

"That's it. Feel it hugging you, sliding over your skin." This wasn't sexual—this was changing the dynamics from boss and lover to Dom and sub. Then he realized Robert's eyes were glistening. Toby didn't say a word, but let Robert weep, seeing the tears for what they were. This was nothing to do with his panic attack—this was a reaction to letting go of all his inner turmoil. Eventually, the tears dried up, and by the time Toby was done, Robert was at peace.

Toby helped him to stand, and wiped his eyes and cheeks with gentle fingers before guiding him backward until his calves met the couch. "Sit."

Robert complied, and Toby sat beside him.

They had all morning, and he was going to use all of it to get Robert's focus back where it should be.

Robert Thorston had never felt so free.

Which had to be the most ironic feeling ever, seeing as he was lying on the couch wearing only his jeans, bound in a Shibari harness. His head rested on Toby's lap, and Toby was reading. Occasionally he would stroke Robert's head, his shoulder, or chest, but there was always that connection between them. He couldn't return the touch—his hands were bound too.

Robert loved it when Toby did this. Being fucked while tied to the bed was amazing, but *this*... Shibari was so much more intimate and emotionally binding.

He smiled to himself at the intentional pun.

"What just went through your mind?" Toby set his book aside on the small table next to the couch.

"Me, trussed up like a turkey. I should feel trapped."

Toby smiled. "But you don't."

Robert managed a slight shake of his head. "Quite the opposite. It feels as though I've let go of everything that was worrying me."

"That was kinda the point." Toby caressed his cheek. "You've been worrying all this past week, haven't you?"

Robert nodded.

"That's why I had to do something." Toby leaned over and kissed him.

"And I trusted you to take it all away." He swallowed. "I... I'm sorry I cried." He hadn't been able to stop the tears, and he had no clue why he was weeping.

"Hey, never apologize for something like that. It happens, sometimes," Toby told him. "But they were happy tears. I guess you could call it a kind of euphoria." He gazed into Robert's eyes. "What are you feeling right this second?"

Robert smiled. "Connected."

Toby's face lit up. "Me too."

Maybe he was right. It *had* been kind of cathartic.

"Ready for me to untie you?"

He chuckled. "The untying part is just as good."

Toby raised Robert's head, cradling it in his hands, stood, and lowered him back onto the seat cushion. He loosened the knots, and little by little, Robert regained control of his limbs. He knew what was coming.

Making love after a session was the best.

Toby knelt on the rug beside the couch, the ropes removed, and bent over to kiss him, a slow, sensual kiss that promised they weren't done. Then Toby perched on the edge of the cushion, studying Robert's face.

"What do you need?"

Robert smiled. "Just this. Us on the couch for a while."

"You *can* come with me to San Francisco if you want. I don't mind."

Robert took Toby's hand and kissed his palm. "You'll only be gone a couple of days. I think I can cope that long without you.

And someone has to run this place."

Who was he kidding? Teague was more than capable. He'd done it for the past five years, after all, when Robert's willingness to get involved had been MIA.

I'm back though.

And that was thanks to Toby, one hundred percent.

"Sean's got some papers he needs me to sign." Toby's fingers traced patterns through the mat of salt-and-pepper hair on his chest, now and then tugging gently on it, sending a shiver through him.

"And you want to see how the club is doing without you." Robert peered at Toby. "Do you miss it?"

"Yes—and no." Toby let out a sigh. "There's always something going on. And then there are the noises." He gave a wry chuckle. "I swapped whips and paddles for cattle lowing, horses neighing, and cries of *yee haw.*"

Robert laughed. "Who around here yells that?"

"Zeeb, when he's teaching a guest how to throw a lariat. It's kinda cute."

"You're going to have your hands full when you get back." The first guests for Salvation's new venture were due September twenty-fourth, and in his more panic-filled moments, Robert had visions of them arriving to find pipes sticking out of walls, floors not laid, no beds…

No wonder Toby had taken him in hand.

Toby got on top of him, his weight pinning Robert to the couch, and looked him in the eye. "Stop that."

He feigned innocence. "Stop what?"

Toby's eyebrows went skyward. "You know what I'm talking about." He kissed the tip of Robert's nose. "It's going to be fine. Everything is working out according to plan. Tomorrow the carpenters and plumbers will arrive—even if we have to find new plumbers—and by the end of the week, you won't recognize the place. Neither will I, probably. Think what a surprise I'll get when I return."

"But we've only had one firm booking so far." And that was his second biggest fear. Toby had invested so much into Salvation's specialist stays. *What if it's a flop? What if no one comes?* The hamster inside his head was moving so fast, its wheel was about to come off its axle.

Toby cupped his chin. "Do I need to tie you up again?"

"No, Sir."

That was clearly the right answer. Toby climbed off him and resumed his perch on the cushion. "You need to have a little faith. Word will get around."

God, Robert loved his confidence, but not nearly as much as he loved his man.

His Dom.

To be able to say those two words felt like a miracle. In the middle of the deepest, darkest night, he'd believed there would never be anyone who could replace Kevin, in his bed and his heart, but Toby had achieved both.

"You haven't heard a word I've said, have you?" Amusement laced Toby's voice.

"I *was* listening. You said word would get around."

"Mm-hmm. And *then* I said I'll be talking up a storm about Salvation when I go to the club. Sean says he'll advertise it too."

"That's good of him."

"Hey, it's a two-way street. We get any clients who are interested in becoming members of the best BDSM club that side of the Rockies?" Toby grinned. "We'll send 'em Sean's way." He laid his hand on Robert's chest. "We *will* make this work, all right? You have to trust me."

"I do." Then Robert recalled his words of a moment ago. "But I'm a little curious. You told me about the things you'll miss in San Francisco. What's the stuff you w*on't* miss?"

"That might surprise you."

Robert blinked. "Try me."

"Being me. Well, the me that existed in San Francisco, in the club."

"Come again?"

Toby said nothing for a moment, and Robert covered Toby's hand with his.

"I was always so in control of myself. I didn't let anyone get too close. And if they did, I pushed them away. There was no reason for it—that was just how I was, okay?" He joined their hands. "I didn't connect with anyone outside of a scene. And those are not just my words. Sean said the same thing. Then I came here.

I met you, Teague, Butch, Zeeb, Paul, Walt, Matt, Diana... and for the first time, I found people I wanted to be around, who had nothing to do with my BDSM lifestyle." He fingered the gleaming metal chain around Robert's neck, tracing the chunky links to the small golden padlock nestled at the base of his throat. "People I love."

Robert's breathing hitched. The day Toby had collared him had been his happiest in such a long time. Toby's light touch on it brought home its truth—they were Dom and sub, lovers...

Except neither of them had yet to utter those three little words.

Robert knew why he hadn't said them. Toby had come from a non-romantic side of BDSM, and in that world, collaring would speak for him in ways he couldn't.

Robert was waiting on Toby, his heart pounding.

Toby leaned in, and their mouths met in a kiss that blew him away with its sweetness, a gentle brushing of lips, Toby's tongue tracing the seam, parting them, exploring him...

Then Toby pulled back. "I told you a few weeks ago that I'd fallen for you."

"I'm not likely to forget that part." Robert brought his fingers to his collar. "This is a constant reminder."

"Yeah, but I think I need to elaborate on that." Toby's forehead met his. "The collar says we're committed to each other, that we share so much. It says something else too, something I haven't been able to voice, but maybe it's time." Another gentle kiss sent Robert's heart soaring, but Toby's words sent him into the stratosphere. "There's no one I love, the way I love you."

Aw fuck. Something broke inside him, and tears pricked the corners of his eyes. "Love you too."

Shock ricocheted through him when he caught the sparkle in Toby's eyes.

Toby swiped at them with his fingertips. "Look at us. What a pair."

Robert took his hand, brought it to his lips, and kissed Toby's fingers. On impulse, he sucked on Toby's thumb, flicking it with his tongue, watching Toby's pupils dilate, hearing that delicious catch in his breathing. He let go and met Toby's heady gaze.

"Got anywhere you need to be right now?"

Toby's eyes gleamed. "Only in our bed."

Robert's dick reacted as his blood took a detour south.

Toby noticed, of course.

He rose, holding his hand out, and Robert took it. "Then let's go upstairs where I can show you how much I love you, without Matt or Teague—or your sister—walking in on us."

Robert could go with that plan.

CHAPTER 5

Tuesday, August 9

San Francisco

Toby leaned back in his chair. "Is that everything?"

Sean chuckled. "Wanna tell me why you came all this way just to sign a few documents? Which you could've done digitally, by the way." He grinned. "Aw, you've missed us."

Toby laughed. "I was only here a month ago. And I haven't had time to miss you. I've been too busy getting ready."

"Then it's full steam ahead?"

He nodded. "We're still on course for the twenty-fourth of next month. Well, the accommodation will be ready—we just don't have that many bookings yet." And while he would never admit it to Robert, that had given him a few sleepless nights.

They had a lot riding on this.

"Of course, your website is ready too. And your social media links."

Toby stared at him.

Sean shook his head. "Yeah, I thought so. You never were any good at the socials. Why haven't you gotten around to this yet?"

Toby glared. "Are you kidding? It's been *three weeks* since we decided to do this. Personally, I think we've achieved a helluva lot in that time."

Sean tapped on his keyboard, then turned the laptop around. "I've been busy too."

Toby had to admit, the club website looked fantastic. "That background... is that leather?" The site had a slick, professional appearance.

"Yup. We took a shitload of photos around the club. The hardest part was keeping the site from straying into NSFW territory, but Sol managed it. That guy is a genius. I mean, how the fuck do you design a website for a BDSM club so that it doesn't have people clutching their pearls when they come across it by accident, and yet has enough to catch the attention of those who are looking for what we offer?"

"*Sol* did this?" Sol Davenport had been a member of the club ever since it had opened its doors four years ago.

Sean nodded. "We got talking after your last visit. I knew about his counseling work—I had *no* idea about this."

Toby felt a stab of guilt.

When did I last speak with Sol? Certainly a few months before he'd taken the fateful trip to Montana. *For all I know, he could've met someone in the intervening time.*

Except that didn't seem likely, knowing what he did about Sol's history.

"Has anything… changed with his situation?"

"He's still single, if that's what you're asking."

Yeah, no shocker there.

He leaned in to take a closer look at the website. "Something knocked the stuffing out of Sol, before he ever came to San Francisco."

"Lemme guess. Some guy broke his heart."

"Sort of." Toby wasn't about to go into details. He'd only heard the story because he and Sol had gotten drunk at a party not long after he'd moved to San Francisco, and it had poured out of Sol in an unstoppable torrent. They'd talked long into the night until both of them had fallen asleep on Casey's couch. The following day, it had become obvious Sol did *not* want to discuss it any further, so Toby withdrew and left him to his own devices.

One night that had cemented a friendship.

Toby gazed at the laptop screen. "Do you think he'd have time to make something similar for us?"

"How about you go find him and ask? He's here." Sean inclined his head toward the door. "Ivor—he's a new sub, joined last week—wanted to know about sounds, so Sol said he'd talk him through using them." Sean's eyes gleamed. "I'm pretty sure he thought he'd be getting a TED talk."

Toby laughed. "Oh, I think I know where this is going. Sol's using Ivor as a visual aid, isn't he?" It wouldn't be the first time.

"Got it in one. As we speak, Ivor's on the stage. Sol's probably removing the biggest sound and Ivor is gonna come like a fucking geyser."

Toby had to see this.

As he rose, Sean cleared his throat. "Everything's okay then, over there under the big sky?"

Toby frowned. "Yeah, everything's fine." Then it hit him. "So… did you bet on me staying in Montana, or did you think I'd come crawling back here with my tail between my legs?"

Sean flushed. "Hey, you can't blame us. Toby Merrow in love? None of us saw *that* one coming."

"You haven't answered my question."

Sean's eyes twinkled. "I bet you'd stay the course."

Toby smiled. "I hope they were good odds, and you win a packet."

He excused himself and left Sean's office. The stage wasn't huge, just big enough to demonstrate suspension, floggers, and occasionally they dragged a St. Andrew's Cross onto it. A crowd stood around; all attention was focused on the demonstration.

Two chairs sat in the center of the stage, Sol on one, the other facing him. Ivor was a skinny guy wearing nothing but a harness and boots. He sat upright, gripping the edge of his seat, his body rigid, his thighs quivering.

His dick was like a flagpole, pre-cum sliding down it in a thin trickle.

Sol was the picture of calm, dressed only in jeans and boots. Toby had to admit that when it came to demonstrations, Sol was pretty amazing. He exuded patience and humor, and the feedback on his demos was always good. From first glance, he appeared to have a new tattoo to add to his collection. Toby had once dared him to have his bald head tattooed, but Sol had laughed off the challenge. Anyone meeting him for the first time would think he was in his early forties, but Toby knew the truth.

I hope I look as good as he does when I reach my fifties.

Toby edged closer through the group of men standing around to get a better view. Sol was oblivious to the crowd, as he always was during such events.

The submissive claimed all his attention.

Sol leaned forward, his hands on Ivor's knees.

"Feels good, doesn't it?"

"Yes, Sir." Ivor was panting, his cock twitching.

Toby got close enough to make out the flat end of the grey

silicone rod, protruding slightly from the top of Ivor's dick head, only an inch or so visible. Sol tapped it a couple of times with his fingers, and Ivor groaned.

"You're hard as a rock," Sol murmured. He rotated the rod until the end was flat against Ivor's slit. Then Toby had to fight the urge to laugh when Sol picked up a bullet vibrator.

Oh, you are evil.

Sol pressed the button on the base, held its rounded end to the rod, and the effect was instantaneous. Tremors rippled through Ivor, and his knuckles went white as he gripped the chair even harder.

Sol nodded. "You want to come, but you can't."

Ivor squirmed, his moans constant, and it was all he could do to manage a single nod.

Sol kept up the vibrations for a minute more, then clicked it off. Ivor sagged into his chair.

"Ready?"

Ivor swallowed. "Yes, Sir."

Slowly, Sol eased the silicone rod free of Ivor's cock, and Ivor creamed over Sol's fingers curled around his shaft, long ribbons of cum pulsing from it, Ivor trembling as wave upon wave of his climax crashed over him. When he was spent, Sol smiled and caressed his cheek.

"You did good."

Ivor fucking *beamed.* "Thank you, Sir."

Around them, the group applauded, some of them voicing their appreciation before the crowd dissipated, leaving the two of them alone on the stage. Sol lifted Ivor into his arms and held him against his chest, cradling him, murmuring compliments.

Toby brought his hands together and clapped, and Sol jerked his head in the direction of the sound. He broke into a wide smile, then refocused on Ivor.

"You okay?"

Ivor nodded, smiling. "Thanks. That was awesome."

"If I let you go, do you think you can make it off the stage?"

"I'll be here to catch him if he stumbles," Ryan called out. Ivor gave him a warm glance, and Toby had to smile.

Aha. It was about time. Ryan had been looking for a sub for a while, but no one had caught his eye. Judging by the glances Ivor was flashing in his direction, it appeared his search might be over.

Sol stroked Ivor's head. "Well, when we do Secret Santa this year, I bet I know what's going to turn up in his sack with *your* name on it."

Ivor stood, a little shakily. "I don't think you'd fit into Santa's sack, Sir."

He laughed. "Sweet kid." He patted Ivor's shoulder, then waited until Ivor was in Ryan's capable arms before jumping down from the stage, grinning at Toby. "Hey. Looks like a grizzly hasn't had you for breakfast. You obviously don't taste good."

They hugged. "Well, I found one bear that likes the taste of me," Toby quipped.

"So I hear. That's still working out?"

Toby rolled his eyes. "Does no one around here believe in a happy ending?"

"Sure, but probably not the kind *you're* talking about." Then Sol's face tightened. "If it's going well, I'm glad. Enjoy every minute of it, because none of us know how long we get, right?"

Toby's stomach clenched. "I hear ya."

Change the subject.

He indicated the door to Sean's office. "I saw your handiwork. Very nice."

Sol's face lit up. "The website? Yeah, it turned out great."

"I had no idea you did that kinda thing."

He chuckled. "I do have a life outside this club, you know. And even in these do-it-yourself days, there are still people out there who don't feel confident enough to build their own site."

"Is business good?"

"Better than good. I'm not here as often as I used to be, because of work demands. Can't tell you the last time I took a vacation. In fact, I think I was still living in Wyoming."

A germ of an idea took root.

"Can I put some more business your way?"

Sol blinked. "You need a website?"

Toby cackled. "I see. Everyone knows I've fallen for someone, but no one's talking about our new venture." Which was the main reason for his visit, if he were honest.

"What new venture?" Then Sol pointed in the direction of the bar. "Let's sit over there, and you can tell me everything over a soda."

"Can you spare the time?" Toby teased. "I know how busy you are."

Sol smacked him on the back. "Sure I'm busy, but for you, I'll make time."

Two ideas were colliding in Toby's head. Bringing off one of them would be great.

Both would be awesome.

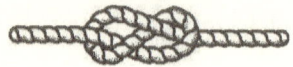

Sol studied the photos on Toby's phone. "It looks like an amazing place."

"It is. And in just over six weeks' time, we open our doors."

"Is Sean going to help spread the word?"

Lord, Toby hoped so.

"Yes, but that's where you come in. Would you build us a site? Like the one you did for Sean?"

He frowned. "Sure, I could do that, but…"

"But what?"

Sol handed Toby's phone back to him. "Those are good photos, don't get me wrong, but they aren't good enough to use on a site."

Toby couldn't have wished for a better opening. "So come stay at Salvation. Take your own pictures. Get a feel for the place."

"But… you said you're not open yet."

"No, I said the *BDSM* part isn't open yet. Come as a guest at the dude ranch. One week. You can spare a week, can't you? If there's work involved."

Toby knew he was begging, but he didn't care. What shocked him was his motivation. Sure, he wanted Sol to put together a stunning website, but he also wanted Sol to unwind a little. He might have left tragedy behind him in Wyoming, but he'd also left any semblance of a life there too.

Sol tilted his head. "A dude ranch. Me?"

"Why not? Hell, the way you look, you'd fit right in." Toby locked gazes with him. "My instincts tell me you need this."

"Your instincts, huh? Are those the same instincts that made you come up with those rules of yours?"

Toby had left those in San Francisco. He was making up a whole new set of rules—for him and Robert.

"Letting Tyler go was the best thing I could have done for him." The sub had found happiness, fulfillment—and love—with Will, which was what he'd wanted all along, and Toby couldn't have been happier for him.

Sol huffed. "You may be right there. That boy is *glowing*. Love'll do that to you." His Adam's apple bobbed sharply.

"At least think about it. I can't remember exactly how many guests we have booked in between now and opening day, but there's always room for one more. Wide open spaces, fresh country air, good food—"

"You forgot big skies in your sales pitch," Sol quipped. Before Toby could utter another word, Sol got his own phone out. "When would you want the site up and running?"

"Preferably by the end of the month. The first week in September at a pinch."

Sol's eyes widened. "Wow. You don't want much, do you?"

Toby laughed. "I have complete faith in your ability to work miracles."

"Now hang on a second. I need to look at my schedule. What if I *can't* squeeze you in? We're talking an awful tight deadline."

Damn it. Toby'd known it wouldn't be easy. He'd expected way too much of Sol.

"But I *will* do what you suggest." When Toby caught his breath, Sol held his hand up. "I'll think about it, all right? But only if I have the time."

Toby knew when to stop pushing rope.

"Okay, fair enough."

"When do you fly back?"

"There's a flight at five-eighteen." It'd get into Bozeman just after midnight, but it was better than the alternative, arriving about ten the following morning.

Toby was already missing Robert.

Good Lord, I've got it bad.

He hoped he got to hold onto Robert for longer than Sol had gotten with Liam.

CHAPTER 6

Wednesday, August 10

Salvation felt like one of those deserted mining towns they used to put in the movies: there seemed to be no one around. Toby's truck was parked beside the barn, so he must've returned at some point during the night—it had been there at five when Butch stepped outside to grab that first lungful of crisp morning air.

Butch glanced up the hill toward the house.

I guess we won't be seeing those two for a while.

A low melodic humming came from the stable. That meant Paul was spending time with the horses. Butch pushed the door to the bunkhouse open and peered inside.

The only person in sight was Matt who was sprawled on the couch, his phone in one hand, the other cupping his crotch.

Butch coughed loudly. "Not interruptin' you, I hope."

Matt snorted. "Nope." He didn't even break eye contact with the screen, his thumb busy swiping.

He didn't let go of his package either.

Butch waited, but it soon became obvious Matt wasn't about to engage in conversation.

"Where the fuck is everyone?" Butch headed for his bunk to stow his purchases. He'd gone into Bozeman to buy bulbs for his night light—the old one had died on him two days before, and he was stocking up. He also needed a few other things, and was glad to find the place empty.

Zeeb seeing him with a box of condoms? Yeah no. Butch didn't think Zeeb would let *that* go without comment. Butch shoved them into the drawer he used for his underwear.

"Teague's up at the house with the boss and Toby. Paul's in the stable. Zeeb took the guests up on the Shafthouse trail, and Walt's feeding the herd."

Butch returned to the couch. "And what are you doing? As if I didn't know."

Matt tilted his head toward Butch and grinned. "Me? I'm on Grindr, finding myself a guy for the weekend. Gonna go to Bozeman." His eyes sparkled as he held up his phone. "I keep thinking one of these days I'm gonna find *you* on here."

"And what would I be doin' on an app for gay guys? Hmm? Fuck, I've never even seen it."

That wasn't to say he hadn't burned with curiosity now and then.

"Well, now's your chance. No one else around." Matt waved his phone in the air. "Wanna take a peek? See what you're missing?" He grinned. "It's not as if you're gonna see dicks. Grindr's more... tasteful than that."

"Yeah right." Butch strolled over to the couch and sat, while Matt straightened. He peered at the screen. "So this is what you use to find yourself a date?" It seemed to be a collection of photos—guys of all shapes and sizes, some clothed, some in just their underwear—some of them in *wet* underwear that left nothing to the imagination...

That led to another snort. "'S not exactly a date, more of a hookup."

"Where'd you take these guys? To a gay bar?" As if he didn't already know the answer to that one.

Matt laughed out loud. "Are you kidding? There are no gay bars in Bozeman. Livingston's okay—if you're a lesbian—but there are still no bars." He shrugged. "Bozeman's safe enough. It's not like I'm going to walk down the street holding a guy's hand, right? We just take a room in the hotel off Highway 191. It's a 1-star, but we're not renting it for the decor, if you catch my drift." He grinned. "At least the Wi-Fi's free so we get to watch porn."

It seemed little had changed in thirty years.

Matt jerked his head toward the door. "Sounds like they're back from the trail. I'd better get on with lunch." He held his hand out. "Can I have my phone, please?" Matt waggled his eyebrows. "Unless you want to take down a guy's particulars?"

"And why would I wanna do that?"

Christ, does he think I'm gay or something?

Butch tossed Matt his phone, and Matt lurched off the couch and through the door that led to the bunkhouse kitchen. Butch propped his feet up on the coffee table strewn with magazines, gloves, used mugs, hats, and the odd pizza box.

Guess I'd better clear this shit up. He didn't want Teague gunning for him. The bunkhouse *was* his area, right?

Matt's words rang in his head.

Livingston again. Two mentions in the last five days. It was almost as if something was determined to remind him of his past.

Butch hadn't been there for about five years, not since that one time when Teague had shown up. But before that, he'd been a regular visitor. Not that there'd been a pattern to his visits—he'd gone there whenever the urge took him, and sometimes that meant it could've been two, three months since the last time.

Before Livingston, however, there had been visits to Billings. Race Prettyman had found himself a place there, and that had been a two-hour drive from Salvation. From July to October after they'd first met, Butch had headed over there to shoot some pool in Race's basement, eat pizza and drink beer, and talk for hours about anything they goddamn pleased. He'd loved those little breaks, driving there every two to three weeks. Race was easygoing and fun to be around.

He'd also been a good-looking dude, and Butch had lost count of the number of times errant thoughts strayed into his head, thoughts of Race bringing guys back to his place, not to shoot pool, not to talk, but to get busy doing other... things. He'd tried to push such thoughts from his mind, but *Lord*, they were persistent.

It was none of his damn business.

And as for why he never imagined Race getting down and dirty with a woman—the guy was bi, after all—Butch didn't care to delve too deeply into that.

Only thing was, part of him had yearned to know more, and when that inner voice piped up with its habitual *Stop thinking about this* warning, Butch shoved it way down deep.

Except it never stayed there for long.

Throughout those four months, Race had remained the perfect gentleman, so Butch guessed he'd lied when he'd said Butch was his type.

If that was so, he'd have done something, wouldn't he? Made a move or something?

Then he'd given himself a mental shake.

But I don't want him to make a move, so why do I keep thinking about this?

Yeah, he already knew the answer to *that* question.

Then came the day when he'd finally gotten up enough nerve to cross the line.

November, 1992

"Gonna put the eight-ball in that corner pocket," Race told him, half of him lying on the pool table, lining up his cue for the long shot.

Butch wasn't thinking about pool—he was staring at Race's ass.

His tight, denim-encased ass.

And you'd better quit that, right fucking now, *because he could turn around at any second and catch—*

"What exactly is it about my behind that has you so captivated?" Race's eyes glittered.

Well fuck.

Butch jerked his head in the opposite direction, staring at a poster Race had stuck on the wall. "That new?"

Race snorted. "It was there the last time you visited. Now, can we get back to why I caught you getting an eyeful of my ass? Not that this is the first time."

"Don't know what you're talking about," Butch mumbled.

Race's eyebrows shot up. "Mm-hmm."

"You got any beers left?"

"Nope, but I've got a bottle of tequila if you're interested."

Butch wasn't too sure about that. Bourbon? He could handle that.

Race grinned. "What's wrong? Tequila too much for ya?"

Oh, *now* he'd gone and done it.

"Where are the glasses?"

Race cackled and pointed to the cabinet on the wall. "In there. So's the tequila."

Butch retrieved the bottle, filled two shot glasses, and handed one to Race.

"Down it in one," Race demanded.

Butch could play that game. He tipped the glass up, and the fiery liquid hit the back of his throat. "Christ, it burns."

"Second shot's always better." Race grabbed the bottle and poured, then raised his own. "Come on, Princess. Don't worry about getting back to the ranch. I've got a sofa bed with your name on it." His eyes twinkled with good humor.

His referral to the night they'd met made Butch smile. "Is it a big enough sofa this time?"

"You know it."

Fuck it.

The more the level in the tequila bottle dropped, the more he noticed stuff. Like Race's lips. They were full and kinda soft-looking, and Butch got to wondering how they'd feel if they were wrapped around his—

Whoa there, cowboy.

He grew hot. Cold. Hot. Hard.

That last part was no surprise. He hadn't been with anyone since Diana, and he'd done a whole lot more jerking off since then.

"You wanna tell me what's going on?" Race sounded sober, the bastard.

"Nothin's goin' on," he retorted.

"Sure. I can hear the cogs turning from across the room." Race frowned. "We're friends, right?"

"Course."

"Then you know you can talk to me about anything, right? Because it looks to me like you need to take a load off your mind."

The words were out before Butch had time to think.

"Is it so different, bein' with a guy?"

Race stilled. "We talking sex?" Butch clammed up, and Race arched his eyebrows. "Okay, where did *that* come from?"

Ice won out over heat. "Forget I asked, okay?" He held his shot glass up. "An' pour me another."

Race shook his head. "Uh-uh. Not until we've talked about this." He stretched his long legs out in front of him, and Butch couldn't miss the bulge in his jeans. "I'm not sure I can explain it. It's kinda like describing the taste of chocolate to someone who's never tasted it."

Say it. For fuck's sake, just say it. You know you want to.

"And... and what if I wanted a taste?"

Race stared at him. "Why would you want that? You're into women."

"Maybe... maybe I'm curious."

Race bit back a smile. "You wouldn't be the first. I've met enough curious straight guys in my time, that's for damn sure."

"Have you ever thought about... me in that way? You said I was your type, but—"

"But I've kept my hands to myself, is that it?" Race leaned forward, his gaze locked on Butch's face. "We talked about this, you remember? That small but vital word—consent?"

"But what if I... give consent?"

Race's breathing hitched, and his pupils enlarged just enough to let Butch know he'd hit his mark. Then Race leaned back. "If I was to... give you a taste..."

In that second Butch *knew* Race was talking about his dick, and the prospect sent tremors up and down his spine.

"I'd want to be one hundred percent certain this was a genuine request." His eyes focused on Butch's. "You understand? You need to be sure about this. We've built up a good friendship these past few months. I don't want to ruin that."

"Would it ruin things? If we did... other stuff besides shooting pool and drinking beer?"

Say it wouldn't. For the love of God...

Butch's heart thumped.

"That all depends on how you react when I get your cock in my mouth."

Sweet Jesus. Butch was on fire.

Race widened his eyes. "And you like that idea, don't you?"

Butch swallowed. "Yes." The word came out as a croak.

Race studied him for a moment, then stood. He walked slowly to where Butch sat on his recliner, knelt in front of him, and stroked Butch's hard-on that pushed against his zipper, almost as if it were demanding to be freed.

"You sure about this? Last time of asking."

Butch was close to breaking point. He popped the button on his waistband, lowered the zipper—carefully, because his dick was like a steel pipe in there—and lifted his ass off the chair to shove his jeans over his hips. His shaft stood to attention, the foreskin already peeling back to reveal the wide head.

Race caught his breath. "Damn, that's pretty."

And before Butch could thank him for the unusual compliment, Race leaned forward, and Butch *finally* got what he'd been thinking about since he was seventeen years old.

Oh FUCK.

Race left Diana in the dust when it came to oral skills.

"You takin' a day off?"

Butch jumped. Zeeb stood beside the couch, grinning. Behind him the two male guests were removing their hats.

"Don't sneak up on a guy like that," Butch groused.

"Who was sneaking?" Zeeb's eyes sparkled. "I got no clue where you were just now, but it seemed to be a nice place. I was almost sorry to disturb you. Almost." He gazed at the coffee table. "You might wanna do something about the mess," he muttered. "Teague was on his way down the hill just now, and he'll have your ass if he sees this." He glanced around to see where the guests were, but they'd gone to the bathroom at the rear of the bunkhouse. Zeeb's grin came back full strength. "Although I'm sure he wouldn't complain about getting a piece of your ass."

Butch was about to reply that *no one* ever got a piece of *his* ass, when he thought better of it.

That was one can of worms he did *not* want to open.

CHAPTER 7

Friday, August 12, 2022
San Francisco

Sol's fingers were as busy as his mind, and the website for the Redbridge Theater was looking good. He estimated a couple more days, three at the most, and it'd be finished. It was one of his more interesting jobs.

He had a list of others that promised to be a whole lot less interesting, but hey, the boring stuff paid the bills too, and it filled the hours when he wasn't working as a counselor.

Sol was never one to stand still for very long. He had to be doing something. As far as he was concerned, inactivity only led to one thing—too much time to think—and he'd done enough of that in recent years to be in gold medal qualification.

Right on cue, his gaze drifted to the framed photo on his desk. Liam's eyes held their habitual light, and he was laughing. Sol remembered the moment as if it were yesterday. Liam had tried to keep a straight face, but at the last minute Sol had cracked a joke, and that was that.

Hey babe.

Time might have diminished the pain, but not the memories, thank God. They were still as fresh and vibrant as ever.

His phone pinged, and he glanced at it. Sol smiled. *Wow. Four days.* He was impressed. He'd expected some communication from Toby way before now.

Maybe that cowboy of his is slowing him down a little.

He scanned the text.

I've checked. Aug 20-27 would be good for a visit. No pressure.

Yeah right.

Sol peered at the desk calendar sitting next to his keyboard. It'd be tight, but if he worked all week and avoided the club, he could manage it—if he wanted to, of course. He picked his phone up and messaged back, smiling to himself. He wasn't about to capitulate *that* easily.

I said I'd think about it.

He set his phone back down and resumed tapping on the keys, anticipating the arrival of another message, maybe one laced with more persuasion.

Nothing.

That made him smile even more. The Toby he'd known prior to this summer wouldn't have stopped at one text. Maybe life in Montana was teaching him to slow the fuck down. The change of pace had to be huge. He tried to picture Toby in a cowboy hat with spurs on his boots, but it wouldn't compute.

Now, a whip in his hand? That was something else entirely.

What was the name of that place again? Salvation?

He opened a new window and typed in the search field, *Salvation dude ranch Montana*. The header for the website was a stunning photo of a lush green pasture, with a huge expanse of cloudless sky, and in the background, a couple of figures on horseback.

When was the last time I did that?

Except he knew. He and his sister Alli had learned to ride pretty much as soon as they were tall enough to grab a saddle. It was something they'd done often, as natural as breathing.

What came as a shock was that he'd missed it, and the image tugged at him.

Sol switched into developer mode and scrolled through the website. Once he'd seen enough, he reached for his phone again.

You don't need me for your new site. Whoever did the dude ranch website is good. Let them build it.

It didn't take long for Toby's reply to appear.

But I think you can do a better job. Plus I want someone who knows the lifestyle.

Sol knew a good designer could turn their hand to anything, provided they had all the information at their fingertips. Still, Toby had a point. Plus, he'd liked what Sol had done for the club.

That header image kept on tugging.

His thumbs got busy. *Okay to call you?*

Less than ten seconds later the phone rang. "I've got thirty minutes before I have to be someplace. What's up?"

Sol settled back in his chair. "Tell me more about your plans."

For the next ten minutes, Toby talked, with Sol interrupting here and there to ask questions. It sounded like a bold venture—and totally Toby-like. Sol could already think of three or four guys at the club who might be interested. But three or four wasn't enough. Toby needed a site that would drag them in, and once word got around…

Sol glanced at the scribbles he'd made during the conversation.

"Have you incorporated an aftercare section in the design for the new space? You know, a place to rest, talk, with lots of aftercare products…"

Crickets.

He grinned. "Aha."

"No, I haven't, but that was because I had two possible spots in mind. I was hoping you'd help me decide… when you see the ranch."

Sol chuckled. "I'll say this for you—you're persistent." He tapped his pen on his notepad. "Is everything completed then?"

"Not yet."

"Can you make any changes? This new barn you've had built… Is there a part of it that could be used for aftercare? Preferably near whatever space you're using for scenes, demos, et cetera. Or is that one of the spots you've identified?"

"Yeah, it was." Toby sighed. "I'll talk to Robert. We need to make a decision on this."

"And this website… you're planning a section where guests can access consent forms, supply medical details…?"

"Already looking into that." Toby's confident tone was back.

"Good." Sol paused. "Have I just given you a headache?"

"Kind of, but it was already brewing. I'll get right on it." A moment's pause. "And now I'm even more determined to get you on board with this."

Sol chuckled. "You're pushing again. What was that you said about no pressure?"

"Sorry."

Sol fought to restrain his snort. "You are *not* sorry at all." Toby knew what he wanted—and what the ranch needed. "I do have one question, though, and it's related to the building you've got going on."

"Fire away."

"Suppose you do get me to come visit. Will there be anything to take pictures of? What I mean is, you'd want photos of the accommodation, the space for scenes… I'm not going to turn up if there's nothing to see. I know you said you want the site ready for the end of the month, but is that feasible?"

"I guess if I want you in on this, it'll have to be ready." He sighed. "I'd better go break the news to Robert. If we're going to do this, he needs to light a fire under the asses of our contractors. Let's talk soon, okay?"

"Sure." He ended the call, then glanced once more at his diary. Once the theater's website was done, there was the dental surgery, the site for that CPA… Both as interesting as whale shit, but work was work.

Toby's venture, on the other hand…

Sol had loved creating the club's website, and this promised to be as much of a challenge. His gaze flickered back to the laptop screen, to those green pastures, rolling hills, dense forests, and trickling streams. The accommodation seemed pretty basic, but Sol didn't give a shit about that.

Toby had been right about one thing.

I need this.

A week would be plenty of time to discover more about the place. He could take a shit ton of pictures, and he was reasonably sure Toby wouldn't be averse to putting on his leathers for a few photo ops. Maybe his cowboy, too—Robert, that was it.

More than that, he wanted some time to reconnect with the great outdoors. How many times had he thought about going to Yosemite or Lake Tahoe, only to back off at the last minute, telling himself the demands of work were too great?

Yeah, he was always busy, but he knew that was just an excuse.

His phone rang, and he laughed. *Maybe Toby hasn't mellowed all that much.*

Then he saw it was Alli.

Sol stabbed at *Answer.* "Hey."

"Hey yourself. Is this a bad time?"

"You're good. What's up?" They usually called each other every two to three weeks. "How's the painting business?"

She chuckled. "Painting makes it sound like I splash paint on walls. I am an *artist*, sweetheart."

"Does it pay as much as house painting?"

She laughed. "It paid off the mortgage so I can't complain." A pause. "I'm calling about Thanksgiving."

Sol went quiet. *Aw shit, here we go again.*

"Sol? You still there?"

He forced himself to be patient. "Sis, it's August. Can't we even get Labor Day out of the way before you start planning Thanksgiving?"

"Uh-uh. I'm tired of you saying you're busy. So I'm putting my request in early."

"I can't plan that far ahead," he lied, trying not to look at his schedule.

"Yes, you can. And the invite includes whoever you decide to bring with you."

He retreated into silence again.

"Sol... When did you last go on a date?"

"None of your business." His tone was harder than he'd intended, but hell, this was not the first time they'd had this conversation.

"Then I'm going to assume you haven't dated anyone since—"

"Stop." Sol's stomach clenched. He took a couple of deep breaths. "Okay... One? I don't do dates. I meet up with guys and we get up to pretty much everything you can think of. Not gonna go into details, because I believe we did that once, and I don't think you ever recovered."

Or looked at me the same way.

"Yeah, thanks for that."

"Two. Dating implies the possibility of romance. I don't do romance."

"But you did." Alli's tone was soft.

"That was then."

Don't go there, Alli. Please.

He did *not* want to talk about Liam.

"Sol... ever heard the phrase 'Lightning doesn't strike the same place twice'?"

He let out a snort. "That's bullshit because it does. And I don't intend to be there when it happens. The only way to truly avoid that is by not letting myself get into that situation again."

He didn't need romance.

Romance developed into love, and Sol was the kind of man who believed you only got one chance at that.

Unfortunately, his chance had been way too brief, and the aftermath had carved his heart up enough to keep him from ever letting anyone in again.

Falling in lust was just fine.

Alli's gentle sigh reached his ears. "I loved him too, okay?"

Sol closed his eyes, as if that would stop the brief pain that lanced through him.

Fat chance.

"But that won't bring him back," he said, proud of the fact he'd kept the tremor from his voice. "And before you start believing I'm still grieving for him, you need to know something. I've moved on, all right? It's been four years and I've finally moved on." That was God's honest truth. "It still hurts, but at least now it's an ache, not a knife through my fucking chest."

He caught the hitch in her breathing, but he wasn't done.

"But you know what? I've learned. I won't put myself in that position again. So I'll hook up with as many men as I damn well please, and that's about as deep as it's going to get. So fine, if it'll make you happy, put me down for Thanksgiving."

"You mean it?" God, the note of joy in her voice nearly unraveled him.

"Yes, I mean it. And you've got my permission to tell Mom and Dad I'm coming home. That way, I won't back out, not if I've given my word. But I'll be coming alone, you got that?"

A pause. "I got it. I don't like it, but I got it."

"We all have to put up with disappointment, right? And now I'll get back to work."

"Sol…. Love you, okay?"

As if he could miss hearing that love in her voice.

"I love you too. Say hi to Hugh and the rest of the family for me, okay? Tell them they'll be seeing Uncle Sol at Thanksgiving this year." It had been ages since he'd seen his two nephews and his niece, not to mention his new grand-niece.

"I will. And I'll let Mom and Dad know." She hesitated. "You could always call them yourself."

"It's easier this way."

And less painful.

They said goodbye, and he hung up. He glanced at the desk calendar once more. August twenty to twenty-seven was a line of pristine white squares.

And isn't that a sign right there?

Yeah, Toby was right, damn him. Sol *did* need this.

He pulled up Toby on WhatsApp and typed.

I'll be there on the 20th. Book me in, and I'll do the rest online. As an afterthought, he added *So you'd better have something for me to take pictures of, okay?*

Then he switched the phone off and went back to work.

He could safely lose himself there.

CHAPTER 8

Saturday, August 13

Butch scanned the interior of the bunkhouse. The guests had all been taken into Bozeman, and it would be a while before the next guests would begin to arrive. Plenty of time to get the place cleaned and ready, and everyone pulled their weight to make that happen. Zeeb stripped the bunks downstairs, Walt did the same on the upper floor, and Matt cleared away anything that belonged to the kitchen.

Butch got the worse job—the bathroom—but he was used to that. To be honest, he preferred it that way. He'd seen the results when Zeeb 'cleaned' it. More often than not, it required a second going-over.

How did the saying go? *'If you want something done, do it yourself.'* Except Butch would've paraphrased that by adding the word *well*. He hated half-assed jobs, but Zeeb readily acknowledged he wasn't the world's best cleaner. What he lacked in domestic skills, he more than made up for with his talent for teaching the guests how to rope steers. Added to that, his natural garrulousness put them at ease.

"Coffee's out," Matt hollered from the kitchen area.

"'Bout time. I'd hate to cross a desert with you," Butch called back. The showers were sparkling, and he'd done his weekly battle with the mold that loved to grow in the thin lines between the tiles.

The smell of bleach would be gone by the time the next guests arrived.

Butch washed his hands and ambled through the bunkhouse. The others were already seated on the couch or at the table, and the welcome aroma of freshly brewed coffee permeated the air.

"How many are coming in?" Walt asked, pouring himself a cup. His eyes lit up when Matt cracked open the plastic box that sat in the middle of the table. "Oh please, tell me those cookies are for us, and not the guests."

Matt cackled. "Relax. They're for us. Help yourself." He sat at the table, his gaze locked on his phone.

Walt grinned and grabbed a couple. "Chocolate chip. My favorite." He picked the box up and hugged it against him. "What are you guys havin'?"

Butch gave him a mock glare. "Put. The box. Down. If you want to keep your fingers."

Walt rolled his eyes but complied.

"Teague says we're expecting seven. Four guys, three girls. And Paul's gonna have his hands full. All newbies." Butch glanced at Zeeb. "You're gonna want to pick out some real easy trails to start with." He pulled out a chair next to Matt and flopped into it.

Zeeb nodded. "Sure. I can do that. The forecast is good the whole week too."

Butch helped himself to a cookie. "Matt, one of these days your neck is gonna lock into that position." The guy was always on his phone. "Found something—or someone—to drool over?"

Matt snorted. "I take an interest in what's going on. Current affairs. Nothing wrong with that."

"So you're telling us you're readin' something about world politics, is that it?" Zeeb guffawed. "Sure you are." He gave a couple of sniffs. "Can any of *you* smell that?"

"Smell what?" Walt frowned. "All I can smell is coffee."

"It's real faint but it's there." Zeeb's eyes sparkled. "The whiff of bullshit."

Chuckles and cackles erupted around the table.

"So what's going on that we all need to know about?" Butch demanded. Matt flushed, and he snorted. "Busted." He glanced at the others. "Y'all know what he's doing, don'tcha? He's on that app of his or he's watching porn, one of the two." He craned his neck as if to get a better look at Matt's phone.

"I am *not*," Matt remonstrated, holding the screen to his chest.

"Then tell us the name of the site you're on." Butch grinned. "If you dare."

Matt's cheeks reddened. "It's the *New York Post.*"

Laughter rebounded off the walls.

"Well, obviously," Zeeb declared with wide eyes. "I mean, they have their finger on the pulse of current affairs, right?"

"If you must know, I read their reports on freak accidents. Every week they talk about all the weird shit that happens."

"What kind of weird shit?" Butch asked. "It's all fake, isn't it?"

"No," Matt protested. "It's in their 'Weird but True' section. Stuff like the guy who had a scary work accident, and had hiccups for sixty-eight years after. Or the woman who said she had a rock in her eye for fifty years, and doctors didn't believe her."

"Are all the stories like that?" Walt inquired. "And I don't know about the weird part, but they sure sound like shit to me."

"Not all. Some of them are just awful though. Like the California dad who was struck by a car while he was helping a family of ducks cross the road. Or the one I read this morning, about an old guy who died at a drive-thru."

"Lemme guess." Butch straightened his face. "Food poisoning."

Matt shook his head. "He'd opened his car door to pick up the credit card he'd dropped. The car rolled forward, colliding with the restaurant building, and he got pinned between the car door and the vehicle frame."

"He died?" Walt stilled. "That *is* awful."

"Yeah. They tried to revive him, but he died at the scene. The report said his husband was devastated."

"Where was this?" Zeeb asked.

"Atlanta. Guy was sixty. It said he'd been with his husband for twenty-three years, and that they finally married in 2016 when it became legal." Matt's face fell. "I've got a few gay friends in Atlanta. I'll ask them if they knew the guy who died."

Zeeb blinked. "Is that likely? Atlanta must be huge."

"Yeah, it is, but it's got a close-knit gay community. And with a name like Prettyman, they might know the couple."

Butch froze. "The guy who died… what was his first name?"

"Race. His husband was called Lee."

No. Aw fuck, no.

His stomach plummeted, and his hands were like ice.

"Butch? You okay?" Matt's voice broke through.

Christ, why was it so difficult to breathe?

"Butch?" That was Zeeb.

With an effort, he forced air into his lungs.

Matt stared at him, aghast. "Did you know him?"

Butch nodded. "A long time ago. He… he was a friend."

The words tasted like betrayal on his tongue. Race had been

more than a friend.

Lord, he needed a cigarette. Or a drink.

"Jesus. I'm sorry."

Butch struggled to regain his mental balance. "I haven't seen him since '98 when he moved to Atlanta. He messaged me to tell me about Lee."

Pull yourself together. It's been twenty-four years since Race said his goodbyes. And how long was it before you found a replacement?

Except with Race, it had been more than sex, and Butch knew it.

"How did you guys meet? And where?"

Butch did *not* want to talk about this. All he wanted was to get the fuck out of there. Because he could see what was coming right at him.

You had a gay friend?

How come you never mention him?

And worse still… Teague could get to hear about this, and Butch just *knew* he'd want the whole story.

Well, *no one* got to hear that. Ever.

He stood and headed for the door. "I'll be back in a while." He expected complaints about how much work there was still to be done, but surprisingly, none came.

Butch strode toward the stable. Inside, Paul was brushing Lightning's mane and crooning to him. Butch stood for a moment, letting the calm of the space seep into him like it always did. Up in the rafters, birds nested, and the only sounds were Paul's melodic humming and the horses' breaths. Butch inhaled the scent of dust and hay, grain and mud, and the warm sweet smell of horses. The hint of ammonia lurked beneath the surface. He could smell leather and wood, but the musky aroma of horse overwhelmed them, a fragrance that brought back memories of childhood.

"Something wrong?"

The spell was broken.

Butch strode over to where Paul stood.

"I need to take a horse out." And then he was going to head out to the pasture where he could be alone for an hour or so. The first guests' flight wasn't due in for another couple of hours.

Paul gazed at the stalls behind Butch. "You can take Bailey. You've ridden him lots of times." He nodded toward the saddles.

"Help yourself. I've already groomed him." Then he went back to his task.

Butch grabbed everything he'd need and led Bailey out to the paddock. He took his time making sure the saddle was correctly placed and secured, and it wasn't long before Butch had Bailey trotting along the trail that led to the pasture, past the cabin the boss and Kevin had used when they wanted privacy.

Not that it was a secret. Hell, *everyone* knew.

Butch let Bailey trot at his own pace. The meadow gave way to tall grass, and then the trail led toward the edge of the forest. Birds sang, and he could hear the trickle of water. Soon they were in the trees, and the trickle had swelled into a creek. It wasn't long before he saw the cabin. No one would be around, and he needed a quiet place to think.

He came to a halt at the hitching post, got down, and wound Bailey's rope around the wooden rail. "You haven't learned how to untie knots yet, have you, boy?" Butch wouldn't put it past him. Goddamn horse was smarter than a lot of humans.

The cabin sat on the other side of the creek, and Butch had to admit, a fresh lick of paint had worked wonders. The boss had replaced the wooden porch with a brand new one, and the two Adirondack chairs were glossy white. Butch knew Toby had suggested making the place available to any guests who wanted a little alone time.

BDSM guests.

Butch couldn't help but think about what those cabin walls might witness, what sounds those walls might muffle.

He patted the breast pocket of his shirt, feeling the pack of cigarettes and the lighter. He glanced at Bailey. "You're not gonna tell on me, are ya?"

Bailey's snort didn't require translation.

Butch crossed the creek, stepping carefully on the boulders, and at last he stood in front of the cabin. He sat on the steps that led to the front door, removed a cigarette from his pocket, and lit up. That first inhale was perfect, marred only by the knowledge that if the boss found him, he'd be in trouble.

I keep saying I'll quit. Maybe it was time he did. "You were always on at me to stop, weren't ya?" Butch had always argued that it was his only vice. A lie, of course—he had plenty of others—

but it had shut Race up.

For a while, at any rate.

Butch stared into the sparkling water.

"Race, I don't know if you can hear this, but I'm sorry, dude."

He wasn't sure what he was apologizing for. Race dying? Or was it more the fact that once their connection had been severed, Butch had been the one who'd let it stay that way.

"We had six years, longer than either of us thought it would last when we first started. And yeah, it was fun. Nothing heavy, just two guys scratching each other's itches."

One taste had been enough to make Butch feel as though he'd won the lottery. It was amazing how good sex could be when there were no complications. There'd only been that one time when—

Nope. Not going there.

Thank God Race had been happy with the way things developed.

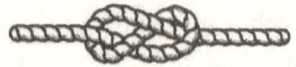

Friday, October 16, 1998

Butch loved that slow-pulsing, cream-in-his-veins kinda feeling that always followed an orgasm. Lord, if he could bottle it, he'd make a fortune because it had to be the most natural high, not to mention addictive as fuck.

Six years on, it still blew his mind, the direction his life had taken. He loved the lack of complications, the tacit understanding that existed between him and Race. No messy emotions, no explanations—just sex. He didn't make demands of Race and vice versa. And once they were done, their urges sated, it was back to beer, pool, and the TV. They didn't discuss the sex, because they didn't need to.

Butch's life was perfect.

True to form, Race was already in the bathroom taking a shower, the way he always did. Butch was content to enjoy the sensations a while longer until the bathroom was free.

Then it hit him.

Race wasn't singing.

Race *always* sang in the shower. It was an immutable law of nature, right up there with night following day, and red wine gravitating toward a cream-colored rug. A ribbon of unease unfurled in Butch's belly, and all pleasurable traces of what they'd just done dissolved into nothingness. He got off the bed and went to the doorway. What met his gaze was enough to send cold spreading out from his core.

Race stood in the shower, elbows locked, hands braced against the tiles, head bowed, the water cascading off him and hitting the glass panels.

Something's wrong.

Butch waited, leaning against the door frame.

Come on, Race. Don't keep it bottled up. Let it out.

At last Race flipped the water off, jumping when he turned and saw Butch.

"Hey. You want a shower too?"

Butch shook his head. "Not right this minute."

Race opened the door and stepped out onto the white mat, reaching for a towel from the handrail. He wrapped it around his hips and tucked the end in.

That skin-crawling feeling of something being badly out of whack wouldn't go away.

"Wanna tell me what's going on?"

Race blinked. "Isn't that my line?" he quipped.

"I'm being serious. Something's wrong. So what is it?"

Silence.

Then Butch got it. "Oh. We're not doing this anymore, is that it?" Race stared at him, standing so still, and Butch's stomach roiled. "Hey, that's fine. It's not as if we didn't know going in that this wasn't a permanent arrangement."

But it *wasn't* fine.

Everything had been great, so what the fuck had changed?

Race sat on the edge of the tub. "You're right—but for the wrong reasons."

"So enlighten me." Then Race smiled, and the sight felt so incongruous. "What's tickled you?"

Race chuckled. "It's a little difficult being serious when you're standing in front of me buck naked, your dick already twitching 'cause it wants round two."

Butch turned and walked out of the bathroom.

"Where are you going?" Race hollered after him.

"To put my jeans on. Then maybe we can have that serious conversation." He grabbed them from where they'd fallen, squirmed into them and hoisted them up over his hips, taking care with the zipper.

If the guys back at the ranch had ever learned how he'd gotten his dick caught in the zipper's teeth one time, he'd never have lived it down. And that was a pain he didn't want to experience again as long as he lived.

Race came into the bedroom. "I should've said something before we fucked, but I knew it would change things. Call me sentimental, but I wanted our last time to be good."

"What should you have said?" God, this felt so freaking ominous.

Last time? What the fuck?

Race sat at the foot of the bed. "I've been transferred. I'm going to Atlanta." Before Butch could react, Race scowled. "Except that's not true. I owe it to you to be honest." He sighed. "I asked for the transfer. Not because of you," he hastened to add. "You did nothing wrong, okay?"

"Then why ask to be transferred?"

Another sigh tumbled from his lips. "Did you hear what happened in Laramie ten days ago?"

Butch usually tried to avoid goings-on in Wyoming, but that rang a bell. "Some college kid got beaten up, didn't he?" Butch was sure he'd seen something like that on the news.

Race nodded. "A *gay* college kid. And the two guys concerned did more than beat him up. They tortured him, then left him tied to a fence. And on Monday? He died. He was twenty-one. *Twenty-one*, Butch."

He had no words.

Race laced his fingers in his lap. "I guess it brought home to me something I'd been trying to ignore." He raised his chin and looked Butch in the eye. "Wyoming, Montana… these are not good places to be if you're queer. And while I'm pretty sure none of my coworkers harbor secret desires to beat the living crap out of me because I like guys, I'm not willing to put that shaky belief to the test."

"Why Atlanta? Georgia can't be all that welcoming either."

Race let out a wry chuckle. "You're probably right, but Atlanta isn't like the rest of Georgia. For one thing, it has a hub of gay guys, and where there's community, there's strength—and safety in numbers. And while I *am* happy to date both sexes, I don't want to keep watching my back."

"When are you leaving?"

"Sunday."

Butch gaped at him. "So soon?" He narrowed his gaze. "There's no *way* you could've arranged a transfer so goddamn fast."

Race shrugged. "The timing was right, that's all. The news only confirmed what I'd been thinking for a while. I called Head Office last week, just to see if there was anything available. Turns out, there was." He bit back a smile. "And if you hadn't been in such a hurry when you got here tonight, you'd have spotted all the boxes in the living room."

Butch snorted. "*I* was in a hurry? As I recall, you opened the front door stark naked, then turned to let me see the butt plug. So yeah, I might have been a little distracted." He couldn't believe it. Race—leaving. Butch knew he'd miss Race's company.

He'd also miss that tight ass.

"We gonna stay in touch?" Race inquired.

"Sure." Easy to say, right? And he *would* try, but they'd both have their own lives to lead.

Race expelled a long breath. "I'm sorry. I shouldn't have left it until now to tell you. That wasn't fair."

Butch gripped Race's still damp, bare shoulder. "Quit acting like we're breakin' up or something. And I totally get why you told me after we fucked." He'd probably have done the same thing.

Race smiled. "It's been quite a ride, hasn't it?"

Butch chuckled. "Yeah."

"So here's the million-dollar question. You gonna find yourself a girl once I've gone?"

He let out another snort. "Dude, I'm twenty-eight. Any woman looks at me, she's gonna have wedding rings dancing behind her eyes. And I don't need that."

"Not *every* woman wants that, you know. Some of them just like to fuck as much as you do."

Butch frowned. "That doesn't sound like the kind of woman I'd be interested in."

"So it's okay for a guy to fuck around, but not a woman?" Race stared at him. "Ever hear the term 'double standards'?"

"Guys know what guys want, okay? Guys don't complicate things."

Race shook his head. "Dude, you are so deep in denial, you can't even see the daylight anymore."

"Who's in denial?" he retorted. "Why're you coming out with all this bullshit?"

"Coming out. Apt choice of words." Race proffered his hand. "Let's say goodbye on good terms, all right?"

Butch could do that.

They shook, and Race's gaze drifted lower. "Man, does that thing ever sleep?"

Butch cupped his crotch and gave it a squeeze. "Not when your ass is near."

"Then let's make it a goodbye fuck to remember."

Bailey whinnied, and Butch jumped. His cigarette had all but burned away, the ash sprinkled on the ground. He'd been lost in his thoughts.

He raised his eyes heavenward.

"Race, I'm happy you found someone. Truly. You got to spend all those years together, which is more than most of us get." He paused. "But dude… in *denial*?"

The initial shock over, he couldn't get past the idea he should feel more sorrow at Race's death, but grief didn't come into it.

"I'm sorry you're dead, but I'm not gonna go to pieces about it. We had our time, said our goodbyes, and that, as they say, is that."

Like he'd told himself many times, he wasn't a nice guy.

It was only as he was heading back to the ranch that it struck him.

He and Race had been fuck buddies for six years. And five

years ago, he and Teague had agreed on their arrangement.

A very similar arrangement.

*How would I feel if something happened to Teague? Would I be this…
detached?*

He hoped he never had to find out.

He could almost hear Race's voice.

"If you think you're detached, dude, you're fuckin' delusional."

Butch knew better. The detachment was his brain's way of
protecting itself.

With all the stuff shoved in there, he needed that protection.

CHAPTER 9

Monday, August 15

Lord, the day was working its way to being a hot one. Zeeb had had the right idea, taking the guests up to Mirror Lake. He and Walt had taken towels with them, so Butch guessed swimming was on the schedule.

When was the last time I did that? So long ago that he'd forgotten. Maybe he should've gone along too. He recalled the feel of icy water against hot skin, and even the memory cooled him, if only for a few seconds.

He pulled his bandanna from his pocket and wiped his brow, watching the workmen heading to their trucks.

"Must be time for lunch." Paul joined him, leaning on the paddock fence. He indicated the new barn. "Have you seen what it looks like inside?"

"Not yet." But he sure wanted to take a peek. "Have you?"

Paul shook his head. "But I have to admit, I'm curious." He chuckled. "About more than just the building."

"Hey, don't let any of the new guests see that," Butch teased. "Once this is a going concern, they might drag you in and invite you to… well, whatever it is they're gonna do in there."

He was in the dark when it came to BDSM. Sure, he'd seen stuff on his phone—who hadn't? —and they'd all heard about *that* book and its movie, but he had no idea if that was real or made-up shit.

The reality could be totally different, not that he intended discovering that reality up close and personal.

Paul grinned. "So it's not just me who's in the dark here? Good to know. I think I'll take a look before the guests arrive, but I was planning on waiting until it was finished."

Butch spotted Toby and the boss strolling toward the barn. "Don't think I'm gonna wait that long." No harm in asking, right?

"Seriously?"

"Why not?" No time like the present.

"Let me know what it's like, okay?" Paul called after him as he walked away.

The barn sat midway between the paddock and the path that led up to the house. A gravel parking lot had been created beside it with space for a few vehicles. The most noticeable feature of the new structure was the lack of windows on the first floor.

Butch could only guess at why they'd designed it that way.

Maybe their guests don't want to be observed.

He walked up to the wide main door. Toby and the boss were talking, so he hung back. Power tools covered the floor space inside the door: Butch had caught the sound of drills from eight o'clock that morning, and he'd wondered what they were working on.

Those drawings he'd seen had stuck in his mind.

"Want to take a peek?"

The boss's smile made it seem as though Butch's presence wouldn't be an intrusion.

"If that's okay."

"Sure. Go on in. Toby's in there." The boss patted him on the shoulder as he headed out.

Butch stepped carefully around the tools. A wooden staircase rose to the left of the door, turning one-eighty degrees at the wall before rising higher. He peered at the landing above his head.

"It's really coming together." Toby stood in the open doorway in front of him.

"The boss said it was all right for me to have a look." Butch pointed to the second floor. "The bedrooms are up there, right?"

"Correct. Do you want to see them?" Without waiting for a response, Toby led the way up the stairs. "It's got nine bedrooms and one huge bathroom." He chuckled. "Now all we need are the guests to fill it."

The bathroom faced them, and Butch peered through another open doorway. Two of the walls had showers placed at regular intervals, and there were four sinks and four toilets against another. The floor was bare, but there was a stack of tiles leaning against one wall, along with a roll of black fabric. A hole had been cut out in the center of the floor for a drain, and two bidets awaited installation.

"Come see the rooms."

He followed Toby through another doorway to a narrow corridor, with three doorways to the right, and four to the left.

"I thought you said there were nine rooms."

Toby pointed back to the staircase. "There are two more in the roof space."

Butch poked his head through into one room. "Looks exactly like it did on the plans," he commented.

"Oh, so you saw those?" Toby's voice held amusement.

"Yeah, just the once." Butch withdrew. "Is it okay if I take a look downstairs?"

"You can look wherever you please. None of this is a secret, all right?"

Butch grinned. "Yeah, good luck trying to keep any secrets on *this* ranch."

"I'm sure there are a few." Toby headed down the stairs, Butch behind him.

The main room was still a shell, with portable lights here and there, so he guessed it had power. Six wooden pillars lined the center, three on each side, supporting the beams that ran across the ceiling. The room took up maybe two thirds of the space, with another doorway in the center. Beyond it was a dark hallway.

"What's through there?"

"Another four rooms."

"Bedrooms?"

"No. Three of them will be private rooms." Toby gestured to the open space around them. "This will be for those guests who don't mind having an audience."

"'An audience'? To what?"

Toby folded his arms. "What do you think will be going on in here?"

Butch laughed. "No need to be coy with me. I saw those drawings you had done. And I'm not talking about the blueprints. You know, the ones showing what it's gonna look like in here? All those benches? Whips hanging on the walls? Hooks in the beams?"

"When did you see those?"

"I came up to the house a couple of weeks ago to speak to the boss, and they were lyin' on the dining table. So... I peeked." He frowned. "Who does stuff like that?"

"They were drawn by a friend in San Francisco. He does a lot of gay erotic art most of the time, but he jumped at the chance to show me how it could look."

Butch squared his shoulders. "Yeah, well, they told me everything I need to know."

"Yeah? And what did they tell you, specifically?"

"That people who indulge in this stuff are kinky as fuck, and they like pain."

Toby's eyebrows shot up. "Okay, I have no problem with your first assumption—we *are* kinky, no doubt about that—but as for the second? Don't believe everything you read or see. Personally? I don't get off on inflicting pain, although I know plenty of guys who do."

"So what gets you off?"

"Freeing people."

"From what?"

Toby shrugged. "Whatever's on their mind. I help them to let go."

Butch stilled. Letting go… *I could do with a little of that.*

"But how? How do you do that?"

Toby pulled his phone from his pocket, tapped the screen, scrolled for a moment, then held it out for Butch to see. On the screen was a naked man, his body covered in an intricate pattern of rope that bound him as he knelt. His head wasn't visible, however.

Butch inclined his head toward the phone. "Does this guy know you're showing him to folks?"

Toby smiled. "Good question. And yes, he does. This was taken in my apartment in San Francisco, and I asked his permission to show it as an example of what I do. That's why I cut his head out of the shot. Plus, there's nothing else in the photo to identify him."

"Protecting his privacy. I like that." He knew nothing about such things, but he guessed that had to be an important part of it. He took a closer look. "Who is he?" Butch couldn't get over how peaceful he appeared.

"Someone who needed to hand over control to someone else for a while."

"And he just let you tie him up?"

Toby chuckled. "It's called Shibari, and if you really want to know more, I could give you a few links that you might find interesting."

"Not sure I like the idea of losing control."

"There has to be trust."

Butch snorted. "Yeah, I'd believe that." He couldn't explain why Toby's quietly-spoken words made something quiver in his belly, but he didn't *want* to know why.

He pointed to the dark hallway. "So… the private rooms are for when guests *don't* wanna be seen?"

"Exactly."

"And what about the last room? What goes on in there?"

"That's going to be for aftercare."

"What's that?" Before Toby could reply, Butch held his hand up. "Forget I asked. You don't have to tell me a damn thing."

Toby smiled. "What if I want to?"

"And what if what you tell me squicks me out?"

Toby frowned. "What the fuck is 'squick'?"

Butch shrugged. "You know, like gross."

"Then why can't you just say gross?"

Butch grinned. "Because squick sounds so much cooler."

Toby rolled his eyes. "Whatever. All you need to know is I won't tell you anything that could make you feel uncomfortable, okay? Give me some credit?"

Butch nodded. "Okay." He hadn't known Toby all that long, but he got a sense the guy was solid.

The boss wouldn't be with him if he wasn't. And Butch trusted the boss's judgment.

"All right then. Aftercare is important. BDSM brings with it a rush of endorphins and adrenaline, so when a scene ends, all the intensity felt by both participants tends to plummet. Aftercare helps combat that feeling. We call it 'drop' and both submissives and Doms experience it." He peered at Butch. "Do you know what those terms refer to?"

Butch huffed. "I can guess what a submissive is, just by the word, so a Dom must be the other half of the equation."

Toby beamed. "That's right. On a practical level, if a sub's been in cuffs, the Dom will check to see if skin needs to be soothed, you know, medical stuff. There'll be water to drink, to rehydrate, soothing cream to apply. But aftercare also involves cuddling, kissing, positive affirmations… It allows both partners to talk openly about what they just experienced. Sometimes it's easy to get lost in a scene. Aftercare is a way of helping us to reconnect, recharge, regain composure…"

"You mean, you get to talk about your feelings?"

Toby nodded.

Butch took off his hat and scraped his fingers through his hair. "I'll be honest, I had no idea. I mean, I watch TV, I see pictures online. They show a bunch of guys in leather, guys being led around on a leash… Hell, I saw a guy once with a hood on that made him look like a dog." He sat the hat back on his head, a comforting weight.

Toby laughed. "It's called puppy play, and you might see a few such guys here."

Butch blinked. "That's a thing?"

"Oh yeah. And again, it's about trust and giving up control but on a different level. But back to your pain assumption. The only thing you need to remember is everything that happens here is done with mutual consent. That's one rule no one is going to break."

Race's voice was right there.

What was missing was one thing—consent. I don't take something without asking, and I don't take advantage of guys—or girls."

Butch had given his consent, and Race had been an excellent teacher. One particular lesson, however, had taught him the importance of being the one in control, a lesson he had never forgotten.

A cough broke the silence that had fallen. Teague stood in the doorway.

"Do you need me?" Toby asked.

"Actually, I was looking for Butch." Teague held a sheet of paper. "I've got the list of guests arriving Saturday."

Butch switched into bunkhouse manager mode. "How many?"

"Five." Teague proffered the list. "All guys, so we can maybe get away with all of them on the first floor."

Butch took it with a frown. "Might mean putting a roster together for the bathroom. It'll get awful congested in there otherwise."

"We can always use the second-floor bathroom if we need to," Teague suggested.

Butch glanced at the list, and an iron fist squeezed his heart. Cold spread through him, and he reached for a nearby wooden pillar as his legs turned to jelly.

What the everlovin' fuck?

CHAPTER 10

"Butch? You okay?"

Toby's voice sounded as if it came from a mile away.

Butch got his shit together fast. "'M fine."

"You sure about that?" The edge of concern in Teague's tone was unmistakable. "Because you look awful. You coming down with something?"

Yeah, I am. A bad case of No Fucking Way.

He glanced at the sheet in his hand, and his second look fared no better than his first: Sol Davenport's name was still there. In the column for Arrival, there was a flight from San Francisco.

It's not him. If it was the same Sol, he'd be flying in from Wyoming.

Then he realized what utter bullshit that was.

And he can't have moved in the last thirty-four years, numb nuts? Is that what you're saying?

Christ, sometimes he had as much brains as a bucket of frogs.

"Butch?" Teague again.

Butch met Teague's gaze with as neutral an expression as he could muster. "I'm fine. Got a bellyache, that's all. So if you'll excuse me, I'll go see if Matt has got lunch ready."

And with that, he strode out of the barn, almost falling over a drill in the process.

Maybe it was time he took a vacation. He could do that, right? He never took time off, so the boss could hardly complain. A week someplace where he could chill, read, swim in an ocean…

A week anywhere but Salvation.

"Hey! Wait up!" Teague yelled after him. By the sound of it, he was running.

Hell no. Butch picked up the pace.

"Will you just stop?"

So what are you gonna do? Run every time Teague comes near? For how long?

That would make a certain arrangement nigh on impossible.

As for that bucket, it was full to the brim with frogs. Time to stop the insanity and act like a man.

Butch came to a halt and turned. Teague stopped running and walked over to him.

"You sure you're okay?"

He drew in a deep breath and forced a smile. "For the third time, I'm fine. Quit worrying."

"Uh-uh." Teague put his hands on his slim hips. "I love you like a brother, okay?" His eyes glinted. "An annoying, exacerbating older brother who bugs the shit out of me at times. So if there's anything you need to talk about, get off your chest..." He pointed in the general direction of his cabin. "My door is always open. And that includes nights when you want to talk, not just fuck. You got that?"

"I got it. Not exactly sure why you'd want me to talk about my bellyache, but hey, whatever lights your candle." Butch went with humor. "Unless you've got this urge to play doctor? And if that's the case, you can count me out. I hate having to visit the real thing, so *you've* got no chance."

Teague laughed. "Okay, I get it. You're fine. But the offer still stands." And with that he turned and walked toward the sloping path.

Butch waited until Teague was at a safe distance before shuddering out a breath. Talking was out. There was shit Teague knew nothing about—hell, no one did—and that was for a damn good reason.

They'd never look at me the same way again.

Butch gazed at the house. He should go talk to the boss. Strike while the iron was hot, and all that. Because Sol would be there in *six days*. Then it hit him. Butch would be the one who had to pick him up from Bozeman.

Fuck that. Fuck *all over* that.

He headed for the barn. Butch had no idea why the place exerted such a calming influence on him. Maybe it was the association of pleasant memories. He only knew he liked the shadows, the smells, the odd squeak of mice nesting somewhere... No one would be there, and that was just fine.

He pushed the door open and stepped inside. He loved how the sunlight fell in beams, making the corner shadows appear much darker. He glanced up to where he and Diana had hidden more times than he cared to remember.

Bales of hay stood to one side, a perfect place to sit and think, so Butch took his hat off and sat. He leaned back against a bale, ignoring the prickle.

Supposing I did ask for some time off. What's the worst that could happen?

Except he already knew the answer. The boss would get curious, he'd want to know what was going on—and Butch couldn't tell him.

So what's the alternative? Stick around?

The thought made his gorge rise.

Butch could see a few sleepless nights in his future, because sure as shit, his mind was *not* going to let go of this until Sol had been and gone.

I can keep out of his way.

Except logistically, that wouldn't fly. Sol would be there for a week.

A long fucking *week.*

He might not recognize me.

Yeah right.

Thirty-four years had elapsed since he'd last clapped eyes on Sol, but Butch was pretty sure he'd recognize Sol too.

He breathed deeply. A face from the past was about to collide headlong with Butch's present, and it could get real ugly. Because Sol *knew.* Sol had been there, hung around with Butch, seen stuff. Although Butch hadn't been there to see it, he imagined the principal would have spoken to the whole school. He could picture Sol sitting in the school auditorium along with everyone else while the principal spoke about Scott, the deep sorrow felt by all that a promising life had ended so abruptly.

Yeah, and I ended it.

Sol hadn't been innocent—he'd been part of that group, hadn't he? —but Butch knew from balls to bones where the blame lay.

Thinking was only going to make things worse. He had work to do, goddammit, and no time to wallow in self-pity, because that was all it boiled down to. *Save the self-torture for when he gets here.*

There would be plenty of it, Butch was sure about that.

His phone buzzed in his jeans pocket. Butch took it out and

glanced at the screen. Teague's text was short and sweet.

My place tonight if you want to let off some steam.

He couldn't help but smile. Fucking cured a lot of ills, and maybe it was just the medicine he needed.

Teague had been curing Butch's ills since 2017, with that serendipitous encounter in a bar in Livingston.

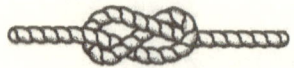

Saturday, May 6, 2017

Butch had a feeling this wasn't his night.

Nine times out of ten, he'd strike lucky at the Murray bar, but no one was biting. It wasn't as if he was there often—maybe every two months or so—and he never stayed long, just enough time to get off, and if that meant getting down and dirty in an alley, then so be it.

He'd gotten good at recognizing the signs. What had one guy called it? His gaydar? Whatever the fuck *that* meant. He just knew it had worked for him so far. No one had punched his lights out.

Yet.

The fella he'd been drinking with was giving off the right vibes, but Butch's tentative forays had met a brick wall. And when the guy thanked him for the beer, made his excuses and left, Butch figured the night was a bust.

Back to Salvation with a severe case of blue balls.

"Well, color me intrigued."

Shit. Shit. Shit.

Butch didn't need to turn around to know who stood there. He'd know that voice anywhere. Teague McKay had been at Salvation for about thirteen years or so. Back then, he'd been a skinny kid and the boss had taken him on.

The *old* boss, he corrected. Robert Thorston had been in charge the last couple of years after his dad's death, and so far, he measured up just fine. It helped that the boss and he were the same age: he didn't think he could take orders from a guy tons younger than himself.

Then he remembered. He was going to have to, because that

very day the boss had promoted Teague. Twenty-nine years old, and suddenly he was the foreman of Salvation.

Christ almighty.

"Oh, *I* get it. You're just gonna ignore me and hope I'll leave you alone? Uh-uh. Not tonight."

A chair scraped across the floor and Teague sat, his hat in his hand. He set a tall frosted glass of beer on the table. His eyes sparkled, his lips twitched, and none of that was a good sign.

"Why don't you pull up a chair and join me?" Butch quipped.

"Don't mind if I do." Teague gave him a lazy smile.

"I hear congratulations are in order." Butch went with polite. He liked Teague, no doubt about that. The guy was lean, with a sparse beard, pretty eyes, and soft-looking lips that reminded him of someone.

Then it came to him. Race Prettyman.

Yeah, he is kinda pretty at that.

Butch shoved such thoughts way out of his mind. The pretty young guy was now his boss too.

Teague beamed. "Yeah, that was a surprise. Can't believe the boss picked me. I thought *you'd* have been a shoe-in for the position."

He snorted. "Who says I'd want it? You'd better do a good job though. You've got some awful big shoes to fill."

Teague's face tightened. "Yeah. Still can't believe he's gone. And I didn't expect the boss to make a decision so soon. The funeral was only last week."

The shock of Kevin Porter's death clung to the ranch. His horse Lightning had stood in the stable since then, with only Paul taking him out for a trot around the paddock. No one wanted to ride him, which was stupid because it wasn't the damn horse's fault.

Kevin had been off his ass drunk, and he shouldn't have gone out riding in the first place.

"The boss is taking it hard," Butch muttered.

"Of course he is. Kevin was more than just the foreman, after all."

Butch stilled. "You knew about them?"

Teague snorted. "*Everyone* knew about them. Hell, I knew the night I came to Salvation, when I hid in that barn. Just because none of us talk about it doesn't mean we were clueless." He drank some of his beer. "It was one of the things about the boss that made me feel safe."

"What do you mean?"

Teague smiled. "Having a gay boss was miles better than having some homophobic asshole."

It took a moment for his words to filter through.

"You're gay?"

Teague nodded.

"I didn't know."

"No one knows—except the boss—and that's the way I like it. That's why I come up to Bozeman and Livingston. I keep that part of my life away from the ranch. It's not ideal, though. Neither place is exactly awash with gay or bi guys."

"Hang on a sec." Butch was having a hard time trying to get his head around this new information. "You don't tell anyone on the ranch you're gay—but you're okay with telling me?"

"Sure, now I know about you."

Fuck.

"Now you know *what* about me?"

Teague frowned. "You're into guys, same as me."

"Says who?" Butch lowered his voice. "I'm just here having a drink, that's all."

"Uh-huh. And what I found interesting was who you were having a drink with."

Oh shit.

"I just met him tonight. We started talking at the bar," Butch explained.

Teague nodded. "And you'd have struck oil too, except for the fact Gordo has a thing for younger guys. Now ask yourself, how do I know this?" His eyes gleamed.

Butch's jaw hit the floor. "You and him... you—"

"Play Hide the Salami? Yes sir, we've been known to do that on a few occasions."

"I had no idea you were seeing someone." Teague was a dark customer.

Teague cackled. "*Jesus.* It's not like that. I hook up with lots of guys. Okay, maybe not *lots,* but when I can." He cocked his head. "But it's only fair I should tell you this is not the first time I've seen you in here."

"Hardly surprising. This is where I come to drink."

"Mm-hmm. I've seen you in Bozeman too at El Camino." Teague's gaze locked on his. "And every time I saw you, you were with someone I recognized." He cocked his head to one side. "It's okay, Butch. I'm not going to tell a soul."

"Tell them what?" Butch's stomach clenched and cold sweat popped out on his brow.

Teague studied him in silence, then took another long drink from his glass. He set the half-empty glass down and leaned forward.

"It's no one else's business who you fuck, all right? And I can see why guys would be interested." He bit his lip. "There's a reason I like hooking up with Gordo. Older guys do it for me every time. They're just pretty thin on the ground in this town."

"It's not what you think," Butch blurted.

Teague arched his eyebrows.

Butch leaned in, his voice low. "I'm not gay. I'm not bi. I... I have sex with guys—now and then—because it's... convenient, that's all. I don't have feelings for any of 'em. It's just sex, a means to an end."

"By what kind of twisted logic doesn't that make you gay or bi?"

"This isn't something I do all the time, all right? We're talking maybe six, seven times a year. And I'm always the top."

Teague blinked, then smiled. "For someone who isn't into guys, you sure have the talk down pat."

This was getting him nowhere. "All I can tell you is... sometimes, I... I have a lot of stuff going on in here." He tapped his temple. "And losing myself in a good fuck helps shut it down for a while."

I need you to understand.

Teague sighed. "Look, I won't make things difficult for you on the ranch. Like I said, it's no one's business but yours." He stilled, then gave Butch a warm smile. "In fact, I could make things a lot easier for both of us."

"How so?"

Teague drained his glass, and wiped his lips. "What you're basically saying is these guys you meet are just a convenient hole?"

"Putting it bluntly, yeah."

"So one hole is as good as another?" Teague's gaze met his. "Even if that hole belonged to a younger guy? Someone you knew? Someone who *definitely* wouldn't be interested in topping?"

Butch couldn't believe what he was hearing.

"You mean you… and me? I'm old enough to be your dad."

Teague grimaced. "Can you *not* say that, please? And I don't care. You're, what, forty-six, forty-seven?" Butch nodded, and he smiled. "That's fine."

"What exactly are you suggesting here?"

Butch needed to hear the words. Then he might be able to get his head around them.

"I'm suggesting an… arrangement that could satisfy both our needs."

"You mean, you and me meet up in Bozeman and fuck? Or here?"

Teague grinned. "Who mentioned either of those places? Do you want to know what's the *best* part about becoming foreman? I get my own cabin. It's clear across on the other side of the paddock. You can't even see it from the bunkhouse. So if you were to get up in the middle of the night when everyone's asleep, creep out, and come knock on my door, we might both get what we want." He froze. "Unless you couldn't ever picture yourself fucking me."

Butch's dick twitched. "I wouldn't say that."

Yeah, part of him was already liking the idea.

Teague's grin would not quit. "I'm glad to hear it. And the feeling is mutual, by the way."

Butch's cock pushed against his zipper.

"Just so we're clear?" Teague counted off on his fingers. "We'd be talking no strings, no complications. We fuck when we both feel like it—for convenience. There'd be no danger of either of us suddenly declaring undying love for each other, now would there?" Butch managed a snort, and Teague chuckled. "Yeah, I thought as much."

"How often do we get to do this?" He needed to nail down the details.

Teague shrugged. "As often as we feel like it. And if either of us wants to call a halt, then that's what we'll do. We'll end the arrangement." He raised his chin. "So? Do we have a deal?"

Butch was seriously torn. Teague had gotten it right on one vital score—it sure would make things easier. But on the other hand...

"What if anyone finds out?"

"We'll be careful. Discreet. And speaking of careful, it'll be condoms all the way, you got that?"

Butch nodded. "I got it." He'd have stipulated the same condition.

"Then it's a yes?"

Butch held his hand out. "It's a yes." They shook in what had to be the weirdest agreement ever.

"And now that we've decided we're doing this..." Teague stood. "I need a hand moving my stuff into the cabin. Think you might be able to help with that?"

"Now?" It'd take him about forty-five minutes at least to reach Salvation, and it was getting late.

"Why not? Unless you *want* to hang around here all night on the off chance you *might* get lucky? When you could be onto a sure thing in my cabin."

Butch grabbed his hat. "Let's go."

He stared at his phone. Maybe letting off steam in Teague's bed would help push all thoughts of Sol Davenport from his head.

Yeah right.

You know, the day is gonna come when Teague's ass won't cure all your ills.

Butch hated that quiet little voice at the back of his mind.

It had a nasty habit of being right.

CHAPTER 11

Friday, August 19, 2022

Butch sat on Teague's porch, warm light spilling through the window onto the wooden boards. He took a drag on his cigarette, relishing the peace and quiet, the cool night air.

That's better.

The dark chasm that had swallowed him up no longer held him captive. He'd fucked it into submission, driving it from his mind with every thrust into Teague's tight ass. It was like he always said—a little fucking was good for what ails ya.

Except this particular form of medicine was proving less and less effective, and he had no clue why that should be. Nothing had changed—

Are you so sure about that?

He took a minute to analyze his situation. Teague was a convenient hole—a term he'd used himself on several occasions—and that suited Butch just fine. Teague hadn't complained, and why the hell would he? They were both getting what they wanted, right? And added to that was the comfort and safety to be found in routine.

Routine? Or a rut?

Fuck it. Middle of the road was just fine too. Butch was content with his lot.

But what happened when middle of the road wasn't enough anymore? When the road ahead went on and on, no divergence, just a straight run that seemed to be going nowhere?

Christ, what the fuck is wrong with me tonight?

The cabin door opened and Teague stepped onto the porch. "You still here?" He'd put on jeans and a tee, his feet bare.

Butch let out a snort. "Fuck, that's blunt. Really feeling the love here."

"I didn't mean it like that." Teague joined him, sitting on the second Adirondack chair. He gestured to Butch's cigarette. "You know you're not supposed to have those."

"Whatcha gonna do about it, Mr. Foreman?"

Teague sighed. "You got one for me?"

Butch reached into the breast pocket of his jacket, removed the pack, and held it out. "That's my last one, but you can have it. Got another pack in the bunkhouse." Then he dug deeper into his jeans pocket and retrieved his lighter.

Teague lit up and took a drag. "Well, isn't this a goddamn cliché."

"What—a smoke after fuckin'?" Butch cackled. "No, dude. A cliché would be me putting two cigarettes between my lips, lighting them both, then handing one to you."

They sat in silence, and that worked. No hearts and flowers shit necessary.

Butch gestured to the ranch. "Something sure lit a fire under Toby's ass this week. I think there were guys working day and night." The barn looked a damn sight better.

"I think he's got someone coming in to take photos for the new website. At least, that was the impression I got." Teague paused. "So what was it this time? Another nightmare?"

Hell no. Butch was *not* going to talk about this. "Leave it." The words came out more gruffly than he'd intended.

"And what if I don't want to leave it?"

Something in Teague's voice registered, a hint of belligerence that tugged him from his safe space of quiet contemplation and thrust him closer to the chasm he'd come there to avoid.

The chasm that lurked in his dreams. The one that contained not only the horrors that usually plagued him, but also a new one. Sol Davenport waited in there. Sol, who would arrive all too soon.

Butch didn't want to stare into its depths again, and fuck, he was pissed at Teague for dragging him back to the precipice.

"Look, what is your problem? I thought you were okay with this."

Teague was silent for a moment, long enough that Butch believed their conversation to be at an end.

I should go. Now.

"I *was* okay with it—at first."

Aw fuck.

"Then what's changed? I mean, it's been five years, for fuck's sake. If you had a problem with our arrangement, I'd have thought you'd have said something before now."

Teague took another drag. "Don't get me wrong, I have no qualms about us fucking."

Butch snickered. "'Qualms'? You've been hanging out with the boss too long. You're starting to use them big words."

Teague glared at him. "Will you stop that? You've got just as wide a vocabulary as I have. You may put on that blunt redneck act around the guests, but I *know* you, okay?" He chuckled. "In the Biblical sense, as my grandma used to say whenever she wanted to talk about people having sex, without actually using the word sex."

Teague's words had hit their mark. Butch frequently hid behind the mask of a dumb good 'ole boy, at least until he got to know someone.

"Just tell me what's on your mind," he said at last.

It was clear *something* had ruffled Teague's feathers.

Teague blew smoke into the night. "I guess what we have going on is what the boss calls a symbiotic relationship—we both get something out of it. And I was totally okay with that."

"But you're not anymore," Butch surmised. It wasn't as huge a blow as he'd imagined it would be, maybe because hadn't he been having the same kind of thoughts?

"I've never said no, have I? I mean, you turn up in the middle of the night, you walk in, strip off, get hard, and we fuck, no questions asked. I knew what I was to you—a convenient hole." Butch opened his mouth to protest but Teague held his hand up. "Don't, okay? We both know that's all I was. And if it comes to that, I wanted my hole filled and you were on hand. Hell, it was my idea, right?"

Butch only had to listen to Teague speak to know whatever they had, it was over.

Using the past tense was a bit of a giveaway.

"But what happens if I meet someone? If I'm no longer... available? Or my ass is no longer available, which I guess is nearer the mark."

That made Butch sit up.

"You got your eye on someone?" He didn't know how he'd feel if that was the case. He'd be happy for Teague, no doubt about that, but...

There shouldn't be a but, *asshole. You should be happy. End of.*

Teague shook his head. "No. This is all hypothetical. I guess what I'm saying is… I feel like I'm being used, physically. Like I don't matter."

"Course you matter," Butch retorted. His chest grew tight.

"So you say, but I know how I feel." He paused. "There's no one on the horizon… but one day there might be, and both of us are going to feel awkward as fuck when you turn up one night and your space in my bed is already taken." Teague huffed. "What if I meet someone who actually wants to kiss me?"

Ouch.

"I don't kiss, okay? I said that right from the start." Butch's stomach was as tight as his chest.

"Sure. You just didn't say why. So I guess I'm asking. What's so wrong with kissing?"

Butch couldn't answer, because saying that kissing was too intimate would feel like he was slapping Teague in the face.

And sex isn't intimate?

Teague stubbed his cigarette out on the wooden porch.

"Why won't you just admit you're into guys? What's the big deal?"

"I like women." Butch stuck his chin out.

Teague gave a nod. "Okay… when was the last time you had sex with a woman?"

Butch's throat seized.

"Was it so long ago that you have to think about it?" Teague demanded.

He stared out at the dark landscape before them. "You sleep with a woman, she'll want to get married. Guys don't pull shit like that."

"Not every woman wants to get married, Butch."

Christ, it was as though he was channeling Race.

"Yeah, but I don't wanna be with someone who sleeps around."

Fuck, Butch was caught up in a time loop, reliving that last conversation before Race left.

Teague gaped at him. "Talk about double standards. Okay. Then answer me this. When did you first have sex with a guy? And be honest." He set his jaw. "You owe me that much."

Butch didn't have to think. It was ingrained, burned into his memory.

"1992."

The silence that followed said much. Then Teague found his voice.

"Thirty years ago? Wow. That's the worst case of denial I've ever seen. Do you always find a way to justify your actions?"

"What are you talking about?" Not someone else who brought up the D word.

"Can you hear yourself? Have you ever heard the phrase cognitive dissonance? I read about it once in a magazine. Look it up sometime."

"Why don't you save me the trouble and tell me what it means now?"

"Basically it's a mental conflict that occurs when your beliefs don't line up with your actions."

"And what beliefs and actions are you referring to?"

Teague rolled his eyes. "Oh, I don't know. How about you believing you're straight, when you've been fucking guys for *thirty years*? My guess is you're going through a helluva lot of mental discomfort right now. And do you want to know why that is?"

"No, but I'm sure you're going to tell me." Butch squeezed the words out.

"It's something we experience only when we know there's an inconsistency. And while you might be tempted to avoid dealing with that discomfort, I wouldn't. That hole you've been digging is only going to get deeper if you don't face up to what you know is the truth."

"Which truth is that?"

Teague expelled a breath. "Butch, you're bi. You like women but you like guys too. You don't fuck guys because it's convenient—you fuck 'em because it feels *good*. Now do yourself a favor and just admit it."

"Is this how you talk to a friend?" It wasn't what he wanted to say, but the words rolled around inside his head and he couldn't form them into a coherent pattern.

"But you're not treating me like a friend, more like a friend with benefits."

Butch stared at him. "You agreed to this, remember?" Then the word came to him. "You gave your consent."

"Okay, fine, there's consent, but this has become a one-sided deal in your favor. When we first started out, it was all about getting *our* needs satisfied. We got off together. But what's going on here?" He gestured to the cabin. "*This* is not equal. So like we agreed back when this started... I'm calling a halt. You deserve better. *I* deserve better."

And there they were, at the end of the road.

Butch finished his cigarette and stubbed it out on the porch. "I guess there isn't a lot left to say."

"I can think of one thing, and it's important." Butch gave him an inquiring glance, and Teague took a deep breath. "I said all these things because I had to, all right? Because someone needed to say them. But we have to work together. I don't want this to sour things between us. I really *do* want you for a friend."

"As well as an aggravating older brother."

He chuckled. "That too. Everyone deserves a little happiness, and I don't think you'll find yours if you keep deluding yourself. So... am I forgiven for speaking my mind?"

Butch didn't want to lose him either.

"You're forgiven." Teague let out an exaggerated sigh of relief, and Butch smiled. "You made for an excellent pressure release valve, though."

Teague coughed. "Well, I've been called many things, but never that." He leaned forward, gazing out into the darkness. "But while we're on the subject, there's something I've been meaning to say to you for some time now, but I never found the right moment."

"This would seem to be that moment," Butch observed. "If you can't say it now, you never will."

Teague paused. "Fucking is not a good coping mechanism."

Butch stared at him once more, and then burst into laughter. "I don't know about that. It's always worked for me."

"Then maybe it's time you found another one."

Butch inclined his head toward the cabin. "Think you could make us some coffee? I don't feel like heading back to the bunkhouse and sleeping. It'll soon be time to get up anyhow."

"Sure—on one condition."

"And what's that?"

"You look me in the eye and tell me I'm right."

It was on the tip of Butch's tongue to deny him that, but a wave of mental fatigue crashed over him.

Teague had been right. Butch owed him the truth.

"I… I like guys too."

Teague's face glowed in the warm light through the window. "Thank you. That means a lot. Doesn't that feel better?" He got up. "And now I'll make that coffee." He squeezed Butch's shoulder and went inside.

Butch wished he had another cigarette. He sure needed one right then.

But he's right. I feel better.

Butch doubted anyone working on the ranch would raise an eyebrow if he suddenly came out and announced he was bi. Hell, they'd probably laugh their asses off and say "About fuckin' time."

That didn't mean he was ready to share other stuff. But with the prospect of Sol arriving within the next twenty-four hours, more revelations were a distinct possibility.

That did it. Butch would be spending most of the following week keeping out of Sol's way. And if their paths should cross?

Sol would be just another guest, nothing more.

CHAPTER 12

Saturday, August 20

At first sight, there was nothing about Bozeman that stood out. Sol could have been anywhere in the west of the U.S. The airport shuttle dropped him in front of the Baxter Hotel, with the restaurant on the first floor, spilling out onto the sidewalk but separated from the pedestrians by black metal railings. Dark green umbrellas provided relief from the late afternoon sun.

The sight of people eating only exacerbated Sol's hunger.

At second glance, Bozeman sure had plenty of places to eat. There was the Backcountry Burger Bar, the Bacchus Pub… The hotel restaurant went by the name of Ted's Montana Grill, with a sign in the shape of a charging bison. According to the sign sitting out front, they served Bison & Burger.

They'd never fit bison in there. They'd never get the insurance anyhow.

A juvenile kind of thought but one that made him smile.

The spirits distillery next door… Now *that* was tempting.

"I've got a bottle of Jack with your name on it back at the ranch, so don't you be looking in there."

He spun around. Toby leaned out of the window of a black truck with the word *Salvation* emblazoned on it. His grin lit up his face, and Sol couldn't help but return it. He picked his bag up from the sidewalk and walked over to the truck.

"You didn't mention you moonlighted as a driver."

Toby inclined his head toward the rear. "Shove that on the back seat, then get in at the front." As Sol opened the door, he added, "And I don't usually do this. It's the job of the bunkhouse foreman, but he's missing in action for some reason. So you drew the short straw."

Sol walked around the truck and climbed in.

"I hardly think the boss's partner counts as the short straw." He peered through the windshield. "So… this is Bozeman, huh?"

"First impressions?"

Sol shrugged. "It's okay. Probably like a lot of small Midwest towns." He sat back and waited for the eruption, schooling his features.

Toby's jaw dropped and his eyebrows went sky high. "What the…. Okay, two things to point out here. One, this is definitely *not* the Midwest. And two, Bozeman is the fourth-largest *city* in Montana. Fifty-four thousand people? That is *not* small."

Sol grinned.

Toby rolled his eyes. "I did it again, didn't I? I let you yank my chain." He chuckled. "Damn, I've missed that." He pulled away from the curb.

"How far is the ranch?"

"About twenty minutes." Toby glanced at Sol's luggage. "You didn't overpack, I see."

"I just brought the basics." Sol's backpack sat in his lap. "All the important stuff is in here. Laptop, camera… Which reminds me. Why did you refund my payment this morning? I saw it when I checked my balance."

"Because you're here as a consultant."

Sol frowned. "You're going to pay me for my services. That's enough."

"Before you go any further, I need to point out this was not my idea. Robert insisted. And speaking of Robert… You're invited to supper up at the house."

"I don't get to eat with the rest of the guests?"

Toby smiled. "You'll be doing that all week. And anytime you want to take a shower, come on up. Robert has plenty of bathrooms, whereas the bunkhouse only has the one and it gets a little crowded."

"That sounds like the voice of experience."

Toby cackled. "Five in the morning, seven guys and only two showers and three sinks. Yup, that was an experience all right."

"I *am* sleeping with the other guests, right?"

"If that's what you want."

"That's what I'm paying for." Then he rolled his eyes. "Except now I'm not. No special treatment, okay? Supper I can deal with. I'm sure me eating with the boss and his boyfriend will raise enough eyebrows. Do the guests take it in turn to cook?"

"No, Matt does all the cooking. He's Robert's housekeeper too. A genuine treasure."

"Seriously?"

"Oh yeah. He cleans house, shops, cooks…"

"Oh my. He's a keeper."

Toby grinned. "It gets better. Take a look on Scruff when you arrive. You'll find him on it."

Sol let out an exaggerated gasp. "He's gay too? Be still my beating heart." He fell silent, staring at the landscape. Civilization had given way to rolling fields and hills, and so much sky that he couldn't take it all in.

It was like coming home, a place he hadn't been in quite a while.

"This is beautiful. Looks so peaceful out there," he murmured.

"Welcome to your first vacation in God knows how many years. And I know you're here to take pictures and learn what you can for the website, but please, *try* and have a good time too?"

Sol had looked at Salvation's site several times during the last week. "I saw the ranch has plenty of horses. Any chance I could ride one soon?"

Toby arched his eyebrows. "You ride?"

"I grew up in Wyoming, remember? I think it's in the genes."

"Sure. I'll introduce you to Paul Stormcloud, the ranch wrangler. He'll find you a horse."

"With a name like that he has to be Native American."

"Yup. He's never far from the stable. If I hadn't seen him in the bunkhouse, I'd have sworn he sleeps with the horses too." Toby took a right onto a long gravel driveway, as straight as an arrow. "Welcome to Salvation."

Sol caught his breath. Ahead of them were two posts supporting a hefty log with the word *Salvation* burned into it, but beyond that were four white barns trimmed in green, a building that had to be the stable, and in the center of them all, a sand-covered corral. Off to the left, an impressive log house sat on top of a hill, overlooking the ranch, and all around was the lushness of green and blue where land met sky.

"I take it back. The site's pictures don't do it justice," Sol muttered. "Looks like my dad's place when I was a kid. Not that he farms anymore."

"Are your parents okay?"

"Yeah, they're fine. Don't see much of them. My sister keeps me in the loop."

Toby stopped the truck beside one of the barns and switched off the engine. "Dude. That was four years ago. They still haven't come around?"

"Uh-uh. No change." Sol shook his head. "Talk about irony. I came out and they freaked. I got involved with an older guy, and they freaked. Then I introduced them to Liam, and it was as if they'd found their second son. Until the day he—" Sol swallowed. "We haven't spoken a whole lot since then."

"They still can't blame you."

He huffed. "Then they're doing a really good job of acting like they do." He held his hand up. "I know, it's illogical. Now, can we change the subject?"

Toby indicated the barn. "This is the bunkhouse. I'll introduce you to everyone." They got out, and Sol collected his bag from the back seat. He strolled toward the paddock, taking in his surroundings. One barn stood out from the others, its paintwork a little fresher.

"Is that it?"

"Yup. And it's almost finished."

"Almost? I'm here to take pictures of it, remember?"

Toby laughed. "Will you just chill? I've made sure there's stuff for you to take photos of. I even got one of the bedrooms upstairs completely ready for that express purpose. As for the main area, the benches and other stuff have arrived—I just haven't gotten around to unpacking and assembling yet." He smiled. "That's on my To Do list for tomorrow. You can help."

Sol laughed. "Wouldn't be the first time. Can I take a look inside after supper?"

"Yeah, we can manage that. We'll give you the five-cent tour." Toby pointed. "That's the stable, and behind that is the main barn."

A figure emerged from the stable and strode briskly toward the barn. Sol didn't get a glimpse at the guy's face, but he couldn't miss his broad back and muscled arms, and then there were those long legs...

"They build 'em big in Montana," he murmured.

Maybe this would be an interesting week.

To his surprise Toby scowled. "What the fuck?" Before Sol could ask what was wrong, he called after the guy. "Hey, Butch! Where were you when I needed you?"

Sol stilled. *Butch?* Then he thought better of it. Butch wasn't an uncommon nickname. And besides, the Butch *he* remembered looked nothing like that guy.

Be serious. We were eighteen, a bunch of skinny dudes that a stiff breeze could've blown over.

The Butch he'd known could be anywhere.

Anywhere.

This Butch clearly hadn't caught Toby's raised voice, because his steps didn't falter.

"Apparently he's suffering from selective deafness. I'll catch up with him later." Toby tugged on his arm. "Let's go inside and I'll do the introductions."

Sol followed him into the bunkhouse, and the place's lived-in look struck him instantly. That end of the building mostly comprised wall cabinets and cluttered countertops, a couch that had seen better days, an armchair that had apparently been on the same journey, and a large wooden table.

Two guys sat at the latter. One was older, his beard flecked with grey at the chin, and the other had to be a decade younger, lean, with a beard that barely hugged his jawline. They regarded Sol with obvious interest.

Toby indicated the older cowboy. "This is Zeeb. He'll be a great help to you."

Zeeb flashed white teeth. "Such praise. Hi. You're Sol?"

He gave a nod.

"Sol is a friend from San Francisco," Toby informed Zeeb. "He's here to do two things—chill, and help us design a website for the new stuff."

"Friend, huh?" Zeeb's eyes gleamed. "We'll have to be careful what we say around you, won't we?"

Toby snorted. "That'll be a first."

Sol had to smile. Toby was already part of the furniture, it seemed. That boded well.

He peered into the darkened room beyond the living area, a large space filled with bunks, but there was no one else to be seen. "So is this everyone?"

Zeeb stuck his thumb out. "Paul's in the stable. He'll be here shortly. Matt's in the kitchen cooking up a storm." He grinned. "It's fried chicken tonight." He pointed to the younger guy. "And this here is Walt, our baby."

Walt rolled his eyes. "Lord, you say that every fucking time."

Toby chuckled. "I should have warned you. They're all a bunch of 'potty mouths'," he air-quoted.

Zeeb's cackle filled the air. "Potty mouths? Tell it like it is, Toby. We cuss a lot around here."

Toby gave him a mock glare. "And whatever happened to toning it down with the guests? At least at the beginning." Before Zeeb could respond, Toby nodded. "Of course. How could I forget? Nowadays you just drop them in at the deep end and see who sinks and who swims."

Zeeb snorted. "Aw, you remembered." He peered at Sol. "You got a problem with that?"

Sol didn't bat an eyelid. "Fuck no. And I was always a good swimmer."

The three men laughed, and Sol had the feeling he'd just passed some kind of a test.

Zeeb gave a nod toward the rear of the bunkhouse. "The guests are getting acquainted with the bathroom. So if you need to take a shower, you're in for a wait."

"I'm good," Sol told him. "Nothing wrong with a little sweat."

That gleam was back. "Oh, I like you." He gazed at Toby. "Teague went to talk to the boss. And Butch was in here a second ago. Don't know where he went."

"Yeah, I saw him. And when he gets back, tell him I want a word."

"Who's Butch?" Sol inquired. He hadn't quite gotten over the shock of hearing that name.

When was the last time I thought about Butch Buchanan?

Decades ago.

"The guy from a moment ago. He's the bunkhouse foreman. You'll see him around at some point." Toby's scowl hadn't faded entirely. "But not if I see him first." He straightened. "Sol's going to eat supper with us at the house tonight, but I'll make sure we send him back early."

"Gotcha." Zeeb glanced at Sol's bag. "I'll put that on a bunk for ya."

"Thanks." Sol didn't relinquish hold of his backpack. "I'll keep this one with me."

"That's fine. Got any preferences for top or bottom?"

Sol blinked. "Excuse me?"

Zeeb's eyes twinkled. "Bunk beds, dude." He grinned. "Or are you happy with either?"

Sol couldn't resist. "I'll take whatever I can get, but I'm happy with a top bunk."

"Yeah, I sorta got that feeling 'bout you."

Toby coughed. "Zeeb."

Zeeb held up both hands. "Just tellin' it like I see it. He's gonna fit right in around here, isn't he?"

Toby chuckled. "And on that note, let's go feed you."

They walked outside, and Sol laughed. "He's a character, isn't he?"

"That's one word for him." Toby smiled. "Zeeb's okay. They all are."

"Even this Butch who seems to have pissed you off?"

"Yeah, him too. I just want to know why he disappeared." Toby pointed to the house on the hill. "That's where I live with Robert."

Sol gazed at him, noting the relaxed stance, the air of contentment. "So it really is working out?"

"Better than I could've believed."

There was something in his voice, a warmth Sol recognized.

"Oh my God. You're in love."

Toby's smile reached his eyes. "And what if I am? No law against that, is there?"

"Toby Merrow, in love. Whatever happened to—"

"Okay, okay. I get it. Yeah, it must be the end of days or something." He looked toward the paddock where a figure stood, leaning against the railing. "Ah, *there's* Butch." He walked quickly in that direction. "Hey Butch. You got a sec?"

As they drew closer, the guy turned, his body stiff, and Sol's heart went into overdrive. The physique had changed, sure, and the man was a damn sight older than the last time Sol had laid eyes on him, but there was no mistaking those green eyes.

I'd know them anywhere.

He'd dreamed of them enough times, hadn't he? Just like he'd dreamed of other stuff too, like watching Butch in the locker room when Sol did his best not to stare.

Butch Buchanan, thirty-four years later and *way* hotter than he'd ever been as a teenager.

Butch Buchanan who showed him not a single ounce of recognition.

Then it hit him.

Butch remembers too.

A yawning chasm of more than thirty years opened up and swallowed him whole, sending him hurtling back to a place and time he did *not* want to revisit, rekindling memories he would rather were left dead and buried.

Memories of a Sol Davenport who no longer existed.

Memories that also explained why Butch was pretending not to recognize him, wiping away Sol's initial flash of pleasure at seeing him.

Lord, he felt so *cold.*

Yeah, Butch remembered, all right.

"Butch, this is Sol Davenport, our last guest. He's here to work on the website design too." Toby patted Sol's arm. "So look after him, okay?" He turned to Sol. "Our bunkhouse foreman, Butch Buchanan."

Butch tipped his hat. "Pleased to meet you, Mr. Davenport." He glanced at Toby. "Sorry about earlier. I wasn't feeling so good. Thanks for meeting the shuttle."

"But you're okay now?" Butch nodded. "And what about just now when I called you? Why did you keep on walking?"

Butch frowned. "You called? I didn't hear. Must've been the wind. Anyhow, I'd best get into supper." Another nod to Sol. "I guess I'll see you later." Then he walked off toward the bunkhouse.

So that was how it was going to be.

Sol stared after him.

What. The. Fuck?

How many thousands of people lived in Wyoming, and the one who turns up in Montana *happened* to be a guy he went to school with?

Any way Sol looked at it, this was one freaky coincidence.

"You okay?"

Sol was most definitely *not* okay.

CHAPTER 13

"Sol. *Sol.*"

He jumped. Toby stood in front of his chair on the porch, holding out a squat glass.

"Sorry. I must've zoned out for a minute." Sol took the proffered glass of Jack Daniels.

"A minute? Try all evening."

It took a moment for Toby's words to seep in.

Sol glanced to his right where Robert occupied another of the Adirondack chairs. Robert's gaze was fixed on him, his brow creased.

I've been rude, haven't I?

Robert didn't deserve that. Sol had liked him from the start, and seeing the way Toby appeared so relaxed in his presence went a long way to cementing that opinion.

He raised his glass to Robert. "Thanks for a great supper, and even better company."

Robert gave a wry smile. "I'll accept the first, but I call bullshit on the second. I don't think the company made much of an impression. Your mind was elsewhere all through supper." He cocked his head. "Is everything okay?"

Toby took the chair next to Robert's. "And that was going to be my next question too."

Sol pushed out a sigh. "I think I owe both of you an apology. I *have* had something on my mind, it's true."

Butch Buchanan had taken root the moment Sol had laid eyes on him.

"Anything you can share? Maybe we can help," Toby suggested.

"Thanks, but…" Then he reconsidered. He didn't intend letting Butch continue with his Hey-we-don't-know-each-other performance, even if it meant confronting him. And that could raise eyebrows around the place.

Sol needed someone to understand what was going on.

He took a sip from his glass before twisting to face Robert.

"You and me, we're the same generation."

Robert smiled. "Which is probably why I invited you to eat with us. After everything Toby told me about you, I had a feeling we'd get along."

Sol had experienced pretty much the same feeling.

"So there's something I'd like to ask you."

"Sure."

Sol stared out at the landscape below them. "Nowadays it seems as though every time you turn the TV on or read posts on social media, someone's coming out."

Toby chuckled. "An exaggeration, but I know what you mean. That has to be a good thing, right?"

"Oh, I agree, but you have to know it wasn't that easy for guys like Robert and me. It wasn't something you did, especially if you lived someplace like my hometown."

"And isn't that the truth?" Robert's face tightened. "Good Lord, how I hated all the secrecy."

Toby reached for his hand and squeezed it. "Yeah, but now everyone knows."

"When did you first know you were gay?" Sol asked Robert.

He leaned back, his head resting against the painted wood. "I was eighteen, I guess. You have to understand, I grew up surrounded by men, ranch hands of all shapes and sizes. Not that I'd have ever said a word to one of them. But yeah, I started to notice them round about then." He smiled. "And then two years later, one of them noticed *me*."

Sol chuckled. "Man, I love that smile." It spoke of pleasant memories.

Robert's expression grew sad. "It only lasted a couple years. He left kinda abruptly, and just recently, I found out why that was. Not going to go into it, but my daddy had a hand in it." His gaze met Sol's. "His name was Clay Kirkham, and he's dead now, but he loved me once, a long time ago."

Sol raised his glass. "To Clay." Robert clinked with him. Then Sol peered at Toby. "And what about you? When did you first know?"

Toby grinned. "In high school. And I most definitely had a thing for jocks back then. All those lithe bodies…" His eyes gleamed. "Especially after practice. Some of them had no problems strutting naked around the locker room. And oh my God, the showers…Talk about a feast for the eyes."

"You were a horny little fucker, weren't you?" Sol said with a smile.

Toby blinked. "What do you mean, I *was*? I'm still a horn dog and I'm not ashamed to admit it." He peered at Sol. "Your turn. What's your story?"

Sol took a gulp of Jack, his heartbeat quickening.

"I was in high school. Sixteen and wedged in that closet because coming out? *Telling* anyone? Hell no. I saw what happened to *anyone* who gave off the slightest queer vibe."

Toby sighed. "You're right. It *was* easier for my generation, especially in California. There were still kids who could be real assholes, though."

Sol took another drink. "It might surprise you to learn I was one of the assholes."

Toby stared at him. "Seriously?"

Sol nodded, then shivered. "I'm not proud of some of the things I did back then."

"What kind of things?" Robert's voice was quiet.

Sol swirled the dark liquid. "You know how these days we say a homophobe is probably just a guy who's too scared to confront what's lurking in his own closet? That bullies home in on stuff they see in themselves?"

Robert and Toby said nothing, and Sol's shivers multiplied.

"I picked on kids who seemed like they were queer. I wasn't the only one doing it—there was a bunch of us. All you had to do was scratch the dirt and up popped a bully. And I felt like shit doing it because I knew deep down I was gay."

"Better to be on the attack than on defense?" Robert suggested.

"You know it. And I couldn't tell anyone so I took out all my fears, my anger, my frustration, you name it, on kids that were too scared to fight back or tell me to shove it." He raised his chin. "Like I said, I'm not proud of how I was, all the shit I pulled. Thank God I grew out of that and became a human being."

"Is that why you went into counseling?" Toby asked. "As a kind of penance?"

"Yeah, but mostly it was to help people understand stuff they're going through."

"Let's get back to your story." Robert gazed at him. "So there you were, sixteen, in the closet... How did you first have an inkling you were gay?"

Toby grinned again. "I got it. You had the hots for the captain of the football team."

Sol managed a wry chuckle. "I was never into jocks." His heart beat faster. "No, I was secretly lusting after a tall drink of water called Brian Buchanan."

"Buchanan?" Toby laughed. "Oh my God." He turned to Robert. "Didn't you say once that Butch came from Wyoming? They could be related." He inclined his head toward the ranch below. "You met Butch earlier. Our bunkhouse foreman."

Here we go.

"Yeah, I did, didn't I?"

"So what was this Brian like? Apart from being a tall drink of water."

Sol rolled his glass between his palms. "He never knew I was interested, that's for damn sure. I knew better than to let anyone see that. Unless I *wanted* to be beaten to a pulp."

"He wouldn't have done that, would he?"

Sol shook his head. "He dealt all his blows with his tongue, not his fists. In that respect, we were a lot alike. But no one called him Brian. He hated that name, so we all called him by his nickname—Butch." He didn't break eye contact.

Crickets.

Toby and Robert stared at him, openmouthed.

"No. Fucking. *Way*," Toby said at last.

"*Our* Butch?"

Sol nodded.

"But..." Toby frowned. "I was there. He... he acted like you'd just met for the first time. And you didn't say a word."

"That was because he was looking at me like he didn't know who I was. I wasn't about to make a scene."

"Maybe he didn't recognize you." Robert sounded hopeful.

Except Sol knew better.

"Look, I have no qualms telling you about Butch, because I know Toby would have told you anyway. But confidentiality is one of the things we live by in our lifestyle, right? And you *are* Butch's boss."

Robert frowned. "Is there something I need to know? Beyond what you've already said?"

"No, nothing at all." Not now he knew the truth.

Prior to fourteen years ago, however, he couldn't have given the same answer.

"Then I don't see how telling us you knew him in high school changes anything."

Sol knew it would change things for Butch.

"He might feel a little awkward, that's all, given that we knew each other, and we were both assholes. No one likes to be reminded they were a dick in high school."

Robert coughed. "Can we go back to the part where you had the hots for Butch? Because... really? What are the odds on you guys meeting again after all this time?"

Sol smiled. "I know, right? I'm sure I wasn't the first gay kid to fall for a straight guy." Toby and Robert exchanged glances, and Sol's senses went on alert. "He *is* straight, isn't he?"

Not that it mattered if Butch was as gay as a nine-dollar bill. The way he'd looked at Sol... And then there was their shared history.

Some things just can't be gotten over, I guess.

"Let's put it this way." Toby bit back a smile. "If there was an award for the gayest straight man, Butch would definitely be in the running."

Robert chuckled. "And that's kind of an open secret around here, so we're not breaking any confidences."

Sol stared back at them. "That's all I get?"

"Yup." Toby's grin was back.

"Because to say anything more would be wrong," Robert added. "Especially as you two don't appear to be on speaking terms." He tilted his head. "Unless you plan to change that?"

Robert had nailed it. No way was Sol going to spend an entire week avoiding Butch or letting him treat Sol like a stranger.

He needs to see I've changed. I'm not that kid he knew.

Sol was intrigued to know what kind of man Butch had grown into, especially after that comment from Toby.

Gayest straight man?

Yeah, Sol was *all* kinds of intrigued.

"I told Teague—he's the ranch foreman—you were interested in riding. He said he'll pass that on to Paul," Toby informed him.

"Thanks." Sol glanced at his watch. "So what time do folks rise and shine around here?"

Robert laughed. "Too early o'clock. You'd better hit the sack." He stilled. "Wait... This business with Butch... Isn't it going to be awkward, staying in the bunkhouse? Talk about forced proximity."

"It probably will be—at first," Sol confessed. "But I won't let it go on for too long, especially if it creates an atmosphere."

He'd take Butch aside and have a few words before he let it go that far.

Toby huffed. "And now I really want to be a fly on the wall when you and Butch go head-to-head."

Robert cleared his throat. "It's none of our business, though. Remember?" Toby arched his eyebrows, but Robert didn't react. "Okay, I'd like to know too, but unless you've installed cameras or mastered the art of out-of-body experiences without telling me, it ain't gonna happen. Besides, the people who work on this ranch are my family, and as such I'll have their backs."

Toby leaned in and kissed Robert on the lips, a slow lingering kiss that warmed Sol's heart to see it. He pulled back and looked Robert in the eye.

"And that's what I love about you."

It was time for Sol to make an exit.

He stood. "Thanks for the excellent supper, and my compliments to Matt, by the way. If that's what I have to look forward to in the way of meals, this is going to be a great week. Tomorrow after I've gone for a ride, you think you could show me the new barn? I'll help you put stuff together too."

"Sure. And I'd welcome the help." Toby rose. "I'll walk you back to the bunkhouse."

Sol waved a hand. "I can find my own way. You stay here." He smiled. "Looks as though you've got a conversation to continue."

Besides, he wanted to think.

I want to be ready for whatever awaits me.

CHAPTER 14

Every time the door to the bunkhouse so much as creaked, Butch froze.

No sign of Sol.

What the fuck is he doing up there all this time?

Except Butch was no fool. He had a pretty good idea what Sol was doing. There was plenty Sol could tell them about him, none of it illegal, but all of it would make the boss and Toby peer at him as though he was a bug to be squashed underfoot.

That was what he feared the most—having people he worked with, laughed with, looking at him differently.

Shunning him.

He's got no fucking right to tell them anything. And if it comes to that, he's not exactly blameless, is he?

Then he realized he could be blowing this up out of all proportions. What if Sol hadn't said anything? What if Butch tore him a new one, only to find Sol had kept his mouth shut, because deep down, he knew he'd played a part in Scott's untimely death too.

Christ, a fella could go mad with all this shit going on in his head.

He took off his boots, then removed his clothing down to his shorts.

"Are you okay?"

Butch jerked his head in Zeeb's direction. "Why'd you ask?"

"You've been awful quiet tonight."

He glanced toward the bunks where the guests were getting ready for bed.

No way was he talking in front of them.

"I'm allowed to be, aren't I?" he retorted. "Now, how about we stop jawin' and get some sleep. These guys have an early start tomorrow."

Zeeb's eyebrows shot up. "Yes sir, Mr. Bunkhouse Foreman sir."

Butch knew what that was all about. He hadn't come out with

his usual shit, and he was if anything a creature of habit.

Of course Zeeb was going to notice.

Don't let Sol get to you. It's only a week. He'll be gone before you know it. Be cool.

Except that was the problem. Butch was ice-cold one minute, burning up the next.

"Is the new guest sleeping here or up at the house?" Walt asked Zeeb, shimmying down under the sheets.

"He's with us. Toby said he'd send him here right after supper, but I think they probably got to shootin' the breeze on the boss's porch. Nice night for it."

That remark did nothing to calm Butch's already fraying nerves.

Paul came into the bunkhouse and hung up his hat. "Rusty's worrying me. He didn't eat much tonight, and he drank more than usual. If he's still like that in the morning, I'll call the vet." He paused at the threshold between the living area and the bunks. "What's going on?" His brow creased in faint lines.

"Nothing," Butch muttered. Paul looked from Butch to Zeeb as if for confirmation, and Butch scowled. "He's gonna give you the same answer. It's time to sleep."

The four guests traipsed into the bathroom and Butch breathed a little easier.

Paul held his hands up. "Whatever you say. I'm just pointing out that there's an atmosphere in here. Felt it the moment I stepped inside."

"Paul, leave it," Zeeb urged. "Have you picked out horses for the guests for the morning? I know Frank, Max, and Eric are newbies. Not so sure about the other two."

"Yeah, Teague's already given me the lowdown. Daisy, Ryan, and Elmer will do just fine. They're all three gentle as a lamb. And Teague came by the stables just now," Paul said in a low voice. "He said Sol wants to go for a ride first thing. Apparently he was around horses a lot when he was a kid. I'll make sure he's okay, then I'll give him Bailey. He shouldn't have any trouble with him." Paul unbuttoned his black shirt.

"How come he didn't eat with you guys?" Butch demanded.

Zeeb regarded him with mild surprise. "How come *you* didn't? Not like you to miss a meal."

Butch sat on the edge of his bunk. "Lost my appetite."

He jerked a thumb toward the living area. "There's a couple pieces of fried chicken in the fridge if you get the munchies." He stripped down to his shorts. "Seems like Sol and Toby already know each other. Toby said Sol's a friend from San Francisco."

Butch froze. "You don't say."

The likelihood of the three of them discussing stuff Butch would rather leave buried in Wyoming had just increased, and the chances of him getting more than a few hours' sleep were shrinking by the second.

The bunkhouse door opened, and Butch averted his gaze.

Show time.

"So where am I sleeping?"

Sol's voice was a helluva lot more gravelly that Butch remembered, but more than thirty years would do that to a guy. He stared at the wooden floor as Sol strolled into the bed area.

"I put your stuff over there," Zeeb told him.

Butch hadn't even noticed, and a trickle of unease worked its way through him when he saw which bunk Zeeb had allocated to Sol.

It was the one across the room from his.

Not that he could say a damn word about it. What excuse could he give? *Hey, you can't put him there because I'll be able to see him*?

They'd think he'd lost it.

Sol walked over to the bed and faced the wall. Butch watched as he removed his dark blue shirt.

Holy fuck.

It was as tantalizing as a strip show.

Sol was still lean, but Lord, just *look* at those muscled shoulders, not to mention his arms and back. The crop of light brown hair was gone, and Sol's bare scalp gleamed in the light. He was slim across the waist and hips, the dark band of his briefs showing above his jeans.

The jeans he was in the process of removing.

Butch didn't want to notice how firm Sol's ass was, how his briefs clung to round cheeks. He didn't want to stare at Sol's muscled, hairy thighs, but he couldn't look away. And he *definitely* didn't want to see Sol's ass revealed as he lowered his briefs to the floor, stepping out of them before reaching into his bag for a pair of white shorts. Butch took in Sol's long naked body, his tanned skin, his sculpted back, but all too soon those firm globes covered in a light brown fuzz were hidden from sight.

Yeah, there seemed little point in denying it any longer. Teague had nailed it. Butch liked guys.

The realization brought a brief flicker of relief.

He was right about that too. It felt good to be honest about it.

Then Sol turned and Butch couldn't miss that long shaft tenting the cotton. He lowered his gaze, holding his breath until Sol climbed between the sheets, thumping his pillow before resting his head upon it…

His eyes focused on Butch.

"Goodnight, guys." Sol smiled. "Looking forward to whatever tomorrow brings."

Jesus, that sounded ominous as fuck.

Butch got into bed, rolled over to face the wall, and closed his eyes.

Except all he could see was Sol.

God, you are such a tease. You could've made him look like a toad, but noooo, you had to go make him a walking sex dream.

With a voice that reminded Butch of Race Prettyman.

Then all traces of lust were swept away by those last words.

Butch had played the 'We're strangers' card, and that hadn't worked. All that left him was avoiding Sol like the fucking *plague*, but that look on Sol's face told him plenty.

He's not gonna keep his distance.

He's gonna want to talk.

Butch was starting to get a very bad feeling about this. And the more he thought about it, the madder he got.

You can't say anything. Not now. Not with everyone around.

Fine. He'd wait until he got Sol alone, and *then* he'd find out exactly what he'd told the boss and Toby.

Butch's life on Salvation wasn't perfect, but it was as close as it could be, and he wasn't about to let Sol fucking Davenport ruin it.

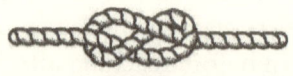

The room was dark, and everyone seemed to be fast asleep judging by the soft snores and rhythmic breathing.

Butch hadn't slept a wink, and the prospects of getting any shuteye before dawn were slim to non-existent.

The nightlight above his head gave his sheets a ghostly green appearance. He turned his head to peer at Sol's bunk. Sol slept on his side, the sheet around his waist.

So what am I going to do? Lie here all night while he sleeps like a baby?

Wasn't it bad enough that his past was never far from his dreams? Sol's arrival had the potential to thrust him into a waking nightmare.

Butch knew he could never forget what he'd done to Scott, not that his tattoo would let him. But he didn't need more reminders in the shape of Sol Davenport. He didn't intend to let Sol ruin his sleep, not when he had an alternative plan.

As quietly as he could, he threw back the sheets and swung his legs out of the bed. Butch eased into his jeans at a snail's pace. Normally he didn't give a shit who heard him—they all knew where he was going, right? —but this was different.

Sol had made it different.

Butch shoved his feet into his boots, grabbed his shirt, and crept out of the bunkhouse. Outside, the moon cast its glow over the landscape, reflecting on the pale gravel that covered the path past the paddock. He stood still for a moment, taking deep breaths.

Bad news comes in threes, isn't that what everyone says?

By Butch's reckoning, he'd had his three. First Race's death, then learning that Sol was coming to Salvation, and finally Teague's decision to call it a day.

He was due a change in fortune.

Butch headed for Teague's cabin, his feet heavy as he followed the path. He wasn't sure what kind of reception awaited him, but hell, they had history, and it was the first thing Butch could come up with.

The cabin was in darkness, and Butch felt a momentary stab of regret before he rapped on the door. It took a minute for him to hear any movement inside, and then a light flickered into existence. The door opened, and Teague stood there in his shorts, rubbing his hand through his hair.

"Something wrong?"

"Can I come in?"

Teague stared at him for a second, then stood aside. Butch went inside, and he closed the door.

"I'm kinda surprised to find you here. Didn't we talk about this very thing not twenty-four hours ago?"

Butch held his hand up. "Now wait a sec. I'm not here because I couldn't get through another night without your ass, okay?"

Teague blinked. "Wow. You know how to wound a guy, don't you?"

"Look, I just need a place to sleep right now that isn't the bunkhouse."

"Seriously?" Teague stared at him.

"I'll sleep on the couch, all right? You'll never even know I'm here."

Please, say yes.

Teague said nothing, and with every second that ticked by, Butch's heartbeat climbed another notch.

At last Teague spoke.

"I don't know what's going on, but it doesn't take a genius to see you're running away from something."

Aw crap.

"You're not gonna let me stay, are you?"

Teague shook his head.

"Go back to bed, Butch. Whatever this is, you need to sort it out."

"You don't understand," Butch protested.

"No, I don't." Teague glanced at his phone on the coffee table. "It's two in the morning, Butch. In a few hours it'll be time to get everyone up and ready for the day. So go back to your bunk, try to switch your damn brain off, and get some sleep. And if you still need to talk, then sure, we can talk. In daylight." He opened the door. "I'm sorry."

"Not as sorry as I'm gonna be," Butch murmured as he brushed past Teague and walked briskly toward the bunkhouse.

"Butch, you're an intelligent guy," Teague called after him. "You can work this out, whatever it is."

He's right. I'm being stupid. I'm better than this.

Butch reached the bunkhouse and opened the door carefully. He crept back to his bed, undressed, and climbed under the covers once more, his heart pounding.

It's only a week. How bad can it get?

"Butch." Sol's whisper made him jump. "We need to talk, but not now."

Shit. He was deluding himself.

It could get *really* bad.

"Go to sleep, Sol," he whispered back.

"I will if you will. But if it helps? I'm not going to make trouble for you, okay? I just want to know what's going on. And I won't let you ignore me, you hear?"

Butch grabbed his courage with both hands. "What did you tell them about me?" he whispered again.

"What?"

"You heard. You were up there for hours. You must've talked about something. So I'm asking… did you talk about me?"

"They know we were in high school together."

"That's it? Just that?"

Silence.

"Sol. What else did you tell them?" His heart hammered.

"I'm not sure what you're getting at, but I haven't said anything, beyond the fact you might feel awkward having me around the place."

Butch suppressed his snort. "'Awkward'? And the rest."

"Please. Don't do this now. Let's talk tomorrow, okay?"

He was right, of course.

"G'night." Butch rolled over to face the wall, pulling his pillow around his head like a cocoon.

Despite Sol's insistence he hadn't divulged a lot, it seemed as if Butch's past was catching up with him, and it could change everything.

Shit always got out, and it always stuck.

CHAPTER 15

Sunday, August 21

Sol woke up and glanced at the bunk opposite.

Empty.

Any relief he'd felt that they'd finally broken the ice and spoken the previous night, vanished.

This is not good.

Little light penetrated the area, and he grabbed his phone to see what time it was. Not even five o'clock, and he was wide awake.

He sat up and looked at the other beds. The four other guests were still out for the count, Walt was hidden under his blanket, and there was no sign of Zeeb or Paul.

Toby's advice came back to him, and he decided to take advantage of the moment. He grabbed his towel and headed for the bathroom. He smiled to himself as he entered, noting the steam coating the mirrors over the sinks. Judging by the low tuneless singing coming from behind the blue shower curtain, he'd located Zeeb.

Sol stepped into the second shower enclosure.

"You're one of those cheerful morning people, aren't you?" he said in a low voice before he flipped on the water.

By the sound of it, Zeeb came close to choking.

"Warn a guy, why don'tcha? And for your information, it's all an act. I'm fakin' it till I get my first three cups of coffee inside me." He paused. "How'd you sleep?"

Sol squeezed bodywash into his palm. "Not great, but then I never do the first night in a strange bed. I woke up a few times. Not that I was the only one having difficulty sleeping."

Zeeb cackled. "You're talkin 'bout Butch not being in his bed, right?"

Sol frowned. "How did you know?"

"Nothing strange about that. It's a regular thing. Don't worry. We all know where he goes." Before Sol could ask what that meant, Zeeb chuckled. "You're a dark horse, I'll say that for ya."

"What's that supposed to mean?"

"You and Butch. You went to the same high school? You kept that quiet."

Well fuck.

"Seems like I wasn't the only one awake last night." At least Butch couldn't blame this on him—he bore some of the responsibility too.

"Hey, if you're gonna talk when there's other folk around… But what *I* wanna know is, how come *he* didn't tell us?"

And now *what do I say?*

Sol thought fast. "Tell me something. When you were in high school, were you the perfect A-student or did you get up to some shit?"

Zeeb hooted. "Dear Lord, the latter. Don't get me started on some of the stunts I pulled back then."

"And that's all stuff you're happy to talk about?"

"Hell no. I was an asshole."

Sol let the warm water rinse away all the soap lather. "I hate to break it to you, but a lot of people feel the same way. So would *you* want someone turning up who knew you back then? Who could tell everyone just how *big* an asshole you were?"

"Okay, fair point. No, I wouldn't. So I guess my next question is which of you got up to shit?"

"We both did. And if you were listening to our conversation, you'll have realized neither of us wants to talk about that. So do me a favor? Don't go spreading this around. If he wants to tell you guys, let him do it in his own time."

"That's probably what he was doin' in the middle of the night—talking." Zeeb snickered. "Among other things."

Okay, one enigmatic statement was one thing, two was pushing it.

"Are you going to keep dancing around whatever it is you're trying not to tell me, or are you going to have the balls to come right out with it?"

There was another pause. "Toby said you're here to work on a new website. So you're not really a guest, are ya?"

Sol laughed. "You don't strike me as the kind of guy who gives a shit what he says or to whom."

Zeeb's rough chuckle rebounded off the tiled walls. "Lord,

you catch on real fast. I guess it's okay to tell you. I mean, you being a friend of Toby's, and you knowing Butch since when the earth was cooling. I mean, I don't suppose he's changed all that much since high school."

Sol couldn't help wondering what on earth was coming.

"Look, it's common knowledge around here Butch don't sleep so well. Sometimes he has nightmares, not that we ever ask him about them. But when he gets them, he goes to Teague's cabin. Whatever they do there seems to help."

That *"whatever they do"* line was bogus and Sol knew it. Sure, he knew what it *sounded* like, but that couldn't be right.

Could it?

Sol turned off the water, pulled back the shower curtain, and stepped onto the cool tiles, still dripping. "Hang on a sec. Let me get this straight." He wrapped the towel around his hips.

Zeeb emerged from his shower and grabbed a towel from the rail. He snorted. "Not exactly the word I'd use to describe Butch, although I'm pretty sure that's how he labels himself."

"You're telling me Butch and Teague…"

Toby's joke about the gayest straight man award suddenly made sense.

Zeeb's eyes flashed. "I've told you nothing, okay?" He bit his lip. "But whatever it is you *think* I'm telling you, you're probably right." He shrugged. "It's not a secret. Everyone knows, even the boss. But can we change the subject before someone else comes in here? Then I really *would* be in the shit."

Sol could do that.

Zeeb dried himself briskly and Sol didn't even try not to stare. He'd met plenty of guys who had a hangup about being naked, but Zeeb didn't appear to suffer from that affliction. Sol took a moment to appreciate his firm body, a few grey hairs here and there on his chest, his nipples standing proud.

It wasn't the only thing about Zeeb that was standing to attention.

"See something you like?"

Sol snapped back into the moment. Zeeb regarded him with obvious amusement.

"Sorry. I was enjoying the view."

"Hell, don't spoil it by apologizin'. Can't remember the last time someone checked me out." He cocked his head. "That *is* what you were doing, right?"

Sol chuckled. "Okay, you got me."

Zeeb raised his eyes heavenward. "Another gay guy. Well, I suppose I'd better get used to it. There are gonna be a lot of you around here once this new shindig gets going." He grinned. "Just so we're clear? I'm not that way inclined. No offense."

"None taken."

Zeeb stilled. "Hey, you *are* gay, aren't ya? I mean, I was makin' an assumption. You could be bi for all I know. We got a few of those around here too."

"Relax. I'm gay."

"Good to know. I'm beginning to feel like an endangered species on this ranch." That grin was very attractive. "The only truly straight guy around here."

Sol couldn't resist. "You know what they say. Don't knock it till you try it."

Zeeb's eyes gleamed. "You offerin'?" Then he burst into laughter. "Just yanking your chain. You wanted a ride, didn't you?" He waggled his eyebrows. "Just not *that* kinda ride. Paul will be in the stable if you wanna head that way. I'll save you some breakfast."

Yeah, Sol could really warm to Zeeb.

"Thanks." An early morning ride sounded a great way to start the day.

"You're welcome, from someone who is still an asshole on occasions but has his better moments." Another cackle. "This obviously wasn't one of them."

The door opened and Walt stumbled into the bathroom. "Lord, you two are noisy." He shucked off his shorts and made a beeline for the shower.

Sol got out of there. Back in the bunks area, there was still no sign of Butch. Sol wasn't going to think about him, though, not with the prospect of getting on a horse for the first time in years.

Butch would keep.

He pulled a clean pair of jeans from his bag, along with socks and a tee. He glanced at Zeeb who was getting dressed.

"How warm is it going to get today?" he whispered.

"Should reach eighty." Zeeb peered at the clothing he'd

selected. "You got a shirt to wear over that? It'll be cool out there this morning."

Sol grabbed a shirt. "Thanks." He dressed quickly.

"And then I guess I'd better find you a hat so you look the part." He grinned. "Don't bother whisperin'. I'm about to give these guys their wake-up call."

By the time Sol was out of the door clutching a dark hat, Zeeb had all the guests up and at 'em.

Sol walked to the stable, enjoying the silence. The ranch lay shrouded in a kind of semi-dark, a morning mist creeping around the buildings, white and ghostly. Inside the stable, the lights were dim, what there was of them, but there was enough to see Paul talking to a beautiful blue-black horse with white socks and a white splash between his eyes.

Paul turned as Sol approached, his serene smile beautiful to see. He wore his long black hair loose, and it reached his waist. A beads-and-bone choker lay snugly around the base of his throat.

Wow. I bet he breaks a lot of hearts.

"Morning." Paul patted the horse's mane. "This is Bailey. And once I've watched you put his saddle and cinch on, he's all yours. I groomed him already. Toby says you're okay with horses."

Sol went over to Bailey and stroked his nose. "He's a beauty. Is he an Andalusian?" The thick mane and tail spoke of the breed.

Paul beamed. "I'm impressed."

Sol chuckled. "Not half as impressed as I am that I remembered the name. It's been a while." He guessed it was true what they said—knowledge never truly died. Everything stayed in the brain someplace.

He grabbed a blanket and saddle then walked Bailey outside where dawn hadn't started yet. Paul stood by the paddock fence, watching as Sol got Bailey ready. He didn't say anything, but his approving glances told Sol a lot.

Sol climbed the fence and mounted the horse. He walked Bailey around the paddock for ten minutes or so before breaking into a trot. Bailey was a gentle, responsive horse, and he couldn't wait to pick up a little speed.

"I think you're ready," Paul told him.

"Any suggestions as to which direction I should take?"

"Head thataway. It'll take you through the meadow to the

creek. Just be careful in the forest, okay? We've had a few instances of wolves lately, not to mention bears." Paul patted Bailey's flank. "He doesn't spook easily. But still, be careful. The sun won't be up for another hour, so watch yourself."

"Gotcha." Sol thanked him and followed the direction Paul had indicated.

The meadow soon gave way to tall grass, and Sol nudged Bailey to go a little faster.

If I thought it was peaceful here last night when I arrived...

The quiet of the morning seeped into him, and a calm settled on him like a soft blanket. He couldn't remember the last time he'd been this relaxed. The first snatches of birdsong broke the silence, and his heart soared to hear it.

Liam would have loved this.

Sol had always meant to teach him how to ride, but Liam had admitted to being nervous around horses. It still amazed Sol how much their interests had diverged. Sol was a lover of the outdoors, whereas Liam was never happier than when he was listening to music, reading books, or watching a movie.

BDSM was what had bound them together—and later, love.

Sol hadn't seen Liam coming, and when he fell, dear Lord he fell hard. But this past year he'd noticed the ache lessening. He could look at Liam's photo and remember the good times, instead of recalling how it had all come to an end. He was single, but content to be so. He played at the club and he had private clients, some of whom he had sex with.

None of whom he was emotionally involved with.

It was a good life.

It would have been a great life with Liam.

As he rode, he debated what he was going to say to Butch. He knew why Butch was uncomfortable—hell, he felt the same way.

Neither of us want to remember what we were like.

Zeeb's revelation added to the intrigue. *Are Butch and Teague in a relationship?* From the way Zeeb told it, Sol didn't think that was likely, not if Butch labeled himself as straight.

Except how could he do that if he and Teague were fucking?

The questions were starting to pile up.

From someplace nearby came the sound of running water, and he followed it. The sound grew louder as he neared the edge of a forest, and he skirted around it. At last he reached the creek Paul had spoken of.

Except someone else had reached it before him.

Two horses stood side by side at the hitching post, a palomino and a black horse. There was no sign of their riders. Then he glanced across the creek and saw a log cabin.

It was an idyllic spot. Large boulders sat in the flowing water, providing steppingstones across. The cabin was small, with a front porch complete with Adirondack chairs. Sol strained to hear, but any sound from the cabin was drowned out by the creek.

Whoever was in there clearly wanted privacy, and they'd picked the perfect place.

He patted Bailey's long neck. "I don't think we should be here, boy." Sol continued along the creek, losing himself in the babbling waters that tumbled over rocks, the cool, dark forest with its abundant foliage, a mix of browns and greens, and the light that changed from minute to minute.

By the time the sun was up, he was starting to get hungry, so he turned around and headed back to the ranch. As he returned to the cabin, he noted the horses were gone.

Sol was dying to see what the cabin was like on the inside.

Paul was waiting for him as he neared the corral.

"Good ride?"

Sol smiled. "You know it." He used the fence to dismount. "By the way... I found the creek, and saw a cute little cabin not far from it. There were a couple of horses there, a palomino and a black horse. Do they belong to the ranch?" He led Bailey into the stable, Paul at his side.

Paul nodded. "That would be Rusty and Lightning." He pointed, and sure enough, there were the horses in their stalls, eating. "They belong to the boss and Toby. The cabin was the boss's mom's. They like to go there most mornings." He smiled. "I think that's a good sign."

"Why?"

Paul's face tightened. "The foreman before Teague was a guy called Kevin Porter. About five years ago, he fell off Lightning down by the creek and broke his neck. He and the boss... Well..."

Sol saw the light. "Then he's exorcising ghosts."

Paul frowned. "Huh?"

Sol returned his smile. "Not literally. But you're right. It's good he can go there again." His stomach grumbled. "And now I'd better see if Zeeb was as good as his word and saved me some breakfast."

Paul laughed. "Good luck with that. Don't worry if it's all gone. Matt's a sweetheart. He'll make you something."

Sol thanked him, gave Bailey one last pat, then walked out of the stable—

To find Butch blocking his path, his hands on his hips, a white hat with brown trim on his head.

He looked Sol in the eye.

"You're right. We need to talk."

Chapter 16

Thank God.

Sol glanced around them. "Here?"

Butch rolled his eyes. "Sure. I want everyone knowing my business." He pointed to the barn. "No one will disturb us in there."

"Then lead the way." Sol walked behind him, drinking in the view. Butch had always been tall, but he'd filled out in other directions since high school. He seemed to be a walking mass of muscle, and Sol was doing his best not to stare.

A muscled body was one of his weak spots.

But he was your weak spot long before those muscles ever put in an appearance. You know, when you thought he was straight?

That had to be the burning question Sol wanted to ask—when had Butch known he was into guys? And if that was truly the case, why would he claim to be straight, like Zeeb said?

Okay, maybe two questions.

Butch pushed the door open. Sol walked in, and Butch peered through the open doorway before closing it. The first rays of sunlight pierced the murky interior, and Sol glanced at his surroundings. Heavy wooden beams crossed the space above their heads, a ladder fastened to one of the pillars that supported them. Bales of hay stood around, and there were more in the roof space. The smell evoked memories of childhood, of playing hide and seek with Alli, hiding from his mom…

Butch came to a halt in front of the bales and turned to face him. "What are you doing at Salvation? Did you know I was here?"

Sol stared at him. "*That's* what you're going to start with? After thirty-four years? You think I came here to find *you?* How could I have known you were here?"

"You're friends with Toby, right? Maybe he told you about me."

Sol sat on one of the bales. "Yes, we're friends, and no, he didn't. And yeah, seeing you was a shock, although you seemed unfazed by my arrival." That was more polite than the words he was striving not to utter.

You pretended not to know me, you bastard.

He was under no illusions. It wasn't as if they'd been best buddies in high school. Sol hadn't hung out with him too much—down that road lay danger. Keeping minimum safe distance was way safer. But they were in the same classes, they lived close by each other—not close enough that Sol had ever visited Butch's home, but hey...

And a bunch of us made life hell for other kids, don't forget that part.

Butch said nothing, but his face flushed.

Sol saw the light. "You knew I was coming. You had to have seen a list of guests, or something."

Butch removed his hat and scraped his fingers through his hair. "Yeah, I knew. Saw the list a week ago." Sol got a flash of a tattoo along his left forearm. It appeared to be Roman numerals. Then Butch lowered his arm.

"Why did you act like you didn't know me?" Sol hadn't expected that to hurt as much as it did.

"It was a shock for me too, okay? I haven't been back home since I was eighteen, and you... You were the last person I expected to see."

"Yeah, I think I got that part."

Butch swallowed. "About last night... You didn't tell them about..."

"I told them I'd done stuff I wasn't proud of, all right? Stuff I tried to... atone for as I got older."

The same stuff you're anxious for me not to tell your boss.

Sol had an inkling what that might be.

Butch's face grew tighter. "I've done my share of atonement these past few years. I just didn't want you telling my boss anything that would put me in a bad light."

Sol couldn't miss the circles under his eyes, the tapping foot, the way he kept scrubbing his hand over his face... Whatever was going on inside him was plainly causing him pain, emotional or otherwise.

"Believe me. I didn't say anything that would jeopardize your position here. I give you my word." That was the truth. Sol wasn't out to hurt him.

Butch's shoulders sagged. "Okay."

Sol couldn't let it go there.

"But I think your fears are groundless. A lot happened after you left, stuff you may not be aware of—"

And just like that, Butch tensed, his back rigid, his neck corded.

"No. We're *not* gonna talk about it, you hear me?"

"But—"

"No buts. I mean it. You start talking about home, high school, whatever, and I swear, I will pack my bags and take a vacation for the rest of this week. Until you're gone." His eyes blazed. "Do you hear me?"

It seemed Sol had touched a raw nerve.

"I hear you." He had to do something. "How about we start again?"

Butch lost a little of his rigidity.

"I can live with that." He looked Sol up and down. "You're looking good."

We're going with compliments? From anger to admiration in one breath. The one-eighty made Sol's head spin.

"Although I think you haven't put on an ounce of fat since then. What's your secret?"

Sol laughed. "I don't think I have one. I work out three, four times a week, I swim…" *And fucking is great for the figure, especially that deep V.* "You're looking pretty good yourself."

Talk about an understatement. The initial sight of him had pressed *all* Sol's buttons, and learning Butch was into guys had lit a fire in him.

"Still can't believe you're here. I mean, what are the odds?"

"I know, right?" Sol cocked his head. "So I guess this means we can actually tell your coworkers we know each other?"

Butch's brow furrowed. "I don't know about that… How would I explain not saying anything before this? I'd look like a real asshole."

"Tell them you didn't recognize me at first. Tell them I've lost a shitload of weight since high school. That would work."

"I guess." Butch leaned against the wooden pillar. "So… What did you do after high school? College, right? That was all planned, wasn't it?"

This had to be the most surreal conversation ever, but if this was how Butch wanted to play it...

"Yeah. I did my degree, then took qualifications in counseling." He couldn't leave it at that. "*My* atonement, if you like."

"Sol..." The word was almost a growl. Those eyes bored into him.

Those same eyes that had sent illicit shivers down his spine when he was seventeen.

Sol held his hands up. "Okay, okay. How long have you been here?" He could play it safe.

"Thirty-four years. The boss's dad took me on." Butch glanced at his surroundings. "Salvation is my home."

Sol frowned. "You meant it? You really haven't been home since then?"

"Nothing to go back for. They're better off without me. Deke's probably running the farm."

Christ, what happened?

Sol had known Butch and his old man didn't get along, but it sounded as though there'd been an irrevocable split. As bad as things had gotten with his own parents, at least Sol managed to get back there now and then.

"What about you? You're in San Francisco now?"

"Yeah. Been there four years." Sol forced a smile, although his stomach churned.

"You get home much?"

He hadn't been home as often as he would have liked, but that was down to his parents. Losing Liam had caused a rift between him and them, and although they'd mellowed a little over the years, their illogical reaction still rankled.

"Not as often as Alli would like."

Butch smiled, and it transformed his face, revealing the lingering details of the young man Sol had known. Butch had always been an attractive kid.

The man he'd become had left his youthful looks in the dust.

"I remember her. Pain in the ass."

Sol laughed. "No change there."

"You never married?"

"How did you know?"

Butch gestured to Sol's left hand. "You're not wearing a ring, and there isn't a pale bit, so you're not divorced either."

"You're observant." Sol smiled. "No, I never married. I came close once, but…"

"Can't say I ever got that close." Butch grinned. "I'm obviously picky when it comes to women. I remember you, though. You never dated, not once. So maybe you're just as picky as I am."

Sol was done hiding.

"Or maybe I just never met the right man." Except that wasn't true. Liam *had* been the right man—until fate robbed Sol of him.

The only sounds came from outside, the muted calls of birds overhead.

Butch stared at him. "You're gay?"

Sol nodded.

"Since when?"

He smiled. "I've known since high school. I kept quiet about it, for obvious reasons."

Butch's brows knitted. "I don't get it. You, me, Cal, Pete… All the stuff we came out with… and you never said a word?"

"Yup. I was a Prince, wasn't I? I couldn't come out so I hid, picking on other kids, calling them names…" They were steering dangerously close to forbidden territory. Any second now, Butch would call a halt.

Sol didn't want to talk about those times either.

"Well if that don't beat all." Butch shook his head. "Is everybody gay?"

Sol blinked. "Excuse me?"

"When we were kids, I could point to one, maybe two people we knew who *might've* been gay. Maybe. Now? You can throw a rock in any direction and you'll hit a gay guy. There's a few on the ranch."

"And where do you fit in that lineup?"

Butch stilled. "Me?"

Sol nodded. "I mean, you're not exactly straight, are you?" He couldn't resist a smile. "At least, not according to what I've heard."

He'd been honest with Butch—he expected the same honesty in return.

Butch narrowed his gaze. "Who's been shooting their mouth

off? And what did they say?"

"Something about you and the ranch foreman… Teague? Not that they went into details. In fact, they were deliberately vague." Sol shrugged. "I kinda read between the lines." He peered at Butch. "So it's true?"

For a moment he got the feeling Butch was going to clam up, tell him to go to hell, or just walk out of there.

Butch shook his head. "Someone up there is laughing his ass off right now."

Sol waited.

"It *was* true, okay? We… we had a thing going on."

Sol chuckled. "Sounds like a line from a song."

"But I'm not gay, all right? I wasn't back then either."

Sol arched his eyebrows.

Butch paced up and down, his hat still in his hand. "I… I've been going through some stuff lately. Personal stuff. Me and Teague? It's over. Not that we were ever an item, you understand? It wasn't like that." He came to a stop. "And I don't have a fucking clue why I'm telling you *any* of this."

"Because we were friends once? Because you get the feeling I might know what you're going through?"

"Maybe."

Sol leaned back against the hay, conscious of bits poking through his shirt. "So… you're not gay."

A sigh rolled out of him. "I'm bi. And you're only the second person I've admitted that to."

"I'm guessing Teague would be the first."

"Yeah." He snorted. "Took me long enough to own up to it."

Sol smiled. "Butch… you just came out."

Butch laughed. "I guess I did."

"But you did know back then you weren't entirely straight, didn't you?"

A shadow crossed Butch's face. "Yeah. And I still don't wanna talk about it."

Sol knew what *it* referred to.

"Who talked, by the way?"

Sol wasn't going to dump Zeeb in the shit. "I cannot reveal my sources. But I got the impression everyone here knows. I mean, about you and Teague?"

"Probably, but no one talks about it." He froze. "Should I tell them?"

"Tell who what?"

"The guys. That I'm bi. Although I don't think they'll be all that surprised, to tell the truth."

"It's your decision," Sol said in a low voice. "If you feel comfortable telling them, fine. If you don't, that's fine too. Screw 'em."

Zeeb's voice shattered the calm. "Hey, breakfast."

Sol peered at Butch. "Have you eaten?"

"Not yet. I woke up early and went for a walk." The skin around his mouth tightened. "Except that's not true. I was hiding out in here, until I figured I couldn't keep doing that. I had to face you sooner or later."

"I'm glad you did." He studied Butch. "Are you? Glad, I mean."

"Yeah. I shouldn't have treated you like that." He shivered. "Gotta say, when I heard you were having supper with the boss…"

"The conversation was mostly about me, honest. We discussed when we first knew we were gay."

He stopped. He'd been about to tell Butch who had caught his eye in high school, but then he reconsidered.

Not going to show all my cards just yet.

"Is there more to this story?" Butch asked.

"For the last time, come and get it while there's still stuff to get," Zeeb yelled.

"We're coming, okay?" Butch hollered back. He rolled his eyes. "If needs be, I *can* rustle up some eggs for us."

"I think we should join the others," Sol suggested. "We've got all week to talk, right? Now that we *are* talking."

"Fair enough." Butch put his hat back on, then held out his hand. "We good?"

Sol took his hand. "We're good." He followed Butch out of the barn and into the morning sunlight.

His week had just gotten a whole lot more interesting.

CHAPTER 17

Butch helped himself to the last of the sausage gravy and spooned it over his biscuits. "Damn, Matt. Your biscuits are better than my mom's ever were."

Matt laughed. "Is that a compliment?"

"Fuck yeah. Hers were awesome." He took a mouthful and rolled his eyes. "I think I've died and gone to Heaven."

Zeeb glanced at the four guests seated around the table. "Now you know why I said eat it while you can."

One of the guests, Max, laughed.

Sol sat facing Butch across the table, eating quietly, not looking in his direction.

Do something. Show him things are different. Talking with Sol had made him feel as though he'd cast off a heavy weight.

"What do you think of Matt's cooking, Sol?"

Sol jerked his head up. "Hmm?"

"Matt's cooking…" Butch peered at his clean plate. "I guess you liked it." He took a deep breath, his heartbeat shifting into a higher gear. "Except that's not saying much. You used to love the food in the school cafeteria, as I recall, and that had to be the most tasteless shit I've ever encountered."

Sol widened his eyes then quickly schooled his features. "It had to be better than those bologna sandwiches you brought."

Butch waved a fork at him. "Ain't nothing wrong with bologna."

"Oh, I agree." Sol's eyes twinkled. "But you can have too much of a good thing."

It was then Butch registered the silence. He gazed at his coworkers.

"Something wrong?"

As if he didn't know.

Walt gaped at him. "Now wait a minute. Are you saying you and Sol knew each other in high school?"

"Seriously?" Matt stared at him.

Butch gave as casual a shrug as he could manage. "Yeah. Didn't recognize him at first." He flickered a glance in Sol's direction. "He looks a whole lot different to how he was back then."

Sol blinked. "And how was I?"

Another shrug. "You'd have given stick insects a run for their money."

"I prefer to think I was a lean, mean machine."

"You go ahead and think that, if it makes you feel better," he replied in a soothing tone. Butch was starting to enjoy himself. He grinned. "Do you still listen to that same shitty music?"

Sol gave a mock gasp. "Excuse me? Michael Jackson was *not* shitty."

"Not talking 'bout him. Although, while we're on the subject... Remember that Christmas your folks gave you a Walkman? Have you *any idea* how many times we caught you listening to that tape of "Bad"? Cal said he was sure you went to sleep listening to it."

Sol put his fork down and folded his arms. "So what music *are* you talking about?"

Butch snorted. "You sure did listen to some weird shit. What was the name of that band? Oh yeah, Talking Heads. And then there was R.E.M."

Sol glared. "There is nothing wrong with R.E.M. either." He smiled. "But if you're going to discuss *my* taste in music, maybe I should share what *you* were listening to back in high school."

Butch narrowed his gaze. "Dude. Don't do it."

Sol grinned. "Aha. *Now* you're scared."

"I mean it."

"Oh, now you *have* to share." Zeeb cackled. "What was he listening to?"

Sol counted off on his fingers. "Poison, Skid Row, Cinderella, Warrant, Alice Cooper—although technically that was his comeback."

Walt chuckled. "How come I've only heard of one of those? When were they playing?"

"In the mid to late eighties," Sol told him. "And they all went under the label of glam metal. It was pretty big back then."

"Which means you weren't even a drip in your daddy's pants," Zeeb added. "And the rest of us were probably still in diapers."

Walt nodded knowingly. "Oh, I get it now. Old guy stuff."

"Fuck you," Butch said good-naturedly.

"You haven't heard the worst." Sol's eyes gleamed. "It was also a time of goodbye denim and leather, hello Spandex, lace, flashy tight-fitting clothing, and make-up."

Zeeb's mouth fell open. "Oh please, tell me there are pictures of Butch in make-up."

"No, there are not." Butch was going to kill Sol. Then he noticed Teague standing by the door, grinning like a fool. "Whatever you're thinking of adding to this conversation, forget it."

Teague gestured to Sol. "You two know each other?"

"Seems they went to high school together," Zeeb said before Butch got a chance to draw breath. "Took 'em a while to recognize each other. Apparently."

That last word made Butch think Zeeb knew more than he was letting on.

Teague's eyebrows went skyward. "Well, what do you know about that?"

"What's up?" Butch inquired, anxious to bring an end to the discussion.

"Just to let you all know Paul won't be around Wednesday or Thursday."

"Is he okay?" Zeeb asked instantly.

"He's fine. The boss has bought a horse from a ranch over in Wibaux, right on the border. It's a six-hour drive at least. So Paul will head over there Wednesday, stay the night, and then pick up the horse the next day and bring it back. Butch, you're going with him."

Butch frowned. "Me? What's this got to do with me?"

"I figured you could handle some of the driving. I can manage the bunkhouse." Teague smiled. "You wouldn't mind a few days away from Salvation, would you?"

Twenty-four hours ago he'd have jumped at the chance, but things had changed.

"Anyway, that's all I came to tell you." He smiled at the four guests. "Today's the first time some of you get on a horse, isn't it?"

Frank, the oldest of them, chuckled. "Remind me, why don't you? I keep thinking I should've done this when I was a kid. Now,

I'm more likely to break something when I fall off."

"You'll be fine," Teague assured him. "And you'll be staying on the ranch today, getting used to being on horseback and learning how to take care of it." He tipped his hat. "Have a great day." Then he was out of there.

"'Scuse me a minute." Butch wiped his lips, pushed back his chair, and followed Teague, who was walking briskly toward the path to the house. "Hey, wait up."

Teague stopped at the paddock fence and turned. "Did I forget something?"

"About this trip Wednesday."

"I'm not about to change my mind. Everyone else will be busy. So that leaves you." Teague looked him in the eye. "Besides, I thought you wanted to get away."

"Yeah, well, that was then."

"Think of it as doing a huge favor for the boss."

When he put it like that...

Teague glanced back toward the bunkhouse before leaning on the rail. "Now that I've got you alone... Are you okay?"

The expression of concern warmed him.

"Yeah, I'm fine."

"I'm sorry about last night. You caught me unawares."

"It's okay. I shouldn't have turned up at your door at that hour in the first place."

Teague inclined his head toward the bunkhouse. "So you knew Sol in high school? Talk about a small world."

"Yeah. We haven't seen each other since then." The conversation over breakfast had gone a long way in eroding some of the intervening years.

Teague cocked his head to one side. "We good?"

Butch took a quick peek to make sure no one else was around. He sighed. "You were right, okay? I guess it was high time I was honest with myself."

Teague smiled. "You have no idea how happy it makes me to hear you say that. I'm proud of you."

Butch frowned. "What did I do to deserve that?"

"It takes guts to admit you were on the wrong path. But it does leave me wondering how this newfound sexuality will change things."

Butch stared at him. "'Newfound sexuality'?"

"Why sure. You told me yourself—you're bi."

"But what do you mean? Why should that change anything?"

Teague stroked his stubbled chin. "Well... My ass is out of the picture, so does that mean you'll be going back to Bozeman or Livingston in search of pastures new? Now that you'd admitted you like fucking guys."

Butch hadn't even considered it. Hell, Teague had only called a halt a couple of days ago.

"I thought you said fucking wasn't a good coping mechanism."

"I'm not talking about finding someone to replace me."

Butch frowned. "Then what *are* you talking about?"

"You, walking into a bar and catching some guy checking you out. A guy you find attractive, even sexy. One who gives you a hard-on just *thinking* about getting him in the sack. Fucking him not because you want to blot out whatever is in your head but because he's hot." Teague smiled. "Someone who might even make you happy, because Lord knows we all need a little of that."

"And you think finding a guy will make me happy?"

Teague shrugged. "Look at the boss. You can't deny how much happier he's been since Toby came onto the scene."

He was right. There was no denying that.

"And if I can give one last word of advice..."

"I don't think I could stop you, so fire away."

Teague locked gazes with him. "Kissing."

He stilled. "What about it?"

"I don't know what you have against it, but you're missing out. It's okay to kiss a guy, all right? Whether you're making out or fucking him, kissing is a good way to connect. And when it's right, it can be... mind-blowing."

"A kiss?" Butch's voice sounded incredulous to his own ears.

"I've spent entire nights naked in some guy's bed, just touching and kissing." Teague straightened. "All I'm saying is, be open to the idea. Because once you start, you might never want to stop."

"I *have* kissed girls, you know." Not many, but Teague didn't need to know that.

"So why not guys?" Before Butch could come up with a

reasonable answer, Teague expelled a breath. "This is about being intimate, isn't it?"

Fuck.

"*Now* it makes sense."

"Now *what* makes sense?"

"All those times you came to my cabin... Do you know that in five years, you never hugged me once? Or sucked me off? We were stuck in a rut of that one act—your dick in my ass—and you wouldn't deviate from it. Were you afraid you'd get too close? That you'd feel vulnerable?"

Butch had never felt so fucking *seen*.

Teague nodded. "I'm right, aren't I? But it doesn't have to be that way anymore. Sex with a guy isn't just a means to an end, not now you've opened that door."

"What door?" Butch wanted this conversation to end, that was for damn sure.

"You've admitted you're bi. That it's okay to like sex with men. So let yourself do what you've never done before." He smiled. "Fall for another guy. Let one in."

"And *you've* fallen for someone before?"

Teague sighed. "Yeah, okay, you got me. No, I haven't, but only because I haven't met a guy yet who makes me want to fall head over heels. He's out there somewhere, though. And in the meantime, I'll go to Bozeman, Livingston, wherever, I'll hook up with someone, and I'll enjoy it. But I'll keep looking for him too."

"You got an ideal type?" Butch rolled his eyes. "I already know about the older part."

"I like a guy with muscles who's softly-spoken, makes me laugh, and fucks me into the mattress. Oh, and he's attractive."

Behind Butch, the bunkhouse door creaked open, and Teague's eyes lit up.

"Speaking of attractive..."

Butch glanced over his shoulder.

Sol was walking toward him.

Teague let out a throaty chuckle. "And while we're on the subject," he said in a low voice, "There are older guys and then there are those who fall into the Holy-fuck-he's-hot category."

Butch had a feeling Teague had someone specific in mind.

"He's gay too," Butch volunteered.

Teague grinned. "You don't say. My day suddenly got a whole lot brighter." His phone rang, and he pulled it from his jeans pocket. He glanced at the screen. "Looks like I'm wanted. You okay about the trip with Paul?"

"Sure." It wasn't as if he had a lot of choice, and Teague had nailed it—he'd be doing a favor for the boss.

Butch wanted to stay in Robert Thorston's good books.

Teague headed up the hill, and Sol caught up with Butch.

"Just making sure I didn't overstep the mark just now," Sol said as he joined him.

"Nah, it was fine. At least it's out in the open." He peered at the backpack in Sol's hand. "What are you doing now?"

"Toby wants to show me around the new barn. I'm going to take photos for the website."

"Then don't let me stop you." Butch laid a hand to Sol's arm. "Did you tell Zeeb before I had a chance to? I sorta got the impression he already knew."

"He did, but not because *I* breathed a word—because *we* did. He overheard us last night."

"Ah." Everything clicked into place. "He was the one who told you about me and Teague, wasn't he?"

Sol bit his lip, and Butch had his answer.

"I was about to leave the bunkhouse when I looked through the window and saw the two of you talking. Seemed like it was a pretty serious conversation, so I waited." Sol's eyes held compassion. "Is everything okay? I know you said you weren't an item, but—"

"Everything is fine. You'd best get along to the barn. Toby will be waiting for you."

Sol studied him for a moment, then gave a nod. "I'll see you later." He walked away from Butch, following the path to the barn.

His stomach churned and his head spun. Teague's words were still bouncing around inside his head.

I don't need a guy to be happy.

Butch *was* happy. Damn it, he *was*.

Except he knew he was fooling himself. There were days when all felt right with the world, and then he'd remember.

Guilt was the ultimate mood killer.

And then there was the light in Teague's eyes when he looked at Sol. Butch wasn't sure why that should bother him. It took him a moment to realize he was jealous.

But I've got nothing to be jealous of. I'm not interested in Sol.

More importantly, Sol wouldn't be interested in him. Too much history. Besides, he knew what Butch was capable of.

He'd seen the results.

CHAPTER 18

"I think you pretty much nailed it, in terms of accommodation," Sol told Toby as they came down the stairs. "That bathroom is amazing." He grinned. "You *know* you're going to have guys putting on a show in there." There was plenty of space for shower shenanigans.

Toby laughed. "Should I put up one of those OSHA signs? *No Fucking In The Showers - Safety Hazard.*"

"I've got a better idea. *Clients Who Fuck In The Shower Do So At Their Own Risk.* That should cover it." They laughed. They walked into the main room, and Sol nodded toward the tall cabinets standing against one wall. "Are they filled yet?"

Toby pointed to the boxes piled in one corner. "No. That's why you're here. We're going to spend today unboxing all the equipment and assembling the furniture."

"So I'm here to be a work horse, is that it?" Sol walked over to the largest box and peered at it. "What's in here?"

Toby chuckled. "A horse. And those two next to it are a flat bench and a sling frame."

"Good choices." Sol was already seeing the place in his head. "This is going to look awesome. How are the bookings coming along?"

"We've had a couple."

He stopped dead. "Wait a sec. If you don't have a website yet, how can anyone make a booking?"

"Word of mouth. I emailed a couple of guys at the club, and they said to book them in."

Sol smiled. "Wait till I'm done. You'll be up to your knees in bookings."

"You really think so?"

Sol was unaccustomed to hearing anything but confidence in Toby's voice. Then he realized what a huge undertaking this had to be for him—for both of them.

"It'll be fine. You're offering something pretty unique here.

I'm sure lots of guys will want to check it out. So I'll be sure to add a section where guests can leave comments after their stay—giving you the option of vetting them, of course."

"That sounds great." Toby's eyes twinkled. "By the way, I'd prefer to be up to my eyeballs in bookings."

"Then I'd better make this a really kick-ass website, hadn't I?" Sol gestured to the box containing the sling frame. "Why don't we start with this one?"

"Sure." Toby picked up a pocketknife from the floor and slit the tape across the top. "So…"

Sol waited, but Toby seemed to have run out of words. "So what?"

"Butch. How's it going?"

"You can relax. We talked this morning."

Toby pushed out a sigh of obvious relief. "Thank God. And? You didn't walk in here with a face like thunder, so I'm assuming the conversation was amicable."

"It was, once we got over a couple of obstacles."

"Is he still acting like you're a stranger?"

"No, he isn't. In fact, he talked about us knowing each other in high school over breakfast." Sol was still amazed by the turn of events. "I thought he'd take longer to get up enough nerve."

Butch was apparently made of stronger stuff.

"That sounds like a win. Good for Butch." Toby sat back on his haunches. "I have to ask… You were lusting after him in high school. Is there still a glimmer there?" He grinned. "Still think he's hot?"

Sol gave him a hard stare. "I know that look. And that was a pretty loaded question."

Toby regarded him with wide eyes. "I have no idea what you're talking about."

"*Sure* you don't. That was a long time ago. Ancient history."

"And you haven't answered my question. Do you still think he's hot? You can tell me," he wheedled. "It's not as if we're school kids and I'm going to go running to him during recess and say, 'Hey, Sol *really* likes you.'"

Sol snorted. "I wouldn't put it past you."

"And you still haven't answered my question."

He pushed out a growl. "For fuck's sake, you are such a kid

sometimes. Yes, he's hot. Happy now?"

"How hot?" Toby demanded. "On a scale from one to ten, where one is lukewarm and ten is burn-the-sheets scorching?"

He's an eight, maybe a nine.

Not that Sol was about to tell Toby that. He wouldn't give him the satisfaction.

"Knock knock." Butch stood in the open doorway.

Sol froze. *Please, God, tell me he didn't hear any of that.*

Toby glanced at him. "What's up?"

"You expecting more stuff? Because there's a delivery for you up at the house. Teague just called."

"Ooh." Toby bounced to his feet. "I know what that is."

Sol laughed. "More goodies?"

Toby grinned. "Spreader bars. Make a start, and I'll be back." And with that, he hurried out of the barn.

"What the fuck is a spreader bar?" Butch asked.

"If you hang around here a while longer, you'll be able to see for yourself." Sol opened the box. "You got a minute? Or do you have to be somewhere?"

"What do you need me for?"

Sol gestured to the box's interior. "Help me get this out and assemble it?"

"Sure, I can do that." Butch came over and peered inside. "What is it?"

"It's a sling frame."

Butch chuckled. "And I'm still none the wiser."

Together they lifted out all the metal pieces and laid them on the floor. The sling bed was wrapped in plastic, and there was a bag containing the chains.

Butch stared at the latter. "What is this, an instrument of torture?"

Sol laughed. "I'll demonstrate it when we're done."

Butch arched his eyebrows. "You know about this stuff?"

"I've assembled a few bits and pieces in my time, helping friends. But this isn't the first website of this kind that I've worked on. I had to familiarize myself with everything that came with it. So yeah, I did my research."

Butch didn't need to know what Sol got up to at the club or in his private life. He was only just getting used to the idea that he was bi, for Christ's sake. While Sol was reasonably certain Butch wasn't a snowflake, learning about Sol's lifestyle might send him running for the hills, or at least make him wary, and Sol did *not* want Butch to feel uncomfortable.

Quite the contrary. He wanted Butch relaxed, content—and open to new situations.

Sol found the two cross pieces that formed the center of the top and base.

"We start with one of these."

Between them, they slotted the upright bars into the corners, assembled the top, and lowered it, sliding the corner posts into position. Sol attached the chains to the corner hooks, then unpacked the sling bed. He pulled the chains through the rings at the head of the leather straps, and secured them using an S-hook, which allowed for a change of height if needed.

Butch stood back and stared at it. "Okay, now I have a better idea of what it is."

"It's not finished yet." Sol reached into the box and removed the pillow. He used its straps to fasten it at the top of the bed. Then he took out the stirrups and attached them to the chains. "*Now* it's finished." He grinned. "And now for that demonstration."

Butch's breathing hitched. "What?"

Sol climbed onto the bed and spread his legs, his thighs resting on the leather straps. He pointed to the stirrups. "Put my feet into those, will you?"

Butch did as instructed, then stood back to take in the whole view. "Whoa. This is some piece of equipment."

"You're too far away." Sol grabbed the chains near his head. "Step closer, between my legs." When Butch hesitated, Sol smiled. "I don't bite, you know."

Butch moved in, and Sol pointed to the bars above his head. "Grab onto those." When Butch was in position, Sol looked him in the eye. "And now you're ready. The height's just right."

"Right for what?"

Sol took in Butch's flushed cheeks. "You're not *that* naive. The sling makes fucking effortless. The bottom has little range of movement, and the top has access to his ass and hole. The sling rocks, and that adds to the overall sensation. See?" He pointed to his ass. "I'm in the perfect position for fucking, rimming, fingering… fisting…"

That last one had Butch's eyes like saucers. Sol noted that he hadn't backed away, however.

"'Rimming'? What's that?"

Sol blinked. "My my, this is turning into Anal Sex 101. I'll tell you about it another time."

So what did you and Teague get up to?

He gestured to Butch's stance, his crotch a hair's breadth away from Sol's denim-encased ass. "So… you can see the attraction, right? The top gets to hold onto the bars and rock his hips back and forth." He gave another smile. "Why don't you try it?"

Butch stilled. "What?"

"Just push against me, see how it moves."

For a moment, he didn't think Butch was going to go for it, and Sol prayed Toby didn't come back too soon. Then Butch really *would* bolt like a skittish colt.

Butch gave a gentle push with his hips and their bodies met.

"That's it. Do that again."

Butch gave another push, only this time with a little more force.

"Keep rocking," Sol urged him, resisting the urge to touch his own burgeoning erection.

Butch's breathing grew shallow, and a sheen of sweat coated his forehead. "I get the idea." He let go of the bars and took a step back. "Maybe I should get back to the bunkhouse."

Sol extricated himself from the sling. "Sure, if you have to. But I've got all these boxes to unpack."

"You don't need me. Besides, Toby won't be long."

Sol got the idea.

I pushed him too far, didn't I?

"Thanks for your help."

"No problem."

"Why don't you come back later today when it's all set up?" Sol smiled. "No more demonstrations, okay?"

"Sure." Butch headed for the door, and Sol picked up the pocketknife to open another box.

"Sol?"

He turned his head. Butch stood there, one hand at the back

of his neck.

"You forget something?"

Butch pointed to the sling. "You were right." He smiled. "I do see the attraction." Then he was gone.

Sol breathed a little easier.

Thank God I didn't ask him to go in the sling.

Butch would be running for the hills by then.

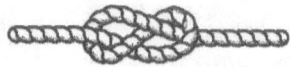

Butch leaned against the barn wall, his heart pounding, heat crawling over and through him, aware of a fluttery sensation in his chest and stomach. Everything was louder, his skin tingled, and he couldn't stop the shivers.

Holy fuck.

That had to be one of the hottest things he'd ever done.

He'd held onto the top bars, Sol's tight ass *right fucking there*, and all he could think of was Sol naked, his hole ready for Butch's cock to slide right in, as deep as it was possible to go. He could feel the warm skin of Sol's thighs as he dug his fingers into the muscled flesh, pulling Sol to him, spearing into him…

Butch knew when night came, he'd close his eyes and those images would be there, making him hard as a rock.

As hard as he was right that second.

CHAPTER 19

Robert left his office in search of coffee. Matt had left him a fresh pot before he'd gone to shop for groceries. Toby was in the barn with Sol, setting up for photos, and the house was quiet.

Robert was still getting used to having Toby in his life. After five years of being alone, it was more difficult than he'd anticipated, adjusting to another body around the place.

The one exception was his bed. Falling asleep wrapped in Toby's arms, waking to find warmth surrounding him, Toby's leg hooked over his, his hand on Robert's chest…

Heaven.

I got so *lucky.*

In his more philosophical moments, Robert liked to believe Kevin had had a hand in it somewhere. Because what were the chances of finding not one lover but two—and two Doms at that—who made his life feel so complete?

Robert Thorston was one lucky son of a bitch.

He paused at the threshold. Toby was standing in the kitchen, staring out of the window.

Robert grabbed a clean cup. "You can't be done already."

Toby smiled. "I'm not. There's still all the unpacking to do."

"Then why are you here and not down there?"

He pointed to an opened cardboard box sitting on the tiled floor by the back door. "I came to collect that."

Robert was none the wiser. "And yet you're still here."

Toby turned and leaned against the sink. "I have news. Butch and Sol are on speaking terms again."

"That's good."

"Oh, it's better than good."

Robert didn't miss the trace of mirth in Toby's voice. "Okay, I'll bite."

"Hmm?"

"You're up to something. Or something's tickled you. So which one is it?"

Toby's grin was apparently all the answer he was going to get.

Robert tried from another angle. "I take it your present mood has something to do with Sol and Butch?"

Toby nodded. "You remember what Sol told us? How he had the hots for Butch in high school?"

"I'm not likely to forget that part," Robert remarked dryly.

"Well, guess what?" Toby's eyes gleamed. "He still does."

The light began to dawn. "Whatever you're thinking of doing, don't."

"Who says I'm thinking of doing anything?"

Robert snorted. "Sweetheart, I don't know if anyone has ever told you this, but you really can't do innocent. And I might not have known you all *that* long, but I do know you can be devious."

"All I was going to do was give them a little push in the right direction."

"Who says they want to be pushed?" Toby fell silent, and Robert stared at him. "Is there something you're not telling me?"

Toby heaved a sigh. "I can't tell you the whole story, because it's not mine to tell. All I *can* say is… It would be good if Sol was interested in Butch. He needs this."

"And what about Butch? Isn't he already… entangled?"

Toby laughed. "Well, his dick might be, but I don't think his heart is."

"Oh, so your intentions are romantic?" Except as soon as he said the words, Robert liked the idea. Butch could do with a little romance.

Hell, we all need that.

"Why not?"

"Do you have a plan to bring this about?"

"Maybe?"

Robert chuckled. "Does it involve me?"

"Maybe?"

"But that still doesn't tell me why you're up here and not down there beavering away."

Toby's grin was full of mischief. "Because I just left the two of them together, and I don't want to walk in there too soon and ruin a moment."

"And what if they're not actually having a 'moment'?" Robert air-quoted. "They could be spitting and snarling at each other."

Toby narrowed his eyes. "They're not."

"Sure about that?"

"No, but I'm going to stay away a while longer, just to make sure."

Robert folded his arms. "I thought you didn't 'do' romance."

Toby straightened and walked over to him. "I didn't—until I met you. And it feels so good, everyone needs to experience it." He stroked Robert's cheek. "There *is* something we could be doing while I'm here."

Robert had a feeling he knew where this was heading. "Oh?"

Toby inclined his head toward the box on the floor. "We could try out one of the spreader bars. You know, make sure it works okay."

Robert chuckled once more. "I don't think there's any way a spreader bar could be defective." His dick stiffened at the thought of him lying on the bed, his wrists and ankles cuffed to the bar, Toby holding onto it while he drove his cock balls-deep into Robert's ass.

There had to be some benefits to being the boss, right? Such as taking time out of his schedule to be with Toby.

"Okay, you're right. I should go." Toby headed for the door.

"Don't you fucking dare," Robert ground out.

Toby paused, grinning. "Something you want?"

Robert knew how to melt his man.

He went over to Toby and knelt at his feet. "Let's go upstairs, Sir." He pointed to the box. "With one of those."

Toby smiled. "I think Sol knows what he's doing." He reached into the box and removed a spreader bar, still wrapped in plastic. "And *I* know what I'm going to do with this."

Robert didn't doubt that for a second.

The bunkhouse was empty, and Butch was grateful for the chance to be alone. It wouldn't be long before the guests returned from the paddock, ready for their supper.

He lay on his bed, arms folded under his head. He needed a little time to process the thoughts swirling around in his mind.

Sol hasn't even been here a day, and already I'm a mess.

Except he knew his present confusion had nothing to do with Sol, and everything to do with the lies he'd been telling himself—lies others had pointed out to him, more than once.

Why didn't I listen?

Race had been right—he *had* been deep in denial.

Teague had been right too, about a great many things. Butch *was* into guys. He *had* used Teague. He'd fucked guys because it felt good. And he was right about something else—they both deserved better.

Does that mean he's right about kissing too?

Butch wasn't going to put it to the test. Not yet, at any rate.

Sol had been right too. Butch wasn't that naive.

I lied to him.

That had been one lie—Butch had been lying to himself for more than thirty years. But if he could admit he liked guys, then maybe it was time to bring an end to all the lies.

Then do something. Now. Before you change your mind.

He got up, grabbed his hat, and headed out of the door. From the paddock came voices, and judging by the laughter, it had been a good day. He took the long way round, not wanting them to see him. As he neared the barn, he caught the sound of yet more laughter from inside. Butch's heart went into overdrive.

Toby's in there. Fuck.

He didn't need an audience. This had to be a private conversation. Then he expelled a breath when Toby exited the barn and walked toward the path to the house.

Thank God.

Butch went inside. Sol was taking photos, and Butch came to a dead stop at the sight. He'd only been away a few hours, and the room had been transformed. The cabinets doors were open to reveal their contents, and Butch wanted to take a better look, but it would have to wait.

He was a man on a mission.

Sol lowered his camera. "Hey. What do you think?"

"Can we talk?" Butch blurted.

"Sure. Why so serious?" He placed the camera on a shelf in one of the cabinets.

Butch walked over to a flat black bench and sat on it. "I... I haven't been honest with you."

"About what?" Sol walked over to stand in front of him.

"Before, when we were putting the sling together… I knew what it was. I even know what rimming is, not that I've ever tried it."

"Then why—"

"I wasn't gonna tell ya I watched gay porn, okay?"

Sol frowned. "Why not? You've told me you're bi, so what's wrong with watching gay porn?"

"Because it didn't fit in with the way I saw myself, that's why." Butch rubbed his hands on his jeans. "But others saw me for who I was—the first guy I ever fucked, Teague—they tried to get me to see the truth, 'cept I wasn't listening."

Sol joined him on the bench. "I'm listening, though."

Butch studied his clasped hands. "I told myself I went with guys because it was convenient. And the guys were always the same kind—guys who couldn't be out at home, straight guys who were curious… In all those years, I got sucked off and I fucked a lot of asses. Never got my lips around a dick, though. And do you know why?"

"I have an idea. Tell me your theory."

Butch nodded. "I think that's because you're another guy who sees through me. I've been fooling myself. I told myself I just wasn't keen on giving blow jobs, but that wasn't true. Because having a dick in your mouth? You do that, and there's no way of denying you're with a guy. And if I stuck with receiving and being the one doing the fucking, then I could close my eyes and pretend I was with a girl."

"You wouldn't be the first man to do that," Sol murmured.

"Thing is, I got stuck in a rut. And I think the reason I got uncomfortable in that rut was because I knew I was lying to myself. Teague calling a halt to us was the best thing he could've done."

"Does this mean there'll be no more hiding?"

"Yeah, no more. And this time I mean it. I'm gonna be honest with the guys too." He turned to look at Sol. "You asked if I knew I wasn't straight back in high school. I did, but that was only because there was someone I was… interested in."

"I guess he never knew how you felt."

"No sir, he did not. But if I'd had the courage to tell him, to be honest, things might have been very different—for both of us."

Butch shivered. "And that's all I'm gonna say on that subject." He felt wiped out.

"So you weren't secretly madly in love with me?" Sol quipped, his eyes twinkling.

Butch laughed, and *Lord*, it felt good. "Thanks. I needed that. And no."

You're being honest, remember?

Butch guessed it was like any new habit—do it enough times and it would become second nature.

He gave Sol a smile. "Always thought you were good-looking, though. Better-looking than I was. I could never understand why you didn't have a girlfriend." He chuckled. "And now I know."

Sol looked him in the eye, and Butch was glad he was sitting down. That searching gaze left him feeling certain Sol could see right through him.

Enough talking.

"Wanna give me the five-cent tour now?"

Sol shook his head. "That can wait for another day. Besides, it's supper time soon. But there *is* something I want to do."

"And what's that?"

Sol rose, stood in front of him, grabbed Butch's hands, and tugged him to his feet before enfolding him in a hug.

A wave of warmth flooded through him at the unexpected embrace, and he relished the sensation of being surrounded by strength in a show of friendship.

Well fuck. Teague was right again.

Then Sol released him, and Butch felt the loss immediately.

"Thank you for sharing all that with me," Sol said in a low voice. "It can't have been easy."

"You have *no* idea."

Sol cocked his head. "But you do feel better for letting it all out, don't you?"

Butch laughed. "Good Lord. First Teague, now you. Yes, okay? Yes, I feel better."

Except better wasn't an adequate description.

He felt lighter.

CHAPTER 20

Sol sat down to supper in the best of moods. Despite spending his day emptying boxes, putting equipment into cabinets, and assembling furniture, he felt wide-awake, warmth radiating through him that had nothing to do with the outside temperature.

Butch had shocked the hell out of him.

His honesty had been unexpected. More than that, he'd made himself vulnerable, and considering his initial reaction to Sol's presence, that was truly humbling.

Right then, Butch was eating his beef casserole, adding comments here and there to the conversations going on around the table. A much more subdued Butch.

No, that wasn't the right word—more pensive.

It took real courage to come out with all that.

Along with honesty, courage was a trait Sol found attractive in a man, but the ability to admit they'd been wrong and show a willingness to make things right? That was even more attractive.

Yeah, Sol was liking this new Butch more and more.

"Where were you all day?" That came from Frank, the oldest of the guests.

Sol pushed his plate away from him. "Working. I'm here as a kind of consultant. But after tomorrow, I'll have time to relax a little and do some riding."

Phil smiled. "I hear that. I really needed this break. I haven't been on a horse in years."

Sol hadn't interacted much with the four other guests. Frank was probably close to his own age, and the others were in their thirties and forties, from the look of them. Phil seemed pleasant enough, and Frank was an open book. Max was a quiet one, but when he did speak, his comments were thoughtful. Eric was a southern boy who'd wanted to ride for a while but had never gotten the chance. From what Sol had picked up, he worked in a high-pressure environment, and Sol figured this was a way for him to de-stress.

"Best thing for the inside of a man is the outside of a horse," Zeeb declared.

"How was the first day on horseback?" Butch asked Frank. He grinned. "There's a packet of Epsom salt in the bathroom cabinet if you need it."

"You know what? I don't feel so bad."

Paul chuckled. "Wait till tomorrow. You'll have aches where you've never had them before. And I'm *still* going to put you back on a horse."

"This sure is a beautiful place," Max commented. "You're so lucky to live and work here."

Walt beamed. "You said it. I love it here." His eyes twinkled. "The only downside is having to work with these guys."

Butch snorted. "Funny. I was thinkin' the same thing about you, junior."

Walt gave him the finger.

Sol liked the banter and good humor. What he liked even better was Butch looking and sounding a whole lot more relaxed.

"We had another talk today with the guy who owns the place. Robert, is that his name?" Max smiled. "Seems like a nice guy."

Teague nodded. "He's a good boss. His granddaddy built Salvation."

"He was with his partner again. Toby, is that his name? So they run the ranch together?" Eric inquired.

Teague leaned back in his chair. "Kind of. Toby hasn't been here all that long."

Phil chuckled. "He's a fast mover, then." When Teague gave him an inquiring glance, Phil flushed. "You know when they stopped by yesterday after we arrived, to welcome us? I saw them a while later. Unless my eyes were playing tricks on me, they were kissing."

Teague smiled. "That's because Toby's more than a business partner. He's the boss's actual 'partner.'" He hooked his fingers in the air.

Eric frowned. "They're… gay?"

Sol's skin prickled. Judging by the way Teague straightened, he had the same reaction.

"Yeah, they're gay." Teague gazed at Eric as if expecting a response, but Eric said nothing.

Frank gave a wry chuckle. "Two guys kissing? That'd be considered pretty tame where I live."

"And where's that?" Sol asked.

"LA. West Hollywood, to be exact."

Sol laughed. "Yeah, I can see why you wouldn't be fazed by guys kissing."

"You know WeHo?" Frank's smile lit up his eyes.

"Sure. Been to the Abbey more times than I can count."

"Not been inside myself—not my kinda place—but it's a popular spot, that's for sure."

Butch gave Sol a puzzled glance. "An abbey? With, like, monks?"

Sol grinned. "Not that kind of abbey. It's a gay bar, and it's famous. Hell. It's probably the country's biggest gay bar."

Eric's frown deepened. "You're saying y'all don't mind working for gay guys?"

Teague tilted his head to one side. "Why should we mind?"

Eric shrugged. "Some people might, y'know. Most might find it… unnatural."

Crickets.

That prickle over Sol's skin morphed into a trickle of unease down his spine.

Teague poured himself a glass of water and downed a third of it. He set the glass on the table. "Then I guess we're not most people. We're an easygoing bunch here."

Sol had the impression Teague was trying hard to be polite.

"I suppose if you didn't like it, you could always find another job someplace different," Eric suggested.

Teague frowned. "What's not to like? Robert's a good boss. Him being gay doesn't affect his ability to run this place. And if it comes to that, some of us are gay too, including the guy who made your supper."

"And some of us are bi," Butch added in a low voice.

Heads swiveled in his direction.

Butch's chin was high, his shoulders held back. "Well, don't act like you didn't know."

Zeeb cackled. "Oh, we knew, all right. We're just tryin' not to faint from hearing you admit it."

Sol's heart swelled. *I am so fucking proud of you.*

Teague's warm expression led him to believe he wasn't the only one.

Then Teague leaned forward, his gaze focused on Eric. "We don't like to hide things around here. You take us as you find us."

"It's that deep end thing again, isn't it? Didn't someone say that last night?"

Smart man, Frank.

Teague nodded. "The boss isn't hiding who he is, so why should we? I think it's better to be upfront about it." His smile was strained. "Makes for fewer surprises that way."

Next to Walt, Phil smiled. "I don't have a problem with it. How does the saying go? 'I may be straight but I don't hate.'"

Walt grinned and high-fived him. "Dude."

Eric blinked, a flush crawling over his cheeks. "Hey. Who's talking about hate? I didn't say I hated gays. Don't put words into my mouth."

"No one said you hated anybody," Walt said in a patient tone.

Eric wasn't listening. "I'm a good Christian, y'hear?"

"Then I'm sure you remember what Jesus said." Butch stared at him. "Something about loving others as he loved you?"

Eric's flush deepened. "I'm entitled to my beliefs."

Butch studied him. "You're a guest. You've paid to be here, to enjoy yourself. And no one is gonna disrespect your beliefs or the way you choose to live. But it goes both ways."

Dear Lord, the man had come a long way in twenty-four hours.

Eric wiped his lips with his napkin, pushed his chair back, and walked out of the door.

Teague let out a sigh. "I'm sorry about that," he said to the others. "We don't usually call guests out—we like to give everyone the benefit of the doubt—but there's only so much we'll take before we have to say something."

"Hey, don't apologize for him," Frank retorted. "I think you were remarkably patient."

"Yeah," Phil agreed. "If anyone should be apologizing, it's Eric."

Sol shook his head. "Do you get many guests like that?"

"Not many, thank the Lord," Teague replied, his eyes fixed on the door.

Zeeb snorted. "I don't think he's thanking the Lord for the fact he now knows he's sleepin' in the same room as a lot of gay and bi guys." He peered at Butch. "You took your damn time."

Butch rolled his eyes. "So I'm bi. Big fucking deal."

His relaxed manner didn't fool Sol for a second. It was a *huge* fucking deal.

Zeeb glanced at Teague. "Anything goin' on we need to know about?"

Teague arched his eyebrows. "Absolutely nothing to report." He glanced at the remaining guests. "So, you guys think you're ready for a trail tomorrow? An easy one, to start with." He smiled at Phil. "It won't be long before they'll be up to speed. Wait and see. By the end of the week, they'll be pros."

Sol knew a change of subject when he heard one.

He switched off as Teague, Walt and Paul discussed the various trails they could undertake. Sol's attention was riveted on Butch, who seemed to be relieved not to be the focus of the conversation.

Then Butch stood. "I'm gonna get some air." He headed for the door.

Sol waited for a minute, then rose. "That sounds like a good idea."

Teague's gaze met his but he said nothing.

Yeah, Teague was another smart man.

Butch leaned against the paddock fence. There was maybe an hour left until sunset, and the world was quiet and still.

Can't believe I said all that.

It had been impulsive, and while Butch was used to opening his mouth before his brain was in gear, that was always about inconsequential matters.

This was new.

"You did good."

Butch jumped. He hadn't even heard the crunch of Sol's boots on the gravel. "You tryin' to give me a heart attack?"

Sol joined him, his forearms resting on the rail. "I mean it. You were awesome."

Warmth surged through him. "Wasn't as scary as I thought it would be." He glanced back at the bunkhouse. "I was right about one thing, though. They weren't exactly surprised."

"Now that I've got you on your own, I really did want to talk to you about—"

Butch spun around to face him. "Does this have anything to do with what went on in high school?" His pulse quickened.

"Yes, but—"

"Then no. I haven't changed my mind on that. Talking about your questionable taste in music back then? That's as far as I go. Everything else is off limits."

Sol's face tightened. "Got it."

Butch resumed his previous position, his heartbeat slowing from its spike of activity. "I guess I won't see much of you while you're here. I'll be gone for two days when I go with Paul to collect that horse for the boss."

"That's a pity, because I'd sure like to see more of you."

Butch glanced at him, and a shiver ran through him when he found Sol staring at him.

Sol didn't break eye contact. He smiled, his eyes sparkling. "Yeah, a whole lot more."

And with that, he wandered back to the bunkhouse.

Butch waited until he caught the creak of the door before expelling a long breath.

Jesus.

Someone somewhere had just turned the thermostat all the way up to *Hotter than Hell.*

Butch lay in bed, wide awake. No shocker there, but what had stirred him from his sleep had not been a nightmare, but another kind of dream entirely.

The kind he hadn't experienced for a great many years.

He had vague recollections of a warm mouth on his dick, but

he'd woken before the finale, with what felt like a steel pipe in his shorts.

Just close your eyes. With any luck, you'll slip right back into it.

The room was filled with the soft sounds of even, deep breathing and the occasional snore from Zeeb's bunk. Butch rolled onto his side—

To find Sol mirroring him. Watching him.

"That's kinda creepy, y'know," Butch whispered.

"I can't sleep." Sol's whisper drifted across the space separating them.

"Try counting cows."

Butch's nightlight didn't give off much illumination, but he could make out Sol's raised eyebrows.

"I thought you were supposed to count sheep."

Butch grinned. "It's a cattle ranch. Duh." He paused, listening for any change in sounds. Zeeb gave a rough snore.

"I've got a better idea." Sol shifted onto his back, his hand beneath the sheet, and the gentle rhythmic movement left Butch in no doubt as to what was happening under there.

What shocked him was the thought that ricocheted through his mind.

I wanna see.

"Oh yeah." Sol let out a sigh.

Butch's gaze drifted back to the middle of the bed, and he froze. Christ, it was sticking up like a flagpole, tenting the sheet. His hand itched to reach into his shorts.

Sol turned his head toward him. "Wanna join me?" he whispered.

What the actual fuck?

"You don't mean—"

"You in your bunk, me in mine," Sol interjected. He grinned. "See which of us reaches the finish line first." He removed his hand, spat into his palm, then slid it beneath the white sheet once more, resuming his previous rhythm.

Butch couldn't move.

Sol stared at him, his hand not pausing once. "You telling me you never jerk off in here?"

Butch was being stupid and he knew it.

"No, not saying that at all." He spat into his hand, then with the other he freed his cock and balls from his shorts. He worked the shaft with his thumb and forefinger, keeping the touch light and trying not to look at Sol.

He could hear, though. More spit, followed by shallow breaths, only served to ramp up the electricity carried in the air. A stifled moan, low and urgent, filtered across, and Butch had to see. He turned his head and—

Sol had thrown back the sheets and removed his shorts. His dick wasn't overly long, maybe six, seven inches, but dear *Lord* it was thick. Butch watched, mesmerized by the fluid motion of Sol's hand, the way he played with his balls, tugging on them, squeezing them, the way he circled the head with his finger before stroking the knot of nerves under it. The bedsprings gave out an occasional grunt of complaint, mingling with Sol's low grunts of pleasure.

Butch threw back his sheet, shoved his shorts to his ankles, and curled his fingers around his turgid length, pressing his lips together to prevent his moans from escaping. He knew it wouldn't be long—that familiar tingle was already snaking its way through him—and he sped up his hand, pulling on it, pausing to add more spit.

No words, just sounds, slicker now, their breathing almost in sync, Butch straining to hear the slightest change in the room.

Then Sol's breathing hitched, and Butch knew he'd lost the race. He covered the head of his dick with his hand, and warmth filled it, seeping through his fingers. He shuddered his way through the jolts of pleasure, until his cock lay on his belly, softened and sticky. Butch grabbed his shorts and wiped himself clean, his breathing resorting to its usual rhythm.

Only then did he turn to look at Sol, who was busy with his own clean-up operation. He tossed his shorts to the end of the bed, then pulled the sheet up over him.

Their eyes met.

"Thank you," Sol whispered.

"Not sure what you're thankin' me for," Butch responded.

"The pleasure of your company? Now close your eyes and sleep. Sweet dreams. I know what *I'll* be dreaming about." Sol smiled. "A certain cowboy with the *sexiest* eyes." Then he rolled onto his side, facing the wall.

Butch lay there, unable to breathe.

He… he wasn't talking about me, *was he?*

Holy fuck.

How in the hell did Sol expect him to sleep after firing a bullet like that?

CHAPTER 21

Tuesday, August 23

Sol closed the folder containing all the photos. "So, what do you think?" His laptop sat between the three of them on the dining table.

Toby's grin said it all, and Sol wished he shared his confidence.

It's missing something.

"I think they look amazing," Robert commented. He smiled. "Now I can't wait to see the website when you're done." He paused. "Are *you* happy with them?"

Sol had a feeling not a lot got past Robert Thorston.

"Sort of."

Toby frowned. "But Robert's right. They *are* amazing. So what's wrong with them?"

Sol opened the folder again and scrolled through the photos. There was the show bedroom Toby had set up, the bathroom, long shots of the main room, close-ups of the equipment, the exterior of the barn…

Then it hit him.

"You got your leathers here?" he asked Toby.

"Dude." Toby smiled. "Everything I *own* is here. I moved here permanently at the end of last month, remember? I sold my apartment in San Francisco. But why do you want my leathers?"

"How would you like to be on the website?"

Toby blinked. "Say what?"

He pointed to a photo of the main room. "It needs people."

"I'm not sure I'm cut out to be a model."

Sol got his phone out and scrolled through his images. "Look." He showed some of them to Toby and Robert. "I take photos of my clients—to show what I can do—but I never include faces. So *we* don't include faces, okay? I can do shots from behind, whatever you want…"

Toby glanced at Robert, who shook his head. "*You* can, but

leave me out of this. I'm not comfortable doing it."

Sol patted his arm. "And that's totally okay." He grinned. "Toby, however, is much more of an exhibitionist." He flashed a quick grin. "Even if he doesn't want to admit it."

Toby snorted. "Wow. It's as if you know me." He frowned. "But won't it look weird if there's only me in the photos?"

Sol had already thought of that. "I *was* going to ask Butch if he'd help out."

Toby gaped. "You really think he's going to let you dress him up in leathers? Besides, I don't think mine would fit him."

Sol chuckled. "I didn't have leather in mind, just jeans and boots. I wouldn't show his face either. Maybe a close-up of his ass with you holding a paddle to it, or him lying face down and your hand holding a flogger, its tails splayed out on his back. That kinda thing. We're not talking porn, more… artistic."

Toby grinned again. "Sure, you can ask him, but I think you already know what the answer will be."

"Then let's go find him." Not that Sol was convinced either. Butch might be more open about his sexuality—it didn't mean he'd be ready to step out of his comfort zone to *that* extent.

Robert glanced at his watch. "They'll be back from the trail by now, so everyone will be in the bunkhouse."

"I won't ask him in front of the guests." Especially one guest in particular.

"If the worst happens and he says no, these photos will be just fine," Robert assured him.

Sol was hoping for a better outcome than that.

Then a thought occurred to him.

"The guys don't know I'm into BDSM. As far as they're concerned, I'm a web designer who happens to be your friend. Even Butch thinks I just did a lot of research."

"And you want it to stay that way?" Toby asked, his head cocked.

"Hey, I share a room with these guys, okay? I want them to feel comfortable around me."

"Fair enough. They won't get to hear about it from me." Toby's eyes sparkled. "But I still don't think you'll get Butch to agree."

Sol smiled. "I'll use my charm."

"Hey, you got a minute?"

Butch tossed the bag of trash into the back of the truck, then turned to face Sol. "What's up?" For the umpteenth time since Sol's arrival, Butch tried to avoid staring.

Dayum. Sol was dressed in tight jeans and a white tee that clung to his lean torso and broad chest, revealing nipples that pushed against the cotton.

Does he have to look so good all the fucking time?

"I need your help with something."

"Okay… what, exactly?"

"You know I've been taking photos of the new barn, right?"

"Yeah."

"Well, I had an idea…"

Butch listened as Sol explained, and his mouth dried up.

Oh. My. God.

"Me? You want *me* to… pose for photos?"

"No one would see your face. I'd shoot from behind, weird angles, whatever it takes to keep your identity a secret. No one will know it's you."

"But what do you want me to wear?" He swallowed. "I've seen stuff, all right? You wouldn't want me… naked, would ya?"

"God no."

What the fuck?

Butch blinked. "Why not? What's wrong with the way I look?"

Sol burst out laughing. "Will you make your mind up, please? You can't be reluctant to show off your body *and* pissed I don't want to show it off, all at the same time. And I was thinking of jeans and boots. Maybe also…"

Butch narrowed his gaze. "Maybe what?"

"A leather collar. Seen from behind, of course, but it would look more authentic."

"And you'd put these photos on the new website?"

He *really* didn't know about this.

"I know, it's a lot to ask." Sol straightened. "You know what? Forget I even mentioned it. I might try some of the others."

Butch's heart hammered.

"Tell you what. If I'm not the only one doing it, sure."

Sol stared at him. "Seriously?"

"Sure," he said, affecting a nonchalance he certainly did not feel. "But only if there's a few of us. If they say no, then it's no from me too."

"I'll go ask them now." Sol walked toward the bunkhouse, but Butch grabbed his arm.

"Don't. Wait in the new barn, and I'll bring them to you. The guests are all taking showers right now. They won't miss us."

"Thank you." Sol headed for the barn.

Butch took a deep breath.

I must be out of my mind to consider this.

He wasn't sure why he hadn't refused pointblank, but he'd said he'd go along with it.

And what if they say yes?

He'd deal with that situation if it arose.

"I'm sure you're wondering why Butch asked you to come here," Sol began.

"Whatever the reason, can we be quick? I've got stuff to do up at the house," Matt told him.

"It'll only take a minute—well, unless you agree. Let's wait and see."

"Wait just one minute." Zeeb narrowed his eyes. "Is this Amway?"

Walt frowned. "What the hell is Amway?"

Zeeb looked heavenward. "Lord, you are *so* young."

Butch chuckled. "Another time, okay? Sol has a... proposal to put to you."

Paul arched his eyebrows. "Okay, you've got me hooked. What's going on?"

"And does the boss know about it?" Teague added.

"Yes, he does."

"Would you just *look* at this place?" Walt wandered over to the sling and gave the chains a tentative stroke.

Zeeb stared at the flat bench. "Why are there two holes in this thing?" He pointed to the one at the end. "That's for your face, I guess, like those massage tables. Oh, is that what this is? Then what's that middle hole for?" Before Sol could explain, Zeeb's eyes widened. "Holy Mary mother of God, it's for your dick, isn't it?"

Sol bit back a chuckle. "I knew you'd get there eventually."

Zeeb was still staring at the hole. "Christ, there are some kinky fuckers out there," he muttered.

Sol coughed. "Zeeb? You think I can drag your mind back for a second here?"

Zeeb flushed. "I'm listening."

Sol gazed at them. "How would you guys feel about playing dress-up?"

Matt's eyebrows shot up. "Okay, I didn't see *that* coming."

Sol didn't waste time. He outlined his idea, making sure to mention the anonymity of the photos, what they'd be wearing, the kind of photos he had in mind… They needed to see the whole picture.

"So you'd be taking the photos in here." Walt gestured to the equipment. "On some of this." His cheeks pinked. "Just checking I've got it all straight in my head."

Zeeb cackled. "Ain't nothing straight about any of this." He shook his head. "Not me. I'd do anything for the boss—within reason—but not that."

"I'm with Zeeb," Paul added.

Sol nodded. "Thanks for being honest." Their responses were pretty much as he'd anticipated.

Looks like it's going to be just Toby after all.

"Well, I'm up for it." Matt grinned. "And I don't mind if you use my face either. I mean, what's the difference between this and Scruff or Grindr?" His eyes sparkled. "It sounds like it could be fun. I've even got a leather jock somewhere." His grin widened. "I wanna play at being a submissive. I've seen stuff online."

Sol laughed. Matt was a regular ray of sunshine. "Okay, you're in."

"Woo hoo!" Matt fist-pumped the air.

"Count me in too." Walt bit his lip. "'Scept I vote for keeping my face out of it."

"That's fine," Sol assured him. He glanced at Teague. "What

about you?"

Teague stroked his lightly bearded chin. "I agree with Matt. This could be fun. But I'm going with Walt. No faces."

Matt rubbed his hands together. "That's great. I get to be the poster boy for this place."

They all laughed.

Sol peered at Butch, waiting.

Butch rolled his eyes. "Fine. But I'm having a drink first."

"Dutch courage, huh?"

He snorted. "You know it."

"When do you want to do this?" Teague asked Sol.

"I've thought about that. Tonight, when the guests go to bed? We won't need daylight—there isn't any in here anyway, except for what comes in through the door—and Toby says if we need extra lighting, the workmen left some portable ones."

"As long as we're not still here at midnight," Teague declared. "We all need to be up early in the morning, remember?"

"And I'm out of here tomorrow with Paul," Butch reminded him.

"That's why tonight is the best bet."

Matt nodded. "Give me half an hour to get stuff ready for the morning, then I'll be here—with my jock." His eyes glittered. "Just so long we're clear about one thing. I am *not* demonstrating one of *those* fuckers." He pointed to the open cabinet containing a shelf of dildos, realistic-looking dicks any elephant would have been proud to possess.

Sol howled with laughter. "Your ass will be quite safe, I assure you."

Matt pursed his lips. "Not sure if I'm relieved or disappointed."

That raised chuckles from the others.

"Just jeans and boots?" Butch reiterated. Sol nodded, and he sighed. "Okay. Can't believe I'm agreeing to this, but okay."

Sol couldn't believe it either.

He waited until everyone had traipsed out before reaching for his phone.

"Toby? You've got half an hour. Be at the barn—and be wearing leather."

"Oh my God. He said yes?"

"Not just Butch—Matt, Walt, and Teague." Sol caught Robert's voice in the background.

"Robert says he's not coming." Toby laughed. "I know why, mister. You just don't want your ranch hands seeing you with a hard-on when you're watching me in my leather pants."

"I'm their boss, for God's sake."

"I have to say I'm with Robert on that," Sol admitted.

"Yeah, I guess you're right." Toby chuckled. "Damn. The next Saturday night supper for the ranch hands, we'd better lay on a pretty amazing spread. Can't believe they're going to do this."

"You got any beer up there?"

"A few bottles. Why—oh yeah. I can bring them with me. Least I can do."

A little alcohol would help with any last-minute nerves. Sol had to admit Matt had nailed it—this could be a lot of fun.

Butch bare-chested, on his knees, however…That promised to be a sight worth seeing.

Fuck. There was no way Sol could hide a boner in *these* jeans.

CHAPTER 22

It had taken longer than Sol had anticipated to get a few shots, but that was mainly due to the guys handling all the toys and speculating about them, accompanied by a whole lot of chuckling.

Like little boys discovering a porn magazine for the first time.

It was on the tip of his tongue to say something, because right then all the guys' comments and laughter was nothing short of kink shaming. He had to remind himself they didn't know any better. He also needed them to relax around the equipment. The serious talk would come from Toby: he and Sol had already discussed the opportune moment. Besides, this was Toby's domain, and Sol wasn't about to overstep the mark.

He let them be while he took photos of Toby in his leather jeans, boots, and harness, checking after each one that Toby was happy with the outcome. Toby walking into the barn in his gear caused a minor ruckus, not to mention an appreciative glance or two from Matt.

Now *there* was someone Sol could see dipping his toes into BDSM at some point in the future—if he hadn't already. All he had on was a jock and boots, and he seemed at ease walking around the room. The leather straps framed his firm ass cheeks, and once or twice, Sol caught Teague looking.

Matt's first comment as he'd strolled into the barn had set the tone for the shoot. He'd grinned at Sol and said, "No nudes, okay?"

An eruption of cackles and hoots had followed.

Sol had discussed a few photo ideas with Toby before they'd gotten started, and Toby set about selecting equipment. He hitched up the long suspension bar to the hook embedded in the rafter, with hand slings dangling from each end. Sol took a great photo of Walt, head bowed, his fingers curled around the slings, his back bare but for a long tail whip snaking down it.

Sol peered at the viewer on his camera. "Awesome, Walt."

"Can I see?" Walt asked, his arms caught up in the shirt he

was pulling over his head. Sol showed him, and Walt's breathing hitched. "That's me?"

"You were the one holding onto that bar, so yeah."

Walt stared at it, lips parted.

Sol squeezed his shoulder. "Like I said, it's an awesome shot."

"Thanks." Walt appeared kind of dazed.

"Hey, Toby." Teague held up a pair of nipple clamps. "Do these go where I *think* they go?"

"If you're thinking nipples, then yes."

"But why?"

Toby went over to him. "They trap the blood, increasing sensitivity." He cocked his head. "You like it when a guy plays with your nipples?"

Teague rolled his eyes. "Are you kidding? Sometimes I swear I could shoot just from a guy sucking on my tits and tugging 'em with his teeth."

"I didn't know that," Butch murmured.

Teague flashed him a glance. "That's 'cause you never asked." He smiled. "Then again, I didn't tell you either."

Matt laughed. "And *how* long have you two been… playing?"

"Playing?" Teague snorted. "You can say fucking, Matt. Especially as everyone in this room probably knows what's been going on."

"And if they didn't," Walt added with a grin, "they do now."

Matt gave Teague a pointed stare. "Well, next time you're *fucking*, get Butch to clamp your nipples."

Butch said nothing, but he and Teague gazed at each other for a moment.

A shiver ran through Sol. *Except according to Butch, there won't be a next time.*

Teague peered at the clamps. "So how do they work?"

"First you get the nipples hard, then you attach the clamps," Toby told him. "I usually don't leave them on for more than ten minutes." He grinned. "When I take them off? That's when things get *really* interesting."

"What do you mean?" Teague asked.

"Well, the sensations can drive you crazy. Some guys have been known to come the minute I touch their nipples."

Teague gaped at him. "Holy fuck."

Sol grinned. "Wanna try them out? Just long enough so I can take a close-up of your chest?"

Butch cackled. "Dude, do it. You know you want to."

Teague bit his lip, his neck and face flushed. "Fuck it. Let's do it."

Toby took the clamps and held them up. "You want these off at any time, you say your name, okay?"

Teague gave him a dazed glance. "My name?"

"Yes. Some guys say 'stop' when they really mean 'Fuck, *don't* stop', but no one says their own name. That'll be a sign you want to call a halt, all right?"

"I got it." He glanced at his chest. "So I need to get 'em hard first?"

"I can do that," Matt piped up. His eyes gleamed. "As long as you understand this is just for the photo, okay? Don't go getting any ideas about me doing this on a regular basis."

"What do you—oh *fuck*!" Teague let out a moan of pleasure when Matt leaned in and took Teague's right nipple into his mouth. Teague grabbed Matt's head as if by instinct, holding him there, while Matt tweaked the left one with his thumb and forefinger. When Matt released him, both nipples were flushed and taut. Toby got in quick and attached the clamps, closing the jaws slowly at the base of the nipple.

"Aw fuck," Teague moaned. "Warn a guy next time, okay?"

Sol moved fast. He zoomed in with the camera to get a good shot, noting the flush spreading over Teague's chest, and clicked rapidly.

"Okay, I'm done."

Toby took hold of the clamps. "Going to take them off now, okay?"

Teague nodded.

Toby removed them with gentle fingers, and Teague's knees buckled. "Jesus fucking *Christ*!" Matt reached toward his chest, and Teague managed a glare. "Keep your hands off them. I mean it." Matt's smile faltered, and Teague growled. "I didn't mind what you did, all right? But if you touch them now, I am gonna come, no word of a lie."

Toby's hand was at Teague's back. "You okay?"

Teague stared at him. "That was intense." His breathing

hitched.

He smiled. "Yeah, I know."

"You did good," Sol told him in a low voice.

Teague raised his head. "Thanks."

Sol turned the camera around. "Want to see? This one shows your face, but I'll crop it before it gets onto the site." He chuckled. "Because that expression on your face?" It was hot.

Without a word, Teague took the camera and stared at the screen for a moment. He raised his chin. "Fuck, I look like I'm having an orgasm." He shuddered out a long breath. "What a ride." Then he looked at Butch. "Thanks for the push."

"Any time. Gotta say, it was pretty intense just watching." Then Butch met Sol's eyes, and he swallowed before quickly averting his gaze.

Okay, what just happened?

"Ooh, look what I've found." Matt held up the black leather paddle Toby had brought out. "Can I be in a photo with this?"

Toby laughed. "I think that can be arranged." He pointed to the horse. "Get up on here, knees on either side, ass in the air."

Matt stilled. "You... you're not really gonna spank me with that, are you?"

"No, I'm just going to hold the paddle against your ass while Sol takes pictures. Okay?"

"That works." Matt climbed onto the horse, straddled it, then brought his chest down to the padded vinyl surface, his knees and elbows resting on the lower shelves, his weight on his forearms. Toby positioned the paddle, and Sol zoomed in for yet another close-up.

Matt chuckled. "Great. My ass is going to be on the website."

"We're done." Sol stepped back, and Matt clambered down. "Let me see?"

Sol showed him. "It's a nice ass," he admitted.

"I'll second that," Teague added.

Matt blinked. "Thanks." He returned the paddle to the cabinet. "Hey, Sol? Can I be in one more photo?"

"Have you seen something else you want to pose with?"

Matt held up the black flogger. "This."

"Sure." Sol glanced at Toby. "Where do you want him?"

Toby shrugged. "He can lean over the bench, I guess."

To Sol's surprise, Matt shook his head. "I got a better idea." He walked over to where the suspension bar still hung. "I could grab onto the handles, and you could hold it against my ass."

"That works," Toby told him.

Sol agreed. Teague and Walt were dressed once more, and he had yet to take a photo of Butch. He had an idea about that, though.

Matt walked over to where the bar hung, and reached for the hand slings. Toby moved to stand beside him, the tails of the flogger covering Matt's ass.

"Okay, hold still," Sol instructed, lining up for the shot.

"Wait!" Matt called out.

"Something wrong?" Sol lowered the camera.

Matt twisted to gaze over his shoulder at him. "No, nothing's wrong, it's just... You want to make the place look good, right? To bring guests here?"

"That's the general idea," Toby commented.

"All right then."

Sol stifled a gasp when Matt hooked his thumbs under the waistband of his jock and shoved it to his ankles, stepping out of it and tossing it to one side. He glanced at Sol over his shoulder once more. "I figured this would make for a better photo." He spread his legs, feet apart, and took hold of the slings once more.

Toby burst out laughing. "Your ass is going to draw them in like flies, huh?"

Matt cackled. "Hey, just using what I've got."

"You said no nudes," Sol reminded him.

"So? I'm doing this for Salvation, okay?"

"Whoa," Walt exclaimed.

Matt glanced over his other shoulder. "What? It's just an ass. One you've seen many, many times, I might add."

"Hey, no fair," Teague called out. "Turn around."

Matt didn't respond, but gave him the finger.

"I think that was a no," Sol told Teague with a smile.

Toby glanced at Sol. "Will we get away with putting this on the website?"

Sol nodded. "I took a few bare ass photos for the club. Had no complaints so far."

"Will you guys hurry up?" Matt muttered. "My dick is hanging out here."

"If it gets cold, I got someplace warm you can put it," Teague suggested with a leer. "Couple of places, now I come to think about it."

Matt guffawed.

Toby brought the flogger into view, and Sol framed the shot, capturing the view of Matt's lower back and ass, the tops of his thighs, and Toby's hand holding the flogger.

"Perfect. I'm done."

Matt went to retrieve his jeans and tee from where he'd left them, keeping his back to the room. Teague broke out into a round of applause, and the others joined in as he dressed. Matt turned, his face red, and gave a short bow.

"That just leaves me, I guess." Butch gave Sol a speculative glance. "How do you want me?" A slight tremor shook him.

"Well, you're keeping your jeans on, for one thing," Sol told him with a smile. He didn't miss Butch's sigh of relief.

Sol went to the cabinet and removed a collar and leash. "I'm going to put this on you, attach the leash to it, then I want you on your knees, facing Toby."

His cock twitched at the thought of it.

Butch stood still as Sol put the collar around his neck. "You really have done your research on this, haven't you?" Butch murmured.

"A little." Sol pushed the metal prong into the hole, then slid the tail of the collar through the loop. "That feel okay? Not too tight?"

"It's fine." Butch reached up to touch it with his fingertips.

"I know, it might feel a little strange," Sol advised him.

"Nah, it's okay."

Sol attached one end of the leash to the D-ring, then handed the other end to Toby before stepping back. "Okay, Butch, kneel down in front of him."

Butch knelt, and Sol peered into the camera. At the top of the frame was Butch's neck in the collar, and beyond him was a great view of Toby's lean torso and the soft sheen of his low-rise leather jeans.

"Perfect," Sol whispered, clicking away. "Butch, put your hands behind your back, one hand clasped around a wrist."

Butch complied, and Sol clicked again.

"Okay, now bow your head."

Butch did as he asked, and Sol caught his breath at the sight of his broad shoulders, his muscled back that narrowed at the waist.

Oh my God, look *at him.*

An image flickered through his mind of Butch kneeling before him, hands behind his back, Sol's fingers through his hair while Butch's head bobbed back and forth, his mouth warm on Sol's steel-like cock—

"Sol?" Toby's voice broke through. "Are we done now? It's getting kinda late."

Sol gave himself a mental shove. "Yup, we're done. Thanks, Butch. You can take that collar off now." He lowered the camera, placing it strategically in front of his crotch.

Butch stood, and once again, Sol caught sight of the Roman numerals tattoo. On impulse, he raised the camera and clicked. That photo was not for public consumption—he wanted a better look without drawing Butch's attention to his scrutiny.

Why would he have a date tattooed onto his arm?

And what was the significance of that date?

"Thanks, guys, you were amazing." Toby beamed. "I can't thank you enough for all this." His eyes twinkled. "And some of you went further than I imagined you would."

Teague nudged Matt with his elbow. "He's talking about you," he said with a grin.

Matt's bashful smile was adorable.

"It was worth it to get to see inside this place." Walt grinned. "And in my opinion? Zeeb missed out. He would *so* have loved this."

"So would Paul," Butch added. "He's been curious about this. Hell, we all have."

"They could've come too," Sol told them. "I wouldn't have minded." He glanced at Matt with a grin. "And Matt *definitely* wouldn't have minded."

That raised a ripple of laughter.

Teague chuckled. "Zeeb's busy planning his fortieth shindig. And Paul said something about not feeling so good."

"That's too bad." Toby frowned. "I hope he's okay."

"He went to bed early," Teague informed him. "I'm sure he'll be right as rain in the morning." He gave Sol a nod. "That was... entertaining."

Sol fired Toby a glance, and Toby nodded.

It was time.

"Er, guys? Before you go?" Toby cleared his throat. "There's something I have to say, and it's important, so listen up, please."

They all stood still, their gazes locked on him. Sol could understand that reaction—he'd heard Toby use that tone so many times at the club, and it never failed to get everyone's attention.

"I know you had a few laughs tonight, but you need to bear in mind that BDSM isn't just fun and games." Toby gestured to the equipment and the cabinets. "All of this? It's a part of people's lives, their relationships. You know, like *my* life?"

The silence was almost tangible.

"Behind all of this stuff, there are people, and you're going to meet them. So get your blushes and giggles out of the way now, because when we open, I want you to be professional. You might not understand some of the kinks our guests enjoy, but I want you to be respectful of them." He paused. "There's a fetish event in San Francisco, called Folsom. And in recent years, it's become a tourist event too. 'Let's go stare at the guys in leather—and more—and take pictures,'" he air-quoted. "So whatever you see taking place on this ranch during those weeks? It's not meant as entertainment. And I'm not just talking about what goes on in here."

"Now you've got me curious," Teague remarked. "What might we see?"

Toby hesitated, and Sol longed to jump in and say something, but they'd talked about this.

"We don't get a lot of couples here, right? And if we do, the men sleep on the first floor, and the women on the second. Well, that right there is an important difference. Above us are bedrooms—and they're big enough for couples, maybe even three people. And yes, you might see that too. We want them to feel relaxed while they're here. They have to know this is a safe space, safe enough that they can be themselves and no one is going to gawk at them or take photos."

"I think what Toby is saying is that these guests have a

different… dynamic," Sol added.

Toby nodded. "If you're going to take anything away from this conversation, let it be two words that are at the heart of what you're going to witness—Domination and submission. Because you're going to see a lot of that. Look 'em up when you get back to the bunkhouse." His expression grew grave. "So… do you think you can remember all that?"

One by one, the hands nodded.

Toby's face glowed. "Thanks, guys. There's a lot riding on this."

Walt chuckled. "And now *I'm* curious too."

The men filed out, chatting among themselves.

Sol packed away his camera equipment, and Toby walked over to him and patted him on the back. "You rock, you know that?"

Sol chuckled. "You come out with stuff like that, and I'm reminded of the difference in our ages. I'm assuming that was a compliment."

"It was." Toby glanced toward the doorway. "Did I lay it on too thick?"

"No, I think you hit just the right note. It was exactly what they needed—a splash of cold reality. They walked in here with one set of ideas, and you showed them a different point of view. You certainly gave them food for thought." He lowered his gaze to take in Toby's leather pants. "I think seeing you in those was probably a revelation too."

Toby grinned. "You know what? I think I'll keep these on."

Sol laughed. "Yeah, I couldn't think why you'd want to do that. Have a good night."

The glint in Toby's eyes said plenty. "I intend to. Switch off the lights when you're done?"

Sol assured him he would, and Toby hurried out of the barn. Sol couldn't help smiling.

Doesn't take a genius to work out what's about to take place up at the big house.

He disassembled the folding tripod and stuffed it into the backpack's side pocket. He'd put all the toys and implements back in their rightful places in the morning. As he went to place the camera into his backpack, a voice startled him.

"Can I see the photo?" Butch stood in the doorway.

"I thought everyone had gone."

He came into the room, and it occurred to Sol that Butch was hot even when clothed. His dark blue tee hugged his body like a second skin.

How come I never noticed what a bear he is?

The kind of bear Sol wouldn't mind encountering on a dark night.

"I waited till you were on your own. I didn't get a chance to see the photo you took of me."

Sol scrolled past the shot of Butch's arm to the photo where his head was bowed. "Here it is."

Butch gazed at it. "You're a good photographer."

"Thank you."

Butch handed the camera back to him. "Well, I guess I'd better say goodnight. I've got a long day tomorrow."

"It'll be weird not seeing you around the place," Sol admitted.

"Ditto." Butch opened his mouth, then closed it again.

"Something you want to talk about?"

Butch shook his head.

"Then I'll walk back with you. I'm done here." Sol fastened the backpack, switched off the lights, and they headed for the door.

Outside, the moon was out, full and bright, set in a swathe of deepest, darkest blue and purple. They walked slowly past the paddock toward the bunkhouse.

"That last part was kinda intense," Butch murmured.

"But you can see why Toby had to say all that, right?"

"Oh yeah, totally. But it made me look at that room in a different way, you know?"

Sol smiled. "I think that was the point."

"Is there anything else you need to do for the website?"

Sol shook his head. "I've taken all the photos I'm going to. The rest of the week is mine, and I intend to spend most of it on horseback while I've got the chance."

"Pity I'm not gonna be around. I could've taken you on the trail to Mirror Lake. It's beautiful up there. The way the thermostat keeps climbing, all I can think about is going for a swim."

"I should've packed my swim shorts but I didn't think I'd need them," Sol confessed.

"You *wouldn't* need 'em, not up there. Hardly anyone else

around."

Sol paused at the bunkhouse door. "Why, Butch Buchanan. Did you just invite me to go skinny-dippin' with you?"

That brief catch in Butch's breathing was delicious, and the little devil on Sol's shoulder took interest.

Sol rested his hand on the door. "Is the water very cold?"

"It can be, especially where it's deep."

"Sounds wonderful. We could go Friday, if time allows."

"You want to?"

"Sure, why not? One thing, though." Sol closed the gap between them and lowered his voice. "If I get cold, are you going to warm me up?" Without waiting for a reply, Sol went inside, smiling to himself.

I shouldn't flirt with him.

Not unless I want to do more than flirt.

And then it struck him.

But I do want to do more.

His stiff dick was testament to that.

CHAPTER 23

Wednesday, August 24

A hand shook Butch roughly from sleep.

"Hey, sleepyhead. You plannin' on getting up this morning?"

Butch opened one eye. "It isn't light yet. That makes it early."
He glared at Zeeb, who snorted.

"Rise 'n' shine, Your Highness. Sol and Walt already grabbed
the showers, but you can have the next one, seeing as you and Paul
are off on your little road trip."

Butch sat up, rubbing his eyes. One glance told him Paul was
not in his bunk. "Is he in the stable?"

Zeeb shrugged. "I guess. He wasn't here when I woke up.
Maybe he's gettin' the horse trailer ready."

Butch swung his legs out of the bed and grabbed his jeans.
"I'll go find him." The previous night Paul had been fast asleep
when they'd returned from the barn, and he and Butch hadn't
spoken about the time they planned on heading out. Butch shoved
his bare feet into his boots, pulled on a shirt, and staggered out of
the bunkhouse.

His intention to get a good night's sleep had flown out of the
window.

That photo session…

It had been fun, especially when Matt stripped off, but what
Toby had said afterward? Butch could still hear his voice.

Never heard him talk like that before.

It was like Butch told Sol—things had gotten kind of intense,
but not in a bad way.

Sure opened my *eyes.*

As for the rest of his sleepless night? He blamed Sol. All that
talk about skinny-dipping, not to mention the fact Sol had been
out-and-out *flirting* with him—because what else could he call that
final remark? —had resulted in a few hours of tossing and turning,
and when he did sleep, his dreams had been…

Hot. They'd been hot as fuck, and it was a miracle he hadn't woken up with a raging boner.

The stable was unnaturally quiet for that time of day. Stranger still, there was no sign Paul had even been in there, and that was just wrong. All the stalls were occupied, so he hadn't gone for a morning ride. Butch headed to behind the stable where the horse trailer usually stood. The blue and white truck was empty.

Butch hurried back to the bunkhouse and grabbed his phone. "Teague? You seen Paul this morning?"

"Nope."

"Well, he isn't here, and he isn't in the stable either."

"I'm coming over for breakfast. I'll stop by the house and see if Toby or the boss know anything."

Zeeb frowned. "This ain't like him."

That was what worried Butch too.

Sol strolled out of the bathroom, a towel wrapped around him, so low that Butch saw the top of his pubes, not to mention the swell of his dick pushing against the fabric.

He's doing it on purpose. It seemed Sol could flirt just fine without a single word.

It took a concerted effort to raise his chin and look Sol in the eye.

"Did you go for a ride before your shower?" he asked.

Sol shook his head. "Paul wasn't in the stable, and I wasn't going to take a horse without his say so." He went over to his bed where he'd laid a pair of jeans, a white tee, and a plaid shirt. Butch got an eyeful of that towel hugging Sol's ass.

Dear Lord, kill me now.

"Butch?" Zeeb pointed to the bathroom. "Grab a shower."

He waved his hand. "The guys can take theirs first." He gave himself a mental shove. Paul's absence was a deviation from the norm, and Butch didn't like things he couldn't explain.

When Toby walked into the bunkhouse, Teague behind him, Butch knew something was up. For one thing, neither of them was smiling.

Toby beckoned them. "Butch, Zeeb, Walt, you got a minute?"

Yeah, something was wrong.

They joined him, and Toby lowered his voice. "Guys, we've got a problem. Paul is sick."

Butch couldn't recall Paul having even one day of illness in all the years he'd known him. "What's wrong with him? And where is he?"

"He's at the house. The doc's coming."

Zeeb stared at Toby. "He needs a doctor? How bad is he?"

"We're not sure at the moment. But one thing is certain. He isn't fit enough to drive to Wibaux."

"That can wait, can't it?" Walt frowned. "I mean, it doesn't have to be today, does it?"

"Apparently it does." Toby held his hands up. "And no, I don't know why that is, so don't ask me, okay? All I know is that horse has to be collected first thing tomorrow morning."

Butch folded his arms. "I am *not* driving all that way on my own."

"And we wouldn't ask you to," Toby assured him. "But... well, there *is* a solution." He glanced in Sol's direction. "If Sol will step in at the last minute."

Butch and Sol blinked in unison.

"Me?" Sol stared at him with an incredulous expression.

"I know," Toby agreed. "It's a lot to ask. But I can't go, and neither can Robert. He's got a meeting with the governor and the cattlemen's association in Billings. With four guests, we can't really spare any of the others. We were stretching them thin by taking Butch out of the equation. And we really don't want to send him on his own." He gave Sol a beseeching gaze. "You'd share the driving. We'd pay for your room at the inn. What do you say?"

Sol glanced at Butch. "I guess it all boils down to whether Butch can put up with my company for two days."

Butch snorted. "Only if I get to choose the music for the trip."

Sol chuckled. "Damn. You saw straight through me." He turned to Toby. "Paul's the expert around horses. What makes you think I'll be any use?"

"The horse won't give you any trouble," Toby assured him. "He's a fifteen-year-old Quarter Horse called Sorrel. Robert says he's had a full life so far, and he'll only be used in the paddock for first-timers and on easy trails. Strictly light riding because he's arthritic."

"And Robert's buying him?"

Toby nodded. "He knows the owner, who also knows what kind of horses Robert has here. Sorrel will have the best life."

Butch put Sol's apparent reluctance down to one thing.

He doesn't want to spend a couple of days with me for company. Not that Butch could blame him for that. They hadn't exactly gotten off on the right foot.

Maybe this trip would give Butch a chance to make amends.

Butch nudged his arm. "It's okay with me if it's okay with you."

Sol sighed. "Fine. I'll do it." He fixed Toby with a hard stare. "But you owe me, okay?"

"No argument there." Toby handed Butch a folder. "Here's the address of the ranch, a photo of Sorrel, the online receipt, and your reservations at the Rodeway Inn."

"Then I'd better grab that shower. If we leave after breakfast we can stop along the way for a bite to eat."

His good intentions had backfired, because there was something he hadn't considered. The prospect of at least thirteen to fourteen hours' driving opened up one possibility Butch didn't want to think about too deeply.

What the fuck are we gonna talk about for all that time?

One thing was certain. High school would *not* be on the list of topics.

Sol checked the map Toby had given him before they'd left. He'd just spotted the sign for Bighorn, which meant they were roughly at the halfway point. They'd stopped in Big Timber for coffee, and in another hour they'd reach Rosebud where they were going to stop for a bite, and Sol would take over the driving. Then two, two-and-a-half more hours before they arrived at the inn.

Thank God the seats were comfortable. He'd thought the map was pretty cute too. *Who uses a map these days?* Maybe that had been Robert's idea.

Music had filled the pauses between small talk, but there hadn't been any awkward silences, more of a peaceful, contemplative kind of mood that had felt comfortable.

Except Sol figured he'd listened to as much country music as he could take in one sitting.

"You're the same age as Robert, right?"

"Uh-huh." Butch kept his faze focused on the road ahead. The I-94 stretched in front of them, low, tree-covered hills on one side, and nothing but green fields on the other.

"What was he like when you first knew him? He seems such a calm person. Was he always that way?"

Butch chuckled. "He's calm, all right—most of the time. I was nineteen when I got to Salvation. To be honest, I didn't pay him much attention. I was too busy trying to impress his daddy, because I wanted to keep working on the ranch."

"Was his dad difficult to please?"

Another chuckle. "He had eyes like a hawk, and a tongue as sharp as its talons. But he took me on when I needed a job." Butch smiled. "I always wondered if he knew about me and Diana."

"Who's Diana?"

"The boss's sister. She's about three years younger than him. Married to a rancher. They've got a dude ranch too, only theirs is fancier than Salvation."

"So you and she…"

Butch turned his head for a second, his eyes twinkling. "Uh-huh." Then he returned his attention to the road. "Every chance we got. Her daddy kept her on a tight leash, but once she hit eighteen, I guess he figured there was no holding her back after that. He married her off to Newt Webster as fast as you please, and that, as they say, was that. Well, it was for me. I don't fool around with married women."

"So you fool around with the unmarried kind?"

Butch's cheeks flushed. "Okay, you got me there. But the whole situation is kinda ironic."

"In what way?"

"I used to visit Bozeman or Livingston when I wanted to let off some steam. I'd go to a bar for a drink, and then I'd cast my net, so to speak. See what I caught. Well, a lot of the guys who showed an interest were straight married men."

"I'm guessing you didn't feel guilty having sex with them," Sol surmised.

"Most of the time, no. Not that I made a habit of it. I was trying not to draw attention to myself. Then, everything changed."

"What happened?"

Butch let out a snort. "Teague happened, that's what. No more trips to Bozeman, not when I had his ass on a plate whenever I wanted it."

"You said you had a thing going on. How long did that last?"

"Five years. We ended it the day before you arrived." His face tightened.

"Was it a bad split?"

Butch's eyes widened. "No, not at all. It's just…" He pointed to the bottle of water in Sol's door. "Pass me that, would you?"

Sol removed the cap, handed it over, and Butch took a long drink, his Adam's apple bobbing. "The last few days, I've begun to feel real bad about those years."

Sol took the bottle. "Why?"

"Teague said he deserved better, and you know what? He was right."

"I'm sure it wasn't as bad as you think."

Butch sighed. "Oh, it was. He complained last week that I never once kissed him, or hugged him. And although I didn't feel like it at the time, right now, that makes me feel like a fuckin' asshole."

"I think I can understand why you didn't, you know."

Butch's gaze flickered in his direction. "You can?"

Sol nodded. "You kiss, there's hair where there shouldn't be, stubble even, and you know instantly you're with a guy. A guy feels different, smells different…"

Butch stared at him. "Exactly."

Sol pointed. "Hey. Eyes on the road, remember?"

Butch jerked his head forward. "Compared to the others, I had it easy."

"What do you mean?"

"All I had to do was go to Teague's cabin. If Matt wants to hook up, he rents a room in a cheap hotel. I don't know what Walt does. He doesn't talk about his sex life. Paul neither. And before Teague, I was doing the same. I'd meet someone in a bar and we'd get off as fast as we could, then I'd drive back to the ranch. Salvation's the only home we've got, but that doesn't mean we can bring our own kinda guests there."

"I guess it's not an ideal situation." Sol cleared his throat. "So, back to Teague…"

Another heavy sigh rolled out of him. "It couldn't have been satisfying. I think I owe him an apology. I was a selfish jerk. When he ended it, all I could see was how it affected *me*. Now, I can see it from his point of view."

"You both did the right thing. Because now, you get to move on." Sol smiled. "You have so much to look forward to."

"What do you mean?"

"You spent all that time trying not to think about the fact that you were with a guy. Now, you can let yourself enjoy it."

Butch managed a half-smile. "Years ago, I asked someone if sex with a guy was all that different."

"I can't speak about being with a woman—not something I've ever experienced—but I know what gets me going about being with a guy." He closed his eyes. "The feel of muscles under my fingertips. The sounds he makes, low, urgent noises that tell me he's loving what I'm doing. The smell of him, a rich musky scent that goes straight to my dick. The way his body wraps around my cock, sucking me in, holding me there. Being manhandled, rough one minute, then slow and sexy as fuck the next. The hardness of his body." Sol smiled. "Sharing the taste of bourbon on his lips, his tongue claiming my mouth…"

Silence.

After a minute, Sol chuckled. "Something I said?"

Butch groaned. "I'm discovering for the first time how difficult it is to drive with a hard-on."

Which was exactly the outcome Sol had been aiming for.

"Want me to shut up?"

"Yes. I mean… no." Butch growled. "Christ, you've got me so fuckin' hard I can't even think straight."

"There's a reason for that." Sol grinned. "You're not straight."

Butch fired him a glance. "You're not gonna keep this up all the way to Wibaux, are ya?"

Sol figured not answering that question would tell Butch all he needed to know. Because he'd be doing his damnedest to make sure part of Butch's anatomy stayed up.

Once they reached the inn, he'd have to decide if he was going to do anything about it.

CHAPTER 24

Butch held the key card against the door and went inside. "Let's see what we've got here." So far he'd spied a coffee machine in a little alcove near the front desk, and a vending machine. The swirling pattern on the carpet made his eyes ache, and he prayed the bed was comfortable.

Then he stopped. "Aw shit."

Only one bed.

Sol dropped his bag to the floor. "I'll go to the front desk, see if they've got another room."

"Don't bother."

Sol frowned. "You're obviously not happy about sharing, so—"

"Didn't you hear the guy? They've got some huge-ass wedding in town tomorrow, and they just rented out the last room. So this is it. At least it's a king." Then he spotted the small couch against the wall, and that was enough to crack him up.

"What's so funny?"

"I got a case of déjà vu," Butch told him. "Doesn't matter. I guess we're sharing the bed." *Wouldn't be the first time, right?* He had to ask himself if he would have batted an eyelid if he'd had to share it with Paul. There was no difference, right?

Except there was, and he knew it.

"Then how about we go into town and find somewhere to eat?"

Butch could get behind that plan. Anything to put off the hour when he had to get into that bed.

Sol went into the bathroom, and Butch shook his head. Somewhere, Race Prettyman was laughing his ass off. *Big enough to build a pillow fort in the middle.* He could almost hear Race's voice.

"It's real easy. You strip off, get in, cover up, turn out the light, and go to sleep. You won't even know I'm there."

Butch doubted it would be that easy. Because things had changed. Sharing a bed with Race had been fine, right up to the point where he'd woken up with a boner.

He was afraid he'd be hard as a rock just *thinking* about slipping between the sheets with Sol. And hiding a hard-on was *not* the easiest of tasks.

It was time to face the truth.

Sol Davenport turned him on, and there wasn't a damn thing Butch could do about that.

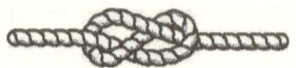

Butch rinsed his toothbrush. "Damn, that was good. The cook at that place could give Matt a run for his money." Matt made fajitas now and then, but the chimichangas and the delicious fried ice cream at Vaqueros had been unbelievable, not to mention the Mexican spicy shots.

Lord, I hope I don't let one rip in the night.

Then he figured Sol would probably be doing the same thing. Dear God, being in the bunkhouse after Matt made beans one time had been like a scene from that movie his dad used to watch, where all the cowboys sat around the campfire, adding their own musical accompaniment to the crackle of the firewood.

"What time do we collect the horse in the morning?" Sol called out from the bedroom.

"Eight. Then I aim to drive back so slow, it'll make a careful little old lady look like a Grand Prix racing driver." He wasn't going to take any chances.

"Hey, could you come in here a minute?"

Butch dried his mouth on the towel, and went into the bedroom. "What's up?"

Sol stood beside the bed, his toiletries unpacked. He held a small bottle of Jack Daniels in his hand.

Butch grinned. "Now that's what I call great planning. You kept that quiet."

"Except I didn't pack it. I just found it in my bag." He frowned. "Didn't *you* put it in there?"

"And when would I have done that?"

"When I asked you to put my bag in the trailer."

"But I didn't—Toby did, remember? He turned up to wave us off." Butch chuckled. "Wow. Remind me to thank him when we get home." Sol removed a folded piece of paper from his bag. "What's that?"

"The bottle was lying on it." Sol scanned it, his brow furrowing. He jerked his head up. "Do me a favor? Call one of the guys and ask how Paul is, will you? Just don't call Toby."

"Are you gonna tell me what this is all about?" Butch pulled his phone from the pocket of his jeans.

"When you've finished the call."

Butch scrolled through his contacts and called Zeeb, who answered after three rings.

"You're missing us already? Aw. We didn't miss you at supper. Some of us even got second helpings."

Butch ignored the barbed comment. "How's Paul?"

"That's kinda sweet, but you've got no cause to be concerned. He was back in the stable about an hour or so after you left. Said he was absolutely fine, and it must've been somethin' he ate. Then he got on with his day as normal."

"Really?"

"Honest, he's okay. I'll tell him you were askin'. Now get off the phone. It's my bedtime. Some of us have to be up at the crack of too damn early o'clock. See you tomorrow. Drive careful." He hung up.

Butch chuckled. "Paul is fine. In fact, he's been fine most of the day. *Now* are you gonna tell me what's going on?"

Sol waved the paper at him. "We've been conned. This is from Toby." He peered at it. "'I'm sorry, okay?'" he read aloud. "'I thought you needed a push in the right direction. You'll thank me later.'" He hesitated.

"Is that it? Or is there more?"

Sol sighed. "I might as well read it all. There's always the possibility you'll see it at some point before we leave here in the morning." He cleared his throat and continued. "'Now tell Butch the story you told us, about when you were sixteen.'"

"What's he sorry for? And tell me what?"

Sol tossed the note onto the nightstand. "I might be wrong, but I think we're going to discover Paul was never sick."

"Then why did he say he was?"

"But did he?" Sol locked gazes. "Who told us he was sick? Toby. Neither of us saw Paul. No one did. You know what I think? Toby told us that story to get me to go with you."

"But why? And what is it you're supposed to tell me?"

Sol sat on the bed, his legs stretched out in front of him, the bottle still in his hand. "I think we're both going to need a drink." He unfastened the top button of his shirt, enough that Butch could see the white tee he wore under it. Sol crossed his legs at the ankles, then uncrossed them again.

Butch studied him. Sol seemed jumpy, and that wasn't something Butch expected of him. His usual cool appeared to have packed its bags and gotten the fuck out of there.

"What's got you so rattled?" He glanced at the note. "Look, just because Toby says tell me something doesn't mean you have to."

"I hate being manipulated, that's all."

Maybe a drink wasn't such a bad idea.

"Let me get the glasses from the bathroom." Butch went in search of them, then joined Sol on the bed. "Okay. Crack it open."

Except Sol didn't.

"On second thoughts, maybe I should do this while we're both sober."

Butch's stomach clenched. "You're scarin' me."

"Nothing to be scared of." Sol leaned his head against the padded board, the bottle sitting between his thighs. "Okay. I was sixteen when I first realized I was into boys, not girls. I mean, I liked girls, but I couldn't ever imagine kissing one."

Butch smiled. "So what gave it away?" Talking seemed to be the medicine Sol needed.

"The fact that the one person I *could* imagine locking lips with was a guy."

"Yeah, I'd say that was a clue right there." Butch was trying to keep the tone light. Whatever it was Sol was about to divulge, it meant something.

"Just the thought of him made me shiver. I used to lie in bed at night, all kinds of dirty, sexy fantasies running through my head. Of course, we both know why there was no way I could ever tell him."

Yeah, he knew all right.

Butch's frown deepened. "But I don't get it. Why does Toby want you to tell *me* all this?"

"Because..." Sol opened the bottle and took a swig. He coughed.

"Hey, take it easy."

Sol stared at the bottle, his breathing quickening. "I told Toby and Robert the name of the guy who'd got me all hot and bothered. Thing was, it was a name they already knew." He raised his chin and stared at him. "Because he works for them."

All of a sudden, Butch was the one getting hot. "You have *got* to be kidding me." His breathing caught. "*Me?*"

No way was this happening. No fucking *way*.

Christ, he was shaking.

Sol's dry mouth called out for another drink, but he was on a roll and there was no going back now.

He needed to get the whole story out into the open.

Sol nodded. "So there I was, being shown around Salvation, and who should be standing by the paddock? My first goddamn crush."

Butch's face tightened. "And I blanked you."

"Hey, how were you to know?" The last thing he wanted was for Butch to catch a case of the guilts. This conversation could lead them in different directions, sure, but that couldn't be one of them.

"I can't believe this," Butch muttered. His eyes widened. "And the boss and Toby know?"

"Oh yeah."

Butch stared at him. "I... I don't know what to say."

That wasn't quite the response Sol had been hoping for.

He took a deep breath. "I've been with a lot of guys since I came out. Loved one of them. But I never forgot you." He forced a chuckle. "Well, not quite. I hadn't thought about you in years, and then, when I saw you..."

"Don't tell me—you thought, 'Damn, my taste in men got better as I got older. What the fuck did I ever see in *him?*'"

There was no way Sol was about to let Butch indulge in a little self-deprecation.

"Not even close," he murmured. Butch became so still, and Sol knew it was crunch time. "I thought you were even hotter than you were as a teenager."

Butch blinked. "You're yanking my chain, right?"

"Wrong." Sol looked him in the eye. "I'm telling you the God's honest truth."

Breathe, damn it.

He was always so calm in a scene. That was his job, to keep his head, to be aware of the sub's needs. But that same calm had deserted him in the wake of Butch's reaction.

I need him to believe me.

No, it was way more than that.

He needed Butch to *want* him.

"I think it's time for that drink now," Butch said with a rough chuckle that sounded a little forced.

"Good idea." Sol opened the bottle and raised it to his lips.

"Hey, whatever happened to using a glass?" Butch retorted.

Sol's heartbeat quickened. "I had a better idea." He took a mouthful of bourbon, swallowed a little of it, then leaned over until his face was mere inches from Butch's.

Dear Lord, his eyes were fucking *huge.*

Butch's chest heaved. "What... what are you doing?" Then his lips parted, and Sol took that as a sign.

He cupped Butch's nape, closed the gap between them, and kissed him, sharing the last of the bourbon. Butch's lips were warm.

More importantly, Butch didn't back off. He shuddered, and all of a sudden his hand was on Sol's face as he filled Sol's mouth with a low moan. "More," he murmured against Sol's lips.

Sol took another drink, and this time he snaked his tongue into Butch's mouth, his ears filled with Butch's harsh breaths as Sol sucked on his top lip, tugging it gently with his teeth. Another drink, only now Butch gave as good as he got.

Thank fuck for that.

"Don't stop," Butch whispered.

Sol drew back to look into his eyes. "Are we talking about sharing the Jack—or kissing?"

Butch swallowed hard. "Kissing."

Sol set the bottle on the nightstand, knelt in the middle of the bed, and crooked his finger. "Come here."

Butch moved forward, his breathing labored, until he knelt facing Sol, sitting back on his haunches. Sol cupped his face and took his lips in a slow intimate kiss, not closing his eyes but meeting Butch's gaze as they kissed, drinking him in. He tempered the urge to claim that soft mouth with hungry passion, choosing instead to breathe deeply, slowing everything down. Butch kept his eyes open too, staring at Sol in a kind of dazed wonder.

Dazed was goddamn perfect.

Butch moaned into his kiss, his hands on Sol's shoulders, his nape, his back. Sol pulled him closer until he could feel the heat of him, the tremors that rocked his body, his fingers digging into Sol's arms. The flush on his face and neck said a lot, but Sol wasn't prepared for the elation rocketing through him when he saw Butch's slow smile that built until it reached his eyes, making them shine.

Holy fuck. There is *a God after all.*

Butch didn't want to breathe for fear this wasn't real. The feel of Sol's lips against his was sublime, heady as fuck, and he didn't want it to stop.

Then Sol broke the kiss, and the moment shattered—until Sol leaned in to kiss his neck, and holy *fuck*, he wasn't prepared for the heat that raced through him, *surged* through him, all the way to his dick. Sol sucked on the skin, and Butch couldn't keep in his groan that filled the air. Sol kissed him again, moving to his nape, setting off rockets inside him. Butch bowed his head, allowing Sol better access. He didn't know what to do with his hands except hold onto Sol to anchor himself to the bed.

"You taste good," Sol murmured between kisses.

Butch would've let him do that all fucking night.

Then Sol moved forward, kissing his cheek, his nose, his forehead, until at last their lips met once more, and Butch didn't hesitate. He opened for him, reaching out for him, his hand on Sol's face, his head, trembling when Sol unfastened the buttons on his shirt, slipping it off his shoulders.

And then Sol eased him down onto the bed until he lay on his back. Sol's fingers danced over his chest while they kissed, never breaking the connection, his hand slipping under Butch's tee to stroke his belly, to tease the hair covering his chest, following his treasure trail down to the waistband of his jeans.

Butch's breathing hitched as Sol gave his crotch a leisurely rub, his dick so hard it fucking *ached*. Sol paused, their gazes locked on each other.

"Do I stop?"

"Fuck no," Butch groaned.

Then Sol kissed him again, sucking on his bottom lip, their tongues dancing, their noses rubbing, no urgency but that same slow movement that felt like gentle waves lapping the shore. And while they kissed, Sol rubbed his bulge, slow as you please, until Butch's moans were constant.

Sol stretched out beside him, leaning over to plunder his mouth again and again while he unbuckled Butch's belt.

Butch's heart pounded.

Button unfastened.

Butch's cock hardened.

Zipper lowered.

His breathing quickened.

Finally, Sol inched his hand inside, freeing Butch's cock. It lay rigid on his stomach, pointing toward his face.

"Oh fuck." He hardly recognized his own voice, strained with need, with urgent desire.

Sol's face was right there, his eyes focused on Butch with an intensity that made him shiver. "Asking again—do I stop?"

Butch stared into those eyes. "No."

He shuddered at the light touch of Sol's fingers as he trailed them up the shaft toward the head. Then Sol sat up, pulling Butch with him until he was upright before removing his tee, tugging it over his head. Butch unbuttoned Sol's shirt, and Sol wrestled out of it, removing his own tee in one fluid action. Sol bowed his head and kissed Butch's chest, flicking his tongue over Butch's nipples. Then he tilted his face upward and their lips met, only now there was hunger in their kiss.

A hunger Butch wanted to consume him.

"Your mouth feels amazing," Sol whispered between kisses.

Butch didn't have words to describe how Sol's kisses felt.

Sol gave him a push, and Butch fell backward onto the pillows. Sol knelt between his legs, bending over him until warm breath fanned the head of his dick. He grasped Butch's jeans and tugged on them until they were around his knees, not stopping until he'd removed them. Butch's shaft jerked, tapping against his belly, and Sol smiled.

"Lord, but you have a nice cock. Uncut too." He got off the bed, unzipped his fly, pushed his jeans past his hips, and after stepping out of them, he straightened, his dick jutting out. "I thought that the first time I saw it. That night we jerked off, remember?"

Butch wasn't likely to forget it. Sol's cock was as thick and heavy as it had been that night, and the sight sent waves of want rippling through him.

This wasn't simply getting off.

This wasn't fucking to chase away a dark dream.

This was a longing that made him ache, made it difficult to focus on anything but the moment.

Sol got back onto the bed and lay between Butch's legs. He pressed gentle kisses to his thighs before moving higher to flick Butch's balls with his tongue.

Fuck.

Then Sol's eyes met his. "I watched you, and all I wanted to do was this." He raised Butch's cock with a single finger, kissed his way up the underside of the shaft, kissed the head, and then took it into his mouth.

There was no way Butch could stay quiet.

He moaned, his hips pumping, his hand on Sol's head, mesmerized as he watched his glistening shaft slide in and out. He shuddered when Sol played with the foreskin, sucking on it, pushing his tongue under it. Then he pulled free to kiss his way up Butch's body until he reached his lips, and Butch melted into another deep, lingering kiss. Sol's hand was on his hip, and Butch covered it with his own, their fingers lacing as Sol took his mouth again and again. The intimacy of the gesture threatened to unravel him even further, and Butch cupped Sol's head, deepening the kiss.

Then Sol broke off. "You know what else I want? Your cum."

Jesus fucking Christ.

He shifted lower on Butch's body, moving slowly, taking his time, and with every passing second, Butch's need spiraled ever higher. Sol's lips were warm on his balls, and Butch groaned when he sucked one into the warm cavern of his mouth. Then Sol licked a path up his shaft and a cry fell from Butch's lips to feel his dick surrounded by wet heat. He pushed up with his hips, both hands on Sol's head, the ending in sight, racing toward them, no attempt at leisure but a hungry passion Butch understood, the same passion he felt from balls to bones.

"Sol... so close," he ground out.

Sol pulled free, his hand curled around the base of Butch's cock. "Then come," he demanded. "Let me see you."

Butch moaned, his shaft throbbing as he pulsed warmth over Sol's hand. Jolts of pleasure wracked his body, his heart hammering, and through it all, Sol gazed at him, lips parted, eyes shining, his fingers still curled around Butch's dick.

He shuddered out a low moan. "Oh my God. That was something else."

The words didn't even scratch the surface of what he'd experienced. This was every blow job he'd ever received, but pushed to the nth degree, an explosion of sensation that left him weak—and wanting more.

Sol let go of his dick, raised his hand to his lips, and with a leisurely tongue, lapped up every trace of cum. His Adam's apple bobbed as he swallowed, and then he lay beside Butch, leaned over to caress his cheek, and kissed him.

Fuck. The intimacy of the act went beyond anything Butch had ever encountered.

They kissed, slow and tender, all urgency fled, all passion spent. Sol's breathing was in sync with his, and little by little, Butch's heartbeat returned to its normal rhythm.

Sol's hard dick tapped against his hip, and a wave of torment rolled over him. He stiffened, unable to hide his reaction.

Sol stilled. "What's wrong?"

"I'm a selfish asshole, that's what's wrong."

"What do you mean?"

Butch gestured to Sol's erection. "I didn't touch you once."

To his surprise, Sol smiled. "This was all about you, okay? We'll have time enough before I leave for you to reciprocate." His eyes twinkled. "I thought you invited me to go skinny-dipping at Mirror Lake. Does that invitation still stand?"

"Of course."

"Well then, that sounds to me like the perfect opportunity for a lot more kissing and touching. Don't you think?"

"I guess."

Sol bent down and kissed his forehead. "Good. Then on that note, maybe we should clean up and get some sleep." He pulled back. "Though I should warn you. If there's a warm body in my bed, I tend to gravitate in that direction in my sleep. Is that going to be a problem?"

Butch hadn't shared a bed with anyone since Race. "Not at all."

Apparently there'd be no need for a pillow fort.

Sol went to get off the bed, and Butch caught hold of his arm. "Sol..." When Sol gave him an inquiring glance, Butch smiled. "Still finding it difficult to get my head around this."

"Around what?"

He didn't think he could make Sol understand.

"I thought I knew what... what it was like being with a guy. But you... you just blew all that out of the water."

Sol kissed him, slow and deep. "That's because you'd already let go of so much baggage before we even got naked." His gaze flickered downward. "And speaking of which..." He grinned. "I like you like this."

Butch laughed. "Well, make the most of it. Because we sure as shit can't do *this* back at the ranch. Not without raising a few eyebrows and getting a shit ton of comments that I'll have to live with when you're gone."

Then it hit him. Sol would be leaving Saturday morning.

Warm, strong arms wrapped around him. "But I'm not gone yet, so let's enjoy what time we have, okay?"

How did the saying go? *All good things must come to an end.*

And that was the problem. Butch had only just discovered what he'd been missing out on.

He didn't want this to end.

CHAPTER 25

Thursday, August 25

Butch knew he'd been too quiet most of the trip back, but Sol didn't seem to mind. He'd tuned into his favorite station, Montana Radio Cafe, that claimed to provide front porch music, playing a mix of bluegrass, blues, folk, jazz and a whole lotta country. Sol didn't appear to mind that either, and Butch caught him humming along several times on the way home.

He'd taken it easy, conscious of Sorrel in the trailer. They'd made a couple of stops along the way, just to check on him, but so far all was well.

"Okay, I'll admit it. I like this station," Sol confessed.

His words barely registered. Butch wasn't listening to the music—he was too busy replaying the previous night in a loop. As in, every damn minute. He wanted to burn it all into his brain: Sol's deep, drugging, intimate kisses; the feel of his hands on Butch's skin, making him quiver; the way he looked at Butch, even when they kissed; the sounds he made when his lips were stretched around Butch's shaft, sending delicious vibrations all the way to his balls; and the smell of him, a scent that got him hard and wanting.

All those things he said he liked about being with a guy…

Sol had nailed every last one of them.

Butch never wanted to go back to what he'd had before. How could he? That would be like going back to candlelight after the discovery of electricity.

I don't want to go back.

The only thing was, there was no way forward. Because Sol was going to leave.

"Penny for them."

He roused himself from his thoughts. "Huh?"

Sol glanced at him with a smile. "I guess I don't have to ask where your mind was, do I?"

Butch chuckled. "Okay, you got me."

"No regrets?"

"Why would I have those?"

Sol grinned. "I offered to help you with your morning wood, but you turned me down."

Butch wasn't sure why he'd said no. Maybe because he wanted their next time to be him giving instead of receiving. One thing was certain—he'd loved waking up to find Sol hadn't lied. He'd curved his body around Butch's, his solid cock pressed against Butch's bare ass, and it had felt like the most natural thing in the whole wide world.

"I lost you again, didn't I?"

Butch's face and neck were on fire.

"We still on for Mirror Lake tomorrow?" he asked. The prospect of spending more time with Sol lit him up inside.

"I said so, didn't I?"

"I know, but I thought you might wanna do something with Toby."

Sol snorted. "He's cute, but he's not my type." He reached across and squeezed Butch's thigh. "I'd rather do something with you. And I don't mean just a repeat of last night."

Lord, he knew how to make a guy feel good.

"I could get Matt to make us some lunch, and we could eat there." Matt wouldn't mind.

"And you're sure me riding off with you isn't going to raise those eyebrows you were talking about?"

"They can raise 'em all they like."

What shocked him was that he meant every word.

Sol chuckled as they drove the trailer to the stable.

"Don't look now, but we've got a welcoming committee."

Three figures stood ahead of them, and at the sight of Paul's smile, Sol reminded himself he needed to have words with the other two.

Toby had some explaining to do. Robert too, if it came to that. He might not be entirely blameless.

"Are you gonna say anything?"

Sol glanced at Butch. "About what?"

"The bottle of Jack. Your theory we were set up."

He snorted. "I'll thank Toby for the bourbon, but that's all he's going to get out of me." Then he grinned. "I wouldn't give him the satisfaction. He'd only get smug."

He stopped the trailer and switched the engine off. Paul had the side door open in a heartbeat, and Sol caught his low crooning as he stepped inside to untie Sorrel.

"Oh, you're a beauty. Come on, boy. I'm going to take good care of you."

The *clomp* of hooves followed as Paul led the horse down the metal ramp.

Butch grabbed both their bags from behind the seats, and they got out.

Robert was stroking Sorrel's nose and neck. "Hey there," he said softly. He gave Sol and Butch a broad smile. "Thank you, both of you."

Sol studied his expression, but couldn't detect a trace of artifice.

So this was Toby's idea. Not that he was all that surprised.

"You're welcome." He returned Robert's smile.

Robert and Paul led Sorrel toward the stable. Butch inclined his head in the direction of the bunkhouse.

"I'll drop these off, then I'll be right back."

Sol nodded, then waited until he was out of sight before turning to stare at Toby, who had the good grace to flush.

"Good trip?"

Sol narrowed his gaze. "Not sure I should be speaking to you after the stunt you pulled." He glanced toward the stable. "Robert doesn't know about your little subterfuge, does he?"

"No, and I'd like to keep it that way. He'd be pissed if he thought I took advantage of you."

Sol shook his head. "You'll have to tell him at some point. Shit has a habit of making its way to the surface, no matter how deep you bury it, and secrets are never a good thing in a relationship."

Toby rolled his eyes. "Okay, okay, I'll tell him. Happy now?"

"Not yet." Sol wanted to extract a little more revenge.

"Well? Did you tell him?"

"Yup." Sol handed him the keys to the trailer.

"And?"

Sol gave him a sweet smile. "Sorry. That's all you get."

Toby's mouth fell open, but then he nodded. "I guess that's fair."

"Payback is tomorrow. Butch is going to take me on the trail to Mirror Lake. Apparently it's beautiful up there. And seeing as I spent most of this week working, I didn't think you'd mind."

Toby scrunched his face up. "I was going to talk to you about that."

Alarm bells started clanging in Sol's head. "About what?"

"We've got a month before we open. How long would it take you to have the website up and running? I mean, how long does it usually take?"

Sol huffed. "How long is a piece of string?" Then he took notice of Toby's strained expression.

Fuck, he really is worried about this.

Sol knew what he could do to alleviate that concern—he just didn't want to do it, because that would call for a little self-sacrifice on his part.

Damn my overactive duty gland all to hell.

He sighed. "You could make the task a lot easier by choosing a starter website. There are tons of packages out there. All you have to do is make the pages, add photos, links…"

"Yes, but I wouldn't know what to—"

Sol held his hand up. "Let me finish? If you chose a package this evening, I could start first thing tomorrow after breakfast, work all day, and I could *probably* have it done by tomorrow night. Making no promises, okay?"

Toby's face shone. "Seriously?"

Yeah, that look broke him.

"Sure," he said in a resigned tone.

Toby grabbed him in a tight hug. "Thank you," he said in Sol's ear. "Really."

Sol extricated himself with a smile. "You're welcome. And now I'll go to supper."

Eating would have to take a back seat until he explained the situation to Butch.

Damn.

"Robert asked if you'd have supper with us. It's the least we can do after all you did to help us out."

Fuck. Something *else* to rob him of time with Butch.

The Lord had a rotten sense of humor.

Then he recalled part of the conversation from the drive to Wibaux. That flicker of an idea he'd gotten...

"You know what? I'd like that. There's something I want to discuss with Robert before I leave, and over supper is as good a time as any."

Toby nodded at something over Sol's shoulder. "Then I'll see you up at the house in about an hour." He tipped his hat and headed for the stable.

Sol didn't need eyes in the back of his head to know who was right behind him. He turned to face Butch.

"You're not going to like this."

Butch's face fell as Sol brought him up to speed. When he was done, Butch grimaced.

"You're right, I don't, but I guess it can't be helped. We'd better go eat."

"Yeah, about that..."

Butch raised his eyes heavenward. "What does a guy have to do to get a fucking *break*?" His shoulders slumped, and he shook his head slowly. "Seriously?"

What became crystal clear in that moment was that all the disappointment and frustration Sol was feeling?

Butch's feelings were the equal of his.

Sol gestured to the barn. "Can we go in there for a second?"

That earned him an inquiring glance. "That depends on what you have in mind."

"I just want to talk without an audience, that's all."

Butch nodded, and Sol followed him into the dark barn filled with the sweet scent of hay. Butch pushed the door shut, and Sol didn't hesitate.

"Okay, I lied." Then he cupped Butch's head and drew him in for a leisurely kiss, his heart singing when Butch responded, feeding him low noises of pleasure. Butch's hands were on his shoulders, his back, molding Sol's body to his, close enough to feel his erection rubbing against Sol's.

Sol did a slow grind, making sure Butch felt every inch of it, and Butch's eyes widened. Sol rocked his hips, and the cutest little whine escaped Butch's lips. Then he poured his heart and soul into yet more kisses, Butch's face warm beneath his fingertips, his breathing loud and harsh.

When they broke apart, Butch chuckled. "I think I've found my new favorite thing. I may even become an addict."

Sol knew it was wrong of him, but he didn't want to think about Butch becoming addicted to another guy's kisses, another guy's touch.

I set him on this path, remember? I told him so much lay ahead for him to discover.

Butch was about to set sail on a new adventure, and Sol wouldn't be there to see what he discovered.

"That was the kiss I can't give you before we go to sleep tonight."

Butch gave a slow nod. "Yeah, I got that." He took a step back. "You'd better grab a shower before supper. I'll see you when you're done, all right?" And with that, he walked out of the barn.

Sol told himself he should be happy for Butch, that the man who'd just left him was nothing like the man who'd ignored him six days ago.

And I did that.

He'd helped to set Butch free, to be the man he was born to be. That had to be a good thing, right?

Then why don't I feel happy about it?

Sol put his coffee cup down and wiped his lips with his napkin. "My first morning here, I went for a ride, and I saw a cabin near a creek." He'd also seen their horses tethered to the hitching post.

"What about it?" Robert poured himself another cup.

"Do you have plans for it?"

He frowned. "Not really. We go there now and again. It's a quiet little spot, with some happy memories."

Sol pondered how best to present his idea. "That sounds wonderful, but it's not as if you two need a cabin to be alone, right?" He gestured to their surroundings. "You have this place."

Toby's brow furrowed. "Where are you going with this?"

Sol leaned forward, his hands clasped on the white tablecloth. "Your ranch hands could get a lot more use out of it."

Robert blinked. "How?"

Sol pointed toward the kitchen. "Let's take your housekeeper Matt as a for instance."

"What about him?" Toby got up and poured bourbon into two glasses. "You want one?"

Sol managed a grin. "Thanks, but no. I've had enough bourbon this week."

Toby coughed, and Sol guessed he hadn't told Robert yet.

"Did you know that when he hooks up with a guy, they rent a cheap hotel room for the night?"

"How do you know this?" Toby inquired.

"Butch told me. Anyway, the point is Matt can't exactly bring his hookups here, even though it's his home. I suppose the same applies to all the others."

"I don't follow you." Robert's frown was still in place.

Toby expelled a breath. "But I think *I* do." He stared at Sol. "You're suggesting Robert should make the cabin available for the hands if they want to bring someone back to Salvation."

"As long as it's their day—or night—off, why not?" He relaxed into his chair. "Right now, it's as if they're living with their two dads. Let's be blunt here. They go elsewhere to fuck because they can't do otherwise when they share a bunkhouse with guests. Surely they should enjoy the same freedom you two do."

Robert's face tightened. "You know, I never thought about it like that. I always tell the hands Salvation is their home, but at times I forget."

"So what do you think?"

He smiled. "I like it."

"You could make it a rule that anyone using the cabin leaves it in a fit state for the next... occupants."

Robert stroked his beard. "You think they'll like the idea?"

Sol regarded him with a straight face. "No." Then he rolled his eyes. "Are you kidding? They'll love it."

"I love it too," Toby added. He glanced at Robert. "What do you say? Can we look into this?"

"Definitely. We'll put it to the hands and get their input too. If it's going to be their space, we should make sure it provides everything they need."

"Condoms and lube," Sol and Toby intoned at the same time.

All three laughed.

"So… how did the trip go?" Toby's eyes twinkled.

Sol shrugged. "We got Sorrel here in one piece. I count that a success."

He loved being a tease sometimes.

"Now wait a minute. You got to spend the night with the guy you were crushing on back in high school, and that's all we get?"

"Yup." Sol rose. "And on that note, I'm going to grab some sleep. I have a lot to do tomorrow."

Robert laughed. "A gentleman never tells, isn't that right?"

Sol grinned. "Exactly. I'll see you both in the morning, bright and early." He said goodnight and headed for the front door. The sun was setting as he strolled down toward the bunkhouse, bathing the landscape in a golden light. Then he spied a familiar figure at the foot of the path.

Sol smiled. "Are you here to protect me from wolves and bears?"

Butch snorted. "Idiot." He fell in step, and they walked slowly, side by side. "How was supper?"

"It was fine." Sol wasn't about to mention his proposal. That would be up to Robert.

"You remember suggesting we had a little race last Sunday night?"

"Race? What are you—oh. *That* race." Sol grinned. "If I recall correctly, I won."

"Yes, you did—that time."

Sol got where Butch was headed. "*Oh.* You want a rematch."

Butch nodded. "Tonight. When everyone's asleep. In our own bunks," he added.

Sol hoped Robert went ahead with his plan for the cabin, but right then he didn't want to think about Butch bringing someone back to the ranch.

Someone who isn't me.

220

"I can do that." He paused at the paddock. "Just as long as you don't mind me looking at you while I jerk off—and wishing it was my mouth on your dick, instead of your hand."

Butch adjusted his package with a stifled groan. "And there you go again, gettin' me hard."

"Only one thing wrong with your idea." Sol's fingers ached to touch him, stroke him, but he couldn't take the chance of someone spotting them.

Butch had to live with these guys long after Sol had taken his leave, and Sol didn't want to make his life awkward.

"And what's that?" Butch moved a little closer, and Sol knew beyond a shadow of a doubt that he wanted the same thing.

"With you on one side and me on the other, we don't get to kiss."

Butch bit his lip. "Then I guess I know what I'm gonna be dreamin' about tonight."

The bunkhouse door opened, and they sprang apart like two horny teenagers surprised by a parent's unexpected return.

"Hey you two," Zeeb called out. "We're gonna have a few rounds of poker, if you're interested."

Butch snorted. "As long as it's not strip poker again. You know what happened the last time."

Zeeb pulled a face. "Spoilsport." He went back inside.

"I'm afraid to ask. What did happen?"

Butch rolled his eyes. "Teague walked in just as one of the guests got down to his shorts. Then he tore us a new one." He studied Sol for a moment. "Fuck. All I can think about is—"

Sol stopped his words with a finger. "I know, okay? I feel the same way."

And the closer he got to leaving Salvation, the worse it got.

This is my fault. I opened the door a crack, and he slipped inside.

A door Sol had been determined to keep shut.

CHAPTER 26

Saturday, August 27

Butch came back into the bunkhouse as Sol was stuffing the last of his belongings into his bag.

"Okay, that's Eric and Phil on their way home." His gaze met Sol's. "Guess that just leaves you."

"I guess so. Are you taking me to Bozeman?" His flight wasn't until one-fifteen, so he had maybe an hour before he needed to be out of there.

No long goodbyes, all right?

He'd come to Salvation to do two things, and one of them had been accomplished—the website for the BDSM venture was now operational, and Toby and Robert seemed more than happy with it. As for the relaxation he'd planned?

Yeah, no. He blamed that on a certain cowboy with sexy as fuck eyes, broad shoulders, and a dick and balls Sol could enjoy all day long.

Think of it as a hot interlude. Nothing more.

Except it was *way* more than that.

Finding Butch again had rekindled a lot of memories, not all of them good, and there'd been one more thing he'd wanted to discuss, but Butch refused to be budged on that one, so that was that.

Scott was apparently off limits.

He needs to know. Because Sol was damn sure Butch had no idea about what had really been going on back then.

None of us did.

Sol liked to think things might have been different if they had.

"Toby called me when I was on the way back. Said he was gonna do it. He also said you were to go on up to the house when you're done here." Butch glanced at the bag. "And it looks like you're ready."

Before Sol could reply, Teague walked into the bunkhouse, smiling.

"Sol, you are a fucking *genius*." His eyes sparkled. "I just saw the website."

Sol grinned. "That photo of you was awesome. Turned out better than I thought."

"*All* of it is awesome." Teague held his hand out. "I gotta say, it's been a pleasure meeting you."

They shook, and Sol gazed at the others who'd gathered around. "Guys, the pleasure was mine. You're a great bunch, and if any of you make it out to San Francisco, come look me up."

"Any chance you'll be coming back to Salvation for another visit?" Walt asked.

Sol heaved a sigh. "Never say never, right? I don't know. Work keeps me busy. I only just managed to squeeze *this* week in." He avoided looking in Butch's direction.

It was just sex, right? That was all it could be.

The farther he got from Salvation, the more he might actually believe that.

There was no putting off the goodbyes a moment longer.

Sol shook hands with all of them, leaving Butch to the last. To his surprise, Butch didn't offer his hand.

"I need to see the boss, so I'll walk up with you."

"Fine." Sol was no fool.

They walked out of the bunkhouse, Sol's bag in one hand, his backpack slung over his shoulder. He caught sight of Paul in the paddock with Sorrel, grooming him. Paul raised his hand in a wave, and Sol waved back.

"Sorrel seems content."

Butch smiled. "He's a sweet one, like Bailey."

Sol stared at the white and green barns, the stable, the house on top of the hill, and the horizon where the land met the huge expanse of sky, so blue it hurt the eyes. "I love your home."

"Pretty fond of it myself." He lapsed into silence.

Sol had expected something more personal, but it appeared Butch wasn't one for goodbyes either, and the realization brought some slight relief.

Butch seemed to be as much a realist as he was.

They reached the old barn, but instead of strolling past it, Butch grabbed his arm and steered him through the door so fast that Sol didn't have time to react.

Butch closed the door behind them. "I had to get you alone. I was awake most of the night, thinking about what I wanted to say to you before you left."

"Butch, I—"

That was as far as he got before Butch's lips stopped the flow of his words.

Yeah, not much of a realist after all.

For someone who'd never kissed a guy until a few nights ago, he sure was making up for lost time, and *fuck*, he was a fast learner. He didn't close his eyes, his breathing slow and deep, as if Butch was learning the taste of him all over again.

Sol dropped his bag to the straw-covered floor and pulled him in, his hands on those wide shoulders, savoring the strength in them, the feeling of muscle beneath his fingertips.

"You're a good kisser," Sol murmured against his lips.

Butch chuckled. "I had a good teacher." He took a step back. "Gotta tell you, I felt kinda lost yesterday, not having you around."

"I'm sorry we didn't get to go riding."

Butch waved a hand. "Couldn't be helped. And it sounds as if you did good." His chest rose and fell. "I know I shouldn't have dragged you in here, but I couldn't let you leave without telling you something."

Sol's stomach muscles tightened and his pulse quickened.

Don't let this be what I think it is.

It happened sometimes. A guy's first experience of intimacy could lead him to make all kinds of wrong assumptions, and Sol didn't want to be the one to dash Butch's hopes.

"About that night in the inn..." Butch breathed deeply. "Can't tell you how important that was to me. Saying 'You opened my eyes' just doesn't cover it." He reached down and cupped his crotch. "You see this? Your fault. This is what kissing you does to me."

Sol chuckled, a wave of relief flooding through him. "Am I supposed to apologize?"

Butch laughed, and the natural sound was such a lift. "I guess not. And I was sorta hoping..." He smiled. "We got time?"

"Time? For what?" Sol saw the light. "Oh. One last taste before I go, is that it?"

It seemed he'd panicked over nothing. Butch was simply a

man who wanted his itch scratched.

What surprised him was that despite wanting that very outcome, the realization stung.

Looks like it really is *just sex after all. That* was *what you wanted, right?*

For fuck's sake, hadn't he told Butch he couldn't have it both ways?

"*Now* you're gettin' it." Butch removed his hat and placed it on a hay bale.

Sol was never one to refuse a morning shot of protein.

He put his backpack next to Butch's hat, then placed his hand on Butch's chest, his fingers brushing over the nipple that pushed against the cotton. Butch's shiver was all kinds of delicious, and he recollected the nipple clamps Teague had discovered almost a week ago.

Oh dear Lord. An image of Butch came to mind, seated, his wrists bound at the back of the chair, clothes pegs on his nipples, his chest flushed, lips parted, low moans tumbling from them—

His dick standing to attention, thick and flushed with blood, a cock ring around the root.

Stop that. He doesn't play your games, remember?

He forced the delightful pictures from his head and unfastened the top three buttons on Butch's shirt. He glimpsed chest hair and smiled. "You didn't wear a tee today." Then he slid his hand down over Butch's belly until he reached the button on his jeans.

Butch grasped him by the wrist. "Not what I had in mind."

Before Sol could inquire further, Butch sank to his knees in front of him, unbuckled Sol's belt, unzipped his fly, and eased his jeans and briefs over his hips, his stiffening cock springing up with a life of its own.

Oh my God.

Butch swallowed, his staccato breaths the only sound in the quiet barn. "So thick," he murmured.

Sol tilted Butch's face toward him, his fingers under Butch's chin. "You don't have to do this."

Their eyes met, and Sol shivered at the look of naked desire he saw burning there.

"No, I don't. But I want to. And if I'm gonna give anyone my first blowjob, I want it to be you. You got that? I *want* to do this for you, okay? You blew my mind the other night." He smiled as he wrapped his fingers around the base of Sol's dick. "Now it's my turn."

Sol's pulse raced. "Remember how I sucked you off. What felt good?" Butch nodded, and he smiled. "Then do the same for me.'"

Butch grinned. "I think I can manage that." He sat back on his haunches, staring at Sol's erect cock once more, his breathing shallow, his fingers fumbling as he unfastened the rest of his shirt buttons, revealing that mat of salt and pepper chest hair.

Sol stroked his hair. "Start with the head," he said softly, his senses primed for that first contact.

Fuck, I want this too.

Butch leaned in, one hand on Sol's hip, and gave the wide head a cautious lick before taking it into his mouth, his nostrils filled with a musky, earthy scent that went straight to his dick.

"Oh yes," Sol said with a sigh, his hand at the back of Butch's head, not applying any pressure. The tremor coursing through him was all the encouragement he needed to take Sol a little deeper, then deeper still, his lips stretched around its girth.

"That's it," Sol whispered. "Just a little more. Careful with your teeth." He unbuttoned his shirt and pulled the flaps aside, revealing his bare flesh, the vein on his stomach like an arrow pointing south to his dick.

Butch bobbed his head forward, coughing when Sol's shaft went too deep. He pulled free, his eyes watering.

"Talk about a mouthful."

Sol grabbed his cock and held the shaft upright against his belly. "Lick my balls. Drag your tongue over them." He took Butch's hand and brought it to his torso. "Touch me while you suck me."

Butch licked Sol's balls, the skin wrinkling against his tongue, that scent almost overpowering. He buried his nose in the crease between thigh and groin, Sol's stomach so firm under his fingertips, the skin satiny and warm.

"Take one in your mouth," Sol demanded, the husky edge to his voice as hot as the act Butch performed.

Butch did as instructed, careful to shield his teeth as the orb filled his mouth, Sol's moan of pleasure making him harder than ever. Sol worked his shaft, his breathing quickening, and Butch kissed his balls. Then Sol fed the head of his dick into Butch's mouth.

"No hands, okay? Just rock back and forth."

Butch complied, bobbing a little faster, only taking about half Sol's length into his mouth, his palms on his thighs.

"Fuck, yeah. Look at me while you suck my cock."

Butch raised his eyes and Sol locked gazes with him, hips pumping.

"Yes, just like that." Sol cupped his head. "Take your dick out. I want you to come when I do."

Butch fumbled with the button on his jeans, almost breaking the zipper when he yanked on it, but finally he freed his shaft, tugging on it as he sucked, letting loose tiny grunts and moans.

"Fucking *perfect*," Sol gasped, and suddenly both his hands were on Butch's head, holding him still while he rocked into his mouth, never venturing too deep.

Butch's first blowjob had somehow morphed into his first face fuck, and exhilaration surged through him to hear Sol's words. He tugged faster on his dick, moaning around his mouthful of hard cock.

"Feels too good," Sol groaned. He let go with one hand to grab his dick, pulling on it, and warmth spattered Butch's cheeks, lips and chin. "Aw, *fuck*." Cum dripped onto Butch's chest, and Butch worked his cock faster, his own climax in sight. His body tingled, his knees ached, and he couldn't get enough of the way Sol looked, the smell of him, the low moans that fell from his lips.

And then he too was coming, his dick pulsing onto the barn floor, electricity zinging through him from head to toe. Sol shoved his hands under Butch's pits and hoisted him upright, their lips reconnecting in a fervent kiss.

"My cum tastes better from your lips," he murmured before licking the skin clean and sliding his tongue into Butch's mouth, his arms around him, holding him close, his cock warm and sticky against Butch's skin.

Butch locked his arms around Sol's neck, clinging to him, his legs trembling. He had no idea how long they stood like that, their bodies connected from chest to groin, so close that Butch could feel the thumping of Sol's heart as they kissed, unhurried, lingering kisses that were the perfect ending.

The perfect way to say goodbye.

Butch glanced at his chest, the remnants of Sol's cum still visible.

"Hang on." Sol reached into his bag, pulled out the tee he'd worn on the way to Wibaux, and wiped it over Butch's chest. Then he repeated the action with his spent dick before placing the garment in Butch's hand.

"You keep this."

Butch frowned. "But… it's yours."

"And now it's yours." He took hold of Butch's wrist and raised it until the soiled tee was an inch from Butch's nose. "Tell me what you can smell."

Butch sniffed. "Spunk—and you."

"And it'll stay that way. You might want to wash it eventually. Before you ask, no, I don't want it back. Keep it as a souvenir." He smiled, then glanced down at Butch's limp dick. "Can't leave you like that," he murmured before dropping to his knees. Butch gasped as he licked the sensitive head clean, then tucked the shaft into his jeans, zipped him up with obvious care, and fastened the button.

Sol grinned. "Well, that was one hell of a goodbye."

Butch's stomach churned. "Does it have to be? Walt's right, you know. You could come back. San Francisco isn't *that* far away, is it?" Not that he had a fucking clue.

All he knew right then was that Sol was about to walk out of that door.

"And like I told him, never say never." Sol stroked his cheek with gentle fingers.

Something in his eyes told a different story, however.

Butch put his hat back on. "I guess you'd better go on up to the house. Toby'll be wondering where you've got to."

Sol nodded. He slung his backpack once more over his shoulder, and picked up his bag. "You have a good life, Butch

Buchanan." He smiled. "Find yourself a good man—or woman. It's never too late to grab onto some happiness." And with that, he pushed the barn door open and stepped out into the sunlight.

Butch stood rooted to the spot.

I thought I'd finally found it.

Except that was a pipe dream, and he knew it. Sol could never be in his life.

He knew where the bodies were buried.

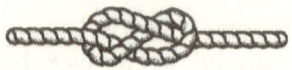

"Robert and I discussed your idea," Toby said as he pulled up outside the Baxter Hotel.

"Hmm?" Sol had been aware of Toby talking during the ride, but not much of what he'd said had sunk in.

Sol's mind was still in that barn, gazing down at Butch on his knees, sliding his dick between Butch's lips, hearing him moan. He could still feel Butch's hair beneath his fingertips, taste his cum, *smell* him, for God's sake…

"Your idea about the cabin? We've decided to go ahead with it. We'll share the proposal at the next ranch supper."

"That's great," he murmured.

Toby's laugh filled the truck. "Your enthusiasm is overwhelming."

Sol abhorred rudeness in others—there was no way he'd tolerate it in himself.

"Sorry. I guess my mind is someplace else."

"Or *with* someone else," Toby observed.

Sol fired him a warning glance. "Stop that right now." He held his backpack against him. "You're happy with the site?"

"God yes. You really delivered. Robert says to email him with your invoice."

Sol frowned. "Hey, you paid for my stay, remember?"

"Yeah, and then you lost a whole day putting it all together. You worked like a Trojan yesterday."

"I hope the bookings start rolling in. I added the link to two or three BDSM forums, by the way, not to mention a kink message board."

Toby beamed. "Thank you."

Sol glanced at the clock on the dash. "I'd better go. The shuttle will be here any minute."

"There *was* one last thing I wanted to mention."

As long as it isn't Butch.

"What?"

"September twenty-fourth… why don't you come back for the opening? We'd love it if you could."

"Toby, I—"

"Don't say no right away. At least say you'll think about it, you know, like you did last time?" His eyes twinkled. "Then I'll wear you down until you say yes. And you can bring a guest with you."

"That assumes I *have* someone to bring with me."

"Hey, that's fine. We got our first booking this morning—a single guy—and the site hasn't even been up for twenty-four hours. I call that a success." He paused.

Sol knew the signs. "Okay, out with it."

"Well, the guy who booked? He said he wants to, quote, 'push his boundaries.' And I thought of you right away. You do demonstrations at the club all the time, don't you? Why not do some here?"

Sol laughed. "*Now* I get it. That's why you want me to come, isn't it?"

Toby let out an uncharacteristic sigh. "I pride myself on being a good Dom, but you? You're an even better Master. You're a damn sight more patient than I am. You're way better at teaching. You've got guys lining up to have sessions with you, both at the club and privately. And don't deny it—Sean told me. We'll need someone like you if we're going to make a success of this."

"You're pushing again. And didn't anyone ever tell you flattery gets you nowhere?"

"I still say there's something else you're not seeing."

"And what's that?"

Toby smiled. "There's Butch."

Sol stilled. "Leave it."

He held his hands up. "Don't get me wrong. I'm not trying to matchmake here—I wouldn't do that, not with you—but I think he needs someone like you too."

Sol snorted. "Let me guess. You think inside that gorgeous exterior, there's a submissive trying to get out."

A supposition that sailed dangerously close to his own fantasies.

Toby's lips twitched. "Okay, a couple of things. Did I *say* he's a submissive? No, I did not. He might not be dominant either. He could even be a switch. But I'd bet my bottom dollar there's a kink or two out there with his name all over them. Because *everyone* is kinky in some way or another, and we both know it. Don't deny that either. *You're* the one who brought up him being a possible submissive. And secondly…" He grinned. "So he's gorgeous, is he?"

Sol had walked right into that one.

A bus drew up outside the hotel, and the driver got out, a clipboard in his hand.

Thank God. Saved by the shuttle.

"Sorry, but I have to go now." Sol reached over onto the back seat and grabbed his bag. "Thanks for a great week, and good luck with everything." He got out of the truck and hurried over to the driver without a backward glance.

He had to get out of there. Every persuasive word Toby uttered chipped away at his resolve, and it wouldn't take much more for him to cave.

He didn't *want* to leave.

He just had to.

CHAPTER 27

Tuesday, August 30

The talk over supper was all about the guests' first day on horseback with the cattle. Kyle and Owen had spent the day showing them how to round up any strays, but Butch knew most of the time had probably been about drinking coffee and enjoying the great outdoors. He wasn't really paying attention to the animated conversation.

His mind was elsewhere, the same place it had been since Sol's departure.

His thoughts were all over the place, veering between disbelief that he'd sucked Sol off, and relief that he'd gone and life could get back to normal.

Except what the fuck is normal? Butch wasn't sure anymore.

His nights were filled with replays: Sol's mouth on his dick. His mouth on Sol's. And those kisses that addled his brain, made his head spin, and his cock hard as a fucking rock.

"Hey!"

Butch jumped. Zeeb was staring at him in obvious amusement.

"What?"

"I *said*, I guess you an' Sol got plenty of time to gas about the old days, what with that trip an' all."

"Yeah, we did." *And the rest.*

"I really liked him," Walt said with a smile.

"Me too," Paul agreed. "It's hard to dislike a guy who knows his way around a horse."

"That's your stick for measurin' a person's worth? Whether or not they get on with horses?" Zeeb snorted. "I don't wanna know how *I* measure up."

Paul narrowed his eyes. "Hey, mock if you like, but horses are a damn good judge of character. If they get a bad feeling around someone, you know about it." His face tightened.

Butch got the feeling Paul had someone specific in mind, but he didn't pry. Paul wasn't one for sharing much, and everyone respected that and let him be.

"Anyone want to come for a stroll before bed?" That was Ian, the oldest of the three guests.

"What—you didn't get enough fresh air today?" Zeeb quipped.

"I'm in." Mike stood. "It's a beautiful evening."

"Yeah, me too." Jake joined the other two. "Got to make the most of this wonderful view while we can, right?" The three headed outside.

Zeeb stared at his fellow ranch hands. "Okay, 'fess up—which one of you farted and drove 'em all outta here?"

That earned him a ripple of laughter.

Teague stood and collected the dishes. "And now we're alone…. Have any of you seen the website? Those photos Sol took of us… Wow. He even made *me* look good."

Zeeb grinned. "Are you fishing for compliments? You're hot as fuck. Hell, *I'd* do you, and I'm straight."

Walt laughed too. "*Sure* you are, Zeeb. You keep right on telling yourself that."

Teague gave Zeeb a speculative glance. "Hey, it's just us. You can be honest. You *have* taken a peek, haven't you?"

Zeeb rolled his eyes. "What do you take me for? *Course* I peeked. And y'all looked awesome. Gotta say, Matt, though… Now *that* was an eye-opener."

"I don't think he'd have done it for anyone else but Sol," Walt remarked. "The guy made you feel comfortable." He poured himself another cup of coffee. "I hope he does come back, though."

Butch rolled his eyes. "Can we just stop yacking about Sol for one goddamn minute? Talk about something else, for Christ's sake." He pushed his chair back, scraping it across the wooden floor, bounced to his feet, and strode out of the bunkhouse, not stopping until he reached the paddock.

His chest heaved, his heart pounded, and something heavy rolled around in his stomach. It felt like a rock.

I am such a hot mess.

"Hey!"

Judging by Teague's strident voice, Butch was about to be

torn a new one.

He turned to face him, his tone apologetic. "I'm sorry. I shouldn't have blown up like that, even if the guests were out of earshot."

Teague came to a halt in front of him, hands on his hips. "No, you shouldn't. What concerns me more is why. It's not like you to vent."

"Just antsy, I guess."

Teague frowned. "You're not nervous about all these leather guys coming to Salvation, are you?"

Butch blinked. "'Leather guys'?" he repeated, hooking his fingers in the air.

Teague flushed. "Okay, I've been doing a little research ever since Toby gave us that talking to. What can I say? A lot of them wear leather."

Butch leaned on the paddock fence. "I'm not nervous, exactly. I don't know what to expect, that's all, and I don't wanna let Toby and the boss down."

Teague squeezed his shoulder. "You won't." He paused. "You miss Sol, don't you?"

Butch jerked his head in Teague's direction. "What?"

Fuck. How much did he see?

Teague shrugged. "It's okay to admit it. He was part of you growing up. Must've brought back a few memories."

Yeah, that was the problem. Most of them were not good.

"I meant what I said." Teague's voice softened. "You ever need to talk, you know where I am." His eyes held a twinkle. "Planning any trips to Bozeman?"

"Not at the moment." To be honest, right then Butch wasn't sure he'd ever reprise his old habits.

Everything had changed.

"Teague?" Robert hollered. "You got a minute?"

He patted Butch's arm. "Just think before you let off steam. Next time there could be guests around. Take a breath first." He hurried over to where Robert stood.

Butch stared at the changing colors in the sky.

How long is it gonna take to get Sol out of my goddamn head?

Butch had no idea what time it was—he only knew he couldn't get his brain to shut down and let him sleep.

The bunkhouse was quiet except for Zeeb's snores, but Butch could maybe put a stop to that.

"Roll onto your side, Zeeb," he said in a whisper loud enough to reach Zeeb's top bunk.

Regular as clockwork, Zeeb rolled over, and peace was restored.

Share a bunkhouse with a guy for a few years, and you learn a trick or two.

Such as how to rub one out without attracting too much attention. Butch usually resorted to jerking off in the bathroom, or biting a pillow.

Now there's a remedy for insomnia.

He groped under his pillow for Sol's tee. He brought it to his face and held it there, burying his nose in the soft cotton. *Fuck…* He could smell cum, sweat, and something that was pure Sol. He breathed in the heady scents, his hand sliding under the waistband of his shorts to wrap around his stiffening shaft, eyes closed so he could focus his thoughts—

So he could see Sol.

Fuck it.

Butch shucked off his shorts, grabbed his pillow, and folded it in half. He flipped onto his belly, stuffed the pillow under him, and drove his dick into the crease, rocking his hips as he dry-humped it, his hands holding Sol's tee to his face. The bed springs squealed in complaint, and he rocked slower, his breath warming the cotton pressed to his nostrils that were filled with the rich scents of Sol.

It wasn't long before he rolled onto his back, sheets thrown back, legs spread, his feet planted on the mattress, the pillow once more beneath his head. He spat into his palm and slicked up his cock, sliding it through the tight funnel of his fingers while he rubbed Sol's tee over his chest and belly. On impulse, he held it against his balls, slowly rubbing them before wrapping the fabric around his shaft, fucking it, his thumb and forefinger tweaking his nipples, tugging them until he was incapable of lying still.

Holy fuck, that feels amazing.

He ignored his cock and focused on teasing his nipples with both hands, his shaft jerking constantly, smacking against his stomach.

Christ, what I wouldn't do for another hand right now.

Butch focused once more on his dick, squeezing his balls as he worked the shaft, his breathing rapid, his body on fire as he closed in on his orgasm. The zing of electricity that traveled all the way to his cock heralded its arrival, and he tilted his hips, aiming for his chest. A string of cum arced through the air, landing on his beard and cheeks, and he stifled his moans with Sol's tee. He gripped his cock in a tight fist, his body shaking as the last drops connected with his skin.

Butch lay there, covered in sweat, Sol's tee held to his nose, his breathing labored as he exulted in the sensations. Never mind another hand—what would have improved the situation beyond all else would have been if Sol were there beside him in the dark, the two of them cramped into the small space, Butch lying in his arms, their lips locked in kiss after kiss while Sol gave leisurely tugs on Butch's shaft to expel those final drops…

Before he licked them from his fingers and shared the taste with Butch.

He wiped his chest and cock with the tee, then remembered the spunk probably already drying in his beard. When he was sure he'd gotten all of it, he shoved the tee under his pillow in a bundle. Once it was washed, the smells that turned him on would only be a memory.

On the other hand, he now had a cum rag that would remind him of Sol every time he jerked off.

As if I could forget him.

CHAPTER 28

Friday, September 2

Sol scrolled through the photos he'd taken of Salvation, smiling to himself.

That night in the barn had been a lot of fun, and Toby's vanilla boys had hopefully learned something. Although he figured one of them might not stay vanilla for long.

Then his screen filled with the image of Butch on his knees, his broad back to the camera, head bowed, the collar around his neck, and Toby's hand in the shot, holding the leash.

Boy, look at you...

Not that he needed the photos to remind him. A day hadn't gone by this past week when he hadn't thought about Butch. He kept scrolling, gazing at all the photos until he reached the last one in the folder.

The one showing Butch's tattoo.

Sol opened a new window and did a search for Roman Numerals. He typed in the letters, and when the result popped up, he stared at it, frowning. It *was* a date, after all, one that rang a bell.

May 5, 1988.

Then it hit him.

That was the day Scott died.

Butch had etched it into his fucking *skin*.

His throat tightened, his stomach roiled.

I should've ignored him when he said he didn't want to talk about it. I should've sat him down and told him.

Sol knew why Butch didn't want to talk about Scott. If anyone did, he did. But learning the truth had lessened the guilt Sol had carried around, and if it had done that for him, there was every reason to believe it would do the same for Butch.

If he'll listen.

Maybe he could put it all in a letter. Except he knew he wouldn't do that. This was a task that required a face-to-face conversation. Sol just wasn't sure seeing Butch again was such a good idea.

So what do I do? Leave it? Let him go on believing we were somehow responsible? Me, him, Cal, Pete… We weren't exactly blameless, but we didn't know the whole story.

Sol had only learned it by chance.

His phone rang, and he peered at the screen. The sight of Alli's name dispelled a little of his internal torment. "Hey, sis."

"Did you really go to Montana?"

He chuckled. "I said so, didn't I? It was a beautiful place. You'd love it. They have horses, trails…"

"Does that mean you'll be going back there?"

I really don't know about that.

"Sol? It wasn't *that* difficult a question."

He got up from his desk, walked over to the liquor cabinet, and poured himself a glass of Jack. The first mouthful took him instantly to that inn. That bed.

Sucking Butch's dick.

Claiming Butch's lips.

"Sol? Want me to call back at some other time?"

He returned to his desk and scrolled back to Butch's photo. "It's just that… well… I have a kind of dilemma."

"Tell me about it. Maybe I can help."

He smiled. "I appreciate the thought, but I don't think you can."

"Try me."

Why not? A problem shared, right?

He took another drink. "I got an invite to go back to the ranch, but it would be a different kind of week. My friend who helps run the place is offering a new kind of experience. For one thing, there'd be no horses involved." *Unless someone comes who likes a little horse play.* It wasn't beyond the realm of possibility. Not that he was about to share *that.*

"This *experience*… Might it have anything to do with that stuff we don't talk about but which I'm totally aware of?"

He laughed. "It might."

"Okay. What's stopping you?"

He sighed. "Last week at the dude ranch, I ran into someone I knew from high school."

"Oh wow." There was a pause. "Not wow?"

"The thing is… we share some baggage, okay?"

"Okay."

"And today I realized I might be able to relieve him of some of that baggage."

"Then what's the problem? Do it."

He sagged into his high-backed chair. "It's more complicated than that."

Another pause. "I have to be honest here… I'm not seeing the dilemma."

Sol wasn't sure he was either.

"So… this high school friend…"

"What about him?"

"Is he also part of this whole other world we don't discuss apart from that one time?"

Sol chuckled. "Alli… you can say BDSM, you know? The words won't kill you."

"Okay—is he?"

"No."

"And does he know *you* are?"

"No."

"So if you did go back, *then* he'd know?"

"Yes."

"And you like him."

"That doesn't sound like a question."

"That's because it wasn't. Come on, you wouldn't be getting into all these knots if you didn't."

"Okay, fine. Yes, I like him."

And there lay the heart of the matter. Sol knew it wouldn't take much to shift the balance from *like* to something a whole lot more complex.

"So that's the dilemma." He couldn't miss the note of triumph in her voice. "You think if he sees what goes on in your life, he'll run a mile."

He lapsed into silence.

Alli heaved a sigh. "Okay, here are my thoughts. I can see three levels to this situation. Number one. You want to accept this invitation because *duh*, this is what you do. But that would entail revealing all to High School Guy."

Sol said nothing. She was doing a pretty good job so far, all on her own.

"Number two. You want to go back to help him get rid of some of his baggage, and that's probably more of a reason to go than number one."

"So what's the third level?"

"That's easy. You want to see him again, but you just don't want to admit it."

Well fuck. Am I that *easy to read?*

Sol coughed. "I thought *I* was the one with a degree in psychology."

"You want to know what *I* think is the best way forward? Go with your gut. What is it telling you?"

Go back to Salvation. Like, yesterday.

That was *not* for sharing.

"By the way... I know I acted all shocked when you first confessed—"

"'Confessed'? That makes it sound as if I was ashamed of the way I live."

"And you're not. I know that. Bad choice of word on my part. But I wasn't all *that* shocked. I've read stuff, you know?"

"I dread to think what." Opinions in the media varied from BDSM being deviant behavior to a sign of mental illness.

Yeah right. Some of the kinksters Sol was acquainted with were the most well-adjusted people he'd ever met.

"Plus, there's something you don't know, and it has to do with your nephew."

"Which one?" Alli had two boys, except they were hardly that anymore: Luke was twenty-eight and Jem was twenty-four.

"Jem. He and I got into this huge discussion over the weekend."

"Is he okay?" Sol knew it was wrong to have favorites, but he'd always had a soft spot for Jem. Luke was the jock of the two, whereas Jem was like his mom, artistic and creative.

"He's fine. What got us talking was me noticing a piece of jewelry I hadn't seen before. A chain he wears around his neck, with a little padlock at the front."

Hoo boy.

"I see."

"You know what I'm talking about, don't you?"

"Possibly."

"So anyway, we went for coffee, we got talking, and he said it wasn't a chain, it was—"

"A collar."

Silence for a moment, followed by a sigh. "So you do know."

"Yeah. Did he say who gave him the collar?"

"Yes. Taylor, a guy he's been seeing for the past year. Jem says he's going to bring him to the house to meet me and Hugh."

Sol blinked. "Did you know he was gay?"

"Not until that moment, no. Have to say, it was a lot to take in over two cups of coffee and a Danish. I get the impression it was a big deal to tell me about the collar, but Jem and me, we've always been able to talk about anything—except the fact he's gay, it seems. But my point is, you don't have to sugarcoat stuff, okay? I'm a big girl now. I can deal with it."

Sol was trying to deal with the revelation that his favorite nephew was both gay and a submissive, and that kink might really be in the genes.

"Jem did ask me not to mention it to Mom and Dad," she added.

"Yeah, I can understand that." All they knew about BDSM was what they saw in the media, and that was *not* a good thing.

"But I did tell him he could talk to you. I figured you wouldn't mind."

The way Sol saw it, Thanksgiving was looking more and more interesting.

"Is he going to bring his... boyfriend to Thanksgiving dinner?"

"He says he'll ask Taylor." She chuckled. "Aren't you glad you agreed to come?"

"Yes. Happy now?"

"And about your... dilemma. Let me know what you decide to do."

Sol was going to do what he'd promised Toby—he was going to think about it. Except he knew from past experience that if he thought about it for too long, he'd find a way to talk himself out of it.

He gazed at Butch's image before clicking on the other window. The date was still there.

Butch gets to see that every day. A constant reminder.

Sol could understand why he'd had it done in the first place—maybe—but *damn it*, that wasn't healthy.

I can't let him dwell on the past. I have to help him move on. Like I did.

And just like that, he'd reached a decision. Sol clicked on his email and hit *Compose.*

Looks like Alli nailed it with her second level.

Sol stared at Liam's photo. "I'm deluding myself, aren't I? It's option three all the way, no matter how I dress it up."

He knew what lay at the root of his decision.

I don't want Butch hurting anymore.

CHAPTER 29

Friday, September 2

Robert finished his bottle of beer, set it down on the porch table, and peered at Teague. "You're not just here to shoot the breeze, are you?" Teague didn't seem agitated or restless, but Robert knew his foreman. Their Friday night beers on the porch routine had come to an end once Toby had moved in, but Robert figured that was because Teague was giving them space.

Teague chuckled. "Not exactly." He turned his head toward the door. "Where's Toby?"

"Working, but he said he'll be down in a minute. We've had some more bookings. For the BDSM ranch," he added.

Teague grinned. "That's awesome. By the way, I love what you called it." His eyes sparkled. "*Deliverance*. Course, the first thing that came to mind was those damn banjos. That movie might be as old as Methuselah, but play that tune and *everyone* knows exactly where it comes from."

He laughed. "It was Toby's idea, and I said the same thing." He gestured to the pail filled with bottles nestling in ice. "Want another?"

"Sure."

Robert took one, popped the cap, and handed it to him. "Okay... what's on your mind?"

"It's more of an FYI kinda thing, to be honest." Teague took a long drink. "You remember a conversation we had back in June? You were concerned that if the *thing* I had going with Butch—that *was* the word you used, right? —went belly up, it might affect us working together."

"I do recall the conversation."

He took another drink. "Well, you can stop being concerned. It's over."

Robert blinked. "Oh. This a recent thing?"

"Yup. Two weeks ago, to be exact."

"No bad feelings, I hope."

Teague shook his head. "I was the one who called a halt, but it was what they call an amicable split. We just came to the end of the road, that's all. And so far, everything's just fine. At least, I think it is. Butch and me, we're still on speaking terms, and he isn't giving me dirty looks."

"Thanks for letting me know. And thanks for all your help with the photos for the website." Robert smiled. "Looks as if you all had some fun."

"If anything, it's made me curious to see who turns up. How many guests so far?"

"If I remember rightly, we've got three couples, a throuple—"

"A what?"

Robert laughed. "Three guys."

Teague frowned. "But how does that work? I mean, with BDSM. Who does what, exactly?" He rolled his eyes. "And I'm not talking about what goes on in the sack—that part I *am* familiar with—more the... dynamic? That was Sol's word."

Robert counted off on his fingers. "It could be a Dom with two submissives, or a Dom and a sub, with a voyeur..."

"Someone who just likes to watch?" Robert nodded, and Teague shook his head once more. "Takes all sorts, I guess."

"You know, some guys—even straight guys—like sessions with a Dom that don't include sex."

Teague's eyebrows shot up. "That's a thing? Why would they do that?"

"They're into it for physical stimulation, stress relief, like flogging, restraints, but their bits and pieces are out of bounds."

Teague cackled. "And there you go, talkin' all coy again. Dude, sometimes you are such a paradox. But back to your... throuple... Any other permutations I should be aware of?"

"It could be a Dom, a sub, and a switch."

Teague chuckled. "The only switch I know is the one my daddy used to take to my butt when I was a kid, and I'm sure that isn't what you're talking about." He bit his lip. "Well, *pretty* sure."

Robert opened another bottle of beer and took a drink. "A switch is basically someone who's happy to swap between being a Dom or a sub during sex."

"You mean, like being vers, but kinkier?" Teague widened his eyes. "So it's not like you choose a role and stick with it? It's not a permanent thing?"

Robert laughed. "No. Well, it is for some. But that's like saying just because you liked women when you were younger, you can't fuck guys later on, or vice versa. People are more fluid than that. And BDSM is pretty fluid too. It's whatever you and your partner—or partners—make of it. As long as there's consent, you're golden. Everyone who comes to BDSM is different. That's one of the best things about it."

Teague chuckled. "Every time I talk with either you or Toby, I learn something new."

"Plus, we've got a single guy staying too."

"Make that two single guys," Toby announced as he joined them on the porch. He greeted Teague with a nod before helping himself to a beer. "We just got another one." He beamed. "I guess Sol couldn't stay away after all."

"Sol's coming back?" Then Teague's frown returned. "Wait a sec—Sol's into this too?" Toby nodded, and he let out a long whistle. "He's a dark horse."

"Could you do me a favor? Sol meant to give Butch his phone number before he left, but I guess it slipped his mind. I was going to come down later and give it to him, but seeing as you're here..." Toby reached into the back pocket of his jeans and removed a piece of paper. "Here you go."

Teague took it and stuffed it into his jeans. "I'll be sure to pass this on. They *should* stay in touch. Butch could use another friend."

"And can you remind everyone about Monday? Matt's got everything in hand." Robert chuckled. "I think he's planning on feeding half of Bozeman too, by the look of the grocery list."

"I'll do that too. Not sure how many of 'em have gone into town tonight. The festivities have already started." He gave Robert a smile. "Thanks for the beer." He stood.

"You're welcome."

Teague tipped his hat to Toby, then headed for the path.

Toby watched him go, grinning.

"What's tickled you?"

He inclined his head in the direction Teague had taken. "He has *no* idea." He flopped into the chair beside Robert.

"And *I* have no idea what you're talking about, so that makes two of us." He drank some more. "You finally wore Sol down, huh?"

Toby stared at him with widened eyes. "Hey, I didn't do a thing. I haven't been in contact with him since he left last week."

Robert chuckled. "My, how restrained. Then you must've been pretty persuasive when you asked him to consider staying."

Toby's smile was definitely smug. "I don't think him coming back has anything to do with me. I think it's *all* about Butch."

Robert gave him a puzzled glance. "Something I don't know?"

Toby shrugged. "My little push must've worked, that's all."

Something clicked into place. "You mentioned something about giving Sol and Butch a push a while back. What did you do?"

Silence.

Robert stared at him. "Toby? What did you do?"

Toby's cheeks flushed. "I was going to tell you about it, actually."

"Fine. Then tell me now." The words came out with a little more weight than he'd intended.

"Wasn't much. I…"

Robert didn't think he'd ever seen Toby flustered. It was a revelation.

"Toby Merrow. What. Did. You. Do?"

"I just got Paul to pretend he was ill, that's all."

It took a moment for all the pieces to fall into place.

Robert looked him in the eye. "And that's the last time you do anything like this, do you hear?"

Toby blinked. "What harm did it do? Might even have helped the situation."

He took a deep breath, his heartbeat pounding, heat flushing through him.

"I get that Sol is your friend, but he came here to consult for us—and to relax. Your *stunt* put him in a horse trailer for two days. I don't call at least fifteen hours of driving a form of relaxation."

Toby's lips parted, but he didn't speak.

"And in case you haven't caught on yet, yes, I'm pissed, but not just with you. I'm angry Paul agreed to this. That isn't like him." He narrowed his gaze. "What did you say to him?"

"I told him he'd be doing them a favor," Toby said at last. "He didn't actually tell anyone he was ill. He went into Bozeman for me on an errand, and as soon as Sol and Butch were on their way, he showed his face again and said whatever it was, he was over it. I just needed him out of sight to get Sol to go." He swallowed.

Fuck.

Robert was never a fan of rocking the boat, but he couldn't let this go.

"Something I have to say, and I need you to hear me out. We've been a couple for seven weeks. *Seven.* Neither of us has really gotten to know what makes the other one tick." Toby opened his mouth, but Robert silenced him with a raised hand. "I won't deny you've gotten a good handle on me when we're in the bedroom or the playroom, but that isn't twenty-four-seven, nor do I want it to be. I don't think you want that either. Yes, you're Sir when it's just us. Yes, I'm the one on my knees. But when it comes to this ranch, I'm the boss, you hear?"

"I thought we were going to run Salvation together—as a team," Toby said in a low voice.

"And we will. But there has to be communication and trust, just like we have in the bedroom. You didn't tell me what you were planning to do. Maybe if we'd discussed it first, I would have come up with an alternative that didn't involve one of my ranch hands, but you didn't give me that option."

Toby bit his lip. "I lied. I wasn't going to tell you initially. I thought you'd be pissed."

"So you know me well enough to gauge my reaction. That's encouraging."

"Sol told me I should tell you. He said something about how you can never bury shit deep enough—it always comes to light— and that there shouldn't be secrets in a relationship."

"Sol's a good man." Robert's anger dissipated. "Thank you for being honest. And for the record, there are *some* secrets you can keep from me, you know, like birthday and Christmas presents, but not stuff like this."

Toby shuddered out a breath. "Did we just have our first fight?"

Robert smiled. "More like a first-time falling out, and it probably won't be our last. But that's okay. If we agreed all the time, that would be downright weird. An argument here and there is healthy." He stood. "Come here." He held his arms wide, and

Toby walked into them. Robert kissed him on the lips. "I love you, you know that, right?"

Toby pressed his cheek to Robert's. "I know. Love you too. And I *am* sorry."

"I know." He stroked Toby's hair. "I *do* know how you can make it up to me, however."

"Yeah?"

Robert slid his hands down Toby's back until he reached that firm ass. He cupped both cheeks and gave a hard squeeze. "This is mine tonight."

Toby chuckled. "I can go with that." He pulled back and looked Robert in the eye. "I call the shots, though."

Robert laughed. "And I can go with *that*." He took his seat once more.

Harmony restored.

Toby hated to admit it, but as much as he loved seeing Robert's submission, seeing him in full-on boss mode was a turn-on. The change in dynamics was a heady switch.

Make-up sex promised to be even better. Robert had gotten more confident when it came to nailing Toby's ass, and he had a feeling he'd know about it the following day.

He took a bottle of beer from the pail and gazed out at the ranch below. "You still think *Deliverance* is a good name?"

"Have you got a better one?"

He chuckled. "Sol suggested *Bound Salvation*, which I also like."

"Yeah, me too." He paused. "I'm still intrigued how you got Paul to agree to your proposal. Which is not me raking over the coals of our fight, by the way, but just genuine interest."

"Hey, he surprised the hell out of me too." Toby took a drink. "Of all the guys who work here, he's something of a closed book." He smiled. "An enigma, that's what he is."

Robert chuckled. "More than you know."

"What do you mean?"

He rolled the bottle between his palms. "I was twenty-nine when my dad brought him home. A wet, skinny boy of seventeen."

Toby nodded. "Yeah, he'd fallen in the river, hadn't he? And your dad saved him."

Robert didn't meet his gaze but took another drink before speaking. "Sure, we'll go with that."

He frowned. "Well, that's what happened, right? I mean, that's what he told me. He said something else too, about having a—"

"Chip on his shoulder? Something about him resenting the fact that a white man had built this ranch on land that had once belonged to his people?"

Toby stared at him. "That was pretty much word for word."

Robert chuckled. "Anyone who asks, he tells them the same story. I can probably recite that whole *speech* word for word. It's almost as if he memorized it."

Paul had suddenly gotten interesting.

"Where did he come from? Do you know?"

Robert stroked his beard. "I think Dad said northern Cheyenne. He also said Paul was pretty vague on the details. He talked once about taking Paul back to see his family, to let them know he was okay." His brow furrowed. "He said Paul went as pale as new-fallen snow, which when you consider his coloring…" He sighed. "Dad never mentioned it again."

Toby finished his beer. "I think I'd better go see Paul in the morning." Robert arched his eyebrows, and he let out a sigh. "I need to apologize. You're right. I shouldn't have involved him."

More than that, he wanted to see if that story came out the same way twice. Because that was *all* kinds of intriguing.

Robert put his bottle on the table, stood, and held out his hand.

"I do believe I have a date with your ass." His eyes twinkled. "And I'm not in the least bit tired. I could probably go for hours."

Toby laughed as he took Robert's hand. "Payback is a bitch? Is that what you're telling me?"

"I wouldn't call it payback, more… fucking every drop of cum from your body." That twinkle again. "Sir."

Toby followed him into the house.

Topping while bottoming was fast becoming one of his favorite pastimes.

Well—almost.

CHAPTER 30

Butch did a last look around the bunkhouse for any trash to take out. He was taking advantage of the lack of guests and getting a head start for the following changeover day. Besides, staying busy was a surefire way to keep his mind off things.

Except there was only one thing on his mind—Sol.

I wonder how he's celebrating Labor Day.

He smiled to himself. He'd gotten the impression Sol was a workaholic, so he'd probably be on his laptop.

The door opened and Teague walked in.

"So where is everyone this evening?"

"Paul took 'em to Montana Days, up at the Pony Bar. Rich Little Eagle's doing his thing again, talking about First Nation music, and tellin' a lot of stories. They should be back any minute. It was over by nine."

"Why didn't you go too?"

Butch had seen Rich's act a dozen times. The truth was, he wasn't in the mood. He'd seen a tee online that summed up his present mood perfectly.

I don't want to people.

Teague reached into his jeans pocket and handed him a scrap of folded paper. Butch opened it.

"If this is your phone number, I already got it. And if you wanna ask me on a date, I ain't cheap."

Teague laughed his ass off. "It's not my number, you dick. It's Sol's."

What the fuck?

"Then why're you giving it to me?"

"He meant to give it to you before he left. He gave it to Toby."

"Oh. Okay." Butch pocketed it.

Why would he do this? Does he want us to stay in touch?

"I'm glad you two got along. I wasn't sure when he first arrived. The air was a little frosty, to tell the truth."

"Yeah, we got past that part. Sol's an okay guy."

With a wicked mouth. Shivers ran through him at the thought of where that mouth had been.

Teague snorted. "I'll be sure to share that glowing praise when I see him next."

"You planning a visit to San Francisco?"

"Won't need to." Teague grinned. "He's coming back."

Jesus. Butch's heart pounded like he was a teenager all over again. "Really? When?" He did his best to rein in his enthusiasm. The last thing he wanted was anyone getting the wrong idea.

Only, it was the right idea, wasn't it?

Teague's eyes glittered, and Butch knew his attempt at nonchalance had been an epic fail.

"That brightened your day, didn't it?"

Butch schooled his features. "What do you mean?"

"S'okay. You don't have to pretend around me, y'know."

He didn't trust himself to speak.

Teague smiled. "You like the guy. I do too. Well, now you get to spend time around him—if you can drag him away from all the other guys in leather."

Maybe Butch's mind was stuck in neutral, because it took several long seconds for Teague's words to register.

"He… He's coming to *Deliverance*?"

"Yup. He'll be here when it opens. And Toby says we can expect another single guy, and a few couples." His lips twitched. "There are going to be a few interesting permutations around here."

Before Butch could get another word out, the door opened and the ranch hands came in, along with the guests.

Teague greeted them with a smile. "Did you have a good time?"

Ian's eyes shone. "It was great. I'm just sorry we're leaving tomorrow. The rest of the weekend looks great too."

Jake chuckled. "Yeah. I wanted to go to the open mic session on Labor Day, at the—what was the name of that pub?"

Zeeb grinned. "The Fainting Goat. There's another session at the Bunkhouse Brewery too."

"And over at the Emerson Center, they're having a variety show," Walt added. "Kind of a mix of *American Idol* and *America's Got Talent*." He buffed his nails on his shirt. "I was thinking of having a go. I've got a pretty good singing voice." Paul, Matt, Zeeb, and Teague erupted into laughter, and Walt glared at them. "Hey, I can sing."

"Sure you can." Zeeb wiped his eyes.

"Walt, you couldn't carry a tune in a cracked bucket," Matt told him.

"I'm not that bad," Walt protested.

"Maybe he *should* sing," Zeeb suggested. He waggled his eyebrows. "Just think of the entertainment value." That earned him another glare before Walt rolled his eyes and gave up.

Mike smiled. "Now I'm *really* sorry I'm leaving."

"Don't go planning too much," Teague told the men. "The boss says everything's in hand for Monday, as usual."

"What happens here on Labor Day?" Ian asked.

"Boss throws a party for us, and any guests who are stayin'," Zeeb informed him. "A cookout with a ton of food, beer..."

"And these guys get to show off their skills in the paddock," Paul added. "Who can bring their horse to the fastest stop, jumping, roping a metal steer..."

"Sounds like fun."

"It is—as long as they do all that *before* they get their hands on a beer."

Zeeb chuckled. "We know the rules."

Butch wasn't really listening. He was too busy thinking about what Teague had said. His pulse sped up, his heart pounded, and he was trying not to grind his teeth.

"Butch?" Teague's voice cut through. "Can I have a word with you outside?"

"Sure." Butch followed him out of the bunkhouse. No sooner had he closed the door than Teague launched.

"What's up?"

"What makes you think something's up?"

Teague arched his eyebrows. "You went from being excited about Sol's return to looking as if someone had shoved poison ivy down the back of your jeans."

"And what if I'm not allergic to poison ivy?"

Teague gaped. "For the love of God, stop prevaricating and tell me what's wrong."

Butch could've made a quip about Teague using them big

words again, but his heart wasn't in it. He paused to take a breath. He didn't want the others hearing this.

"Sol... He said he wasn't into that."

Teague frowned. "That's not what he said at all."

"Hey, I was there, okay? I asked how come he knew about all that stuff, and he said he'd researched it for websites."

Teague studied him for a second. "You two got off on the wrong foot, didn't you? That's why the pair of you seemed a little awkward at first."

"And I told you, we got over it."

"Fine, but let me run something past you. If things were awkward between you, why would he make it worse by telling you he was into all that? He didn't tell any of us that night, did he? He wanted us to feel relaxed, comfortable. Maybe that's why Toby did all the talking."

"Okay, but things were better between us by the time he left. He could've said something then, but he didn't, like it was a secret."

"Well, it isn't a secret now, is it?" Teague retorted. His frown deepened. "Besides, what difference does it make if Sol's into BDSM? I'll tell you. Absolutely none at all. He's still Sol."

That wasn't helping.

"I'm just not sure what I'm going to say to him when I see him, that's all." Except that was a huge understatement.

Teague let out a noise of exasperation.

"Then isn't it fortunate he won't be sleeping in the bunkhouse with you guys? That way you won't feel uncomfortable." Teague cocked his head. "I don't get it. You're pretty relaxed around Toby. So I'll ask again. What's the difference?"

Butch couldn't answer that, because for the life of him, he didn't know.

Teague let out a sigh. "Quit thinking so much, all right? Sounds like there's a heap of stuff going on in Bozeman this weekend. Why not go see what's going on? You know, let your hair down a little." He snorted. "I forgot. You don't have that much to start with."

"Bastard."

Teague chuckled. "Yeah, but you love me."

"Course I do." Their relationship might have undergone a

monumental shift, but that wouldn't change what they'd shared through the years.

The boss, Teague, Zeeb, Matt, Paul, Walt… They were his family. Give it time, and Toby would be in there too.

Zeeb poked his head around the bunkhouse door. "Lights out in ten minutes. You've got an early morning run into Bozeman, haven't you? You're dropping Ian at the Baxter."

"And don't forget, Butch needs his beauty sleep," Teague quipped.

"Fuck you," Butch fired back with a grin. "Go play with yourself in your cabin."

Teague's grin eclipsed his. "You read my mind." He walked off, and Butch was certain Teague was giving a little wiggle of his hips on purpose.

He went into the bunkhouse a damn sight calmer than he'd been a few minutes before.

Teague talks a lot of sense. Why am I making such a big deal of this? The comparison with Toby had helped put the situation into perspective. *Toby's into all this, and he's okay.*

He got ready for bed on autopilot, aware of the chatter and laughter around him. The guests had been a good bunch, easy to get along with, and he hoped the next lot would be as amenable. But by the time he lay beneath his comforter, his thoughts defaulted to Sol once more.

Toby talked about Doms and submissives. Which one is Sol? Toby hadn't come right out and said he was a Dom, but that was the feeling Butch got after listening to the way he spoke to Walt and Teague, and after that talk he'd given them too. He could picture Toby being the one in control.

And that's what it's all about, right? Control.

At least, that was Butch's take on it. He didn't want to think too deeply about the boss and Toby—whatever they got up to was no one's business but theirs—but he couldn't help wondering how things worked between them.

All that stuff in the barn… Floggers, paddles, benches… He couldn't picture the boss letting anyone spank him or paddle his ass. But then he recalled how Kevin Porter had been around the boss. Nothing was ever said, but he got the feeling Kevin had called the shots in the bedroom. Not that Butch could pinpoint any particular mannerism or words that gave it away—it was just a feeling.

An instinct.

Then it hit him.

For the first time, he realized just how much the boss had lost when Kevin died. Because Kevin had to have been *way* more than a lover, a partner. Butch didn't know a whole lot about BDSM—the sum of all his knowledge could be written on the back of a packet of cigarettes—but he knew enough to realize they must have shared something pretty intense.

And then he lost it all.

Everyone who worked on Salvation had been overjoyed to see the boss happy again, but it wasn't until that moment Butch understood *why* his boss was so damn happy.

Toby was the missing piece. Toby completes him.

And the more he thought about it, the more certain he was that Sol was probably a Dom too.

A Dom who was coming back to Salvation.

A Dom who'd given Butch his phone number.

The math wasn't all that hard—Butch just didn't know what the answer was going to be.

I guess I'll know in a few weeks.

Now all he had to do was get on with his life and stop thinking about what *might* be heading his way.

Yeah right. Wasn't gonna happen.

CHAPTER 31

Monday, September 5 - Labor Day

"Who's got the fastest time so far?" Butch demanded as he dismounted.

Owen sat on his quad bike, ready to drag the metal steer around the paddock one more time. Matt had called to say the cookout would start in about thirty minutes, and two of the guests, Gary and Logan, were waiting to take their turn roping.

Zeeb peered at the chalk board leaning against the fence. "So far, it's you and Teague. So unless one of these guys beats the pants off of you both, there's gonna be a showdown."

The clatter of hooves had all heads turning toward the drive. Butch broke into a smile. "Well, look who's here." He hollered to the boss sitting on the fence with Toby. "Hey, boss? We've got company."

Diana rode up to the paddock, slowing as she approached. "Happy Labor Day, everyone." She waved in greeting to the ranch hands.

"Hey, Diana." Zeeb waved back. "You slummin' it?"

All he got was an eye-roll.

The boss climbed down and ambled over to her. He leaned on the fence. "You rode here?"

"That's all I get?" Diana snorted. "Really feeling the love. And it's not as if I haven't done this before." She narrowed her gaze. "Are you saying I'm too old to ride all the way from my ranch to yours?"

The boss held both hands up. "I wouldn't dream of it."

"Not if you like your balls where they are." She glanced at Toby. "The boyfriend might have something to say about that."

Toby laughed. "Hey, Diana. I wouldn't dream of it either."

The boss stroked the black horse's neck. "I haven't seen this boy before."

"That's because he's new. This is Blackheart." She patted his mane. "We're still getting used to each other, but I figured a ride over here would give us that chance."

"You could've told me you were coming," he grumbled.

"I wanted to surprise you." She grinned. "Surprise!"

"Don't you have guests?"

"Sure. Newt's taken them to the rodeo at White Sulphur Springs. I've seen enough rodeos to last me a lifetime." She gave the boss a hopeful look. "Is there food?"

He laughed. "Matt's cooking steaks, sausages, burgers, chicken, you name it. Plus, there's beans, potato salad—"

"You had me at steak." She gave Butch a smile. "How you doin', handsome?"

"Doing just fine." Age hadn't robbed Diana of any of her sass, thank God.

"We've got ourselves a little contest goin' on," Zeeb told her. "Ropin' the steer."

Diana peered into the paddock and laughed. "You call that a steer? Aw, Robert, couldn't you have given them a *real* one? You know, something that's more of a challenge?"

Gary laughed. "Trust me, ma'am, that is as much of a challenge as I can take."

"Guys, this is my sister, Diana." The boss introduced the three guests, and she nodded at them.

"You having a good time?"

"Yes, ma'am," Logan replied. He glanced at the horse standing beside him. "And it'll stay good as long as I stay on this magnificent beast." He gave a rueful smile. "I've had a couple of tumbles already."

"The thing about falling off a horse? You just get right back on again." Diana scrutinized the board. "Who's winning?" She grinned. "Ooh, neck-and-neck, boys."

Butch stuck his chest out. "You're just in time to watch me beat Teague."

"In your dreams," Teague retorted.

Diana laughed. "There *is* another possible outcome, you know." She nodded toward the paddock gate. "Open up and let me in, and I'll show you boys how it's done."

Teague jerked his head in the boss's direction. "She any good?"

Butch laughed out loud. "I forgot you never saw Diana before she left Salvation."

The boss chuckled. "She's better than me."

"Aw fu—I mean, damn."

Paul opened the gate, grinning. "Come on, Diana, show us what you've got."

"With pleasure." She trotted into the paddock, leaning forward to speak into Blackheart's ear. "Let's show 'em what *you've* got, too."

"Here ya go." Zeeb handed her the coil of poly rope, and Butch watched as she expertly made a loop, holding the excess coils of lariat in her left hand as well as the reins.

Teague groaned. "Oh dear Lord, you weren't kidding."

The boss laughed. "Told ya. Dad taught her."

Owen set off, the quad bike roaring into life as he charged across the paddock, the metal steer dragging behind him, and Diana followed, lifting the loop above her head and twirling it.

Zeeb hooted. "You go, girl."

She turned her head to grin at him. "You'd better be timing this." Then she jolted as Blackheart came to a sudden stop. He bucked and Diana went flying. She landed on the ground with a dull thud.

"Oh my God." Butch ran over to her. Diana wasn't moving, her arm at an odd angle. The boss knelt beside her, hands outstretched, calling her name, and Butch cried out, "Don't touch her! You can't move her, okay? Someone call 911, now!"

"I'm on it." Teague pulled his phone from his pocket. The others stood around, everyone silent.

Dear God, the boss's face was white. Toby tried to help him stand, his arm around him, but the boss struggled to get free.

"Boss… let me take a look at her, okay?" Butch pleaded.

The boss swallowed hard, his gaze locked on Diana's still form, but he nodded, and Toby managed to get him upright. He took a step back and Butch dropped to his knees. His stomach churned when he saw the extent of Diana's injuries. She was unconscious, and he felt for her pulse, giddy with relief when it was weak but still there. Her face looked as though she'd gone ten rounds with a train. Then he saw blood leaking from Diana's ear, except it seemed streaky, thinned down…

As though blood and clear fluid had mingled.

Aw fuck. This is not *good.*

"Why doesn't she open her eyes?" the boss demanded. "She… she isn't dead, is she?"

"She's alive, just unconscious. But we can't move her."

"Listen to Butch, okay?" Toby's voice was low and soothing. "He's the first aid guy on the ranch, isn't he?"

"Butch, what do I tell them about her condition?" Teague asked, his phone against his chest.

"Unconscious, broken arm, bleeding from her face, and from her ear. Especially that last part. Tell them I think there's clear fluid too."

"Got it." Teague went back to his call, his voice strained.

"What does it mean if she's bleeding from her ear?" The boss's voice shook.

"I don't know, all right? I'm not a doctor. But…" Butch looked him in the eye. "There's fluid around the brain, okay? And her head hit the ground with an awful wallop. I'm thinking she could've fractured her skull." He scraped his fingers through his hair. "Look, I don't have a clue what that other fluid is. I just know it shouldn't be leaking from her ear."

He had no idea how bad her injuries were. That would be for the doctors to ascertain.

"Medivac is on its way," Teague announced. "They're going to take her to Bozeman Health Deaconess. They've got a helipad."

"Get all the horses into the stable, then everyone clear the paddock," Toby instructed. "They can land here. All of you, go on up to the house. Let Matt know what's happened." He tightened his grip around the boss's shoulders. "I'll stay here."

"Me too." Butch wasn't budging until Diana was safely on her way to the hospital. He kept praying for her to open her eyes, give some sign of life, but there was nothing.

Paul and Zeeb rounded up the horses and led them out of the paddock, while Owen drove the quad bike over to the barn. Walt directed the guests to the path that wound its way up the hill to the house.

A moment later came the *whirr* of helicopter blades, and dust rose in the paddock as it hovered then lowered itself to the ground. Butch grabbed a horse blanket that hung over the fence and covered Diana with it until the dust settled. The door slid open and two EMTs jumped out, dragging a wheeled stretcher behind them, followed by two more with a board. They hurried over to where Diana lay.

"Okay, stand back, please," the female EMT said in a firm voice.

Butch stood by as she and another EMT carefully fixed a collar around Diana's neck, while the other two slid the back board under her. Once she was secured, they lifted her and placed her on the stretcher.

"Can I go with her?" the boss asked.

The EMT's face fell. "Sorry, sir, but that isn't possible."

"I'll drive him to the hospital," Toby told them.

With one EMT at each corner, they rolled the stretcher to the helicopter, where a nurse waited for them. Once the stretcher was locked into position, the boss, Toby, Teague, and Butch retreated to the fence, standing together in a huddle as the helicopter rose, its blades slicing through the air, stirring up the dust once more. Then it was gone.

"Okay, let's get you to the hospital." Toby sounded calmer than Butch felt. He glanced at Teague. "Make sure everyone gets some food, okay? There's plenty, but I know they may not feel like eating right now. I'll call you from the hospital when we have more news."

The boss leaned into Toby. "I can't lose her," he whispered.

Toby held him. "She's going to get the best care, all right? We have to pray she'll come through this." His gaze met Teague's. "You're in charge."

"Gotcha."

Toby guided the boss toward the path, and Teague stood at Butch's side as they walked slowly up the hill.

"This is such a fucking mess," Butch murmured. He'd never seen the boss appear so... fragile, as if a harsh word would shatter him into a million tiny pieces.

"There's nothing we can do but wait—and pray."

Butch sighed. "I thought my praying days were over a long time ago, but for her? I'd be willing to give 'em another try."

Then Teague paled. "Oh God. Someone needs to call Newt."

"I can do that." Teague had enough on his plate, taking care of the ranch.

Teague laid a hand on Butch's arm. "You okay?"

Butch gave him an inquiring glance.

"Well, you and Diana... I mean..."

He sighed. "That was also a long time ago. And I'm quite capable of talking to her husband."

"Then I'll go up to the house. Lord knows I could sure use a beer right now."

Butch managed a smile. "Save one for me. I won't be long."

Teague nodded, and Butch waited until he was on the path before he looked up the number for Newt and Diana's dude ranch.

Yet another soul about to be crushed by devastating news.

The whole time Teague was on the phone, no one on the patio spoke. All eyes were focused on him, and Butch swore every single man there was holding his breath. When Teague finished the call, he let out a long sigh.

"Well?" Butch demanded.

Teague pocketed his phone. "She's still unconscious."

Groans rippled through the assembled men.

"How long can she stay like that?" Zeeb stared at him. "It's been *hours*." The sun had set about an hour ago, but no one had moved.

Everyone was waiting for news.

"The doctor told Toby it could last as long as twenty-four hours. They're doing a CT scan to—"

"Haven't they done X-rays or something?" Matt hadn't eaten a bite.

"He said X-rays don't help much in cases of head injury. They use CT scans to check for skull fractures and... brain damage." Teague caught Butch's eye. "That fluid you saw? Toby said it was cerebral spinal fluid."

"What does that mean?" Paul asked in a hushed tone.

"It means it's fucking serious." No sooner had the words left his lips than Butch gave Paul an apologetic glance. "I'm sorry. I'm just on edge. Hell, I think we all are. I shouldn't have yelled at you like that."

Paul's dark eyes were warm. "You don't need to apologize. I get it, honest. We know you and Diana were…"

Butch didn't want to talk about that. He didn't want to talk, period.

"I think I'll go back to the bunkhouse," he said, rising from his chair. He glanced at Teague. "If there's more news—"

"I'll let you know," Teague assured him.

Butch's feet—and his heart—were like lead as he walked down the path.

Lord? You can't have Diana, you hear? It isn't her time. And I've already lost too many people who meant something to me, so you're not getting her too.

Maybe arguing with the Almighty wasn't the best way to get prayers answered, but Butch wasn't firing on all eight cylinders. He knew his Salvation family were there for him, but *damn* it, what he needed right then, they couldn't provide.

I want someone to hold me. Comfort me. Kiss away my pain.

His heart quaked.

I want someone to love me.

CHAPTER 32

Robert rested his head against the back of the chair, his eyes closed.

Watching the clock didn't help. Neither did staring at the door to Diana's room.

She'll be fine. I know she will.

She had to be.

He opened his eyes at the sound of approaching footsteps. Toby looked like he felt, so Robert was awfully glad there were no mirrors in the room.

He straightened. "Hey. What are they all doing?"

"Sitting on the patio, not touching a bite of food, and waiting for news," Toby told him. He glanced at the vacant chair next to Robert. "Where's Newt?"

"Gone to get coffee." Robert was grateful for the respite. He'd thought *he* was taking the news kinda hard—Newt was a mess, and then some. Then again, Newt didn't have someone to lean on.

Toby was a rock, and Robert leaned on him because he knew Toby could take whatever Robert threw at him.

Right then he was throwing a *ton* of emotional debris.

"How are you doing?" Toby sat beside him, his hand on Robert's neck.

God, he loved it when Toby did that. Sex was always goddamn amazing, but this touch, the feel of his hand on Robert's neck, away from all the sex, the role-plays… As much as Robert loved all of that, those quiet moments between Dom and Sub?

He loved them more.

He focused on that touch, Toby's reminder that he was not alone in this.

"I've been better," he admitted. "The hardest part is the waiting." He stilled as a nurse passed them and went into the room, closing the door behind them. When a doctor passed them a minute later, heading in the same direction, Robert knew something was going on.

"Was that the doctor I saw a second ago?" Newt walked briskly toward them, holding a tray with three cups sat in it.

"Yeah. He's in there now." Robert sent up another silent prayer.

The door opened again, and the nurse emerged.

"Mr. Webster? Your wife is awake."

Newt deposited the tray on the chair, and hurried into the room.

The nurse gave Robert a warm smile. "You can come in too, Mr. Thorston. And your… partner."

Robert was off his chair in a heartbeat, Toby following.

The room was dark but for the lights that illuminated the bed. Diana was pale, and there were bandages on her face. Her arm was in a cast. Then he realized something.

There were no bandages around her head.

Newt bent down to kiss her. "She looks so small," he murmured.

Robert came around to the other side of the bed. "I thought you said she was awake."

"She came round, but now she's sleeping," the nurse told him. "Right now her condition is guarded but stable."

Newt sat in the chair next to her bed, holding her hand. "When will she be allowed home, doc?"

"What's the verdict, doctor?" Robert kept up a silent litany, hoping for good news.

The doctor stood at the foot of the bed. "Mrs. Webster has suffered a linear fracture of the skull."

"But what does that mean?" Newt demanded.

"It's the most common type of skull fracture," the doctor told him. "There's a break in the bone, but the bone itself doesn't move."

"But what does that mean for her? Will she be able to leave here in a few days, or a few weeks? Has there been any brain damage?"

Newt's words sent Robert into a blind panic, and his heart pounded.

Toby's hand was at his neck, firm yet gentle, and Robert took a breath.

"The longest she might expect to stay is a week, but I think she could be out of here by Friday or Saturday."

"What about the bleeding from her ear?" Robert asked. "Isn't that serious? One of the ER doctors said something about cerebral spinal fluid."

"We did think that for a while, but that proved false. There was a lot of blood from two facial lacerations, and it was this blood you saw running *into* her ear, not from it. The cat scan ruled out the possibility of spinal fluid leakage." He pointed to her arm. "Her arm suffered a complex fracture, and we had to operate. But after five days with us, she should be able to go home, where she'll need plenty of rest."

Diana opened her eyes, and Robert's legs almost buckled under him with relief. She blinked several times. "Where... where am I?"

Newt stood, still holding her hand. "Hey there, darlin'. You're in the hospital."

She frowned. "What am I doing here?"

Robert stroked her forehead. "You had an accident."

Her frown deepened. "What happened?"

"You don't remember?" Fuck, she sounded so confused, so unlike her usual self that a trickle of panic slithered down Robert's spine.

"What happened?" she repeated. "Why am I here?"

"The confusion is normal," the doctor said in a low voice. "She's suffering from concussion."

"You took a tumble off your horse," Newt said in a gentle voice.

"I did?" Her brows knitted together, and she raised her hand to peer at the tubes coming from the canula.

"Gentlemen, she needs to rest," the doctor told them.

"Can I stay with her?" Newt hadn't taken his eyes off her.

In all the years since their marriage, Robert had gotten along with his brother-in-law, but they hadn't exactly bonded. They saw each other during the holidays, at Diana's fortieth birthday party which had been the talk of Bozeman for *weeks*, just fragments of time here and there. For the first time, he felt a connection.

Diana connected them. Their love and concern for her united them.

"You can stay a while longer, until she falls asleep. Then I'd recommend going home and getting some sleep yourself. It's been a long day for you."

"I'll take you home," Toby murmured in Robert's ear. "The doc's right. You need to sleep."

Robert didn't want to move from her bedside, but he knew Toby made a lot of sense.

He leaned over and kissed her forehead. "I'll be back tomorrow, okay?"

Diana didn't respond, but brought her hand up to touch his arm.

Robert gave Newt a nod. "You get some rest too, y'hear?"

"I will." He returned his attention to Diana.

After he'd thanked the doctor and the nurse, Robert walked out of the room a damn sight more hopeful than when he'd entered it.

Toby's hand was right there on his neck, and Robert gave himself up to the touch.

"Let's go home."

Butch helped Matt clear away the dishes and glasses, while Walt and Zeeb carried the food into the kitchen. Paul had taken the guests back to the bunkhouse, and Teague was outside on his phone.

Butch prayed it was good news.

He stared at the mass of untouched food. "I guess no one was hungry."

"It's all going into the refrigerator—and the freezer," Matt told him. "And once we know she's okay, we'll have that party."

Butch loved his optimism. "From your mouth to God's ears, dude."

Teague came into the kitchen. "Good news. Diana's come round. They're on their way back from the hospital. Toby said they're almost home."

Butch had to fight back the tears of relief. "Thank the Lord.

What do the docs say?"

Teague reeled off all the medical jargon, but the two things Butch homed in on were that there was no brain damage, and she'd be home by the end of the week.

It had been a hell of a long time since Butch had gotten an answer to prayer.

"They'll be hungry," Matt announced. "They haven't eaten since breakfast. I'll rustle something up for them." He smiled at Walt and Zeeb. "Thanks for your help, guys." He gestured to the food. "Grab a bite if you're hungry. God knows there's plenty."

Zeeb grabbed a couple of chunks of bread, and helped himself to a bowl of potato salad. "This'll do just fine." His eyes met Butch's. "Might even be able to eat it now." He headed out of the door.

Walt hesitated for a second, then followed suit. "You coming?" he asked Butch as he added a couple of spoonfuls to a bowl.

"I'm gonna wait till I've seen the boss."

Walt nodded, then walked out of the kitchen. Matt was putting two plates of food together, and Teague sat at the kitchen table, a bottle of beer in one hand.

"Christ Almighty, what a day." He glanced at Butch. "You hanging in there?"

He expelled a breath. "Just thankful she's gonna be okay." He paused. "And even more thankful to be wrong."

Teague shivered. "I know. It could've been much, much worse." He smiled. "You did good today. You kept your head."

Butch returned the smile. "Why, thank you, Mr. Foreman, sir."

"I mean it." He inclined his head toward the porch. "Wanna join me outside?"

"Don't mind if I do." Butch grabbed one of the beer bottles from the pail standing by the fridge, and followed Teague. In the night sky, more and more stars became visible, and the air was cooler. They sat in the chairs, and Butch stared out at the ranch below, the barns lit up, their white paint glowing in the lights.

"You calmed down yet?"

Butch frowned. "What?"

"I'm not talking about today—I'm referring to that

conversation we had on Friday night. You remember that, right? Where you lost it because you found out Sol likes to wear leather an' shit."

He smirked. "'Leather an' shit'?" Teague arched his eyebrows, and Butch sighed. "Yeah, I've calmed down, thanks to you." He raised his bottle to Teague. "You talk a lot of sense. I'm still not sure what I'm gonna say to him when he arrives."

"Then don't wait till then. He gave you his number—use it."

Butch blinked. "Seriously?"

"Why not? You'd clear the air before he gets here."

"And why is that so all-fired important?"

Teague turned his head to meet Butch's gaze. "Because he'll only be here for a week, and I want him to enjoy it, not be on edge 'cause of whatever the two of you have going on."

"There's nothing goin' on between us," Butch retorted quickly.

Maybe a little *too* quickly.

Teague widened his eyes. "You want to try that again?"

"Don't see why I need to."

That twinkle in Teague's eyes told him his bluff had been called.

"I guess I was right when I said you liked him." Teague smiled. "Only, you like him in a different way to the rest of us, don't you?"

Shit. Shit. Shit.

The sound of tires on gravel was a blessed relief.

Butch got to his feet. "They're back."

"And in the nick of time too." Teague's lips twitched. He got up and they went into the house, just as Toby and the boss came through the front door.

Robert looked exhausted.

Toby stood slightly in front of him. "Everything good here?"

"Matt's got food waiting for you in the kitchen," Teague told them. "And the party's all cleared away."

"We'll do it again." The boss gave him a weary smile. "When Diana can share it with us."

"You got that right." He tipped his hat. "I'll say goodnight. We can talk in the morning." And with that, he left them.

Toby's hand was on the back of the boss's neck. "You go on into the kitchen. I want a word with Butch."

The boss nodded, and walked along the hallway toward the kitchen.

"Something wrong?" Apart from the fact that the boss seemed to have aged ten years in one night.

"Got a job I'd like you to do for us in the morning."

"Sure."

"Sol came up with an idea. He suggested the cabin down by the creek could be used for any… overnight guests you guys might want to invite."

Butch gaped. "Really?"

"Well, this *is* your home, and Robert and I agreed you should all feel free to have guests. Obviously the bunkhouse is out so the cabin would give you a little privacy."

Way to go, Sol. They owed him, big time. Butch couldn't wait to see their faces when he shared *this* bit of news.

He said as much, and to his surprise, Toby's face fell.

"We were going to get everyone together and put it to you all, get your input, but you know what? Life's too short. *You* know they're going to love the idea, *we* think they'll love it, so let's just go ahead and get the job done, so everybody can start using the place, getting some enjoyment out of life."

Butch knew he was thinking of Diana.

Nothing like a brush with death to make you aware of your own mortality.

"What do you want me to do?"

"Take a ride over there, and see what needs doing to the place. If we're going to have people staying the night, we have to make sure it provides everything they might need." His eyes gleamed. "I'm sure you can think of a couple of things to add to a shopping list."

Butch was no fool. *Dear Lord, he's talking about condoms and lube.*

"I can do that." He frowned. "I get why you want to do this, but why bring it up this minute? Surely it could've waited till morning."

"Because right now I need a distraction, and it was the first thing that came to mind. Added to that, I might have forgotten it by morning. I've got other priorities at the moment."

It didn't take a genius to know Toby's main priority was the boss.

"Leave it with me. I'll report back once I've worked out what the place needs." Then he reconsidered. "Why don't you just let me deal with it? I'll see to whatever needs doing and have it ready to go without bothering you about it." He glanced toward the kitchen. "You can concentrate on the more important stuff."

Toby's smile reached his eyes. "Thank you. That's something else I don't need to think about. And thanks for taking charge this afternoon."

"I'm just happy she's gonna be okay."

Happy had to be the understatement of the millennium.

"I'll say goodnight then." Toby patted him on the shoulder and headed for the kitchen.

Butch was on the path when his rumbling stomach reminded him he'd meant to grab a bite to eat. The boss's arrival had wiped it clean from his mind. He turned around and walked briskly to the house. Inside, the silence was broken only by the tick of the clock in the living room. He went to the kitchen—

And stopped in the doorway.

Toby and the boss were sitting at the table, and although Butch knew he should make his presence known, he didn't want to disturb the scene in front of him. He stood there and drank it all in, hardly daring to breathe in case that alerted them.

He'd seen the boss and Toby together plenty of times, but never like this. There was nothing sexual about the way Toby touched him, or even sensual, but at the same time Butch couldn't miss the connection between them. Robert Thorston had run Salvation ever since his dad died, and every ranch hand knew that if he said jump, they jumped, no hesitation whatsoever.

Yet seeing the two men like this, there was no doubt in Butch's mind his boss wasn't the dominant force in their relationship. The way he reacted when Toby touched him, when he spoke to him...

What struck Butch most was that this didn't seem to make him a lesser man, but quite the opposite. There was such an honesty in the way they acted around each other that it made him ache inside, and he was reminded of his urgent wish of only a few hours ago.

I said I wanted someone to love me, comfort me, hold me...

Well, now he could add to that.

I want someone to look at me the way Toby looks at the boss. Like I'm their whole fucking world.

He wanted that same honesty, that trust.

The scene was an intensely private and intimate moment. Robert laid his head on Toby's shoulder, and Toby whispered to him, words Butch couldn't hear, but then to do so would've been wrong. And through it all, he stroked Robert's neck, the movement slow and gentle, a reminder of Toby's presence.

And right then Butch needed to be someplace else before either of them found him staring at them.

Butch crept down the hallway and out of the house, his thoughts focused on the two men.

For such a simple display, it had shaken him to his core.

CHAPTER 33

Tuesday, September 6

Butch rode through the meadow at a gallop, as though the devil himself was on his tail. Except it wasn't fear that gave him wings, but the phone call from the boss, and they were wings of joy. He and Toby had gone back to the hospital right after breakfast, and the news that Diana seemed much improved had lightened everyone's spirits.

She's going to be okay. She really is.

When he reached the creek, he slowed, letting Bailey drop into a canter. Birds tweeted in the trees that marked the edge of the forest, and ordinarily he'd enjoy their song, but today each note sounded sweeter, purer somehow.

He knew why Toby had asked him to check out the cabin—he wanted to keep Butch occupied. Hell, the night before, everyone had been handling him like he was made of glass.

The boss *is the one who needs all the attention, not me.* Him and Diana? That had been way back when dinosaurs roamed the land. Now she had a husband who was probably over the moon with relief right then.

Butch was in pretty much the same state.

She's gonna be okay. She's in the best hospital in the county. A linear fracture is better than a severe fracture. She isn't leaking spinal fluid. She'll be home in five days.

It was all good.

He came to a stop at the hitching rail, and dismounted. Once he'd tied him up, he patted Bailey's neck, and pulled an apple from the saddle bag. "Brought this for ya," he said in a low voice. He cut it into pieces with his pocketknife and let Bailey take them from his hand. Then he crossed over the creek and climbed the porch steps.

Inside the cabin was cool, and he removed his hat, placing it on the couch. He smiled to himself when he caught sight of the bottle of lube sitting on the coffee table.

Guess I know what someone was up to in here.

Butch took out his notepad and did a quick inventory, making a note of what was missing. He loved the plan to let the hands use the cabin for overnight guests. What pleased him even more was that it had been Sol's idea.

He was looking out for us hands. Good man.

It was only then it occurred to him that Sol didn't know about Diana. He pulled his phone from his jeans pocket and scrolled for the number he'd entered on Friday evening.

Was it only four days ago?

It felt like a lifetime.

Butch went out onto the porch, sat in one of the chairs, and clicked on call.

After four rings, Sol's deep voice filled his ear. "Hello?"

"Hey, it's me."

There was a pause. "Hey, Butch."

Butch's skin prickled. *It's a bad time.* "If you're busy, I can—"

"No, it's okay. I needed a break anyway. I just wasn't expecting to hear from you, I guess."

"Then why else would you make sure I got your number? Which kinda surprised me, I have to say."

"Why?"

"I had the feeling when we said goodbye that I was never gonna see you again. And then you go and give Toby your number."

"I'm glad he remembered to pass it on."

Butch had been momentarily distracted by the lush sound of Sol's voice, and the mention of Toby sent a wave of guilt surging through him.

"I'm calling because something happened yesterday, and I know Toby's got his hands full taking care of the boss, so—"

"Butch. What's happened?" Butch told him about Diana's accident, and Sol's breathing hitched. "Oh my God. What's the prognosis?"

"She's gonna be okay. They're talking about letting her come home in four or five days."

"How's Robert taking it?"

Butch sighed. "I think he'd have fallen apart by now if it wasn't for Toby." He hesitated.

"Is there something you're not telling me? Is Diana really going to be all right?"

"Yeah, she is. It's just…" Butch didn't know how to frame his thoughts. He wasn't even sure why he wanted to share what he'd seen, but it had been so…

Beautiful. Precious. Those two words were the closest he got to describing what he'd witnessed between the two men.

And maybe Sol was the one person who would understand.

"I was up at the house last night when Toby and the boss came back from the hospital, and… I saw something. They were in the kitchen and…" He paused. "It seemed—to me at any rate—like the boss kept sorta flashing back to her falling, and that got him worked up all over again. And then Toby…" He took a breath. "Toby was just… *there*, you know? He was sitting real close, and he never stopped touching the boss. A hand on his shoulder, or his leg, as if he was just reminding the boss he was there. And when the boss got all worked up again, Toby had his hand on the back of the boss's neck, not stroking or anything, just touching, letting it rest there. And the boss seemed to… I don't know… sort of melt into those touches. Toby did all the talking too, and I guess that was his way of shielding the boss, putting himself between the boss and me. Like he was saying to the boss, 'you don't have to worry about anything. I'm here for you.'"

Yeah, it had been beautiful, like nothing Butch had ever seen. The two men were so into each other, like they fitted together perfectly.

There was a pause before Sol spoke. "I think you nailed it. Robert handed control over to Toby, who helped him hold it together."

And there it was, the opening Butch had wished for.

"Is that a BDSM thing? And before you say you have no idea or you'll do a little research, I *know*, all right? That cat is out of the bag and yowling its head off."

"I see." Sol paused. "Okay, then yes, I'd say it is, but let me ask you something. Why does it bother you that it's part of my life?"

"Who says it does?"

"Your reaction says so."

He huffed. "Doesn't bother *me* none if you're kinky as fuck. I don't have a kinky bone in my body." Sol laughed, and he bristled. "What's so damn funny?"

"So you're vanilla, huh?"

"If that's the opposite of kinky, then yes, yes I am."

Sol chuckled. "I bet *I* could find a kinky bone or two—if I looked real hard."

Butch wasn't sure if he'd imagined the slight stress placed on that last word, but it was as if something tugged on his dick.

"Look all you want. You're wasting your time." He kept his tone light.

"Is that a challenge?" The gleeful note in Sol's voice sent a shiver of apprehension trickling through him, robbing him of words.

Don't go looking. What scared the fuck out of him was that Sol might find something.

Sol cleared his throat. "Since I left, have you thought about it much?"

"Thought about what?" Except he knew what was coming. His pulse quickened.

"My mouth on your dick was that forgettable? Ouch. You know how to bruise a guy's ego."

"You saying you've been thinking about me sucking you off?" *Yeah right.* Sol probably had guys lining up to blow him, offer him their asses, begging to be tied up, tied down…

Whatever.

Now, thinking about *that* bothered him, only he wasn't about to let Sol know that.

Sol said nothing for a moment, and Butch's stomach churned.

"Being totally honest? There hasn't been a single day since my return when I haven't thought about how you chose to say goodbye. Never mind 'say it with flowers'—you said it with your lips and tongue, and that was *way* hotter than words."

All of a sudden, Butch was back in that barn, on his knees, Sol's cock filling his mouth, Sol's hands on the back of his head, guiding him, encouraging him, Butch hot, hard—

And loving every second.

"You were right, by the way."

The swift change in direction gave Butch whiplash. "Right about what?"

"I wasn't going to stay in touch, but then I reconsidered." The frequent pauses served to ramp up Butch's anxiety. "Because I came to a decision." Another pause.

Christ, it was worse than watching those goddamn reality TV shows Walt was so freaking fond of, where they paused for what seemed like forever before they announced who was leaving, who was staying, who'd won…

"You gonna leave me hangin' or are you gonna get to the punchline?"

"Okay then." There was the slightest pause this time before Sol spoke. "I want more."

Oh dear Lord.

"I'd be down for another blowjob," Butch affirmed, thankful he'd managed to keep the tremor out of his voice.

God, he was *so* down for that.

"Nope. Not what I had in mind."

Then what is he—

Alarm bells started clanging. "Er, no. Uh-uh. No kinky shit, remember? No nipple clamps, floggers, paddles… no benches…"

"That's not what I had in mind either."

The seed of an idea planted itself in Butch's head, unfurling shoots and tendrils faster than that fucking beanstalk in the story books. "Then what are we talking about?"

"You and me, naked, on a bed, and the only thing between us is a condom."

Holy fucking fuck.

Butch's skin couldn't seem to make its mind up whether it was burning up or ice cold. His mouth dried up, and his heart was beating like a whole battalion of drums.

"Okay, I've got the message," Sol said after a few seconds of silence. "That's a no." He sounded flattened, his usual confidence drained from him.

Wait—what?

"No, it's—"

"Like I said, it's okay. I won't mention it again."

I did that. I deflated him.

"Will you just shut up for a sec and let me get a word in?" Butch blurted out.

Silence.

Butch took a moment to breathe. "I want that too, okay? I mean, who wouldn't? You're gorgeous."

Sol chuckled. "I used exactly the same word to describe you a short while ago."

Butch momentarily forgot his consternation and glowed. "You said that about me?"

"Uh-huh. No word of a lie."

Damn, he felt like a million dollars.

"So if we're on the same page, what's the problem?"

Butch stared at the water cascading over rocks, flowing around them, a happy, bubbling sound that lifted him.

Maybe it was better this way, not being able to see Sol's face while they talked.

"Would... would you want to fuck me?"

He caught Sol's soft exhale. "Ah. Are we talking about who tops, who bottoms? Because I do remember what you said. You've only ever topped, haven't you?"

"About that... I didn't tell you everything."

"Is it something you feel you can share? Because if it isn't, that's okay." Sol's voice was as warm as his words.

Butch's pulse was calm and steady. *Tell him.*

This was Sol, and although he couldn't explain why, Butch felt *safe.*

"The first guy I ever had sex with—his name was Race, by the way, but that isn't important—he always let me top, apart from this one time. It was probably my fault. I said I was ready, and I wasn't, and we were both a little drunk." He chuckled. "Actually, we were a *lot* drunk. The bottom line? I didn't like it, and I told him I wasn't gonna do that again." He winced at the memory. "It hurt."

"Maybe he didn't prep you enough, or—"

"I'm not gonna go into details, all right? Afterward, he was mortified. Kept saying sorry. I think it was the booze, because he usually went out of his way to make sure we both enjoyed it."

It took him a moment to realize Sol had gone quiet.

"Sol? You still there?"

Sol's rough chuckle eased his nerves. "'Bottom line'? Was that a deliberate choice of words?"

Butch laughed. "You know, I didn't even think about it."

"So… just to check I've got this… you *do* want to fuck me?"

He laughed again. "Sorry, but this has to be one of the weirdest conversations ever."

"It's taken your mind off Diana, at least for a while, hasn't it?"

Butch's heart hammered. "That isn't why you—"

"Fuck, no." Sol sounded horrified. "This is *not* me distracting the hell out of you, all right? This is me trying to tell you I want you."

Lord, the relief…

"I want you too. And yeah, I want to fuck you. Although I *am* kinda surprised you'd let me near your ass."

"Why?"

"Well… you're a Dom, right?"

"I never told you that, but yes, I am." A pause. "Oh, *I* get it. You think Doms always top, is that it?"

"Well, yeah."

Sol's soft laughter told him he might have gotten that part wrong.

"No one ever makes you sign a contract that says Thou Shalt Never Bottom, you know. I can't speak for every Dom, but I *love* taking a dick."

"Why? What makes it so good?" Butch had always wanted to ask Teague the same question, but theirs hadn't been an arrangement where conversation had played a huge part.

Theirs was more of a *wham bam* kinda deal.

"I love clenching my muscles tight around it, and hearing him moan because I've brought him to the edge and he can't hold back a moment longer. I love that feeling when he's all the way in, and we're locked together, his sweat dripping onto my skin, his smell filling my nostrils, his groans so fucking loud because he's buried his face in my neck and he's picking up speed. The throb of his cock when he comes…"

Butch's shaft was steel. It was rock.

It was fucking *diamond.*

"So in case you missed it, yes, I want you to fuck me. And when I see you next, that's what we're going to do. But be warned—"

"No ki—"

"Yeah, yeah, I got that part. You know, you can protest *too* often. What I was *going* to say was… I like to kiss while I fuck, whether I'm pitching *or* catching."

Sweet mother of God.

"That'll be a first."

"The kissing? I knew that."

"No, that wasn't what I was talking about."

"Then what *are* we talking about?"

Confession time.

"Race, Teague, every guy I've ever fucked… They were always on all fours, bent over the bed, face down, kneeling on the couch…You get the picture."

A moment of silence had his heartbeat quickening.

"You've never fucked a guy face-to-face?" Before Butch could respond, Sol continued. "Of course you haven't. It's that 'If I can't see who I'm fucking' scenario. But that was *then*. This is a whole new Butch. A Butch who sucks dick, kisses like he invented it…"

A Butch who was sitting on the front porch, his fly unzipped, his cock out, and he was pulling on it, heat racing through him, pushed to the edge by Sol's words, Sol's voice, and the images in his head of his dick sliding into Sol's tight body…

He moaned as warmth seeped through his fingers, his body shaking.

"Fuck, you just came, didn't you?"

"What gave it away?" He glanced at the wooden deck. "Aw shit. I'd better clean up before I leave."

"And now I can't wait to see you again."

What made Butch's heart dance was not Sol's words but the light in his voice, the energy he'd come to recognize as being part of Sol.

Then reality set in.

"You won't have time," Butch remonstrated. "You'll be too busy doing… whatever it is you'll be doing." He didn't want to think about that part.

"Can I remind you of something? I'll have a room to myself. With a bed. In a space where I can make all the noise I want when I come because no one will bat an eyelash. And no one will mind if there's a sexy cowboy sharing that bed every single night of my stay. Robert can work your body during daylight hours—at night, you'll be mine." Sol chuckled. "And I'll be all yours."

"I can't be out of my bed every night for a week," Butch protested.

"Why not?"

"Why not? Because… people will talk, that's why."

"So? Let 'em. Talk can't hurt you."

It was as if Sol had dunked him in ice water.

"We're gonna have to agree to disagree on that one."

Silence fell, and Butch knew he'd hit the mark.

"Listen, Butch, while I'm there, we—"

"Sorry, but I need to go now. I'll see you in a few weeks, although you might not see much of me. It's a busy time of year at Salvation. See ya." He hung up, his pulse rapid, his chest tight.

That was close.

A small part of him argued that he couldn't avoid the subject forever. What if Sol made multiple visits?

The rest of him argued that he'd have a damn good try.

He glanced at his limp cock, his cum-coated fingers.

Clean-up time.

He went indoors in search of tissues, water, and a towel, his stomach churning again.

Three weeks till he's back. And while Butch loved the idea of getting naked again with Sol, the prospect left him torn.

Close enough to fuck is close enough to talk.

Talk about a dilemma.

CHAPTER 34

Thursday, September 8

Sol clicked on *Republish* with a sigh. Another satisfied customer. And only three more sites to create before his next break.

Thank God. Work was kicking his ass. He hadn't been to the club since… well, since his visit to Salvation, and his regular clients seemed to have either disappeared off the face of the earth, or they too were experiencing work/life balance challenges.

Two weeks of no scenes, no sex, nothing.

This is really bad. If it continues, I could apply to be a monk in a monastery.

He snorted. He would *never* let it get *that* bad.

The closest he'd gotten to any action had been inadvertently making Butch shoot his load during their phone call a couple of days ago, and *fuck*, that had been hot, not that he'd let Butch know that.

Bet you couldn't do it again.

Sol had indulged in phone sex on more than one occasion, and listening to a sub breathless with need, waiting for Sol to say the magic words—'You can come now'—was the hottest thing ever.

Saying 'You can't come' was even more delicious.

But Butch wasn't his sub and he didn't play those kinds of games, so while Sol was reasonably certain that yes, he could probably talk Butch into an orgasm, he wasn't going to do it, even if Butch turned him on like no one had in a long time.

And you scared him off last time, remember?

Yeah, he was still kicking himself over that one. He knew the moment the words left his lips that he'd fucked up.

I didn't think before I spoke.

And Butch had ended the call faster than green grass through a goose. The chances of him wanting to speak to Sol again were slim to non-existent. The only problem was Sol wanted to know how Diana was doing. He'd had a text from Toby two days ago, and Sol had thanked him for the update, mentioning that Butch had called.

Toby has his hands full, what with the upcoming launch, taking care of Robert...

Calling Butch for another update was totally logical in the circumstances.

Yeah, he could rationalize with the best of them.

He scrolled through his contacts for Butch's number and hit Call. By the time it had reached five rings, Sol knew it was a bust: Butch did *not* want to talk to him. Not that Sol could blame him for—

"Hello? Your timing sucks, by the way."

Butch didn't sound all that pissed. The note of amusement was a welcome addition.

"Have I caught you at a bad time? What are you doing?"

Butch chuckled. "I'm standing on steps, painting a wall."

"Hell, it's not the side of a barn, is it?" He had visions of Butch falling and breaking his neck. He could see the tombstone already—*He Fell Because An Asshole Phoned Him At A Really Bad Time.*

Another chuckle. "Nope. Did you ever see the cabin down by the creek? The one that belonged to the boss's mom?"

"Yeah, I rode past it when I was staying there."

"I'm prettying it up for Toby and the boss. Well, really it's for the hands. Toby said we can use it if we want to invite anyone to stay over, so I'm getting it ready for guests. And we have you to thank for it."

Sol grinned. "I knew they liked the idea, but I'm so happy they're making a move on this."

"Did you call for any particular reason?"

"Is the paint drying on your brush? You want to get back to it?"

Butch laughed. "I'm using a roller, and I've just climbed down and put it in the tray of paint."

"I was calling to see how Diana is. I didn't want to call Toby."

"She's doing much better. They should be bringing her home Saturday. Course, she'll need to rest up a while."

"That's great. So, what have you done to the cabin? Apart

from painting it." He'd gotten this far and he was reluctant to let Butch go, not while they were talking and laughing, banishing his last epic fail of a call into the trash can of *next time keep your fucking mouth shut.*

Okay, not *all* of it had been an epic fail, just the last part.

The earlier part had formed the basis for his fantasies since his return to San Francisco.

"It's only getting a lick of paint because it hasn't been used in a long time. I've been out buying new bedding, towels, and a new mattress because how anyone slept on the last one is beyond me. It isn't a huge space—it's basically one big room—with a living room, a tiny kitchen, and a separate bathroom. There's an open staircase leading up to a mezzanine, you know, like there is in the big house? Only theirs is much grander. But in the cabin, that's where the bed is, with this teeny window over it. It's kinda cute."

"And they let you do the painting?" he quipped.

There was a pause.

"You saying you don't think I'd be any good at it?"

And there you go again, smartass. Better put a lock on that mouth of yours.

"I'm sure you are," Sol said quickly. He needed to turn this conversation around. He smiled to himself as he added, "You've got a nice steady hand."

Okay, that was wicked and he knew it.

Butch cleared his throat, and Sol tried not to picture him adjusting his package. *Score.*

"Place needed a damn good clean." Butch's voice was gruff.

"You're going to stock up on the essentials?"

"Yup. Shampoo, bodywash, coffee…"

"Those weren't the essentials I was thinking of."

There was the tiniest pause before Butch said, "Yeah, got those too." His voice sounded like a blunt saw driving through wood, and Sol grinned. *Score two to me.* "Course, have to remember we could have male *or* female guests. And we can't have it looking like a whorehouse either. Hell, what if someone's mom or sister comes to visit?"

Sol hadn't considered that. "I see your point. I'd only thought about bringing guests there to—"

"Yeah, that was my thought too. I just wanted to mess with

your head. Call it payback."

This was turning out better than Sol had hoped.

"Who gets to try out the place first?"

"We haven't discussed it yet. Toby only got me working on this on Tuesday. But weekends will be the most popular times, so we might be talking about a roster."

"And will you be adding your name to it?"

"Hadn't thought about it."

The prompt response intrigued him.

"Is that code for 'I *have* thought about it but I don't want to tell *you* that'?"

There was a pause. "Would it bother you if I did?"

Sol had to think about that. What disturbed him was the realization that yes, it *would* bother him—a lot.

Change the subject.

"When will you be done at the cabin?"

"Once I've finished painting and moved all the furniture back inside—not that there's a lot to move—*then* I'm done. What about you? What are you up to?"

"I've just finished setting up a website. Nothing like the one I did for Robert and Toby. This is a site for model railway enthusiasts."

"Seriously?"

"Hey, there are a lot of them out there."

"Takes all sorts, I guess." Then Butch went quiet, and goosebumps pricked into life all over Sol's arms.

"You still there?"

"Yeah, I'm here. Just thinking."

"What about?"

"You remember we talked a few days ago?"

"As I recall, it was a memorable conversation." Butch coughed, and Sol smiled. *Score three.* "What about it?"

"Well, I've been thinking a lot about something you said."

Sol couldn't resist. "Good to know you've been thinking about me, because I've been thinking about you."

"See, you say stuff like that, and whatever I was gonna say goes clean out of my head."

"Okay, I'll shut up and listen."

"You... you were talking about... taking a dick."

Oh dear God.

Okay, Sol hadn't expected that.

"Still listening."

"It's just that… well… I'm finding it hard—I mean, difficult—to match up your description with my experience."

He could have easily resorted to humor, but instead, Sol went with serious. "I can understand that, given your particular experience." He paused. "Can I ask something personal?"

Butch's snort filled his ears. "Dude, I've had your dick in my mouth. I think that's probably as personal as it gets."

Sol fought the urge to tell him it could get *way* more personal than a blowjob, but that would involve a hand—or more—and a *whole* lotta lube.

"Good point. Okay then. Have you ever played with your ass?"

Crickets.

"Butch?"

"Er… no."

"Not even a finger?"

"No."

"But you fingered the guys you fucked, right? You know, *before* you—"

"Did I ever say that?"

Sol stilled. "Seriously? You never prepped them? *Ouch.* And I can say that because I've seen your cock."

"No, they did all that."

What the fuck?

"Every guy you've ever been with… you let them prep themselves? Why? Because sticking your finger in their assholes was somehow more gay than sticking your *dick* in there?"

"And now you're makin' me *sound* like an asshole," Butch groused. "I feel like one, too."

"There's a reason for that. But hey," Sol added quickly, "that was the old Butch Buchanan, remember? I'm talking to the new-and-improved Butch." His heartbeat slipped into a higher gear. "The Butch who's okay with accepting a little challenge in the name of self-discovery."

Butch's voice was rich with caution.

"What kind of challenge?"

"Call me back from the barn, and I'll tell you."

A pause. "Which barn?"

"I think you already know the answer to that question."

Yet more hesitation, and Sol started to regret his impulse.

"You don't have to," he said in a low voice. "No pressure, okay? It was just an idea."

"Tell me more about this idea of yours, and I might consider it. In the name of self-discovery," Butch added.

Sol thought fast. "You talked about the difference between my experiences and yours. Well, I want to show you what you've been missing out on. It's something you can do on your own, in your own time." He paused. "I also think it's something you'll enjoy." He chuckled. "There's only one fly in the ointment."

"And what's that?"

"I won't be there to watch you come like a geyser. And you *will*, trust me."

Butch went quiet.

"You still there?"

He cleared his throat again. "You really think I'll like it that much?"

Sol grinned. "Satisfaction guaranteed."

"So why are you sending me to the barn?"

"Because I want you to go to one of the cabinets in the main room, and pick out a couple of things that are going to help you on this voyage of discovery."

Butch chuckled. "You're enjoying this, aren't you?"

Not as much as you're *going to.*

"How do you know what's in the cabinets?"

Sol clicked on a folder on the laptop and smiled. "Because I'm looking at the photos I took as we speak. Well? Are you going to accept my challenge or not?"

His instincts said yes, but Butch had already surprised him once today, so he wasn't counting his chickens.

Butch sighed. "Give me an hour to finish here, clean up, and get to the barn. But if there's *anyone* around there, this isn't happening, you got that?"

"Got it." When Butch fell silent again, Sol frowned. "You okay? Is anything wrong?"

He's changed his mind.

292

"I'm gonna do this, because I have to tell ya, you got me real curious. But… there's one thing I'm sorry about."

"What's that?"

"You won't be there to watch. Talk in an hour." He hung up.

Sol sagged into his chair.

My *timing might suck, but Butch is a goddamn master at it.*

The next hour was going to drag *so* much, but Sol would be ready for the call. Because now he had a goal.

Butch Buchanan was going to shoot his load again, and *this* time, Sol wanted to hear every sigh, moan and whimper that escaped those soft lips.

CHAPTER 35

Butch stared at the bench Matt had posed on.

How come I never noticed those before?

At each end of the bench were two metal rings shaped like the letter D, and a wave of heat rolled over him. *They're for tying someone down.* He shivered, and it wasn't an unpleasant sensation.

His phone buzzed in his jeans pocket and he took it out, peering at the screen.

It's been over an hour. You need more time?

Butch rolled his eyes and hit Call. "Dude. Impatient much? I had to go to the bathroom, okay?" The prospect of putting anything near his ass had sent him into a panic, and he'd spent almost fifteen minutes getting himself as clean as could be down there.

He was *going* to tell Sol his ass was clean enough to eat off it, but pulled it back at the last minute. That conjured up an image he did not *want* to leave in his head for too long.

"Sorry. And good call, by the way. Are you in the barn?"

"Yup."

"I'm guessing there's no one around then."

"You guess right. Walt and Owen have taken the guests to where the herd are grazing, giving them some genuine cowboy time. They'll be back in an hour or so." Toby and the boss were at the hospital, and Matt was working on supper. Paul was probably in the stable, so Butch was pretty sure he wouldn't be disturbed.

His heart had been thumping ever since Sol had hung up.

Can't believe I said yes to this.

"Okay. You see the two cabinets against the wall? Go to the one on the right and open it."

Butch approached the tall wooden cabinet, his pulse rapid. He gazed at the contents. "Sure are a lot of... things in here." Some of them made his heart beat even faster, and set something fluttering in his belly.

Sol chuckled. "Think of it as a toy chest. Can you see the

dildos and vibrators?"

Butch glanced at the shelf and snorted. "That's not a dildo—that's a traffic cone."

"Turn the camera on. Show me."

"I thought you could see all this stuff in your photos?" Nevertheless, Butch clicked on the icon, and Sol's face filled the screen, his blue eyes bright. There had to be a window close by, because the afternoon sun played over his tanned bare chest, highlighting the curve of his pecs, the dip below his sternum, and the hollow between his collarbones.

Sol smiled. "Hey there, gorgeous."

Whatever he'd been about to say was lost in a rush of warmth. "Hey." He cleared his throat and peered closer. "Are you in bed?"

"Technically, I'm *on* bed. I wanted to be comfortable while we talked. And much as I would love to look at your handsome face all afternoon, I believe I mentioned a little challenge?"

He managed another eye-roll. "I haven't forgotten."

"Then flip the camera and show me the dildos."

Butch did as instructed, pointing to the bronze monstrosity that had caught his attention. "That's not a toy, it's an instrument of torture."

Sol laughed. "Yeah. Toby's favorite dildo was about that size. He named it Gargantua."

"Can't think why," Butch murmured.

"Look at the top shelf. See the pretty little vibrators?"

Butch peered at them. There was one shaped like a long, slim cock, another that was neon-pink, and yet another that looked for all the world like a real dick—

Something caught his eye. "What's this?" He picked up the black object. One end was slightly curved and sleek, made of shiny plastic, and there was a lip in the center, comprising little nubs. The other more bulbous end was made of matte silicone, soft to the touch, also with a slight curve to it.

Butch stared at it, and his hole clenched. "Just so I'm clear on this… you want me to put this in my ass?"

"You got it. Except that one might be a tad ambitious for a first time."

He gazed at the toy. The business end of it was at least as thick as three of his fingers. "I think I'm with you on that." He peered at the shelf. "What about this one?" He picked up the neon-pink tube with a switch at its base. "That's more my kinda size."

Sol laughed. "And such a pretty color too. Okay, we'll go with that one. Third shelf from the bottom. Grab some lube."

He flipped the camera back and stared at the screen. "You don't think Toby's gonna be pissed that I'm using his supplies?"

Sol's eyes twinkled. "If it makes you feel better, I'll bring a brand-new bottle of lube with me to replace that one. And you can wash the toy when you're done. You'll find a spray in there to get it clean as a whistle." His lips twitched. "The lube, Butch. Time's ticking away."

Butch grabbed the nearest bottle. "Now what?"

"You know those rooms off the hallway? You're going to go into one of them."

He gaped. "But what if someone comes into the barn?"

"Then you'll need to be real quiet."

Butch's breathing hitched. "Who says I'll be making any noise?"

Sol grinned. "I do. Now… pick a room."

The toy and lube in one hand, his phone in the other, Butch stepped into the hallway that led off the main room, and tried the handle of the first door on the left. It opened, and he flicked the switch.

There wasn't much in there: a chair, a small table on which sat a folded towel, and—

"There's a bed in here."

Sol chuckled again. "Of course. Sometimes you want more than a bench, a chair, the floor…" He paused. "A wall."

That last one sent a ripple of—anticipation? Excitement? Fear? —through him, and once more, it wasn't unpleasant.

"But it's covered in black vinyl."

"Easier to wipe off spunk and lube than throw sheets in the washer." Sol's eyes locked onto his. "Take your jeans off."

Holy fuck, they were really gonna do this.

Butch placed the phone on the bed, pulled his boots off, and removed his jeans, his dick already at half-mast. He picked the phone up. "Now what?"

He might be nervous but his cock was sure taking an interest.

"Sit on the bed, your back to the wall, feet on the mattress."

Sol paused. "Then spread your legs for me."

He shivered. "This is so fucking weird. Don't know why I'm doing this."

"I do." Sol regarded him with such an intense gaze that Butch's heart lurched. "You need to get out of that rut you've worn yourself into. Push your boundaries. And of course, we both know the main reason why you're standing in that room."

"And what's that?"

Sol didn't break eye contact. "Because I asked you to." Then he smiled. "And if you want, I'll be here the whole time. Your call."

Butch's heartbeat quickened. "I want you to stay."

Sol beamed. "You have no idea how that makes me feel." His lips twitched. "Butch? On the bed, remember?"

He climbed onto it, his head and shoulders against the wall, knees bent and wide, feet planted on the mattress, both the toy and lube within reach. "Ready."

"You know why it feels good to have someone touch your hole? There are a ton of nerve endings around it. So just start by rubbing slowly over it."

Butch held the phone so that the camera focused on his face, then reached down and stroked over his hole with the pad of his finger.

Sol nodded. "Nice and slow. Circle it, feel it contract beneath your fingertip."

He had to admit, it felt okay.

"Right, you're going to need both hands for this part. Squeeze some lube onto your fingers. I'll stare at the ceiling while you do it."

Butch's heart hammered, and his mouth dried up.

"Butch? Something wrong?"

Say it. Say it now, before you change your mind. Say it while you still have the nerve.

"When we were talking before, when I was at the cabin… You remember what I said just before I hung up?"

Sol became still, his eyes fixed on Butch. "You bet I do. That was one hell of an exit line."

"Yeah, about that…" Dammit, he was shaking. "The thing is… you *are* here. So… if you want to watch…" He swallowed. "What I'm *trying* to say is… I want you to."

Sol's eyes shone. "I am *so* fucking proud of you right now."

Butch could hear it in Sol's voice, and fierce exhilaration flushed through him, *surged* through him, leaving him so joyful he didn't know whether he wanted to dance, cheer, whoop, explode, or all of the above at the same time.

"Gimme a sec, okay?"

Without waiting for a response, he launched himself off the bed and grabbed the towel from the table. He folded it, placed it at the midpoint of the mattress, then leaned his phone against it. Butch resumed his previous position, peering at the corner of the screen, his heart pounding when he saw himself, his cock pointing at the phone, legs spread.

Just what in the world do you think you're doing?

This was so far out of his comfort zone, Butch doubted he'd ever find his way back to normality.

Then again, did he want to? *Wasn't this the whole point?* Sol had said he was there to push his boundaries. *I've been on this path for the last thirty years, give or take.*

It was time for a change of scenery.

He realized Sol had gone quiet, and he glanced at his phone.

Sol gazed at him with parted lips. "Look at you."

Butch had never felt this exposed his whole life, but the way Sol focused on him, the light in his eyes, the way his breath caught...

Fuck, that was an *amazing* feeling.

His hand shook as he squeezed lube onto his finger.

"Look at me, Butch."

He stared into those blue eyes, his pulse racing.

"Any time you want to stop this, say your name. You got that? You're allowed to change your mind, okay?"

He took a deep breath. "Okay. But you set me a challenge, and I'm not backin' down."

"Good man." Sol chuckled. "So I guess that means we've gone from FaceTime to AssTime. And it's such a gorgeous ass."

Butch was lost for words. *AssTime?*

He reached over his balls again, but this time he pressed the tip of his slick finger against his hole.

"Go slow," Sol urged him.

Butch glanced at the screen and managed a smile. "I will if you will." He knew it was bold of him, but hell, Sol could always say no.

Sol's eyes widened, and he dropped the phone. "One second!" he called out. A moment later, Butch's screen was filled with the breathtaking sight of Sol, nude, knees apart, his cock pointing to the ceiling, one finger buried deep in his hole.

Despite his nerves, Butch laughed. "You were already naked, weren't ya?"

Sol grinned. "Okay, you got me." His eyes sparkled. "Now catch me up."

Butch watched, mesmerized, as Sol pumped his middle finger in and out, his stomach quivering, his breathing shallow. Butch pushed his own finger into warmth and tightness, stilling for a moment when everything got *too* warm, *too* tight.

"Take a few deep, slow breaths. The more relaxed you are, the easier it'll go in. And remember—you're not so much pushing, as allowing your body to pull it in."

Sol brought his hand to a standstill, and Butch knew he was waiting on him. He squeezed a little more lube onto his finger and tried again, but *fuck*, it was tight.

"Let's try something. Squeeze your sphincter, then relax it a few times. Feel the difference between relaxed and tight. And each time you relax, move your finger in a little deeper."

Butch followed his instructions, and it wasn't long before it slid right in, *so* much better than before.

"That's it. Keep it slow."

Butch did as he was told, and while it was okay—maybe he'd even go so far as good—it wasn't as awesome as Sol had led him to expect. Watching Sol finger his own ass was much more of a turn-on.

"Ready to move out of Neutral?"

He frowned. "This is *Neutral?*"

Sol chuckled. "Hell yeah. Now we get to Drive." He moved his hand lazily up and down his thick shaft. "Coat the vibrator with lube, then slide it in."

Butch slicked up the neon pink tube, then eased it into his hole, noting how Sol followed every motion of his hand.

Sol grinned. "Push the button on the base."

Butch did as instructed, and—

"Oh my God." It felt for all the world as though someone had lit a fire under his feet and it was spreading slowly though his whole body, working its way to his head. There was sensation *everywhere*, not just in his cock, and so much of it. That first incredible rush of pleasure had him hooked, and it just kept on coming.

He didn't know what was happening. Too much sensation, in every part of his body, lighting him up inside...

Sol nodded, his finger still sliding in and out. "Someone stretching me with his dick? The idea turns me on, and yeah, it feels so good, but something nudging my *prostate*? Holy fuck. It's an actual button for sheer physical pleasure." His face glowed. "Fuck, I *love* watching a guy's face the first time he finds it, and discovers what it can do." His gaze drifted lower and he smiled. "That is so hot."

Butch glanced down. His dick oozed cum, nothing like the spurts he was used to when he orgasmed, but a steady trickle sliding down his bobbing shaft. He hadn't even touched his cock.

Then he pressed the button once more, and the vibrations intensified.

"This thing has different *speeds*?" he panted. "And you didn't tell me?" He felt a rush of heat to his face, and soon it had spread everywhere in a slow tide, burning him up until it was like a volcano erupting inside him. The sensations intensified, and he willed himself to relax into them, let them carry him along on a wave of pleasure.

And then it started to feel *really* good, a kind of strange, suspended throbbing, almost as if he had to pee, and he couldn't hold the moans in a second longer. He had to give voice to the toe-curling, *fucking-take-me-now*, eyes-rolled-back out of body explosion that was like nothing he'd ever experienced.

If shooting his load was a ten, this was off-the-scale awesomeness.

He touched his dick, and that was all it took to have him coming, a beautiful, intense and internal drawn-out orgasm that robbed him of breath. His hole spasmed, something else that was new, and he groaned again, chasing the sensation, unwilling for this extravaganza of physical delight to be over.

Then it was done, and that too was nothing like the ejaculations he'd experienced. The usual lightning punch of ecstasy, followed by a thunderstorm of mini-quakes and jolts gave way to an orgasm that was slower, more intense, echoes of thunder that rumbled on and on, stretching out the moment until it finally died, leaving him bereft of spunk and in a heaven he hadn't known existed.

The screen blurred, and Butch realized he was seeing Sol through blotches of cum, Sol's groans loud and heartfelt. A moment later, Sol wiped his phone clean and flopped onto his back, staring up at Butch.

"Back with me?"

Butch managed a weak smile. "I think so."

Sol's face was flushed, his eyes still bright and shining. "So the next time I suggest playing with your hole…"

Butch grinned. "You won't hear any arguments from me." He drew in a deep breath. "Is it always like that?"

Sol chuckled. "First times can be awkward, uncomfortable even, until you relax enough to let it happen." He paused. "You were fucking beautiful when you came. It was the sight of you that pushed me over the edge." The rough, throaty quality to Sol's voice sent a shudder through him.

His words finally registered. "So there *is* going to be a next time?"

Sol's smile was like sunshine on his skin, warm and welcome. "If you want there to be."

Butch grinned. "I think you already know the answer to that." He glanced at the black vinyl slick with lube and spattered with cum. "I think I'd better get this place cleaned up before everyone gets back."

"About that… If you want to do this again, but someplace that's a little more private, there's always the cabin, right? I mean, it *is* for the use of the ranch hands, right? As long as you leave it the way you found it?"

Butch chuckled. "Great idea. Anyone could be forgiven for thinking that was the whole reason behind you suggesting it to the boss." He stilled. "This wasn't some evil plan of yours, was it? To provide a private little spot so we could—"

"Butch Buchanan, just how big is your ego? Are you saying I came up with the idea expressly for the purpose of having my wicked way with you?"

Butch's face was on fire. "Of course not."

"I'm relieved to hear it." That twinkle in Sol's eyes gave the game away.

Butch groaned. "You really had me going for a minute there. You always were good at yanking my chain."

"Then I'll be good from now on." He grinned. "The only thing I'll be yanking is your dick."

Butch had thought his cock was out for the count, but apparently it was listening, and it liked what it heard.

Sol's expression softened. "I meant every word, by the way. You were beautiful. And yes, guys can be beautiful too." He looked Butch in the eye. "Especially when they're in the throes of their first p-spot orgasm." He grabbed a towel. "Now get your butt out of there before Toby catches you."

Butch nodded. He picked his phone up, and Sol's face filled the screen.

"Thanks, Sol."

Sol blew him a kiss. "Anytime, gorgeous." Then he was gone.

Butch got off the bed, not surprised to find his legs trembled.

I had no idea. But now he knew what he'd been missing? He wanted to experience it all over again.

He knew, however, that when night fell, he'd be lying in bed thinking about what had just happened—and recalling every word Sol had uttered.

CHAPTER 36

Saturday, September 10

Teague walked into the bunkhouse just as Gary, Logan, and Rog dumped their bags by the door.

"We're all ready here," Butch told him. Once he got back, it would be clean-up time.

"I'm glad I caught you before you left." Teague took his hat off and addressed the three guests. "I came to say goodbye, and to offer apologies from the boss. It wasn't exactly the week you were expecting, especially the start of it. We've all been a little preoccupied around here."

Gary widened his eyes. "Hey, there's no need to apologize. I'm just relieved she's okay."

"When does she get to leave the hospital?" Logan asked.

"This afternoon."

"I don't know about these two," Rog began, "but I've had a great week. And I'm kinda intrigued about this new venture of yours. I saw the website last night."

"Do you want a look around the place before you leave?" Teague offered.

Rog stilled. "Oh, no, it's not for *me*. Not my scene at all. But I have some friends who'd definitely be interested. I already sent them the link."

Teague smiled, and Butch was reminded what a handsome guy he was. There hadn't been many smiles the past week.

"Thank you." Teague caught Butch's eye. "You ready to take these three gentlemen into Bozeman for the shuttle?"

"Yup."

"Do we have time for a last look at the stable?" Gary asked. "I wanted to say goodbye to Paul too."

"Sure." Butch pulled his phone out and checked the time. "You've got about fifteen minutes before we have to be out of here."

"Great."

"Here." Matt tossed them a couple of apples from the bowl on the table. He grinned. "For the horses."

They laughed and headed outside.

Matt was on his phone a heartbeat later, still grinning.

"And what's got you so goddamn happy?" Butch demanded.

Matt's eyes gleamed. "I've got a date tonight."

Zeeb snorted. "Is that what we're calling it now?"

Matt gave him the finger, then turned to Butch. "You did say the cabin would be ready by the weekend, didn't you?"

Butch stared at him. "We haven't even drawn up a roster yet. The paint's hardly dry."

Matt rolled his eyes. "We're not going there to admire your handiwork, Butch."

Butch put his hands on his hips. "This 'date' of yours," he said, hooking his fingers in the air, "Can he ride a horse?"

Matt's lips twitched. "I don't know. It wasn't listed as one of his skills on his profile." Then he grinned. "Wait—I tell a lie. He did say he likes riding." His eyes held a wicked twinkle. "I just don't think he was talking about a horse."

That earned him a cackle from Zeeb.

"Then take him the back way to the cabin, in a truck."

Matt nodded, smiling. "Good thinking. Thanks."

"Well, that's all settled," Teague announced. "Matt gets first use of the cabin." He frowned. "Wait a minute. Your date might have to be canceled. The boss has moved next week's Saturday supper to this evening."

Matt blinked. "When did he do that?"

"Just now. That's one of the reasons I came down here."

Matt ran his fingers through his hair. "Okay. I guess I can have everything ready for supper time. I was going to meet this dude at eight o'clock." He chuckled. "You'll have eaten everything but the dining table by then. If a couple of you would clean up after, I'd be most grateful."

Walt stroked his excuse for a beard. "Let me see. Volunteer to load the dishwasher while you're out having a good time..." He grinned. "Course we will. We'll just be jealous as hell while we do it."

"Why did the boss move it?" Zeeb asked Teague.

"I think that's because Monday's party sorta fell flat,

understandably. But now he's got something to celebrate."

"When do you think we'll see Diana here again?" Butch had wanted to visit her in the hospital, but Toby's request to work on the cabin had kept him busy, and besides, she had the boss and Newt there every day. She didn't need to see him.

"Don't rightly know." Teague glanced at the bunkhouse interior. "We've got two guests arriving at three o'clock, and two more at five. Just make sure—"

"Don't worry, this place will be shining like a new penny by the time they get here," Butch assured him. "How're we lookin' for the grand opening?"

Only two weeks to go. *My, but the time has flown.*

Teague pulled out his phone. "So far… nine bodies. That's two singles—one of them Sol—two couples, and a throuple."

"A what?" Zeeb gave him a puzzled glance.

"It means three guys, but they're together." Teague grinned. "I thought everyone knew that."

Three?

Butch gazed at his fellow ranch hands.

"Life around here is gonna be mighty interesting."

The new guests had arrived and unpacked, and everyone was due up at the house at six-thirty. The others had already taken the guests there, and Butch was the last to leave. He was more than ready for Matt's meatloaf, mac and cheese, meatballs and pasta, and a chunk or three of freshly made bread.

He swore he could smell it all the way from the house.

Toby stuck his head around the bunkhouse door, and Butch grinned. "You slummin' it? Shouldn't you be getting ready for supper?"

He laughed. "I'm here because of you." In his hands he held a package covered in plain brown paper. "This came for you this afternoon. Special delivery." He shook it. "Well, whatever it is, it doesn't rattle."

"And if it's made of glass, you've just broken it," Butch flung back at him. He held his hand out for the package, but Toby didn't relinquish it. "Can I please have *my* delivery?"

Toby turned it over. "You expecting something?"

"Nope. I haven't ordered anything." He glared at Toby. "Give. Me. The. Package."

"There's a return address label." Toby squinted at it. He straightened, his face one huge shit-eating grin. "Erotique, huh?"

Butch frowned. "That store on Willson Avenue?"

"Oh, so you do know it, then?"

Butch rolled his eyes. "Dude, *everyone* knows it. Little old ladies from churches all over Bozeman have been handing out leaflets warning people not to go in there, 'cause it's a 'den of iniquity'. And before you ask, no, I've never been in there, and no, I haven't ordered anything from there either."

Toby handed him the package with obvious reluctance.

When he didn't move, Butch arched his eyebrows. "*Dude*. I am *not* gonna open it with you standing there."

"Fine. Spoilsport. See you up at the house." Toby turned on his heel and walked out.

Butch waited for a moment just to make sure Toby really had gone, then ripped the wrapping paper off to reveal a cardboard box. He opened it and saw—

The sleek black toy that had caught his attention on Thursday. It was encased in plastic, and there was also a bottle of sex toy cleaner and a bottle of lube.

No card.

His phone buzzed, and Butch set the box down to look at the screen.

It was from Sol.

I know you've got it. Just received a text saying it was delivered a while ago. Thought you'd have messaged me by now.

Butch's thumbs flew over the keyboard.

Toby only just brought it over. Why are you sending me this? It isn't my birthday. And even if it was, this is one weird gift.

Sol: Thought that was obvious. So you don't have to borrow the one from the barn. You seemed kinda partial to this one.

Butch: And just where do you expect me to use it? Remembering where I sleep—and how many others sleep there too?

Sol: I guess you'll have to find a place where you can be private—and bare your ass.

    Butch: You are evil. EVIL.

    Sol: LMAO Not gonna deny it.

    Butch: Can we talk?

    Sol: No. I'm at a conference—counseling stuff. The guy who's speaking is sending me to sleep. Figured I'd have more fun with you.

    Butch: well, I've got supper up at the house, so your fun ain't happening. Later, dude.

He switched his phone off, stuffed it into his pocket, then grabbed the box and went over to his bed. There was no place in his drawers for it, and he wasn't about to leave it in plain sight. He shoved it under his pillow, and hurried out of the bunkhouse.

Any later, and all the food would be eaten by the horde of locusts he lived with.

He walked briskly up the path, his mind still on the shiny toy.

Butch had never bought a sex toy in his life, but he supposed it was never too late to start. At least now he had a name for the fiendish device that had grabbed his attention: the label on its packaging said *Prostate Massager.*

    He's trying to kill me. Death by orgasm, that's what it'll say on my death certificate.

He could almost hear Sol's voice in his head.

Yeah, but what a way to go.

The boss met him at the door.

"We've been waiting for you."

Butch removed his hat and stepped into the cool interior. "Sorry, boss. Had to deal with… something."

He smiled, and Butch was so goddamn relieved to see Robert Thorston happy again. "Got a surprise for you."

Butch wasn't sure he could take two surprises in one day.

He followed the boss into the dining room, and his heart did a little dance to see Diana sitting there, chatting with Toby and Zeeb. Her face lit up when she saw him, and she held her arms wide. "Come here, you."

Butch went over to her, bent down, and found himself hugged so tightly it robbed him of breath. When she released him, he kissed her on the cheek and stroked her hair.

"How you feelin'?"

She bit her lip. "The doctor says no horseback riding until I'm fully healed."

"And you're gonna listen to him, right?"

Diana smiled. "Yeah. I've already had the same lecture from Robert and Newt." She took hold of his hands and squeezed them. "Thank you. Robert says you were wonderful."

"I didn't do all that much," he protested.

"Sounds as if you kept your head. Newt says thanks too."

"Why didn't he come with you?"

She chuckled. "We have guests, remember? He's been running the place single-handed all week." Diana tilted her head to one side. "And what have *you* been up to?" Her eyes sparkled. "You've got this glow about you. I like it. Happy is a good look on you."

I guess I am happy. What shocked him was that it showed.

Diana gestured to the table. "Now sit and eat while there's still food left."

He joined the others, and helped himself to a good-sized portion of mac and cheese. The boss's good mood was infectious, and the atmosphere in the room was jubilant.

Butch pulled his phone from his pocket to check for messages, and was grateful not to have his mouth full at the time.

I bet you'll make the hottest little whimpers when you slide it in and turn it on. Turns *me* on just thinking about it.

Butch wasn't going to reply. It would only encourage him. He placed his phone face down on the table. A minute later, it buzzed, and he peered at it cautiously.

In case I didn't tell you the other day… Your hole is goddamn perfect.

Butch wiped his brow with his napkin, and Zeeb gave him an inquiring glance.

"You feelin' okay?"

Butch forced a smile. "It's hot in here, that's all."

Buzz.

Fuck, now what? He turned his phone over.

Can't wait till it's my fingers inside you.

Walt chuckled. "Someone's popular tonight." He winked at the others. "Maybe Matt isn't the only one who's getting—"

Teague coughed loudly and inclined his head toward the four guests seated with them. Walt clammed up pretty damn fast.

Yeah, it was official. The next time Butch saw Sol Davenport, he was a dead man.

Buzz.

Butch fired a look of pure trepidation at the screen.

You know what else would feel good in there? My tongue.

Fuck. Fuck. Fuck.

Butch was torn between *Really?* and *Oh my God I wanna know how that feels.*

Buzz.

You look amazing when you cum.

He couldn't take a second more. His dick was like a rock in his jeans. He typed quickly, not glancing at the faces around the table.

Will you stop this? I'm having supper, everyone is here, and you're turning me on.

Sol's reply was swift. *Are you hard?*

Nope. Nope. Not going there.

Answer me. Are you hard?

Butch groaned internally. *Yes.*

Touch it.

He gaped at the screen. *Is he out of his fucking mind?*

"You sure you're okay?" Zeeb frowned. "Because I have to tell ya, you're acting mighty strange tonight."

"I'm fine. Something has… come up, that's all." And he was willing it to go down again before he had to stand.

No, he texted back.

But you want to.

Damn it, the man knew him way too well.

Butch?

Okay, okay, I want to. Happy now?

Matt chuckled. "Sorry, dude, but the cabin is taken for the night and I am *not* about to share."

Diana frowned. "The cabin? Mom's old cabin?"

The boss explained what they'd instigated—the safe for work version—but Butch wasn't really listening.

Buzz.

How long are you going to wait before you get that thing humming against your p-spot?

Butch typed fast. *Well, it sure won't be tonight, so quit making me think about it.*

Sol: I'm sorry.

Butch: No you're not.

Sol: SNORT. Okay, I'm not. But one last thing.

"Are we disturbing your obviously enthralling conversation?" The boss's eyes twinkled. "Want us to leave the room and let you continue?"

"I'm gonna tell them I can't talk right now," Butch told him.

"Should've told 'em that five minutes ago," Zeeb muttered. Then he gave Butch a sly smile that told him Zeeb would be asking questions later.

Butch picked up his phone to tell Sol goodnight—and his breathing hitched when he read the words on his screen.

Thank you for trusting me. That was such an awesome thing you did, letting me see you at your most vulnerable—something I'm sure you haven't done before—and it was something I won't ever forget. Goodnight.

It was such a contrast to the dirty flirty texts, and Butch could hear Sol's voice as he read the message once more. Warmth radiated through him, and what filled him was the glorious feeling that all was right with his world.

Diana was right. I am happy.

He was under no illusions—his present state was because of Sol.

Maybe it *was* time to finally let himself be happy, and not feel guilty about it.

Maybe.

CHAPTER 37

Sunday, September 11

Thirteen days till he gets here.

Thirteen more days, and then…

It was the *and then* that set Butch's heartbeat racing, his stomach churning, and his dick trying to bust through the zipper on his jeans. He replayed Sol's words over and over on a loop, and each time the shiver of anticipation got more and more intense.

'I want you to fuck me. And when I see you next, that's what we're going to do.'

'I like to kiss while I fuck.'

'At night, you'll be mine. And I'll be all yours.'

As for spending his nights in Sol's bed, no one would bat an eye, not if they thought it was just him and Teague doing what they'd done for the past five years.

It's not as if either of us has come right out and said we're not fucking anymore, right?

Yeah, that didn't sit well with him, and he felt certain Teague would feel the same way. And there was nothing wrong with telling the others he and Sol were doing a little horizontal dancing, right?

Except they weren't dancing—yet—and Butch wasn't going to breathe a word until he'd talked to Sol.

He could change his mind.

He could hook up with one of the guys who's staying over there with him.

Someone who lives his life the way Sol does.

It was those kinds of thoughts that killed his mood now and then, like a heavy blanket weighing him down, and throwing it off took a real effort.

Sunday afternoon had been drawn-out and lazy. Paul and Walt had ridden out with the guests that morning to hunt deer and elk, getting ready to stock the freezer for winter. And when they'd returned in good spirits, Matt turned up with coffee and snacks, and they'd sat around the bunkhouse table, chatting about their day.

Right then the guests had taken over the bathroom, and Matt was busy preparing supper. Zeeb was sitting on the couch, cleaning rifles. He glanced up from his task.

"Fellas? Y'all know it's my birthday end of the month, right?"

Walt laughed. "No, really? You could've told us." He pointed to the calendar stuck on the fridge door, with the twenty-ninth circled in red, and *Zeeb is 40* written on it.

Zeeb rolled his eyes. "Just for that, I'm not gonna invite you to my birthday celebration."

"You still planning on going to a casino?" Butch asked him.

"Yup, that's the plan. Any of you wanna come along, you'd be most welcome. I'm gonna stay the night in Livingston, and if you wanna do that, you'd better book yourself a room."

"I love the idea," Matt said as he placed bowls on the table. "But the boss won't let us all go."

Zeeb grinned. "Ya think? Well, it so happens that I spoke with the boss this morning after breakfast. He said as long as there's one of us here with the guests, for insurance purposes, it's fine by him. So… Who's comin' with me?"

"I've never been to a casino," Paul remarked. "Do I need to wear a tux?"

Zeeb laughed. "Hell no. You've been watching too many James Bond movies. It's a whole lot more casual than that."

Paul smiled. "Then count me in. I'd better save up for it."

Walt snorted. "You'll need to."

"That mean you won't come?" Zeeb asked.

"Are you kidding?" He grinned. "I wouldn't miss it."

"Me too," Matt added. "And if you want a cheap room for the night, I can recommend a hotel."

"I'd like to go," Butch told Zeeb. "But then there'll be no one minding the store, if you get my drift."

Zeeb grinned. "All taken care of. Owen says he'll do it. He said it would make a change from sleeping with only the herd for comp'ny."

"Then okay, I'm in too."

"I was gonna ask Sol if he wanted to join us." Teague frowned, and Zeeb held his hands up. "I know, I know, he'll be here as a guest, but he's more than that, an' we know it. And he *will* be here that week, right?"

Teague nodded. "Run it past Toby. See what he says before you invite him." Zeeb whipped his phone out, and Teague chuckled. "I didn't mean right this minute."

"Hey, no time like the present." Zeeb went outside to make his call.

"You think Sol will want to come with us?" Butch wasn't sure how he felt about Zeeb's idea, and he couldn't put his finger on exactly what was bugging him.

"He doesn't have to say yes if he doesn't want to," Teague said with a shrug. "He might get a kick out of it. And if Zeeb feels comfortable enough to want to invite him, I think that says a lot."

Zeeb burst in through the door. "Toby says go for it," he announced, beaming.

Teague pointed to Butch. "Get Butch to call him. He's got Sol's number."

Zeeb's eyebrows shot up. "Yeah? Oh, right, you two went to high school together. I forgot. Call him, see what he says."

Butch laughed. "You mean now, don'tcha?" He shook his head and went outside. He strolled over to the paddock to his favorite leaning spot and took his phone out.

You got a minute?

A moment later, the phone rang.

"Are you still talking to me after yesterday? I thought you might be pissed about the texting."

"I was," Butch admitted. "Until that last message. I couldn't stay pissed at you after that. But that's not why I'm calling." He outlined Zeeb's plan, and his invitation.

"I've only been to a casino once. It was a charity event, and it was a lot of fun. Are you going?"

"Yup."

"Okay, then I'll go too." He paused. "Actually, I was going to call you this evening. Something I wanted to ask you, especially after our last... exchanges."

"Oh Lord, do I wanna hear this?"

"How do you manage to jerk off when you share a room with all those guys?"

"Quietly," Butch said with a grin. "There's always the bathroom. In the shower first thing in the morning works for me. Any other time of the day, then it's a little more complicated. I usually wait until everyone's asleep."

"How often do you jerk off? If you don't mind answering such a personal question."

"I think we already covered that last week. Depends. Sometimes it could be every two days, sometimes more like three or four. Nothing like when I was a horny teenager. Getting older sucks."

"I hear ya."

"So why are you asking? You writing a psychological profile of the sexual habits of cowboys?"

"I spend a lot of my time asking subs about how often they come. Sometimes, when I'm planning a scene, I tell a sub he can't come for a day or two."

That one word threw him for a second.

"Sub... that's a submissive, right?"

"You know the word?"

"Toby might've mentioned it. So... you get to tell your sub he isn't allowed to come?" Butch snorted. "Good luck with that. Why would anyone agree to that?"

"Because when they do come, the waiting makes it so much more intense, more... voluminous."

"Now *there's* a big word."

"So I was thinking... would you like to try it?"

Butch blinked. "Me?"

It was on the tip of his tongue to remind Sol he wasn't talking to one of his subs.

"Yes, you. Was I right about playing with your hole?"

"Yeah."

I ain't submissive. Not by a long shot. I've been the one on top ever since I started fucking guys.

Then why wasn't he saying all that to Sol?

"Was it as amazing as I said it would be?"

He had him there. "Yeah."

"So believe me when I tell you this will be just as awesome. Well? What do you say?"

Wait just one goddamn minute.

It felt as though he was standing at a door, one that Sol wanted him to walk through—a door leading into something new, and huge, and scary as shit.

He's treating me like one of his subs.

This is what he does, right?

What shocked the fuck out of him was how much he wanted to see what lay on the other side. Because all this stuff Sol was coming out with had him hooked.

What we did last Thursday… is that the kinda thing he does with his subs too?

If it was, then maybe Butch had already taken a step through that doorway without even knowing it, and he wasn't sure how that made him feel. But the conversation had sewn yet another seed, and he was torn.

What if he's right again?

Would it really matter if this is a sub thing?

Sol hadn't come out and said as much, had he? And after all the internal wrestling Butch was doing, everything boiled down to one crystal clear thought.

I wanna see just how good it can be.

His heart pounded.

Say yes, before you change your mind.

Before he lost his nerve.

"Okay." He was so fucking proud of how confidently he uttered that one word.

"In that case… how about we start with no jerking off for a week?

"A *week?*" he yelled into the phone. "I was thinking a day."

Hell no. Hell to the fucking no.

"But where's the challenge in that? You can already go a couple, three days without jerking off—you said so."

"Yeah, I did, didn't I?" *Me and my big mouth.*

"So how about we say you can't come until I call you a week from today. This time Sunday. Only, you'd better make sure you're someplace private."

"Why?"

"Because when I say Butch, you can come now', you're going to want to shoot then and there."

"I can't see me being that desperate." All of a sudden, it was no longer a matter of simply holding off for a week—he had to *wait* to be told he could come?

What filled his head was the thought of being balanced on a

precipice, his body aching for release—and hearing Sol's rich voice praise him when he obeyed that command.

He *so* wanted to do this.

"Well, you haven't factored in the effect of my calls."

Aw fuck. "What calls? You didn't say anything about calls."

"Or I might text you."

Butch had a feeling he knew what those texts might comprise.

"Tell me one thing. What do *you* get out of this?"

He could hear the smile in Sol's voice. "I get to hear it. Or if I'm very lucky, see it."

"I don't know about this." Except that was a lie. The more he heard, the more he yearned to try it.

"But *I* do," Sol assured him. "Think about it. That feeling of anticipation. You know it's going to happen. You're looking forward to it, thinking about it, *dreaming* about it… You'll have a horny little buzz going on all week. And when you do come, it'll be all the better for delaying it."

"Just so long as you're not gonna be calling or texting me to get me all riled up."

Sol chuckled. "Ooh, I can't promise that. I could make it easier on you though."

"How?"

"I could let you jerk off, but tell you not to come. If you think you could be that disciplined."

Okay, that was reverse psychology and he knew it. "You think I can't make it, don't you?"

Sol laughed. "I don't think any such thing. I'm sure you can go a whole week without coming."

"You put that 'whole' in there on purpose. You're playing with my mind."

And I'm letting you do it. He could see where Sol was leading him from a mile off, and yet it didn't change his mind.

"Then we're agreed. I call you a week from today, and if you haven't come, you get to jerk off. If you have, then next time we'll make it two weeks."

Butch did the math. "Hey, now wait a minute. Two weeks from next Sunday would be after you'd left Salvation."

"Mm-hmm."

"And you're talking about us fucking while you're here."

"Mm-hmm."

"So you'd expect me to fuck you and *not come?*"

"Them's the rules, dude. So you'd better not come between now and Sunday."

One last chance to talk himself out of it.

"Why should I do this?"

"Because it's kinda fun?"

"Hey, Butch," Zeeb hollered. "Is Sol coming or not?"

Sol was coming—Butch, it seemed, was not.

He's right. It's a challenge. And if it's half as good as that vibrator turned out to be, then I want this.

He wanted it *so* badly.

"Yeah, he's coming."

Sol chuckled in his ear. "You got that right." Then he hung up.

I must be crazy to agree to this.

He knew why he'd said yes. He wanted to see Sol's face on his phone when Butch announced he'd gone the entire week without spilling so much as a drop of cum.

I'll show him.

The last thought to flit through his mind before he went back inside was something that messed with his head.

Maybe he sees something in me that no one else sees, because why else would he talk to me like that? Maybe I'm not as dominant as I thought.

And if he wasn't dominant, then that meant…

Fuck.

Butch thought he knew himself.

What if I've been wrong all this time?

CHAPTER 38

Monday, September 12
Sol: You made it to 24 hrs, right?
Butch: [eye-roll emoji] Seriously? You have to ask?
Sol: I have faith in you.
Butch: You should, because I'm gonna do this.
Sol: Good for you. Back to work for me. Later.

Tuesday, September 13
Sol: Woke up this morning thinking of you. This was the result.
[photo of an erect dick]
Butch: 2 can play at that game.
[photo of an equally erect dick]
Sol: You didn't play with that? I wouldn't have been able to resist.
Butch: Are you kidding? I didn't even touch it, except to tuck it in.
Sol: Wise move. I bet it feels silky to the touch. Just looking at it, I want to trace that vein with my tongue.
Butch: UR evil.
Sol: Like I said, not denying it. Now put that pretty cock away and get back to work.
Butch: Hey, you messaged me, remember?
Sol: LOL

Wednesday, September 14

Sol: You doing okay?

Butch: Yes.

Sol: That's all I get?

Butch: Yes.

Sol: You're just scared that anything you say will provide me with ammunition, aren't you?

Butch: [eye-roll emoji]

Sol: So I'm not allowed to show you this?

[video: A close-up of Sol's ass, his finger sliding in and out of his hole, his breathing shallow]

[voice] Can't wait to feel your dick in here. Was thinking about it all last night.

[video ends]

Butch: U fucker.

Sol: I don't need ammunition. My head is already full of you. And soon, my ass will be full of you too.

Butch: Going now. Bye.

Thursday, September 15

Sol: 4 days.

Butch: You like torturing me, don't you?

Sol: Of course. How else would I get my shits & giggles? You're a delicious distraction from my work.

Butch: Working with a hard-on is not fun.

Sol: Are you hard right now?

Butch: Yes.

Sol: Show me.

Butch: No.

Sol: Please.

[photo of Butch's flushed hard cock]

Sol: Look at that. My mouth is watering. My hole is clenching. No, really, it's got a life all of its own, because I'm looking at your dick and letting myself imagine.

Butch: Sol...

Sol: Too much? Are your fingers itching to touch it? Is there pre-cum?
Butch: I hate U.
Sol; OMG there is, isn't there? You feel like you want to pop any second.
Butch: I'm going to do this, okay? 3 more days.
Sol: Go you. And now I'm going too. Hang in there.

Friday, September 16
Butch: Thought I'd text first for a change.
Sol: Nice surprise.
Butch: What have you done to me?
Sol: ???
Butch: I could go for a few days without feeling the need to jerk off. Hell, at my age, I could go for a month without sex. But it's been 5 days and it's all I can think about. I blame you.
Sol: I couldn't make it easy on you, could I? Had to make it more of a challenge.
Butch: You've done that, alright.
Sol: Want to talk about how you're going to cum on Sunday?
Butch: How??? You're kidding, right? I'm just gonna call you, say 'Hey, guess what? It's been a week.' Then I'll drop trou, give it maybe one or two tugs, and that'll be all she wrote.
Sol: Oh sweetheart, you think it's going to be that easy?
Butch: Sol... what do you mean?
Sol: You'll have to wait till Sunday to find out. Now I need to get back to work. I'll be thinking of you.
Butch: Wait.
Sol: What's up?
Butch: This thing we're doing...
Sol: What about it?
Butch: You do this with subs, right? That's what you said?
Sol: Yes.
Butch: So... what does that make me?
Sol: Right now, it makes you a guy who's trying something new, something different. Because your way was getting a little tired, wasn't it? Deep down you wanted to break it off with Teague, but he got in there first.

Butch: How the fuck do you see what's in my head?

Sol: It's a gift. But I'm right, aren't I? You're doing this because you *need* this.

Butch: yeah.

Sol: It's gonna be worth the wait, I promise you.

Butch: Gonna hold you to that.

Sol: Whereas I just want to hold you. Bye for now.

Saturday, September 17

Sol: Still holding on there?

Butch: woke up this morning and started pulling on it without thinking.

Sol: Did you cum?

Butch: No, but fuck, it was hard.

Sol: LMAO. Are we talking about your cock, or the effort it took not to keep going?

Butch: Both.

Sol: I'm proud of you.

Butch: What is there to be proud of?

Sol: You didn't have to do this. You could've lied. If you jerked off, I'd never know.

Butch: But I'd know. I'm not doing this just to prove I can - although that is part of it.

Sol: Then why?

Butch: I'm doing it because you asked me to.

Sol: Fuck. You know what I want to be doing right this second?

Butch: Teasing the cum out of me?

Sol: No. Kissing you, until your lips are red and swollen and you've got beard rash.

Butch: Now you've done it.

Sol: Done what?

Butch: I'm thinking about kissing you, and I'm like a fucking rock.

Sol: Tomorrow night, okay? Find someplace where we can talk without being heard.

Butch: You still want me?

Sol: More than ever. Can't wait to hold your naked body against mine.

Butch: Sol… You're doing it again.

Sol: Then I'll stop. Tomorrow. You and me. A video call, if you think you can deal with that.

Butch: You watched me finger my ass and more. I think I can deal with it.

Sol: Goodnight.

Butch: Night.

Sol: Still hard?

Butch: SOL.

CHAPTER 39

Sunday, September 18

Matt cleared the dishes after supper, and Zeeb dropped a pack of cards onto the table.

"Poker, anyone? We're playing for Skittles, not money."

Walt laughed. "Skittles? Really?"

Zeeb held the bag up and shook it. "Yup. Wanna taste the rainbow?"

"Sure. Count me in."

It wasn't long before all four guests and most of the hands were squeezed around the table. Butch grabbed his hat and phone, and headed for the door.

Zeeb peered at Butch. "You not gonna join us?"

"Nope. I'm gonna take a stroll and watch the sunset." When all eyes focused on the cards, he picked up a flashlight too, shoving it under his jacket when Zeeb glanced at him again.

"You don't fool me none, y'know."

Butch feigned ignorance. "What you talking about?"

Zeeb hooked his fingers in the air. "'Watch the sunset'? You gonna take pictures of it too? That why you need your phone?"

"Is there a law against it?"

Zeeb cackled. "Nope. But I think your little evening stroll has less to do with observing nature and more to do with calling or messaging someone. Now, who that someone is, I don't have a clue, but you've been messaging them at all hours of the day and night, so I *am* mighty curious."

"You know what curiosity did, right?"

"So you're not gonna tell me?"

Butch snorted. "Got it in one." He left them to their game and stepped outside. Fall was definitely in the air: the temperature had dropped to maybe the low sixties. He stood for a moment to observe the changing colors in the sky, then took a photo. He grinned.

There ya go, Zeeb. Communing with nature.

He walked briskly toward the old barn. It would be private: no one was likely to walk in on him, not when they were all occupied with a game of cards. Once he was inside, he closed the door and switched the flashlight on. It wouldn't be long before daylight faded into twilight, and the barn was dark enough even on sunny days.

He'd woken up that morning hard as usual, but with something else—a buzz of anticipation that was almost intoxicating. He enjoyed the feeling of being horny, more aroused than he'd ever been, because all his senses told him his patience was about to pay off. He couldn't wait to experience the sexual high that awaited him.

The week had taught him a surprising lesson, one he wasn't sure he wanted to share with Sol. Yes, it had been an exercise in self-control, but as time passed, the more the idea of Sol directing him not to jerk off, not to come, turned him on. The thought of seeing Sol's expression as he watched what was certain to be an explosive orgasm had made him hard to the point of aching.

His phone buzzed in his pocket, and he took it out to look at the screen.

Ready this end.

Butch had been ready three days ago.

He hit Call, and Sol's warm voice filled his ears.

"You made it."

"Let's do this." He rubbed his crotch, his cock pointing toward his hip.

"Hey, not so fast. Don't I even rate a *Hi?*"

Butch snorted. "You wanna talk about the weather? The price of beef? Politics? Because while I can guarantee they might get my thoughts away from the pressing problem in my jeans, we could just skip to the chase and let me shoot a load."

"Where are you?"

"In the barn."

"*Which* barn?"

"The old one, where I kissed you."

Sol chuckled. "And blew my mind. Okay… take your jeans off."

"I don't need to do that. I could just push 'em down a bit and—"

"Take. Them. Off."

Butch pushed out a sigh of sheer impatience. "Fine." He put the phone on top of a hay bale.

"Wait!" Sol's voice burst from the phone.

Butch grabbed it. "Now what?"

"Turn the camera on. I want to watch."

That made him laugh. "Oh, so you want me to be a stripper?" He clicked on the camera and held the flashlight under his chin, making a noise like a wailing ghost.

Sol laughed his ass off. "You jerk."

"Shouldn't that be 'you jerk *off*'? Like, now?" He propped the phone against the hay bale, then set the flashlight down next to it, aimed at him. "Okay. Can you see me?" Sol was sitting on his bed again, only his head and bare shoulders visible.

"Perfectly. Now, slowly... Take 'em off."

Butch popped the button on his jeans and lowered the zipper.

"Oh Lord." Sol's voice cracked.

He frowned. "What's wrong?"

"Wrong? Absolutely nothing. You've gone commando."

Despite his aching dick and balls, Butch managed a smile. "You like that?"

"I love it! Who doesn't like easy access?"

Butch stared at Sol's face as he slid his hand into his jeans, his breathing quickening when his fingers touched warm, hard flesh.

Sol's low gasp was a delight. "You fucking tease."

"Says you, who've been teasing me all week. Payback's a bitch, ain't it?" He let go of his dick and went about the task of removing his boots and jeans. Once that was done, he put the boots back on. His cock pointed toward the phone, bobbing stiffly.

"Now the shirt. Open it. I wanna see that chest."

Butch didn't break eye contact as he freed each button, working his way down. He pulled the shirt flaps aside, his heart hammering. Sol was once again pushing him out of his comfort zone, and it was heady as fuck.

"Okay... nice and slow... pull on your dick."

Butch's breathing hitched. "Not sure I can do slow. Sol, I... I need to come."

"I know, but not yet."

He arched his eyebrows. "Are you for real?" His voice was

loud enough to raise a squeak or two from somewhere up among the rafters.

"Hush now. They'll hear you." Sol smiled. "Touch yourself. One hand on your cock while you play with your nipples."

Butch curled his fingers around his warm solid dick, feeling it throb in his hand, and tweaked a nipple with thumb and forefinger, sending a zing of electricity all the way to his balls, shooting along his shaft.

"This is torture," he whined.

"Feels good though, doesn't it? And when you do come, it'll feel even better."

"So you say." Not that he had any reason to doubt Sol. *He nailed it about the ass play, didn't he?* Butch slid his fingers up and down his shaft, fighting the urge to shoot his load right then and there.

"Now a little harder."

"Sol, please," he begged.

"Not till I say. Can you do that? For me?"

"I'll try, but if you suddenly can't see, you'll know I shot all over the camera lens." The comment wasn't entirely humorous.

Sol moved forward, and when he sat back, Butch had a much better view. Sol leaned against a mound of pillows, his jeans around his knees, and his hand on his cock, tugging on it with languid strokes.

"See if we can come together," Sol said with a smile. "Think we can aim for that?"

Butch chuckled and gripped his dick. "This is likely to go off at hair-trigger speed, you know that right?"

Sol grinned. "I'm pretty close myself. I've been thinking about this all freaking day."

"Getting one off?"

"No—watching you come."

Damn, that made him feel amazing.

"One hand on your shaft, the other on your balls," Sol directed, his own hand providing quite the distraction.

Butch worked his cock, and all too soon that buzz he'd been experiencing all week morphed into something much more intense, and he knew it wouldn't be long before the fireworks started.

"Sol, for fuck's sake, say the word."

Sol ignored the plea. "You look so fucking beautiful in that light. Your muscles, your pecs…"

Oh dear God, he was seconds away from losing it.

"Sol," he begged. "Not sure I can take much more." He closed his eyes, as if that would help him fend off his impending climax.

"Butch, look at me."

He opened his eyes and found Sol staring at him, his hand a blur on his cock.

"You can come now."

A groan forced its way out of him from someplace deep, his dick throbbed in his hand, and cum pulsed from the slit, his legs threatening to collapse under him as he shot onto the straw-covered floor. It seemed to be a never-ending stream, and he moaned, not wanting the waves of pleasure to stop.

Sol tugged on his own cock, aimed for his chest and groaned as he shot hard, sagging into the pillows, his body trembling.

Neither of them spoke for a minute or two, until finally Butch's brain cells unscrambled enough to try speech again.

"You didn't lie. That was… wow."

"For me too." Sol swiped his finger across his chest, then put it into his mouth. "Wish I was there to taste yours."

Fuck, he wished that too.

"What a rush. So here's my next question." Sol grinned. "Think you can do that again?"

Butch snorted. "Dude, I don't have a drop of cum left in me." He picked his jeans up from the floor and began the process of dressing, conscious of his sticky cock. He'd grab a shower before bed, and his jeans were going straight into the hamper anyway.

"That wasn't what I meant. Do you think you can keep yourself from jerking off again?"

What the fuck?

Even as he reacted, the thought was there. *Why not?*

This was addictive as fuck.

"How long for *this* time?" He narrowed his gaze. "Say a month, and I'm hanging up, right fucking now."

"Not even a week. How does that sound?"

"Like there's a catch."

"Wow, it's like you know me or something," Sol said with a wry chuckle. He smiled. "The next time you come, I'll be right there with you. Next Saturday. Think you can wait that long?"

Now *that* was what Butch called an incentive.

"In your room?" He picked his phone up, and Sol's face filled the screen.

He nodded. "Just you and me."

"Yeah, I can do that."

Sol beamed, and the sight sent warmth barreling through him. "That's good."

Except at some point during Sol's visit, he'd be doing more than jerk off.

"About what you said…"

"Which part?"

"You said there'd be nothing but a condom between us. Is that okay?"

"Of course. I don't use them all the time because I'm on PrEP, but I do with some clients."

Butch had no clue what PrEP was, but he wasn't about to reveal his ignorance. He'd google it later. Then Sol's words registered.

"'Clients'?" *Clients who are subs too?*

"I have guys who come to me for sessions. Bondage, flogging, a little cock-and-ball torture…"

"You fuck 'em?"

"Not all, but yeah, some." Sol cocked his head. "We never really talked about this, did we?"

Butch shook his head.

"You do know what I'll be doing during my stay?"

"I didn't, but I do now."

Sol chuckled. "I'll be there primarily to do demonstrations. I do a lot of those at the club—the one Toby used to run in San Francisco." Sol's eyes sparkled. "Why don't you come along? You might learn something."

"Thanks, but I don't think the boss would be happy about that. I work here, remember?"

And he wasn't sure which made his stomach quiver—the thought of guys getting tied up and fucked, or that it was Sol doing the tying up and fucking.

"Yeah, good point. But back to your question. Condoms work for me."

Butch cleared his throat. "I guess I'd better get back to the bunkhouse. There were already comments before I left."

Sol's warm smile was such a lift. "You feel better now though."

Butch laughed. "No, I feel amazing. Thank you." And he had it all to look forward to again.

A suspicion took root, and he frowned.

"This coming week... It's not gonna be like last week, is it? You know, with all the messages?"

Sol's grin was pure evil. "You'll just have to wait and see. And don't give me that. You liked them." He hung up.

Talk about getting the last word in.

Except Sol was right—he did. Already that same frisson of anticipation and desire was starting to trickle through him, although it did leave him a little perplexed.

What does it say about me that Sol can tell me what to do, and I not only do as I'm told, but I enjoy it?

He knew what it said, all right. He just didn't want to admit it yet.

CHAPTER 40

Saturday, September 24

The last of the guests were on their way home, and a buzz of excitement permeated the bunkhouse. No shocker there—this was virgin territory for everyone.

Butch had a totally different kinda buzz going on.

Sol's coming.

And that meant Butch would be too, pun most definitely intended.

Yet another week of abstinence, but it had felt... different. He'd been surprised by how much he'd enjoyed the anticipation. And Sol had nailed it—he'd been horny as fuck all week, but rather than frustrate him, it only made him focus on what was coming right at him.

Sol's texts? Now, they *did* frustrate him, but they also turned him on and filtered into his dreams. By the time he'd awoken Saturday morning, the idea of shooting his load consumed his thoughts, but coupled with that was the knowledge that if his recent experience was anything to go by, it was going to be *awesome*.

What sent warmth radiating through him was the thought that Sol would be there when he did.

First order of business was a meeting around the bunkhouse table with Teague, and all the hands were there, except for Kyle.

"Feels sorta weird," Zeeb confessed. "I mean, not havin' guests in here."

"That's why I'm here," Teague told him. "I need to talk to all of you before the first guests arrive." He glanced at Butch. "You're off duty today as far as picking up guests goes. Toby's doing that."

"Okay." The news crushed him a little. He'd been looking forward to seeing Sol's face when Butch pulled up at the hotel in Bozeman.

Guess I'll have to catch him later.

"So what are we doing this week?" Paul demanded.

"Your days won't look all that different," Teague told him.

"The guests are still here to chill, and that'll mean riding. So just go about your work as usual. The only difference is, we don't know how experienced any of 'em are on a horse, so you might get guys who know how to ride, and total newbies. Play it by ear."

"If they're stayin' in the new barn—we can't keep callin' it that, by the way," Zeeb remonstrated. "And I sure as shit ain't callin' it the Deliverance barn."

"Then how about the Leather Barn? Just among us?"

Zeeb grinned. "I like that. Okay, if they're stayin' in the Leather Barn, where do they eat? They gonna come over here?"

Teague shook his head. "They'll have their meals up at the house. One of the perks of their stay."

Walt smiled. "I expect they'll feel right at home with Toby and the boss."

"I think that's the idea," Butch murmured. His chances of getting to see Sol were growing slimmer by the second.

"So what happens when they arrive? Do they just… get down to it?" Zeeb asked.

"'Get down to it'?" Matt cackled. "What do our usual guests do on arrival day?"

Zeeb shrugged. "Unpack, chill, have supper, and then early bed."

"Which is probably what these guys will do too, especially if they've traveled a distance to get here."

"It's exciting," Walt remarked. "I've been thinking about it all week." He glanced at Butch. "You have too, I guess."

He frowned. "What makes you say that?"

"You've been real jumpy, like you've got ants in your pants or something."

"You're imagining things," Butch retorted.

Damn. Am I that transparent?

"I keep wondering what they'll be like," Paul mused.

Butch's nerves got the better of him. "You already know that. Just look at Toby and the boss."

"What do you mean?"

"It ain't all leather an' whips an' shit, and it's nothing like what you see on those videos." He stared at the faces around the table. "And don't tell me you haven't looked at 'em, because that's horse shit and everyone here knows it. Of *course* you have. We *all* have.

We're curious as fuck." The memory of the two men in that kitchen, the intimacy he'd witnessed, had lingered with him.

That's what BDSM looks like away from the leather, the spanking, the paddles, all of it. That's the face of it you don't *see on those videos.*

Zeeb gaped at him. "Well, if that don't beat all. This, from a guy who until just recently, wouldn't even admit—"

"You don't have to remind me," Butch interjected. "But a guy can change, can't he?"

"He sure can." Teague's voice was warm. "But guys… if you *do* see some of the guests in leather—or very little clothing—you don't stare, okay?" Teague told them all. "Your job this week is to be there if they need anything. You won't be cleaning up after them—Toby says they'll take care of the barn, because that's what they do. So really, you're gonna have an easy week."

"And don't forget, you're all coming with me on Thursday to help me celebrate the big forty," Zeeb added with a grin.

Butch's phone buzzed, and he glanced at the screen.

On my way.

Fuck, if that didn't make him feel like a million bucks.

By the time supper had come and gone, Butch was pissed beyond belief. He knew Sol had arrived, along with all the other guests, but there'd been no chance to pay a visit. The water heater in the bunkhouse chose that day of all days to die, and it fell to Butch to try and fix it, which ate up a couple of hours, but hell, he wanted another shower before he saw Sol. Then Teague called to say the guy who delivered the containers of drinking water had shortchanged them by two, and when Toby had signed for them, he hadn't noticed. So Butch had to drive to Bozeman to pick up the containers, because the delivery guy was unable to do a return trip due to his wife going into labor a week early, which probably accounted for his mistake—his mind was understandably elsewhere.

When supper arrived, it became clear no one had spied any of the guests, and it hadn't been for want of trying. Then Paul announced he'd seen them all heading up the hill to the house, and that they all looked normal.

He sounded disappointed.

Butch had grabbed a second shower before supper, in the hope that he'd get a moment to go see Sol, but since that morning text, there'd been nothing. And once Matt had cleared away the dishes, he had to accept the situation.

I guess I'll have to wait till tomorrow. What's one more night? Except it was more than the opportunity to come.

He wanted to see Sol.

It was a subdued Butch who undressed and climbed beneath his sheets that night.

He's here, less than five hundred feet from where I'm lyin', and it might as well be five hundred miles. He wasn't about to go knock on Sol's door—for one thing Butch had no clue which room was his—and for another, if Toby got to hear, he would be pissed.

Eleven o'clock arrived, and the bunkhouse was quiet. Butch hadn't slept a wink. He'd even kept his phone under his pillow, set to vibrate, hoping for a goodnight message, a pic, *anything* to show him he was in Sol's thoughts as much as Sol was in his.

His phone buzzed, and he made a grab for it, sending it clattering to the floor.

Fuck.

Butch lurched out of bed and picked it up. The screen was intact, but he didn't give a flying leap about that. What made his heart soar was a message.

My room, upstairs, 2nd door on the left. Don't knock, just come in.

He hurried into the bathroom, brushed his teeth—again— gave his ass a thorough cleaning—again—then crept out of the bunkhouse and over to the barn. Then he turned around and came back, opening the drawer next to his bed as quietly as he could to retrieve a handful of condoms—he lived in hope—and stuffed them into his pockets before heading out once more.

The barn was quiet, and there was a single light on in the main room. Butch crept up the wooden stairs, turning left into the hallway that led to the rooms. He stopped outside Sol's door, heart pounding, his breath leaving him in shallow bursts, and then he opened it and went inside.

Sol sat on the bed, dressed in jeans and a tee, and his face lit up as Butch closed the door behind him.

"I was starting to—"

That was as far as Butch got before Sol launched himself off the bed, zipped across the floor, pushed him against the door, pinning him there with his body, and kissed him with a ferocity that left Butch breathless.

"I thought I was going to explode," Sol muttered between kisses.

"I know. Me too."

"Then no more talking." Sol grabbed his hand and pulled him toward the bed.

Thank fuck.

Sol undressed him, taking his time, unable to resist the siren call of Butch's lips as he unbuttoned, unzipped, and tugged, until Butch was naked and they were both tumbling onto the bed. Butch lay on his back, and Sol stretched out beside him on his side, their bodies touching as he kissed his neck, pulling low moans from him as he sucked on the skin.

Butch gazed at him, his breathing labored. "What about you? Aren't you gonna take your clothes off?"

"Eventually, but it's not my priority right now." He smiled, kissed Butch on the lips, and stroked his chest. "That would be you." He slid his hand lower, grazing his fingernails over Butch's belly, loving the way it quivered, the whimper that escaped him. Then he moved lower still, until his fingertips met the warm, taut skin on the head of Butch's flushed, solid cock that pointed toward his chin. Butch shivered, and with a single finger Sol traced the line of his shaft that jerked up to meet his touch.

Butch's soft sigh was like nectar.

"I've been thinking about touching you ever since I left Salvation," Sol confessed. He curled his fingers around the shaft and rubbed over the head with his thumb. Butch squirmed a little, hips starting to rock as he tried to deepen the contact, and Sol claimed his mouth once more, keeping his kisses languid and sensual. He let go of Butch's cock and slid his hand along Butch's thigh, encouraging him to hook his leg over Sol's, opening him up, spreading him wide.

The hitch in Butch's breathing sent a zing of anticipation down his spine.

Sol cupped his cheek, turning his face to meet Sol's mouth, and they kissed, Butch feeding him low noises and sighs with every brush of Sol's lips against his. He kissed a path from Butch's mouth to his neck, and Butch groaned at the double assault when Sol wrapped gentle fingers around his dick and pulled on it, never ceasing to kiss the fragrant sensitive skin below Butch's ear.

"You like that, don't you?" he murmured between kisses.

"Ugh."

Sol smiled. "I didn't quite catch that."

He took Butch's growl of protestation for agreement, and kissed yet another path from neck to chest, pausing to worship at Butch's nipples, tugging gently on them with his teeth, then sucking them, until Butch's moans were constant. He kept his hand still, and Butch rocked his hips again, pushing his shaft through the funnel of Sol's fingers. Sol matched each sensual motion of Butch's hips, Butch's ass resting on his thigh, and they moved together, locked into a horizontal dance with a slow, teasing tempo he knew would soon explode into a more rhythmic display.

"Feels so good," Butch whispered between kisses.

"It's about to get better." Sol released his dick and trailed his hand lower, encountering the softness of his sac. He paused to roll Butch's balls through his fingers, then moved lower still until he met the warm cleft of Butch's ass. Butch tilted his hips, an obvious demand for more, and Sol ignored the plea, rubbing his thumb over Butch's taint with a slow circular motion.

"Tease," Butch moaned.

Sol chuckled. "Would a tease do this?" He planted a trail of kisses down Butch's torso, getting closer to where Butch's dick jumped as if tugged by an unseen cord, closer, closer, until there was barely an inch between the head where pre-cum glistened and Sol's lips.

"Please," Butch begged. "I'm so close, you have *no* idea."

Sol kissed his belly, the trail of fur that led to the root of his cock, and at last he closed his mouth around the head, holding his shaft steady at the base. He gave it nibbling little kisses, and the noises pouring from Butch's lips ramped up his desire until all he could think about was making Butch come.

Slow down.

He wanted this to last, to draw out Butch's pleasure for as long as he could.

Sol pulled free and turned his face toward Butch's.

"You can't come yet, okay?" And before Butch could protest, he unhooked Butch's leg, shifted further down the bed, and took Butch's cock deep, sliding his lips down the shaft.

Butch's groan of pleasure burst from him. "Aw fuck," he said softly, pushing up with his hips. Sol bobbed his head, gaining momentum, and each time he filled his throat, he was rewarded with a moan. Then he pulled free once more, a chain of saliva from his lips to Butch's cock, and shifted again until they were locked in a heated kiss while he stroked Butch's shaft and balls.

Time to move things into high gear.

Sol drew back and looked him in the eye. "Can you keep going?" Butch had to be perilously close to the edge after a week of no jerking off, and Sol hadn't made it easy for him.

"Yes," Butch croaked.

"Because I'm about to turn up the heat."

Butch's eyes widened. "It's already pretty hot."

"And I'm going to take it to inferno level." Sol smiled. "Flip yourself over, and get on your knees."

Butch's pupils dilated, and he swallowed. "Okay." He knelt up on the bed, and Sol pushed on his back and shoulders, pressing his chest to the mattress.

"Grab onto the pillow, and spread for me, nice and wide."

Butch turned to stare at Sol over his shoulder. "What… what are you going to do?"

Sol locked gazes with him.

"Blow your mind."

"Specifics, please."

Sol rubbed his thumb over Butch's hole. "What I had in mind was eating your ass."

Ice and heat vied for dominance of Butch's skin.

"I… I've never…"

"There's a first time for everything."

"But…" He couldn't find the words to express the tumult of emotions tumbling through his head.

This is gross.

This is wrong.

It's dirty.

And yet buried deep was the desire to know how it felt, why guys indulged in it… The desire to do something so taboo was winning out over all other considerations too.

"Do you want me to stop?"

Yes.

No.

Fuck, I don't know.

Then Sol removed his thumb and caressed Butch's hip. "We don't have to. It really *is* your choice."

"You'd be okay if I said no?"

"Of course." Sol's hand was gentle on his back. "I might call the shots, but not when it comes to something like this. You know your own limits—and I'll honor them."

A mixture of relief and elation barreled through him, and he went with his gut.

"Do it," he said with a groan.

Sol kissed and stroked his ass cheeks, and Butch loved the intimacy of it, the slow teasing, the way his heart raced as Sol spread him with both hands—

And the electricity surging through him when a warm tongue met his asshole.

Fuck.

It was like nothing he'd ever experienced.

It was warm.

It was electric.

It made his eyes pop out with the shock of how *utterly amazing* it felt, and damn it, he wanted to *see*.

Butch twisted his upper body to get a good look. *Fuck.* It was as if the act lit him up, making him notice every sensation: the sight of Sol licking a path over his hole while his thumb rubbed Butch's taint; the feel of his beard brushing against Butch's ass cheeks; his tongue flicking, switching between hard and soft, making out with his hole; the way Sol divided his attention between Butch's pucker and the delicate, sensitive skin around it, drawing with his tongue; and the *Holy Fuck* feeling when Sol went from barely pushing his tongue in, almost tickling it, to thrusting it as deep as it could go, sending waves of exquisite pleasure pulsing through him, his hole twitching beneath Sol's hungry mouth.

Sol's moans mingled with his own, and Butch buried his face in the pillow and let go, groaning into it. The sounds that poured out of him seemed to act as an invitation to keep going, and Sol worked his tongue deeper, tugging on Butch's stiff cock.

"Fuck, you taste good," Sol murmured, pausing to blow cool air on his hole, followed by a gush of warm air that opened him up, made his skin tingle—

Made him want *more*.

Butch hugged the pillow against him, unable to rein in his moans when Sol pressed the pad of his thumb into him. "Aw fuck, yeah." Sol traced a line with his tongue over his balls, pausing to suck them into his mouth, one at a time before carpeting his cheeks with tiny, intimate kisses. Then it was back to making love to his hole, one hand on his dick, the other on his ass, squeezing, kneading, and all the while Sol couldn't stay quiet.

Butch dug his fingers into the pillow as Sol spread him with both hands, fucking him with his tongue, Butch unable to stay still. Then Sol blew a stream of cool air onto his hole, and Butch knew what he wanted.

"Sol… Put your fingers in me," he pleaded, his heartbeat racing.

"You sure?"

Butch raised his head enough to gaze at Sol over his shoulder. "Sol… please."

Sol inclined his head toward the nightstand. "Toss me the lube."

Butch grabbed the bottle and threw it to him, then spread his legs wide, his arms once again enveloping the pillow, his breathing labored as he waited.

The *click* of the bottle cap sounded so loud in the quiet room, and a moment later a slick finger slid into his ass.

Sol paused. "Take a moment to breathe, okay?" He groaned. "Fuck, you feel warm and soft as silk in there."

"Don't stop," Butch begged.

Sol chuckled. "What makes you think I have any intention of stopping?" Soft lips pressed against his ass cheek, and Butch moaned as Sol corkscrewed his finger. The mattress dipped, and Sol straddled Butch's leg, rocking, making him hyper aware of the hard cock rubbing against his thigh.

Sol leaned over, kissed his shoulder and back, and Butch propped himself up on his hands, turning his face to beg another kiss, only now there was a hunger in their connection, Sol's finger moving in and out, faster, deeper...

When Sol pulled free, Butch pushed out a loud moan.

"Onto your back," Sol told him.

Butch flipped himself over, Sol stuffed a pillow under his head, and kissed him, a hard, claiming kiss that made him ache for more. Then Sol kissed a trail down to Butch's cock, and he groaned at the feel of that warm, wet mouth on his shaft. Sol took him deep, head bobbing once more, and Butch couldn't lie still. He sat up, leaned back on his hands, and watched Sol worship his dick with lips and tongue.

"Fuck. So good," he whispered. Then he put his weight on his elbows and spread his legs as Sol rolled his balls in his fingers before moving lower to slide them into his crease.

"Yeah, put 'em back in me," he cried.

Sol added a little more lube to his fingers, then took Butch deep again, except now he slid a finger inside him, settling into a rhythm. He pumped his fingers, matching each thrust with every slide of Butch's shaft into his throat, gaining speed.

Butch's hips bucked, and he knew he couldn't hold on anymore.

"Gonna come," he said, breathless.

Sol didn't slow down, didn't pull free, and Butch's groan was so fucking *loud* as he shot hard, filling Sol's mouth, watching his throat work as he swallowed every last drop. Multiple shivers wracked his body and he flopped onto his back, his chest heaving.

Sol knelt between his legs, unfastened his jeans, pulled his cock free, and gave it three sharp tugs. Warmth spattered Butch's stomach and chest, and the sight of Sol, eyes closed, mouth open, shaking with the force of his orgasm, was breathtaking. Sol scooped up some of his cum on his fingertips, and brought them to Butch's lips.

Butch didn't hesitate. He took Sol's fingers into his mouth, sucking on them, cleaning them of all traces. When he was done, Sol stretched toward the nightstand, grabbed a handful of tissues from the box there, and wiped up the rest. Then he slowly removed his tee and jeans, and lay beside Butch on the bed.

"Every time you make me come, I think 'that's it, he can't beat that.' And then you go and beat it." Butch shivered. "It gets more and more... intense."

Sol leaned over and kissed him. "That was the plan." He stroked Butch's damp forehead. "You don't have to go back to the bunkhouse tonight, do you? I mean, there aren't any guests." He smiled. "And I know this isn't as big as the bed we shared in Wibaux, but I don't mind close quarters so much. I'm all for a little snuggling."

Butch could handle a little snuggling right then. And as for any comments about his absence?

He'd deal with those if—when—they occurred.

All he could think of was spending another night with Sol, and *fuck*, the prospect made him so damn happy.

A little happiness was long overdue.

CHAPTER 41

Sunday, September 25

Butch woke to strong arms surrounding him, Sol's breath stirring his hair, Sol's hand covering his heart...

Sol's morning wood making its presence known, nestled in his crack.

That morning of so long ago came to mind, except it had been *his* dick making a home between Race's ass cheeks, and *Lord*, he recalled how he'd gotten out of that bed so fucking fast, in case Race woke up and got the wrong idea. He also recalled how he'd thought if the roles were reversed, it would've felt weird waking up with a hard-on against his butt.

And here we are, full circle.

Except now it didn't feel weird.

Now he closed his eyes and imagined the slow press of Sol's cock inside him. His fingers had set Butch's hole on fire—in a good way—and the vibrator had awoken Butch to the delights of his prostate, so it felt kinda natural to want to take things a step further.

Because if Sol's fingers and a little vibrator made his ass feel good, how would Sol's dick feel?

Sol's arms tightened around him. "Hey," he murmured, his voice still heavy with sleep. Warm lips met Butch's shoulder. "God, you smell good in the morning." He rocked against him, his cock doing a leisurely glide through Butch's crease, rubbing over his hole...

Making him *want*.

Nope. Nope. Nope.

Butch had a day of work ahead of him, and Sol would be doing his demonstrations, or whatever else he had planned. For all Butch knew, Sol's fingers would be buried in someone else's hole, and that thought made him shiver.

There was so much he didn't know—that he *needed* to know—and maybe it was time to start asking questions.

"You cold?" Sol enveloped him in warmth.

Butch couldn't tell him it wasn't that kind of shiver. "Not now," he murmured.

"What time is it?"

Butch glanced at the window above the bed. The sun was barely up, spilling its warm, golden light into the room. "'Bout seven-thirty."

Sol issued a throaty chuckle. "I thought you were up before dawn, you know, while it's still dark."

Butch smiled. "And so we are, usually, but not this week." He slid his hand down his torso, encountering Sol's fingers along the way, and reached his own hard shaft. "Thanks for that, by the way." He gave it a slow pull—

Until Sol's hand covered his, gently removing it from his dick. "Uh-uh."

Butch rolled onto his back. "You wanna do it, is that it?" He grinned. "I'm down with that." What he really wanted was to find a toothbrush, then get reacquainted with Sol's lips.

Butch had no idea kissing could be so addictive.

"Not right now. I'd forgotten—Toby said we're having an early breakfast up at the house, and I forgot to set my alarm last night." Sol smiled. "I was kind of distracted." He let go of Butch's hand and wrapped warm fingers around his shaft. "And while I'm here? This is off limits for you."

Oh dear Lord, again? Except part of him had been expecting it, if he were honest. "For the rest of the week?" Butch could feign frustration, but inside he was buzzing. He was getting to like this, the anticipation, the glorious release when he finally came…

Sol nodded, his eyes locked on Butch's. "And you only get to come when I say so. That includes when we're in this bed."

A suspicion was forming, and Butch's stomach clenched. "But I *do* get to come, right?"

Sol's cool stare was *not* the answer he was looking for.

What. The. Fuck?

Butch sat up and swung his legs out of the bed. He reached for his jeans where Sol had dropped them the night before, and squirmed into them, his dick still hard, creating a bulge as he zipped up. His heartbeat raced as he faced Sol.

"What's going on here?"

Sol arched his eyebrows. "You mean, apart from you having the best orgasms of your life? That isn't an exaggeration, is it?"

Butch stood there, his arms at his sides. "Okay, fair enough, they've been awesome. Not gonna deny that. But... What we're doing here... you know, you telling me not to jerk off, telling me when I can come... That's what you do with your subs, right?"

There was no putting this conversation off a moment longer.

Sol got out of bed and reached for his clothing, and Butch felt the change in the air.

Things had just gotten serious, and there was no turning back.

"I do it with some of them, yes. It's a favorite of mine."

Butch was aware of the blood pounding in his ears, the quiver of something unfurling in his belly.

"I gotta ask a question here. Do you do stuff like this with every guy you fuck?" Before Sol could respond, he added, "I guess what I'm asking is... is sex *always* a Dom/sub thing with you?"

Sol cocked his head. "Can I ask you something first? Have you liked what we've done so far?"

Butch swallowed hard. "You already know the answer to that."

Sol nodded. "And when I tell you what to do, how does it make you feel?" He didn't break eye contact. "Do you hate it?"

"No!" He hadn't meant to shout, but he couldn't hold back.

Sol walked around the bed to stand before him. "Does it confuse you, that you want to obey my instructions? You take orders every day, right?"

Butch frowned. "Yeah, but not *these* kinda orders. And as for how it makes me feel... I... I like it, but it confuses the fuck out of me." That fluttering in his stomach would not quit, and he felt as though he was starting to overheat.

Sol took a breath. "Okay... what *you* want to know is, am I always a Dom when it comes to sex?" He looked Butch in the eye. "The answer is yes. Do I tie up or flog every guy I fuck? No, but I do call the shots. I can't turn off that part of myself. And yes, sometimes it *can* be an all-night fuckfest where I tie him to the bed, cuff his ankles to a spreader bar, and make his hole mine, his body mine." He paused. "But it can also be as simple as telling him how I like to be fucked, drawing out his pleasure..."

Butch could live with that latter part, but it opened up all kinds of questions in his mind.

One in particular that he had to have answered.

"And where do I fit in? I know you said I'm trying something new, something different, but it's more than that, isn't it?"

Sol gestured to the bed. "Will you please sit down, just for a minute?"

Butch sat on the edge of the mattress, and Sol joined him. He got the impression Sol was as conflicted as he was, as though he was struggling to find the right words.

Sol let out a soft sigh.

"I'm giving you a taste of what I'm like—what Sol the Dom is like—with a guy he's interested in. And I *am* interested in you."

An unexpected lightness suffused his body, and his mouth dried up.

"But…"

That one word sent a tremor through him.

Sol met his gaze. "When you think of BDSM, you see someone wielding a whip or a flogger. I wanted you to see the man *holding* that whip. I wanted you to see *me*, learn about *me*—my likes, my fantasies, what turns me on, what gets me off." That tilt of his head again. "You want to know why that was so important to me?"

Butch couldn't speak, he could only nod.

"Because I wanted you to open up and give me the same back. Yes, I've shown you new stuff, yes, you've experienced feelings you've never felt before. But then I needed you to decide if you wanted more of them."

Butch's head was spinning, his mind racing.

"You said I take orders every day. That's true, but I never saw that as being submissive. And as for how I am with a guy, if you'd asked me, I'd have told you hell no, I've always been the dominant one." *Dammit, when did breathing become such a fucking chore?* He took a moment to force calm into himself, because what he had to say was *so* fucking important. "But with you…" He raised his chin and looked into Sol's blue eyes. "You tell me what to do, and it turns me on. You treat me like one of your subs—and it turns me on. It's as if you flicked a switch inside me, one I didn't even know existed." Another hard swallow. "And now I have to decide if I'm gonna leave it switched on or not."

And there he was, at the heart of the matter, at a fork in the road with two routes ahead of him, and not a fucking clue which one he was going to take.

Sol took Butch's hand in his. "I have so much I want to tell you, share with you... but there was something I needed to see first before I did that."

The feel of Sol's fingers laced through his made him yearn for more of that connection.

"What did you need to see?"

Sol lowered his eyes to stare at their joined hands. "Whether you were doing what I asked simply to please me, or..."

"Or?" Butch pressed.

Sol lifted his chin and smiled. "You nailed it. I had to know if there was a switch inside you, if it had always been in you, and I was just bringing that side of you out into the open."

Butch wanted to know the same thing.

A fragment of the previous night filtered back into his head. "Something you said last night... about honoring my limits." He'd wanted to ask about that at the time, but Sol's tongue in his hole had robbed him of all coherent thought.

Sol chuckled. "That's a conversation in itself." Then his expression grew solemn. "We can talk about this, but I need to message Toby to tell him I'll be delayed." He released Butch's hand and reached for his phone on the nightstand.

Butch rose. "No, don't do that. Go have your breakfast, and we can talk later."

What he needed right then was space to breathe, to think...

To process.

"If you're sure..."

He managed a smile. "I'm sure." He finished dressing, his thoughts still in a whirl. "Message me later, okay? There's stuff I need to do this morning."

Such as taking Bailey for a long ride to try to clear up the mess inside his head.

Sol waited until Butch's footsteps on the stairs died away, then sat on the bed, his elbows on his knees, hands clasped between them.

I should've foreseen this.

Butch had come such a long way in a very short time span, but he had to be struggling. Right then his life had to resemble a juggling act as he tried to work out who in the hell he was: bisexual, a (potentially) natural submissive, and maybe even a bottom—the episode with the vibrator and the previous night when he'd begged for Sol's fingers inside him made it all too clear Butch was considering that as an option, despite his first time being an epic fail.

I showed him how good it can feel.

And hadn't that been the aim all along?

Seeing him struggle brought all of Sol's caring instincts to the fore.

I just want to bring out the best in him. To let him enjoy experiences that had been denied him—or more accurately, that he'd denied himself.

Sol had used the miles between them to hang back, allowing Butch space to grow.

But into what? And does he want that?

Sol knew he was pushing Butch, but he had to know if he could coax out the submissive he was certain lurked inside him. There was so much Butch needed to know, the ins and outs of the BDSM lifestyle the videos he'd undoubtedly seen *did* not show. And such a conversation would have to be handled delicately, carefully…

When he's ready to talk, I have to be ready to lay it all out for him.

It was only then that the truth dawned.

I'm not doing this so he can discover himself and become another man's submissive.

Hell no.

Sol wanted Butch for himself, but there was still a long way to go before that could happen—if it could even get that far.

CHAPTER 42

Butch sat on his unfurled bedroll and gazed out at the calm, crystal clear waters of Mirror Lake. On the other side, majestic mountains rose up from a swathe of dark green pine trees, and rocky outcrops sloped down to the water's edge. The sky was eye-hurtingly blue, not a wisp of cloud to be seen, and the temperature was just right.

Summer wasn't ready to call it a day, apparently.

The peaceful landscape was not a reflection of the state of Butch's mind, however. He lay on his back, hands folded beneath his head, and stared at the sky above.

What the fuck am I doing?

Where do I want this to go?

The conversation with Sol had raised more questions than it had answered, and most of them were dancing around in his head. He could acknowledge a few home truths: he liked it when Sol gave him commands. He even liked the abstinence, although he wasn't sure how he'd cope without jerking off for longer than a week or two. The prospect of sex without an orgasm, however…

I'm not sure how—or if—I would cope with that.

What shocked him was part of him wanted the chance to find out.

Discovering Sol was always a Dom when he fucked had brought one question to the top of a long list.

He has subs… clients… How would I feel if I watched him in the barn? Watched him make someone else shatter the way he makes me shatter? Watched him fuck someone who wasn't me?

Because sure as shit, if he continued along this route with Sol, Butch would not be the only guy along for the ride, and he had no idea how he would feel about that.

He said there's stuff we need to talk about. Then I guess that's a conversation we're gonna have, and sooner rather than later. All this clatter and noise inside his head made it difficult to concentrate, to function, and he couldn't saddle Bailey and ride off every time he needed to think. He had a job to do.

Right now I don't have the full picture.

Maybe when he did, it would be easier to come to a decision.

Then why the fuck am I sitting here?

The answers were not to be found in the still waters of Mirror Lake—they were back at Salvation. And it wasn't until he was riding home that something occurred to him, something he hadn't realized until that moment.

Part of him wanted to be the only man Sol fucked, and he knew that was unreasonable and impractical—this was what Sol did, right? —but it also implied that somehow he was already connected to Sol, with ties that had nothing to do with sex or lust, but emotion.

Butch led Bailey into the stable. Lunch had been and gone, but he wasn't hungry. Right then he had more important things on his mind than food.

Paul smiled. "Good ride? You looked as if you needed to clear the cobwebs away."

Butch stroked Bailey's flank. "He's a good cure for that. Want me to brush him?"

"Nah, you're good. Besides, Teague was looking for you just before lunch."

"Then I'd better go see what he wants." Butch walked out of the stable, removing his phone from his pocket and switching it from mute. As he drew nearer to the bunkhouse, he caught the sound of laughter from inside, and he came to a dead stop.

I don't think I want to people today.

The only person he wanted to talk to was Sol, and he knew where to find him. What he *didn't* know was what Sol would be doing when he got there, and cold trickled through him.

I don't wanna interrupt anything.

If he had questions, there had to be other sources of information, right? And he wasn't thinking about videos involving gags, whips, paddles.... Hell, one conversation with Toby had provided a goldmine of information.

He just had to know where to look.

Butch headed for the old barn. It'd be quiet there, and he could peruse the Internet undisturbed.

Thank God my phone is fully charged.

He had a feeling this could take a lot of time, and even more battery juice.

Butch's phone buzzed, and he opened his messages. It was from Teague.

Where are you?

Damn it, he didn't want to talk to Teague right then. And then he noticed the time.

Three hours? I've been in here three fucking hours? Where the hell did the time go?

Down the goddamn rabbit hole, that was where.

He knew more now than he'd known that morning, and all of it made his head spin. On an impulse, he'd searched for the website for Toby's former club in San Francisco, and while there was a huge section dealing with kinks—and *holy fuck*, there were a lot of them—there was an equally large one that dealt with what went on behind the scenes.

LMAO. Scenes. That's funny.

He'd learned about SSC, starting with looking it up to find out what the letters stood for. One glance at the last word of the acronym brought Race to mind, and that had made him smile.

Safe, Sane, Consensual. You'd have approved of that, dude.

He'd read through the bit on aftercare, and then he'd found his way into a part all about contracts. There appeared to be a lot more protocol than he'd realized—respecting boundaries, limits, stuff like that—and a section about informing a Dom of any allergies, medical conditions…

I had no idea.

He'd already realized there was more to BDSM than kinky sex—he had Toby and the boss to thank for that—but now he was seeing everything laid out, the practicalities, guidelines, concepts...

It was no good. He needed to talk to Sol.

He's gotten me into something, and I'm not sure I wanna get out.

He wanted to know more, that was for damn sure.

Butch slipped out of the old barn and headed for the new one, steeling himself for whatever sight awaited him through those wide doors.

"Butch!"

Fuck. Teague.

He turned, pasting on a smile he certainly didn't feel. "Hey."

"You got a minute?" Teague strode toward him.

No, I do not. I've gotta see a man and get a shit ton of questions answered.

"Sure." He kept his tone light, leaning against the paddock fence.

Teague caught up with him. "Paul said you went for a ride."

He arched his eyebrows. "You got a problem with that? I didn't have any chores to do."

"That's right, you didn't. But because you hightailed it outta the bunkhouse so fast after breakfast, you missed a really interesting conversation." Teague's eyes gleamed. "Well, *I* found it interesting."

Something in that glint set an alarm bell ringing.

"Do tell."

Teague folded his arms. "You weren't in your bed last night."

Butch smirked at him. "You got cameras installed in there or something?"

"Nope, but when I get nods and winks about how little sleep I must've gotten, I put two and two together."

Aw fuck.

"So I wasn't in my bed last night. Big deal. As far as I know, I'm not under a curfew, and there ain't no rule about where I choose to lay my head." He managed a teasing tone.

"The deal, as you put it, is that you were in someone else's bed, and I think I know whose." Teague straightened. "You found a new friend to play with—except he's an old friend, isn't he?"

"None of your business." Butch fought to remain cool.

Teague stared at him. "Apart from the fact you're fucking a guest? Hey, I know Sol is a different kinda guest, but that isn't what's bothering me."

"Then what is?"

Teague narrowed his gaze. "You've swapped my ass for his."

What the everlovin' fuck?

"Who says that's what happened?"

"Hell, I *know* you, remember? Mr. *I Only Ever Top*? And it's *still* not a good coping mechanism."

Okay, now he was pissed.

"Get off my back."

Teague stuck his chin out. "Not when it comes to this. How'd you think Toby and the boss would react if they found out?"

"You gonna tell 'em?"

Teague looked him in the eye. "I thought you'd changed—for the better. You were finally owning up to what you are, but I guess you haven't found another cure yet for those bad dreams. Because we both know that's why you were in his bed last night. You woke up from a bad dream again, and you couldn't come running to my door so you went to his. Does he know you're using him? Or why?"

Fuck, he was this close to sending Teague flying with a punch so hard he'd see stars for a week.

He had to get out of there before his temper got the better of him.

"You know fuck all about it," he ground out, then stormed off in the direction of the barn. "And you call yourself a friend," he flung back without turning his head.

"It's because I *am* your fucking friend that I'm saying all this," Teague hollered.

If that was his definition of friend, he could keep it.

It isn't like it was with Teague. Not the same thing at all.

Butch opened the door to the barn, his heart thumping. He heard voices from the main room, and he paused at the inner door, listening. From the sound of it, whoever was in there was just talking, and he breathed a little easier. He pushed the door open and stepped into the room.

Sol was standing in front of four seated guys, and beside him on a table was an open case containing rods of varying thicknesses, some in shiny metal, others a matte gray. There was also a bottle of lube and a towel. Judging by the disarray, he figured he'd missed the—whatever Sol had been doing.

Butch didn't stop to think too much about that. He marched up to the group, his chest tight, sweat popping out on his brow, and a jittery feeling in his belly.

"Sol? You got a minute?"

He frowned. "Is there something wrong?"

"No, I just …"

He was going to sound *so* stupid. *I shouldn't be here.*

"You know what? It can wait. Sorry I interrupted." Butch turned and walked out, berating himself for acting like a fucking idiot, and feeling flustered, overheated, and vexed, all at the same time.

"Butch!" Sol called out to him, and he froze.

"You're busy. Like I said, it can wait."

"Actually, I've just finished my demonstration, so perfect timing." Sol hurried over to him, and laid his hand on Butch's arm. "Something *is* wrong, isn't it?"

He swallowed. "I can't… not here…"

Sol studied his face for a moment, then nodded. "Come to my room. We won't be disturbed there."

It took him about two seconds to come to a decision. "Okay."

He followed Sol back into the barn and up the stairs. Once inside, Sol closed the door and pointed to the bed. "Sit." He went over to the sink and filled a glass with water, then handed it to Butch. "And drink this." Butch opened his mouth to protest, and Sol's eyes flashed. "Don't argue, just do it."

He sat on the bed and drank, not stopping until he'd drunk all of it. Sol took the empty glass, put it on the nightstand, then sat beside him. Before he could utter a word, Butch got in first.

"Fuck me," he blurted out.

Sol blinked. "Excuse me?"

"You heard right."

"Oh, I heard. I'm wondering why you're asking, though." He paused. "Just so we're clear… We *are* talking about my dick in your ass, right?"

Butch nodded.

"So why ask now? And in such an abrupt manner?"

His throat seized.

Sol expelled a long breath. "Okay, when you can answer that to my satisfaction, *then* I'll fuck you." He stood, picked up the glass, refilled it, and gave it back to him. "I think you need some more."

Butch drank it, the water easing the tightness in his throat and cooling his mood. He set the glass down, and stared at the wooden floorboards.

"Teague got me all riled up."

"I can see that. What did he say or do to get you in this state?"

Breathe, goddamn it. Breathe.

"He... he worked out where I spent last night, and he made an assumption."

Sol's hand was on his thigh, not moving, just a slight pressure as if to make Butch aware of his presence. "It's a reasonable assumption. So what if he thinks we fucked?"

"That's not what I meant."

Sol lapsed into silence, and Butch knew he was waiting.

He sighed. "We... we didn't fuck all that often, Teague and me. Mostly when..."

Sol's cool fingers raised his chin, until he was looking into Sol's eyes. "When...?" he prompted.

Butch shivered. "I... I have bad dreams sometimes, and fucking seemed to be the only thing that scared them away. So when I woke up in the middle of the night, I'd go to his cabin, we'd fuck, and then I'd come back to my bed."

Sol smiled. "I call that a great form of medicine. I wish my doctor would prescribe that."

Butch breathed easier. "You're sayin' that to get me to calm down, aren't you?"

Sol leaned in and gave him a light kiss on the mouth. "Got it in one." He sat back. "So what did Teague assume?" He stilled. "Ah. He thought you'd swapped his form of medicine for mine?"

Butch nodded. "But that wasn't why I was with you last night."

"Of course it wasn't. I know that." Butch shuddered out a breath, and Sol kissed his forehead. "Now...tell me about these dreams. What are they about?"

Butch frowned. "You already know."

He blinked again. "Then let's pretend I don't. Tell me."

Butch's stomach was hard as iron, and he had difficulty swallowing past the lump in his throat.

"Because..." The word came out as a croak, and he took

another sip of water. "Because I've never forgotten what I did." He put the glass down, then wrung his hands. "I've tried to be a better person, but the guilt just never goes away. It's always there, gnawing at me."

"'Guilt'?"

Butch gaped at him. "Don't act like you don't know what I'm talking about. It's my fault Scott Nelson died. You were there, for Christ's sake. *I'm* the reason he never made it past seventeen-years-old."

Sol could've been cast in marble, he was so still.

"You don't know that," he said in a quiet, flat voice.

Butch snorted. "Oh yes I do. I pushed him too far, and that was why he killed himself. And I've lived with it ever since. Even his mom knew it was my fault."

Sol stared at him. "She *told* you that?" Butch nodded, his heart heavy with misery. "When?"

Butch couldn't look him in the eye.

"The morning after he hanged himself."

CHAPTER 43

May 6, 1988

"Sweetheart, are you okay?"

It took a moment for his mom's voice to register. Butch glanced up from the milk and cookies he hadn't even touched. "'M fine."

Her brows knitted. "You don't look fine. You've hardly said a word since you got home from school. Did something happen today?"

It was more a case of what *hadn't* happened, but he couldn't tell her that, not unless he wanted to be on the receiving end of a barrage of questions.

Scott Nelson hadn't been in his English class, and as soon as Butch noticed his absence, his stomach had gone into churn-mode, big time.

He couldn't face me, not after yesterday. He probably couldn't face anyone, if it comes to that.

That wasn't surprising, seeing as Butch had called him a fag and a queerboy, he'd demanded to know who Scott was dating, when he was gonna start wearing lipstick and mascara, and all kinds of similar comments designed to detract attention from himself and make it clear to everyone there that Butch Buchanan was no fag.

Which was ironic as hell, seeing as the main recipient of his barbs was the person Butch had fixated on for almost a year, and was probably the least gay of the two of them. Not that Scott had a clue how Butch felt—Butch had been *so* careful around him. And offense was better than defense any day, right?

Scott was good-looking to the point of almost pretty, with light brown hair he always wore kinda long, down to his shoulders, except when it was tied back in class. His eyes were hazel, framed with long lashes that made Butch's heart skip a beat every time he caught sight of them, along with the fine, chiseled cheekbones that made him yearn to cup that sweet face in both hands, lean in, and—

Such thoughts usually resulted in a more vicious verbal attack than usual, while his stomach roiled in a mess of self-loathing.

He couldn't be attracted to Scott Nelson. *He* wasn't gay—*Scott* was. Hadn't he caught Scott looking at him in class sometimes? Did he think Butch hadn't noticed? Didn't he see all the girls that flocked around Butch like moths to a flame? Butch had made sure to kiss Veronica Chapman in the cafeteria, where everyone could see—especially Scott.

He knew he'd treated Scott badly, but hey, Butch wasn't the only one, right? There was Cal, Pete, Sol… They'd come out with just as much shit. Except he knew where he led, they followed.

"Are you going to eat those cookies or just stare at them?" Dad said as he came into the kitchen. "Your mom made your favorites—the least you can do is take a bite out of one of 'em, and tell her they taste great." He scowled. "You should show more appreciation."

Butch was about to protest that he *did* appreciate everything Mom did, when he heard the squeal of brakes outside.

Dad shook his head. "That'll be one of those assholes you run around with."

"Honey, language," Mom murmured.

Dad ignored her. "Pete Calhoun's dad bought him a car when he turned eighteen, didn't he? Well, don't *you* go getting any ideas—I can't afford it. You want a car, you're gonna have to work your ass off for it, which means doing a damn sight more on the ranch than you do right now." Another scowl. "Why can't you be more like your brother?"

Butch tried his best to let the tide of words flow over him. His dad had been like this ever since Butch reached his teens, and he had no clue why. Maybe it was a male thing, but Dad wasn't the same way with Deke.

Loud hammering on the front door made him almost jump out of his skin.

"I'll get that," Mom murmured, rising from the table.

"If it's one of those yahoos, tell 'em Brian won't be joining them on any joyride," Dad hollered after her.

He cringed.

Why can't he call me Butch? What's so bad about having a nickname?

Then he heard raised voices, and his heartbeat quickened.

Something's wrong.

"You can't just barge into my house." Mom sounded... pissed? Scared? Butch couldn't decide. A moment later, the door was flung open, and a woman burst in, her gaze darting around the room. Her eyes were red, her face blotchy, and it didn't look as if her hair had a passing acquaintance with a hairbrush.

What he couldn't miss was the fact she wore a nightgown under her coat, and slippers on her feet.

She saw him, and lurched toward the table.

"You, you little bastard. You're the one I'm here to see." There was a slur to her voice that reminded him of Saturday nights when his dad came back from the bar where he'd spent a few hours with his friends.

His dad frowned. "Melissa? You alright?"

It took Butch a moment to recognize her. He'd seen her at their church on Sundays, but she hadn't attended for a long time.

The look in Scott Nelson's mom's eyes sent his heart plummeting.

She paid his dad no mind, but slammed her hands down onto the kitchen table.

"You did it, didn'tcha? You finally pushed him too far."

"What's all this about?" Mom put her hand on Mrs. Nelson's back, but she squirmed away as if the touch burned her. She jerked her head to stare at his mom, her eyes wild, her breathing erratic.

"My boy is dead, and *your son* drove him to it."

It felt as though time slowed down. The *tick* of the clock on the wall was sluggish. Pain tore through Butch's chest, and bile rose in his throat. He couldn't speak.

Scott dead? He can't *be.*

"Scott?" Mom brought her hand to her mouth, her eyes huge. "Melissa, what happened? And how can it have anything to do with Brian?"

Mrs. Nelson pointed a thin, trembling finger at Butch. "What did you do yesterday? He came home in such a state. I knew something had happened at school, but he wouldn't talk about it. His uncle tried for hours to get through to him." She let out a sob. "And finally he told us the truth. He was being bullied." She stared at Butch, her gaze unwavering.

Then he caught the hitch in his dad's breathing, and he turned.

Dad stood there, rigid, gaping at her. "You saying Brian had something to do with this?"

She nodded, never taking her eyes off Butch. "He said there were a few boys involved, but his was the only name Scott mentioned, not that he told us why he was being bullied." She slammed her hand down again. "What is *wrong* with you? What did Scott ever do to *you*? He was the sweetest boy ever. He'd do anything for anyone. Wasn't it bad enough he lost his dad a few years ago? Did you and your friends have to make his life even worse?"

Another knock at the door made everyone jump, and Dad left the room. Butch caught the murmur of voices, and then the door opened once more. A man came into the room, flustered. He hurried over to Mrs. Nelson, and put his arm around her.

"Aw, Mel, you shouldn't be here."

She stiffened at first, and made as if to shrug off his embrace, but as Butch watched, she crumpled in on herself and turned to the man, sobs wracking her body as she buried her face in his neck.

"I thought I'd find her here," he told Mom, stroking Mrs. Nelson's back. "She's been under sedation most of the day. I went to get her some water, and when I came back, she'd taken my car keys. It didn't take a genius to work out where she'd gone." He glared at Butch. "So *you're* the one. I hope you're feeling proud of yourself. My sister lost her husband, so Scott was her whole world. And now she's lost him too."

Butch finally found his voice. "How did Scott die?" he croaked.

He shivered. "I found him this morning in the barn. He'd taken some rope and..." Another violent shiver coursed through him. "I cut him down. Mel was hysterical, and who can blame her? She wouldn't eat, but then I found the whiskey bottle. She said something a few hours ago about coming here, and I told her not to do it." He held Mrs. Nelson close. "Come on home now, Mel. You shouldn't be here."

They walked out, Mrs. Nelson weeping, and Mom followed them.

Dad closed the door behind her and turned, his eyes so freaking cold.

"You had something to do with that boy's death, didn't you?"

"N-no, sir." Butch couldn't stop shaking. All he could see in his head was an image of Scott the last time Butch had seen him. The haunted look in his eyes.

I did that. We did that.

Except it had been Butch's words that had pushed Scott over the edge. Why else would he have named him to his mom?

Dad narrowed his gaze. "You're lying. I always know when you're lying. I have no idea what you did to that poor boy—only you know the truth—but it'll be on your conscience for the rest of your life, yours and your asshole friends." He glared. "Christ, how old was he? Seventeen? He had his whole life ahead of him, and you robbed him of it." He pulled a face. "You disgust me. Get out of my sight."

Butch pushed his chair back, its feet scraping loudly over the wooden floor, and stumbled out of the room, up the stairs to the attic bedroom he shared with no one.

God, what have I done?

He threw himself face down onto his bed and cried into his pillow. His dad might piss him off on a regular basis, but Butch couldn't deny he was speaking the absolute truth. Scott Nelson was dead, and it was his fault.

When Deke came home a couple of hours later after football practice, Butch was still holed up in their room, unwilling to step out of it. He skipped supper, and no one brought him anything, so he figured they were avoiding him as much as he was avoiding them.

When it was time for bed, Butch lay there in the dark, his mind a rabbit warren of twists and turns, all of its tunnels leading him back to one place. He waited until the house was silent, then grabbed a flashlight. He emptied his backpack onto the bed, then proceeded to fill it with as much clothing as he could. Money was going to be a problem—he only got a small allowance each month, and May's was spent already.

That meant hitching a ride.

He crept downstairs and into the kitchen. A raid on the fridge resulted in a hunk of cheese, some cold meat, and a plastic container filled with meatloaf. He'd have to find water where he could. He cut off a few slices of bread, wrapped them in paper, and grabbed some fruit from the bowl on the sideboard. He squeezed everything into his bag and crept along the hallway to the front door. On impulse he went into the living room, opened his dad's liquor cabinet, grabbed the almost full bottle of whiskey, and somehow found space for it in his bag. Then he headed back into the hallway and let himself out as silently as he could.

He paused at the driveway, glancing back at the only home he'd ever known.

I can't stay there, not now.

His dad would never let him forget this.

Once the kids at school found out, he'd be a pariah.

Hell, there was still Scott's funeral to come, and no way could he stick around for that.

Other kids leave home at eighteen, don't they? He'd manage somehow.

The one thing he focused on was putting distance between himself and home, and if that meant walking all the way to Montana, he'd do it.

I'm never coming back.

Those bridges were burned, and a chasm had opened up between him and his family. What lay before him was an unknown road.

I'm gonna make it a better road than the one I just left.

Butch walked slowly, but it didn't feel as though he walked alone.

Scott was with him, and Butch had an idea he'd always be there at his shoulder.

Sunday, September 25, 2022

Part of Sol had always known, but hearing his suspicions confirmed had been a harrowing experience. He kissed Butch on the forehead.

"I'm so sorry you went through all that. It must've been awful," he murmured. "When we heard the news, everyone was so shocked. I looked for you at school. I don't know who found out first, but word finally got around that you'd gone, only, no one knew any more than that. Where did you go?"

"I walked for miles that first day. I snuck into a barn and spent the night there." Butch grimaced. "I also drank all my dad's whiskey, until I threw up. The next morning the ranch owner found me, and I must've looked pretty pathetic because they gave me breakfast before they sent me on my way." Butch sighed. "And that became the pattern for my days. I walked as far as I could, ate when I could, and after weeks of walking and begging, I came to a small farm. I had no clue where I was, but the farmer was an old guy who was struggling. His son used to do a lot of the heavy work, but he'd gone away with his friends before they all started college. He couldn't afford to pay me, but they fed me, three meals a day, they gave me a bed, and I worked my ass off. I stayed long enough to help get the harvest in, then I left—and went back to walking." He smiled. "I found places to work, and I did all kinds of jobs—working with horses, laboring for a house builder, painting, you name it."

"And then you reached Salvation."

"After about a year, yeah. I didn't recognize myself. I'd put on weight, but a lot of it was muscle. I didn't know when I got here that it would be my last stop."

The pain etched into Butch's voice tore at Sol's heart, and he knew he could do something about that.

I can help him heal, if only a little.

"She was wrong to lay the blame at your door. You weren't the only one at fault. We were just as guilty." Sol pushed out a sigh. "Scott was in my thoughts for such a long time."

"Whether it was my fault, yours, Cal's, Pete's…" Butch stared at him, his face drawn. "What the fuck does it matter? It still doesn't change the fact Scott died. We pushed him, and he couldn't take it."

"Butch…" Sol spoke calmly, waiting until he had Butch's attention. "Please… let me speak."

Butch blinked. "Okay."

Sol expelled his tension with a long breath. "I can't tell you how many times I've thought about that last year. I know it didn't matter that we didn't hit Scott: the verbal bullying we did that day—and all the days that led up to it—would have been enough to put him through hell." Sol held his hands up. "I'll be honest. I screwed up there, big time, and it taught me a lesson that I take into every goddamn scene I do." He stared at Butch. "You already know what I learned, don't you? That words can bring someone to their knees just as easily as blows." He swallowed. "Scott lost his dad, and we should've thought about that when we were taunting the fuck out of him. We should've remembered he was hurting in other ways, but we didn't. We didn't think, and dammit, we *should've* done. Me, you…we were swamped with fighting our own sexuality, and Scott got caught in our battle, except he was already drowning." He gripped Butch's upper arm. "But you need to remember one thing. None of us wanted him dead. *You* didn't want him dead."

"So what if it was just words?" Butch protested. "We were dicks, sure, but I treated him horribly, and it drove him to—"

"Stop," Sol interjected. He squared his shoulders. "Ever since I saw you here, I've been trying to tell you something, and you kept shutting me down."

"Can you blame me? I didn't wanna talk about this."

Sol grabbed Butch's wrists and held them tight. "But you're going to listen to me now, okay? Because there's something you need to hear." He looked Butch in the eye. "I might have believed it once, but that was before I learned the truth. Scott did *not* kill himself because of either of us."

Butch gazed at him with a pained expression. "You don't know that."

Sol sighed. "Actually? Yes, I do."

CHAPTER 44

Sol lay on his side on the bed, his head resting in his hand, and gestured for Butch to join him. They faced each other, and Sol's heartbeat raced.

He has to know.

He took Butch's left hand in his and raised it into the air, gazing at the Roman numerals etched into his skin. "When I saw this tattoo for the first time, its significance was lost on me—until I Googled it. *Then* I knew what it was. And I also knew I had to tell you what I'd discovered." He lowered Butch's arm.

"I still think you—"

Sol covered Butch's lips with his fingers. "Nope. This is where you get to listen to *me*, remember?" He waited until Butch nodded before removing them. "Okay then. After college I didn't return to Casper. I found a job in Gillette, and although it was only two hours away from home, it was enough. I didn't want to live in Casper, maybe for the same reasons you left. Why would I stay and be surrounded by people who'd known me in high school? I didn't want to see them, didn't want to be reminded of… everything."

"I hear that," Butch murmured.

"Eventually I ended up in Cheyenne." He smiled. "From the north of Wyoming to about as far south as you could get. And I was happy there—for a while—but that's not what I want to talk about. *This* story takes place in 2008, when my parents were celebrating forty years of marriage. Alli organized a big shindig, and I went back to Casper." He chuckled. "That was some party. Anyhow, I was there for a week, and before I left, Mom got a call from Melissa Nelson."

Butch blinked. "Scott's mom?"

He nodded. "She was finally leaving Casper. I think she'd only stayed because her brother Errol came to live with her after her husband died, and he'd made a home for himself. But then he decided it was time to make a move, and she didn't want to stay there on her own. She'd found a place in Rock Springs, a retirement community, so she wouldn't be alone. Only, there wasn't going to be an awful lot of space, and she was downsizing like crazy. So there she was, packing up all her stuff and trying to decide what to keep and what to either sell, give away, or simply put in the trash. She called my mom and asked for some help. Mom and Mrs. Nelson were good friends. I think my mom felt guilty when she learned about... Scott."

"I was gonna ask if your mom knew."

Another nod. "I told her. I didn't want her hearing it from someone else. And yeah, that's another story for another time. So Mom went over there, and I thought she'd be gone a couple of hours, but it was nearly midnight when she got home." His throat tightened at the memory. "I'd never seen her in such a state. She walked into the living room, over to the liquor cabinet, and poured herself a belt of whiskey. And I *mean* a belt." Sol shuddered. "Except Mom never drank more than a sip at New Year's, or maybe Christmas Eve. So I asked her what had happened."

His stomach clenched. He could still hear her voice.

Wednesday, September 17, 2008

"Mom, you're scaring me." In all Sol's thirty-eight years, he couldn't recall ever seeing her so distressed. He couldn't even call for his dad—he'd gone fishing with Sol's two uncles.

Sol knelt beside the armchair she'd almost stumbled into. "What's wrong?"

Her hand shook as she drank a little of the whiskey. "Twenty years that boy's been dead, and she'd kept everything, y'know? All his clothes, his books, his toys, even the ones from when he was a little kid. But she wasn't upset. Like I said, it was twenty years. She'd done her grieving."

"It might look like that," Sol told her quietly. "But you can't know what's going on inside her head. Some people never stop grieving—they just get better at learning to live with it. The memories are always there."

Mom stroked his cheek. "And there's the counselor talking."

He sat on the floor beside her chair, wanting to stay close. "Something happened, didn't it?"

She nodded. "We were packing up Scott's things, and she was talking about sending the clothes, books, and toys to Goodwill. And then... she found something." Mom swallowed hard. "It was wrapped up in an old T-shirt, squirreled away at the bottom of a drawer. She said she hadn't looked in there in years."

"*What* was squirreled away?"

She met his gaze, and he winced to see the pain there.

"A journal."

Sol's heart lurched. "Scott kept a journal?"

She nodded. "And clearly he didn't want anyone reading it. So anyway, Melissa sat there on the bed, opened it, and started reading. She said the first entry was written in 1985, and that had to have been around the time his dad died, so I understood why he might have kept a journal. I left her to it while I folded clothes and put them in boxes. I figured this was important. She cried a little, wiping her eyes now and then, and I didn't make a big thing of it, I let her be." She shivered. "Then she went so quiet. It was eerie how all the sound seemed to die. I swear, I couldn't even hear her breathing." A hard swallow. "And then she just... lost it. I mean, completely. She broke down, and she made such a noise that Errol came running in to see what the hell had happened. Well, Melissa picked up a lamp, a real heavy one, and she threw it at him. He sidestepped it, and the whole thing hit the wall behind him and shattered." Mom's voice quavered. "Then she told him to get out, that she didn't want to see him ever again. He got angry about the lamp, and when it didn't look as if he was going to leave, Melissa glared at him, and... I'll never forget her expression when she said this. She looked him in the eye, her face red, her cheeks streaked with tears, and she said 'I *know*, okay? I know everything. Because Scott wrote it all down. *All* of it, you hear? So you'd better start packing, because I'm goin' downstairs to call the police. They might tell me it all happened too long ago for them to do a damn thing about it, but I'm gonna tell 'em anyway.'"

371

Sunday, September 25, 2022

Cold spread out from Butch's core, reaching his extremities within seconds.

"I think I know what's coming. Because for her to say all that, it can really only mean one thing."

Sol gave a nod. "As soon as Mom said that, I froze. She tried to get Melissa to calm down, but it was as if she couldn't hear her anymore. Then she thrust the journal into Mom's hands and told her to read it." He sighed. "She said it made for horrific reading. It turns out Scott's Uncle Errol—you know, the kind man who moved in to be near his poor grieving sister? —had been sexually abusing him since not long after his dad died. The last entry was the night Scott killed himself." He scowled. "Remember you told me his uncle had tried for hours to calm Scott down when he came home so upset?"

"Yeah."

"Well, that wasn't true. His uncle had taken him into the barn—where they could talk freely, he said, but Scott didn't buy that—and then he'd fucked him. And that night, something inside him just… broke, I guess. He couldn't take it anymore."

Butch frowned. "Now wait a minute. There'd have been an autopsy, right? Wouldn't it have picked up on the fact that he'd had sex recently?"

"Possibly—if there *was* an autopsy. I don't know for sure. But what if the uncle told the authorities Scott had a boyfriend, only he never told the uncle who it was? That'd sound plausible enough."

"Did his mom say if he'd ever tried to tell her about the abuse?"

"If he did, she either missed it entirely, or she didn't mention it to my mom. But his journal made it clear he couldn't go on." There was an ache in Sol's chest. "So now we know. Scott's home life was a shitshow, and yes, everything we did at school didn't help, but we weren't the reason he killed himself. That rat bastard of an uncle abused him sexually—and probably psychologically too—while his mom was busy trying to keep things together. No wonder she didn't notice what was happening."

Butch's throat tightened. "I've thought a lot about Scott over the years, about what kind of guy he was. You know what I remembered? He always had a smile—except when we were around, of course. It was like he was always trying to please everyone, help everyone."

"He probably was," Sol remarked. "It could be he was desperate for positive recognition, to maintain what was left of his self-esteem. But I don't want to talk about Scott right now—I want to talk about you." He cupped Butch's chin. "*Now* do you see why I wanted to share this with you? You've been torturing yourself all these years. You've been haunted by the memory of his death—and don't deny it because I've been there, okay? I know how it feels to be haunted." His fingers were gentle on Butch's cheek. "But it's time to exorcise those ghosts. It's time to be kind to yourself, to allow yourself to be happy." He stroked Butch's arm. "That isn't going to go away, nor do I think it should. It's a reminder of the person you used to be." Sol looked him in the eyes, and Butch's stomach quivered at the intensity of that gaze. "But that isn't you anymore, Butch Buchanan. As of right now, you are a new man."

Butch stared at him, hardly daring to breathe.

And then the dam burst.

Sol held him as he wept, his tears soaking into the pillow, Sol's tee, his body shaking, trembling, unable to hold back the tide of emotions sweeping through him, *crashed* through him, raw, fierce and liberating. And through it all, Sol's strong arms enveloped him, and he leaned into that strength, needing it with every cell and fiber of his being. He knew the tears were for Scott, for all he'd suffered, but they were for him too, a cleansing, cathartic release that had been a long time coming.

The tears dried up, the emotional waves receded, and he lay in Sol's arms.

He felt safe. Cared for. Wanted.

"You okay?" Sol asked.

Butch's head was on Sol's chest, and his ear was filled with Sol's heartbeat. "Better than okay." He couldn't recall the last time he'd felt so at peace.

Sol kissed him, and it was a gentle, sweet kiss. "Right now you have to be emotionally exhausted. I know *I* would be after all that."

"Yeah, I guess I am."

"So what I'm saying is, don't try to think beyond what's going on inside your head. Let all that emotion drain out."

"But I wanted to—"

Sol stopped his words with a kiss. "Let's cuddle up and sleep. Shut out the world for a while. There's no place I need to be— how about you?"

A cuddle and a sleep sounded perfect.

"There's no place I need to be, except right here."

CHAPTER 45

Now and then Sol would invite a client to stay the night, simply to enjoy the sensation of holding a man in his arms, breathing him in, waking to find a warm body in his bed…

Waking up in the semi-darkness with Butch brought mixed emotions.

On a physical level, it felt good. *So* fucking good, and they'd fallen asleep with their clothes on too. The thought that warm cuddles might lead to heat and sweat and cum quickened his heartbeat. They'd talked about it, they both wanted it, and the prospect of Butch fucking him made him hard as a rock.

What trickled through his mind was the knowledge they were connected, that this could be more than sex. Somewhere along the line, Sol's emotions had become entangled, and that was *not* good. Added to that was the burgeoning desire to guide Butch across the steppingstones into BDSM, because his instincts told him Butch's interest was genuine.

I need to keep my feet on the ground here. Okay, he might want to know more. Sure, there's a connection, emotional as well as physical.

What scared him was the feeling that this connection could develop into something more—something deeper.

Something that might last longer than his stay would allow.

Then Butch stirred in his arms, and Sol had to switch off his internal meandering.

"What time is it?"

Sol didn't have a clue. Time seemed to have lost all meaning.

"I think we slept right through supper," Butch murmured. "Lord, I can't wait to hear the comments when I get back to the bunkhouse."

Sol grabbed his phone from the nightstand and peered at it. There were three messages from Toby. "I think I'm in the same boat." He grinned. "You could stay a little longer. You know, *really* give them something to talk about?" Darren, a Dom who was there with his two subs, wanted Sol to join him in a scene later that day, and they'd already discussed boundaries and the subs' limits. And Stephen, the other single guest, had made noises about trying something new—he just hadn't shared any ideas on what direction he wanted to take.

While the suggestion to have Butch stay had been playful, he realized something deeper lay at the root of it.

All Sol wanted to do right then was stay right where he was, and he couldn't help feeling that was kind of dangerous.

Butch hadn't slept that well in years, and he relished the warmth and the feelings of well-being that cocooned him. The exchange with Teague seemed like a distant memory, but then again, he'd been put through an emotional wringer not once, but twice since then.

Then he remembered why he'd been coming to see Sol in the first place.

"I've been doing some research," he murmured.

Sol tilted his chin with his fingertips. "What kind of research?"

"If I said Safe, Sane, Consensual, would that be a clue?"

It was Sol's turn to blink. "What else did you find?"

"So many things I wanna talk about. I had no idea there was so much to it."

Sol smiled. "You just realized it's not all whips and paddles, didn't you?"

"Exactly!" Then he stilled. "And while we're on the subject, I gotta say, they might not be my thing, okay?"

Sol's smile didn't fade. "Do you have an idea of what might be your thing? Did your research turn up something that made you go 'Ooh, I wanna try that?' Or even 'I'm not sure about that, but it's a maybe'?"

Butch had an inkling—he just wasn't sure what admitting it would say about him.

Sol tightened his arm around him. "You *do* know I'm not going to judge you, right? You're in a safe space. The safest, if it comes to that."

His words were exactly what Butch needed to hear.

"I… I saw pictures of these little cages… You wear 'em on your dick."

Sol chuckled. "That's a general *you*, isn't it? Because *I* don't wear one. *You* might, though." He stroked Butch's arm. "Tell me how the pictures made you feel."

"Not sure I could put it into words. I guess it was like the feeling I got when you told me I couldn't come for a week, that I could only come when you said so… only… bigger, somehow." He raised his chin to meet Sol's gaze. "Could we do that before you leave?" His pulse raced. "Just so I know how it feels?"

Sol's broad grin was all the answer Butch needed. He kissed Butch's forehead. "I think that could be arranged. But we'd need to talk first, and I mean a serious discussion."

"I worked that much out for myself." Butch's heart thumped. "Do we have to talk right now?"

"Did you have another activity in mind?" Sol's lips twitched, and Butch had never felt so seen. Then he grinned and added, "Because if it involves condoms and lube, I am *so* ready for that."

Fuck.

Then he recalled Sol's stipulation of the previous night. "And would I get to come?"

Sol grinned. "Greedy boy. You came last night, remember?"

He widened his eyes. "You expect me to fuck you and not shoot a load?"

"Is that asking too much of you?" Sol regarded him with a neutral expression.

It was on the tip of his tongue to say *Fuck* yeah, *it's too much*, but something held him back, a desire to prove to Sol that he was serious about learning more.

Then Sol smiled. "I won't ask that of you, not this time. But after today, you won't come again until I say so."

Relief flooded through him, and Butch claimed Sol's lips with a fervent kiss. Sol responded, their bodies moving together as heat bloomed inside him, making his heart race, his blood pound. Impulsively, Butch rolled on top of Sol and did a slow, sensual undulation, loving the feel of Sol's warm, firm body beneath him. He kept up the rhythmic rocking, moaning when his own hardening shaft met the steel of Sol's dick. Sol reached down and grabbed Butch's ass, molding him against his erection, grinding, and Butch realized the whimper that broke the silence came from his own lips.

He pulled back, breathless. "I… I can't do this right now."

Sol's breathing caught. "You could've fooled me." He snaked his hand between their bodies and cupped Butch's solid crotch. "This says you can."

"No, it's not that, it's just…." Butch grimaced. "I need to take a shower, all right? I mean, I slept in my clothes, for God's sake."

"So did I." Sol smiled. "You smell just fine to me, I assure you." His eyes sparkled. "Nothing wrong with a little sweat. I have subs who fight for who gets to sniff my jock after a scene."

He gaped. "Seriously?"

Sol laughed. "Oh sweetheart, the things you're going to discover about yourself."

"This isn't me being prissy, okay?" Butch rolled his eyes. "Look, I want your tongue in my ass again. And I'm not letting you within a foot of my hole until I've cleaned it, understand?"

Sol's lips brushed against his ear. "Then why don't we both grab a shower?" His chuckle tickled. "I was going to take one anyway, but I was enjoying the feel of you so much, I got distracted."

Yeah, Butch knew all about being distracted.

He threw back the sheets. "I won't be long." He bent over to put his boots on.

"Where are you going?" Sol demanded.

"To the bunkhouse. For a shower. Didn't I just say that?"

"Why go there when there's a perfectly good bathroom here?"

Butch wasn't sure how Toby or the boss would feel if they got to hear about that.

"It's still early. No one will know," Sol assured him. "And we'll be fast."

The idea of a quick clean-up rather than braving the bunkhouse only to leave it again won out. "Okay." He stripped off, and Sol did the same, then they walked barefoot out of the room and along the hallway to the bathroom. Not a sound came from the other rooms, and Butch guessed all the guests were still sleeping.

Light filled the room, glinting off the tiles. The first thing

Butch saw was a shelf above the sink, where a toothbrush stood in a glass.

"Damn it," he muttered.

"Something wrong?"

"There was another reason I was gonna head back to the bunkhouse—I wanted my toothbrush."

Sol chuckled. "Gotta love a man who likes to be clean all over." He opened a wall cabinet, and removed a brand-new toothbrush wrapped in plastic. "Here. There's toothpaste too. Toby thought of everything. So while you brush your teeth, I'll get a head start, which is probably a good idea." He grinned. "The less time I spend in the shower with you, the better." Sol looked him up and down, his gaze lingering on Butch's erect cock. "Yeah, *definitely* a good idea."

Butch brushed his teeth, but instead of watching his reflection, he watched Sol beneath the jets of water, the languid slide of lather over his skin, the gleam of the lights on Sol's head, his concentration as he cleaned his ass with a soapy hand, working his fingers into his hole.

Then Sol glanced up and grinned again. "Don't think I don't know what you're doing."

Butch got on with his task, averting his eyes to prevent further distractions. When he was done, he crossed the floor and joined Sol under the stream of warm water. Butch filled his cupped palm with bodywash from the wall canister, but when he reached behind to clean his crack, balls, and hole, Sol stopped him.

"That's my job this morning." And before Butch could get a word out, Sol slid a lathered hand down Butch's back, rubbing slick fingers through his crease, pausing at his hole to push a fingertip inside. "Hands on the tiles, arms straight, eyes front, and arch your back."

Okay, that was hot.

Butch didn't hesitate, groaning when Sol penetrated him. He leaned in, his lips close to Butch's ear. "Are you good to go?"

It took him a second to work out what Sol was asking, and heat surged through him. "I'm good." He groaned as Sol's fingers did a little dance inside him. "Any more of that, and I'm gonna be cleaning my cum off the tiles."

"Not today, you're not." Sol's tone told him that outcome was not up for discussion. He pulled Butch's hips toward him, and water ran down his spine. Sol spread his cheeks, allowing the warm water to rinse away all traces of the soap. Butch thought they were done, until a warm tongue lapped his hole, and he let out a moan.

"Fuck, Sol. He sounds amazing. Where've you been hiding him? And are you going to share?"

Aw shoot, a guest.

Butch froze, then straightened without thinking, and Sol's reaction was instantaneous. He placed himself between Butch and the guest, and Butch had only to look at Sol's rigid stance to know he was pissed.

"What are you doing here, Darren?" Sol's voice had an edge to it, a touch of steel, and Butch shivered.

"I heard the shower running. I didn't realize you weren't alone."

"Then why, when you could see I was plainly *not* alone, did you think it okay to walk in here without making us aware of your presence, and then make that unprofessional comment? You know nothing about him, but you *do* know about boundaries, right? And you also know Toby would be as pissed as I am right now if he knew you'd breached them. So turn around, go back to your room, and be ready to explain yourself to me later. Because we *are* going to discuss this."

Butch peered over Sol's shoulder. Darren stood there in a pair of black briefs, his face pale.

"You're right. I'm sorry. I should know better. But I really didn't know you weren't—"

"Not now, Darren."

He gave a single nod, then turned around and left.

Sol turned to face Butch. He expelled a breath, and Sol's arms enveloped him.

"I'm so sorry about that." Sol's brows furrowed. "I hate it when guys don't respect boundaries, especially a Dom who should know better. I know I only met the man yesterday, but that was very unprofessional of him. If he's an example of the kind of Dom they have over there in Atlanta, I don't think I'll be going there any day soon." He curved a hand around Butch's cheek. "You okay?"

Butch took a deep breath. "Yeah. I was more concerned he'd report *me* for being in here."

Sol snorted. "I don't think that's likely, not if he wants to come back here in the future. Right now, he's probably sweating about me reporting him to Toby." He grabbed a towel from the wall rack, and dried Butch off.

Butch was beginning to learn Sol had two sides, and Darren had definitely gotten on the wrong side of one of them. "Has he been a Dom for long?"

Sol arched his eyebrows. "I think you already know the answer to that question."

"I know something else too." Butch leaned in and kissed him on the lips. "You said this was a safe space, but *you're* the one who makes it safe."

Sol's face lit up. "Let's go to my room."

Butch wrapped the towel around his hips and followed Sol out of the bathroom and along the hallway. Once inside, Sol closed the door behind them.

"Would I be right in thinking you've never been naked with two men before?"

Butch nodded. "Fucking one guy was more than enough."

"Which is why I was so angry with him. He doesn't know you, and yet he thought it was okay to make those asinine comments when you were standing there at your most vulnerable."

"You make me sound like a snowflake," Butch murmured.

"No—like a man who until very recently was unsure of his sexuality. That makes you vulnerable, which is why he needed to back the fuck off."

"And he did," Butch said in a low voice. "So please, don't let him spoil the mood. Because we had plans, remember?" He took a step forward, his hands on Sol's bare, damp chest, but Sol gripped his wrists and lowered them to his sides.

"Before we get to those plans, how flexible are you, physically speaking?"

Butch stared at him. "I'm the same age as you, and I'm in good shape."

"Nothing to do with age," Sol told him. "I'm asking because I need to know if I fold you in half, you're going to be okay with that."

Butch got where he was coming from, his heartbeat quickening at the prospect.

"In that case… I'm limber enough. I can't get my ankles around my neck anymore, but I doubt you could either, if it came to that."

Sol smiled. "Good to know. And you'd be right. My contortionist days are well and truly over. Any medical issues I need to know about?"

Butch blinked. "Do you always ask these questions?"

"Yes." He paused, and Butch realized he was waiting for an answer.

"No, no medical issues."

Shit just got real.

Sol cupped his chin and looked him in the eye. "And that's it. No more talking about Darren, and no more questions—for now. Tonight it's just us—no whips, no gags, no toys…And if you want me to stop at any—"

"I say my name," Butch concluded.

Sol's smile reached his eyes. "I want to enjoy you, and I *definitely* want you to enjoy me. Everything beyond that can come later." He grinned. "Probably right after you do."

Butch hardly registered Sol's attempt at humor.

This is new. Huge.

Not fucking a man—he'd been doing that for years—but this was different.

This was sex with someone he cared about. Someone he felt connected to.

Except it was still more than that.

This went beyond the physical and entered emotional territory.

This was what a relationship between a Dom and sub was really like, two men forming an intimate pattern that wove itself through their lives.

"Hey."

Butch snapped back into the moment. Sol stood naked in front of him, his towel on the floor, his dick jutting out.

Sol smiled. "Kiss me."

Butch had never received a sweeter invitation.

CHAPTER 46

Butch sat on the edge of the bed, his towel still wrapped around him, relishing the feel of Sol's hands on his neck as they kissed, Sol's tongue going deep. Then Sol cradled Butch's head, as if he was something both precious and fragile, their lips locked in ever more intimate, deepening kisses that made Butch's toes curl.

"So handsome," Sol murmured against his lips. He pulled back, grasped Butch's hand, and guided it to his cock. Butch wrapped his fingers around the thick, heavy shaft.

"You're so hard."

Sol chuckled. "That's because you're here. Only explanation needed." He gazed at Butch. "Do whatever you feel like."

Butch smiled, then rubbed his face against Sol's chest before kissing his belly and nipples, his hand still working Sol's length. Sol cradled his head once more and held him there.

"I like it when you hold me like that," Butch confessed.

Sol stroked his hair. "I like it too." A chuckle reverberated through him.

"What's so funny?"

Sol bent over to kiss him. "I'm about to discover if you're as limber as you say you are." He gave Butch a gentle shove onto his back, loosening the towel, allowing Butch's dick to bob up, the foreskin peeling back to reveal the wide head. Butch held his breath for that first electric touch of Sol's fingers on his shaft, but Sol avoided his dick, grabbing his knees instead and pushing them toward his shoulders.

He grinned. "Yeah, you're limber, all right." He leaned over to claim Butch's lips once more, only this time he rubbed his thumb over Butch's taint, exerting a little pressure. Butch tried to stifle a moan when Sol circled his hole with his fingertip.

"Oh no you don't," Sol murmured against his lips. "You make as much noise as you like. No one here will give a damn." He withdrew his finger, and Butch groaned.

"Now you're just teasing," he groused.

Sol's eyes held amusement. "What do they say about good things coming to those who wait?" He lowered his head and kissed Butch's stomach, a trail of soft kisses as he followed Butch's treasure trail to the root of his cock. Butch's heart hammered as Sol placed both hands on his thighs and spread him wide.

He smiled. "*Very* limber."

Butch moaned at the touch of Sol's lips on his balls, the feel of his nose pressing there, the sigh of satisfaction that escaped Sol's mouth. Then he buried his face in Butch's crease, and there was no way Butch could keep quiet, not when Sol's tongue danced over his hole, teasing, probing, kissing... His dick jerked as if demanding to receive the same treatment, so hard it ached.

Sol raised his head, his eyes sparkling, then *thank the Lord*, his mouth was on Butch's cock, and he tried to push up with his hips. Sol chuckled around his cock, and *holy fuck*, how come no one had ever done *that* before?

Sol pulled free. "I love the taste of you." Before Butch could thank him for the compliment, Sol sucked one of his balls into that warm mouth, and Butch arched his back, wanting more.

Sol kissed his sac. "Have to get you hard if you're gonna fuck me."

A wave of heat and desire crashed over him, leaving him shaking in its wake.

"What if... what if that's not what I want?"

Okay, *now* he had Sol's full attention.

Sol knelt on the bed, his hand curled around Butch's shaft, working it as though he could do it all fucking day. "What *do* you want?"

He'd thought about it, fantasized about it, and here he was, finally at the point where he had just about enough nerve to ask for what his body craved.

"I've had your tongue in my ass, your fingers..." Butch breathed deeply. "I think I'm ready for your dick."

There. Said it.

Sol didn't speak for a second, and then he gave Butch a searching gaze that made him hot and cold all at the same time. "You didn't enjoy that. You told me so."

He wasn't about to be deterred, not now he'd gotten this far.

"That was the old Butch. The *new* Butch knows you'll make it good for him, you'll take care of him, and you'll make it just as awesome as everything else we've done."

Sol's lips twitched. "Wow. Talk about pressure."

Butch's eyes flickered to Sol's still rigid cock. "But not too much pressure, right?"

Sol crawled up Butch's body and kissed him. "You're trusting me. I won't let you down." Another kiss, and then he moved lower, flicking Butch's nipples with his tongue, circling Butch's navel, until at last his mouth was where Butch wanted it, giving the head a hard suck.

"Have I told you how much I love it when you do that?" He watched the bob of Sol's head, groaning when Sol pulled gently on the foreskin with his teeth. He stroked Sol's gleaming scalp, shuddering as Sol took him deep.

Then Sol pulled free, reached over to the nightstand, and grabbed the bottle of lube sitting there. "We're going to need this." He squeezed the viscous liquid onto his fingers.

Butch's heartbeat raced. "Kiss me?"

Sol smiled. "As if I could stop doing that." He leaned over and their lips met in another toe-curling, heart-melting kiss while Sol teased his hole. Then he cradled Butch's head yet again as he slid a finger into him.

Butch kissed him open-mouthed, his cock jumping as Sol fingered him, his breathing loud and harsh.

"Fuck, you're tight," Sol whispered.

"That's a good thing, right?" Butch groaned when Sol nudged that glorious spot inside him. "Aw fuck."

Sol stroked Butch's belly, his own dick leaking pre-cum that dropped like a thin strand of glass from his slit. Sol smiled. "Taste it."

Butch applied the pad of his forefinger, drawing the sticky fluid away and bringing it to his lips. He raised his gaze. "Can I suck it?"

Sol grinned. "Like I'm going to say no." He shuffled across the bed until he was at Butch's side, his shaft pointing right at Butch's mouth, his finger wedged in Butch's body. Butch held Sol's dick steady and kissed along the length of Sol's thick cock before taking the head into his mouth, moaning around it as Sol explored his hole, nudging his prostate with firm strokes.

"Lie on your front," Sol instructed.

Butch obeyed, propping himself up on his elbows to take Sol's dick into his mouth again, sliding his lips along the shaft, picking up a little speed.

Sol leaned over him toward his ass, there was a finger inside his hole once more, and Butch let out a whimper he could no longer contain, spreading his legs.

"Want me to stop?"

"Fuck no," he replied with a groan. He worked Sol's shaft while he sucked, aware of Sol pushing his finger deeper, then adding another. "Aw fuck, that's a stretch." His ass felt as if it was on fire.

"Stretch is good," Sol told him. "Gotta open you up." He moved his fingers in and out, and it wasn't long before the fire gave way to much more pleasurable sensations, and Butch was rocking his ass up to meet each thrust.

Then his hole was empty, and Sol cupped his chin, tilting his face upward.

"Ready?"

"Maybe?" he quipped.

Sol kissed him. "You know the drill. You want to stop, any time, you say your name." He got onto the bed and lay on his back, reaching over to the nightstand drawer.

The sight of a condom wrapper made Butch's heart lurch into overdrive.

Sol's hand covered his. "Second thoughts?"

Butch remembered how to breathe. "No."

Sol's smile reached his eyes. "Good boy."

That word should've been an insult, but instead it made him feel warm.

Safe.

Sol tore the wrapper, unrolled the latex over his hard cock, and applied lube, spreading it all over. He tossed the bottle aside and held his shaft steady around the base. "You're going to ride me. Best way ever to take a dick for the first time."

Butch managed a smile. "Not my first time, though."

Sol's gaze didn't waver. "It is with me. And we stay like this until you're ready for more."

Butch straddled Sol's hips, his pulse rapid, his chest heaving.

"Reach back and guide me in." Sol stroked his thigh. "And remember to breathe. It helps."

Butch brought the slippery head of Sol's dick to his hole and held it there as he sat back, slowly, so slowly, aware of pressure and heat, and solid flesh penetrating him, stretching him, filling him. He took his time, doing his best to take deep breaths, willing himself to relax.

"That's it." Sol's voice was warm with praise, adding a layer of pleasure to the experience. His hands were on Butch's hips, not exerting pressure but simply *there*, a reminder of their connection. And when Sol's cock was all the way home, Butch let out a moan that came from so fucking deep inside him.

Sol shivered. "Fuck, that feels so good."

Butch didn't move, but sat there, adjusting to the sensation of being full.

It felt *nothing* like the first time. That had been an exercise in discomfort—this filled him with elation, pride, and the desire for more.

He began to move, a gentle up-and-down motion, riding the head and half the shaft, and it wasn't long before everything became that little easier, the sensations more acute, the need in him growing, spreading...

Then Sol squeezed his thigh. "On your back, and bring your knees to your chest again."

Butch lifted himself up and off Sol's dick, then lay on the bed. Sol stuffed a pillow under his ass, applied more lube, then eased back into him.

The change of angle brought with it a whole slew of new sensations, and Butch groaned. "Feels good," he confessed.

"Happy to hear that." Sol worked Butch's cock, all the time moving in and out so goddamn slowly, working his cock further in with each glide, until at last he was balls-deep.

Sol paused. "I'm all the way inside you. How does that feel?"

"Like you need to move," Butch blurted.

Sol smiled. "You read my mind." He slid his arm under Butch's neck, kissing him, their tongues in play. And then he was moving again, his hips rolling fluidly, and Butch had to touch him, stroking Sol's bicep, feeding him moans when Sol's dick connected with his gland again.

Sol broke the kiss and grinned. "I knew it was there somewhere." He went back to cradling Butch's head, an intimate embrace Butch never wanted to end, while he rocked in and out, the kisses constant and demanding.

"You weren't lying, were ya?" Butch ground out. "You like to kiss while you fuck." Except what Sol was doing was nothing like the frantic pounding Butch had given every man he'd ever had sex with.

This was unhurried, sensual, intimate.

And then everything changed.

Sol took hold of Butch's wrists, brought one hand to above his head, then did the same with the other. Sol's arms were under his, Butch's elbows resting in the crooks of Sol's arms.

He was pinned there, held there, and then Sol picked up the pace.

The bed bounced, and Butch moaned into every kiss, locked in place by Sol's body, Sol's cock sliding into him faster now, faster, driving his dick in and out, his hips rocking, snapping…

Butch couldn't hold in his whimpers, unable to form words, just noises that sounded raw and primal. Sol let go of his hands, and Butch held onto Sol's shoulders, deepening their kisses, digging his fingers into the muscled flesh.

Sol cradled his head with both hands, holding him steady while he slid into him, slowing the pace for a brief moment before returning to his previous frenetic pace.

Butch knew he was getting close. "I'm gonna shoot," he cried out.

Sol propped himself up on his hands, hips rolling, dick going deep. "Touch yourself. I want to watch you come."

Butch worked his cock, his body alive with sensation, skin tingling, and then he came, crying out, unable to contain the overwhelming feelings of pleasure inside him. Warmth coated his chest and belly, and Sol scooped it up on his fingers and licked up every drop.

Butch shuddered with every jolt of his orgasm, and then he felt it, a throbbing inside him, accompanied by Sol's groan. Sol stilled, but the throb of his dick continued, and Sol made it perfect by joining their lips in another kiss.

Butch didn't want to move, didn't want to shatter the

moment, but eventually Sol eased out of him, leaving an ache that was more than physical. Sol dealt with the condom, then pulled Butch into an upright position, Butch's legs over his, and kissed his neck, his lips, his hands gentle on Butch's back.

It was the perfect ending.

Butch looped his arms around Sol's neck. "Wow. I feel cheated."

Sol blinked. "What do you mean?"

"If my first time taking a dick had been like this… I keep thinking of all those years when I kept saying no, I don't do that."

Sol laughed. "Better late than never, right?" He stroked Butch's cheek. "Imagine what it would feel like fucking me—with a butt plug in your ass, nudging your prostate every time you drive into me."

Butch gaped at him. "You had to go and say that, right?"

Sol chuckled, then cupped Butch's nape and drew him in for a tender kiss. "I have things to do today, and I'm sure you do, but I'm hoping you'll be back in my bed tonight."

Butch bit his lip. "As long as you don't have any plans for my ass. Because I don't think I could manage that twice in one day."

Sol smiled. "Your ass will be in safe hands. But I do have plans for you tomorrow. I just need to do a little research first."

Butch cocked his head. "That all I get?"

"For now, yes."

He had to say something. He couldn't leave it like this.

"Sol… That was…" He swallowed, lost for words.

Sol kissed him. "I know. And later, we'll talk, okay?"

He nodded. Talk would have to wait until his brain cells decided to work again.

CHAPTER 47

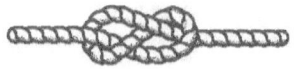

Monday, September 26

"Hey, look what the cat dragged in." Zeeb's eyes sparkled. "So you *do* still work here, right? The boss didn't fire your ass?"

Butch had expected Zeeb to be the first one to comment. "Nope, you don't get rid of me that easy. And it *is* time for breakfast, so where else would I be?" He pulled out a chair and sat at the table. "How's today looking?" It still felt weird, not having guests in the bunkhouse.

"I'm checking the fences," Walt told him. "Me and Owen are riding out to see what needs repairing and where."

"And I'm riding a trail with Stephen, one of the guests," Zeeb added. "He got along great yesterday morning, considerin' it was his first time on horseback, and he wants to go for a ride."

Matt bustled in, his arms full. "Eggs, bacon and sausage. I'll be back in a sec with the hash browns." He deposited the food, then disappeared through the door.

Butch made a beeline for the eggs. "I'm starved."

Zeeb snorted. "Color me not surprised. You've been expendin' a lot of … energy lately."

He didn't bother to comment.

Matt returned with hash browns, biscuits and sausage gravy. "Dig in. I've already fed the guests, so I'm going to have breakfast with you before I go to the house to clean up."

The guys attacked the food with gusto.

"Have y'all found a bed for Thursday night, or are you driving back to Salvation?" Zeeb asked between mouthfuls.

"Matt booked us a couple of rooms," Paul told him. "I think you're lucky your birthday fell this week—if we'd had guests, there'd be no way the boss would let us all do this."

"I know, right?" Zeeb rubbed his hands together. "There's gonna be shenanigans, that's for damn sure."

"There'd better not be," Butch warned him. He grinned. "The boss'll be pissed if he has to bail you outta jail."

The door opened, and Teague walked in. "Great, there's food left." He joined them at the table. He glanced at Butch before helping himself to the food, and it took Butch a second or two to realize what was missing.

Teague wasn't smiling.

Aw shit.

With everything that had happened since the previous evening, Butch had forgotten the sour taste of their last conversation.

I guess I need to mend some bridges. Not that he'd been the one at fault—*it takes two to tango, right?* —but someone had to make the first move.

Everyone lapsed into silence as they ate. Butch shifted a little on his chair, aware of an ache where there hadn't been one before. His mind drifted to Sol's mysterious plans.

He's up to something.

The thought sent shivers of excitement and trepidation coursing through him in equal measure.

"One of the showers has gone on the fritz," Walt told Butch. "Think you can use those magic fingers of your and fix it?"

"I'll take a look." Butch chuckled. "What would you do if I wasn't around?"

Zeeb let out another snort. "Call for a plumber, wait for two weeks to get a reply, then pay through the nose to get it fixed, like everyone else."

"Have any of you seen the three guys?" Teague poured himself a cup of coffee.

"I was gonna ask you about that. What's the deal with them?" Walt frowned. "Is it like a permanent three-way or something?"

"The boss says yeah. There's even a word for what they've got going on— they're a throuple."

Zeeb blinked. "That's a thing?"

"Apparently."

"So how does that work?"

"I don't know how it works for them specifically, but from what the boss said, there are many permutations."

Zeeb rolled his eyes. "I swear, you sound more like the boss every day."

"I watched them at breakfast," Matt told them. "There's

obviously one of them who's in charge of the other two."

"Not sure *in charge* is how I'd put it," Teague observed, "but you're on the right track. I'll be honest, I'm curious."

Behind Butch, the door opened, and Zeeb's face lit up. "Hey, stranger? How's it hanging?"

"I don't know. I haven't measured it in a while."

Butch forced himself not to react to the sound of Sol's deep voice. Finally coming out as bi to his coworkers was one thing—letting them know every detail of his private life was another, and right then Butch wanted to keep things private.

Zeeb laughed. "Good to see ya, Sol. How's life over there in the Leather barn?"

Sol chuckled. "Seriously? That's what you're going to call it?"

"Gimme a minute, and I'm sure I can come up with something better." Zeeb grinned. "And definitely dirtier. Tied anyone up lately?"

"Not yet, but it's only Monday." That brought a few chuckles from around the table.

Teague cleared his throat. "Was there something you wanted, Sol?"

"He came over to see us," Walt interjected. His eyes gleamed. "You missed us, right?"

Sol laughed. "You know what? I did. I've thought a lot about this place since I left. It's good to be back. And I came over here because I have to go into Bozeman this afternoon, and Toby said Butch would take me."

"Not sure Butch can fit that into his busy schedule," Zeeb quipped.

Butch rolled his eyes. "Quit being a dick." He glanced at Sol. "What time?"

"I need to be there by two. That okay?"

"Sure." Butch couldn't help wondering if this trip was part of Sol's plan.

"You still okay for Thursday night?" Zeeb asked Sol.

"I wouldn't miss it. I've already ordered the male stripper to join us at the casino." Sol regarded Zeeb with a deadpan expression.

Zeeb widened his eyes. "Tell me you're joking."

Sol arched his eyebrows. "Did I choose the wrong gender?

Want me to change it?"

Zeeb huffed. "Hey, if a guy wants to show off what God gave him, that's okay by me, but the casino owners won't be too happy about it. They'll throw me out." Then he narrowed his gaze. "There isn't any stripper, is there? You're yanking my chain." His eyes sparkled. "Now, if you were to order one for my hotel room, that'd be just fine." He waggled his eyebrows. "Why else d'you think I booked a room all to myself?"

Butch had a feeling if he didn't call a halt to the banter, Teague would lose it.

"I'll be ready at one-thirty," he told Sol.

"Thanks. You're going to have to wait a while for me. This could take a few hours."

"Hey, Butch. Don't forget to take your needlepoint with ya," Zeeb joked. Butch gave him the finger, and Zeeb cackled.

"You got time to grab a cup of coffee with us?" Matt asked. "Or do you have plans?"

"The latter. I'm giving a talk this morning." Sol smiled. "Seems some of the other guests need a refresher course on boundaries." He gave Butch a nod. "I'll see you at one-thirty." He smiled at the hands. "It's good to see you all again." Then he was out of there.

"And there was me thinking it was all hot, dirty sex," Zeeb remarked. "They got classes too? Who knew?"

Teague finished his coffee. "Okay, I need to get on with my day. I'll be back later with the guest list for next week." He pushed his chair back, stood, and headed out of the door.

Butch wasn't about to leave things hanging.

"Back in a sec." He rose and followed Teague out of the bunkhouse. "Hey, Teague?" he hollered.

Teague stopped and turned. "Something up?" His eyes were cool.

Butch caught up with him. "Yeah. We need to talk."

"Whatever you've got going on with Sol is none of my business—until the boss or Toby find out. *Then* it'll be my business."

"I'm not using him, all right?" Butch flung at him. "You're about as wrong as you can be. I haven't swapped your ass for his. I didn't go to him because of any fucking bad dream. And I'm not gonna go into details, but this is fucking huge, I mean, *crazily* huge." He paused to draw breath. "Don't be giving me a hard time over this. It's not what you think." His chest heaved.

Teague stared at him. "I guess I'll have to take your word for that." He tipped his hat. "Just… be careful, okay?" He resumed his previous brisk pace, heading for the house.

Butch wasn't sure what that last comment meant.

What do I have to be careful about?

Butch pulled into the curb and switched off the engine. "So, where's this appointment of yours?"

Sol pointed across the street. "There."

Butch followed his finger, and frowned. "Sacred Images? The tattoo place? You're getting another tattoo?" As far as he knew, Sol only had one—the strip of barbed wire around his upper right arm.

Sol studied him. "I wasn't thinking of one for me—but for you. Two, actually."

What the fuck?

"You think you might've *asked* me first?" he retorted. "Tattoos are kinda personal. You don't just—"

"Please," Sol entreated. "Let me speak?"

Butch fell silent, perplexed.

"It was your tattoo that gave me the idea. I wanted to leave you with a reminder that you're not the same man." Sol pulled his phone from his pocket and scrolled. He held it up for Butch to see. On the screen was a stylized picture of a lotus flower.

"Pretty, but why would I want that?"

"Because it has a meaning that fits you perfectly." Sol smiled. "The lotus flower signifies new beginnings."

Butch's throat tightened. "That's beautiful."

Sol scrolled again, and this time he showed Butch a tattoo of a compass.

Butch chuckled. "I don't think that'll work, y'know."

Sol laughed too. "I chose this one to show you're moving in

the right direction."

Fuck.

He swallowed hard. "You've put a lot of thought into this, haven't you?"

Sol nodded. "Your first tattoo will always remind you of the past. Like I said, I wouldn't change that. But you need new tattoos for the new man you've become." He squeezed Butch's thigh. "Here's the important part. You don't have to do this. If you really don't want them, then I'll cross the street, cancel the appointment, and you can drive me back to Salvation." His eyes were warm. "I know it was presumptive of me, but I just wanted to give you the opportunity."

Yes, it *was* presumptive. A tattoo was a very personal choice, but the meanings behind the images had overturned Butch's initial objections.

Sol's right. So much has changed in my life. And looking at the flower and the compass would also be a reminder of Sol when he returned home to San Francisco.

That last part? That was the clincher.

His heart quaked. *Don't think about that part. You've got four whole days left before that happens.*

Butch squared his shoulders. "So… where do you think they'd look good?"

The rest of the afternoon was kind of a blur.

Sol sat in a chair, watching Tanner work on Butch's left inner arm and his right forearm. He'd booked a big enough block of time so Butch wouldn't have to come back: part of that decision took Butch's job into account.

He still couldn't believe Butch had agreed to it. The idea had been a gamble, but he'd given a great deal of thought to what images to use. In the end, he'd researched images with specific meanings, and he had to admit, the compass and flower were perfect.

Butch was quiet, and Sol wasn't sure if that was because he

didn't like the feeling of Tanner's needle, or because he'd retreated deep inside himself to think and reflect. The compass on his left arm was completed relatively quickly, but the lotus flower required more time. Every now and then, Tanner would check Butch was okay, but for the most part he worked in silence, and the only sounds in the salon were the buzzing of the needle and the soft music in the background.

Three hours later, Tanner was done. He covered the tattoos with clear wrap, and secured them with tape before handing Butch a leaflet about caring for a new tattoo. Butch kept staring at the lotus flower, executed in shades of red, orange, and yellow, with glossy, lush green leaves surrounding it.

"It's even better than I expected," Sol admitted. And when the redness faded, the colors would be awesome.

Butch glanced at the clock on the wall. "I'd better get you back to the ranch."

The hint of reluctance in his voice mirrored Sol's own feelings.

I don't want the day to end like this.

He wanted more time with Butch.

Sol paid Tanner, and Butch appeared uncomfortable.

"I should pay for these."

Sol shook his head. "This was my idea. I'm not going to let you pay for them." He inclined his head toward the door. "We'd better go."

They both thanked Tanner once more, and then walked out into the sunshine.

"Where were you planning on sleeping tonight?" Sol asked as they crossed the street.

"With you—if that's okay."

Sol beamed. "More than okay. Have any of the guys commented about your absence the last two nights?"

"Sure they have, but I'm sayin' nothing." Butch unlocked the truck. "There's only one thing I need to know."

The pause that followed intrigued the hell out of him. "And what's that?"

"Will we be doing much sleeping?"

Sol's laughter caused several heads to turn in their direction.

"Not much, no, but I'll be sure to be careful around your

tattoos. And I hope you enjoyed last night, because whatever we end up doing, you don't get to come."

"How long this time?"

"That depends on how long I decide to leave you in the cock cage."

The hitch in Butch's breathing was delicious.

CHAPTER 48

Butch found Sol in the main room of the Leather barn, peering into one of the cabinets. There was no one in sight, but voices came from over their heads. Cries. Moans. Groans.

Butch's face grew warm when he realized what he was hearing, and he had to adjust his crotch.

Sol glanced at him and chuckled. "Well, that isn't going to work."

"What isn't?"

He pointed to Butch's erection. "You need to be soft if I'm going to get this on you." He held up a shiny metal contraption, and Butch saw instantly that it was one of the cock cages he'd seen on the club website.

He grinned. "You could help me get rid of it."

Sol snorted. "Nice try." He closed the cabinet. "Come on up to my room. We won't be disturbed in there."

Butch followed him up the stairs, unable to tear his gaze away from the cage in Sol's hand.

How is that gonna feel? Will I be aware of it all the time? How long do I have to wear it? Can I pee while it's on?

And underneath all the questions there was a ripple of anticipation, excitement, and maybe a little trepidation.

If someone had told me I'd be doing this—and wanting *to do this—I'd have laughed my ass off.* But he couldn't deny everything Sol had gotten him to do had been so damn good. And when Sol said it would be worth trying, Butch believed him.

Butch trusted him.

Hell, it was more than trust, and Butch knew it.

Something had shifted inside him, and for the first time, sex wasn't a cure-all. It wasn't just a case of getting off, or a distraction from the guilt that had plagued him. And a big part of that shift was to do with Sol.

The previous night, he'd lain in Sol's bed, Sol's arms around him, and while it had felt so fucking *right*, what had come to mind was the strangeness of it all. Not only strange, but scary too.

I never felt like this about anyone, not even Diana.

Theirs had been a physical relationship, and they'd both known that. Butch had been fond of her, sure, but hell, he'd been twenty-one, twenty-two, and what had filled his mind every time she'd been around had been lust, pure and simple. Race had been a good friend, albeit one with benefits, but again, there hadn't been this *connection* he felt with Sol.

The connection that scared the fuck out of him.

Butch prided himself on being open and communicative with his coworkers and the boss, but as for sharing his true feelings? Hell no. Yet here he was, yearning to be open and honest with Sol, but at the same time, scared of the consequences if he spoke out.

What would I say to him? 'Sol, I never cared about anyone the way I care about you. And I don't want this to end. It's way more than all the stuff you're showing me, teaching me…I know you have to leave, but I need to know you're coming back. Or that I can come see you.'

All of which he could sum up in six words.

I think I'm falling for you.

Not that Butch would recognize such feelings. He'd never fallen for anyone, and he hadn't thought it would happen for him.

The fact that it had?

Butch didn't know if he was elated or scared shitless. And until he got the slightest indication from Sol that his feelings might be reciprocated, he was keeping his damn mouth shut.

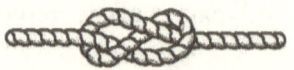

Sol closed the door. He'd been thinking about the upcoming conversation all the way home from Bozeman.

I have to find a balance between sharing too much and not enough.

With a little more than four days before he had to leave, he wasn't about to cover all the guidelines, protocols…

Butch doesn't know yet if he wants this.

Sol's task was to give him enough to enable him to come to a decision.

Butch stood beside the bed. He had an air about him, a kind

of what-am-I-doing-here? vibe, so unlike the man who'd blanked him all those weeks ago.

That's because he isn't the same man.

It felt as though Butch had done more than change—he'd evolved. And Sol was about to help him take a few more steps along the path he was following at present.

The problem was, Sol wanted to be around when Butch reached the end of the path, but that was *not* a good idea. The more time he spent with Butch, the more convoluted his feelings became.

This is about opening new doors for Butch.

Except Butch was the one who'd opened a door, one Sol had thought was closed, the lock rusted beyond repair, and the key lost, never to be found again.

Never to be sought again, either.

I can't let him in. I just can't.

He'd been there, done that, and gotten his heart broken in the process. It was a pain that had stayed with him, a pain he did *not* want to suffer again, and that meant not letting himself get into that position.

Ever.

Letting Butch in opened the door to potentially losing him one day, and although there were risks associated with anything worthwhile in life, he wasn't prepared to take that risk.

None of it made sense.

It was illogical and he knew it.

"Sol?"

He gave himself a mental kick for getting so lost in his own head that he'd forgotten he wasn't alone. He gestured to the bed. "Sit, please."

"Don't I need to take my jeans off?" Butch smirked. "It might be a little difficult to put that on otherwise."

Sol set the cock cage aside. "That's for later. Right now we need to talk."

Butch sat. "Sounds kinda serious."

"To be honest, we've already begun this conversation. Remember I asked if there were things you wanted to try—or not, as the case may be?"

"Sure."

Sol perched on the foot of the bed. "Well, that's one of the things we need to discuss. There's an awful lot we could talk about, but time is not on our side. So... think of this as an introduction." He noted Butch's intense gaze. "You're dipping your toes into a whole new world of experiences, and it might be that you decide 'hey, you know what? This isn't for me.'"

Butch frowned. "'An introduction'? I see. But what happens if I *like* how it's going? Where do we go from there? Will you show me more?"

Sol's heart raced. Dear *Lord*, he wanted that. He forced himself to be practical, however.

"See, *that's* what I want to talk about. You'd be starting on a journey, but your guide might change along the way." Sol was dancing around the subject, instead of coming right out with it and speaking plainly, but he couldn't help himself.

Butch leaned back on his hands. "So let me see if I understand you right. What you're saying is, I might *start* with you but that's not necessarily who I continue with?"

Sol smiled, relief flooding through him.

"It makes sense. You're here, and I'm in San Francisco. And while I *do* know a couple of Doms who have subs in other states, and they manage to make things work at a distance, I'm not sure I could do that."

His stomach clenched at the lie. *I don't want to do that.* Putting distance between them would prevent him from falling further than he already had.

I can be honest about that much. He could even pinpoint the moment when he'd first recognized Butch could be important to him.

I didn't come back to Salvation to help Toby out. I came back for Butch.

And that had been a mistake. He should've seen the way things were going, recognized the danger signs.

It isn't too late. I can still walk away.

Then he noticed how quiet the room was.

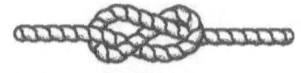

Butch gazed at him, doing his damnedest not to appear disappointed.

"Oh. Yeah, I can see how that might not work."

But why *can't it?*

Fuck, that hurt, more than he'd imagined it would. He didn't *want* another guide—he wanted Sol. Okay, so Sol had to leave. He had a life in San Francisco. Butch got that. *But he could always come back, right? We could make it a regular thing, couldn't we?*

He could boil everything down to one question that made his heart ache.

Is this all I get?

Because if this was it, he was determined to get as much out of their time together as possible. A vague hope stirred inside him.

Spending time with Sol could have an unforeseen consequence.

He might change his mind.

Yes, Sol would leave—Butch knew that was a given—but there was a greater chance he'd return if there was a stronger connection between them.

A bond neither of them wanted to break.

It was a plan. Not a great one, but at least it was something.

Butch took a deep breath. "That website I looked at... the one from Toby's club? I saw a list. Is that what you're talking about?"

Sol nodded, smiling. "I could show you a list. We could talk about the activities, and you could tell me which ones interest you."

"Sure. Let's do that." He glanced at the cock cage, and realized his dick was limp.

The prospect of losing Sol killed his libido stone-dead.

Butch unfastened his jeans and shoved them to his knees. "Better do it now, while you've got the chance. We can talk once you've got me all trussed up."

"Not so fast. Talk first, cage later."

Butch sat, not bothering to pull up his jeans. "You're gonna lock my dick in a cage. What else do I need to know?"

"How long it can be worn generally and how it will feel? How *you* will feel?"

He stilled. "How *will* it feel?"

"A little strange at first. After a few hours, it might feel a little uncomfortable, especially if you get a boner. You can urinate with it on—you just can't come." Sol smiled. "Except that can happen. One time a Dom held a vibrator against the cage, and *oh my God*, that was intense."

He blinked. "You've worn one?"

Sol smiled. "Of course. I never ask a sub to do something I haven't experienced firsthand." He squeezed Butch's shoulder. "As for how you will feel, mentally and emotionally it can be a bit of a rollercoaster. You're handing over control of your sexual desires." Sol tilted his head. "Still want to do it?"

Butch nodded. "Will it hurt when you put it on?"

"Only if the process gets you all excited. But to be honest, that just makes it difficult to attach it."

"And when does it come off?"

Sol shrugged. "Experienced subs can last for weeks, even months with care taken over hygiene. It *can* be removed at night, or alternated with an on-off approach over nights—"

Butch figured his face told a story all on its own because Sol buried a smile, or tried to at least. "I said *experienced* subs. With you? I'd say a few hours to see if you can tolerate it. But I'd be here the whole time, watching for signs that you can't, you know, like bad circulation. If everything's okay, it comes off when I say so." Sol cupped his cheek. "Unless you call a stop yourself because you simply change your mind."

Butch breathed a little easier. "I can do that?"

"Of course. That happens, okay? Sometimes you'll like the look of something, try it, and find it's not for you." Sol smiled. "That's when you learn handing over control is a borrowed gift, one you can take back at any time." His smile faded. "And if the Dom shows no signs of handing control back to you, you resist headbutting the bastard, you get out of there, and you don't let him use the word Dom around you ever again." Sol narrowed his gaze. "Because he won't ever be one, not in *my* eyes at any rate."

Butch didn't want to think about another Dom. "Let's do this." He looked Sol in the eye. "This is me giving consent, okay?"

Sol kissed him on the lips. "Understood."

He grabbed the bottle of lube from the nightstand, opened it, and applied it liberally to Butch's cock and balls before squeezing a small amount inside the cage. The base was a heavy ring, and Sol slid it over Butch's shaft and balls, taking his time, working at a slow and steady pace, easing each testicle through one at a time and bending his flaccid dick downward to get it through. At last it sat snugly against his body.

"Okay so far?"

Butch managed a nod, and Sol arched his eyebrows. "It's fine," Butch told him.

Sol guided his cock into the cage, lining up the locking pins with the holes on the base ring and sliding the cage toward his body until it was in the correct position. Then he aligned the device, hooking the padlock through and clicking the locking pin into place.

"Does that feel okay?" Sol asked.

"Yeah. Weird, but okay."

"Almost done."

Butch's eyebrows shot up. "There's more?"

Sol placed the key in his hand. "Only one thing. This opens the padlock."

Butch rolled his eyes. "I just saw you lock it, so *duh*."

Sol held his hand out. "And now you give it to me."

His heart pounded, something Butch hadn't expected. His hand shook a little as he handed over the key. "And when does it come off?"

"When I say so."

Okay, this was heady as fuck. Then a horrible thought occurred.

"You… you're not gonna try and turn me on while I'm wearing this, are you?"

Sol widened his eyes. "Would I do something so evil?"

Butch let out a loud snort. "Never play poker, Sol."

"And now we'll talk."

There was one thing about wearing the cock cage—it concentrated the mind wonderfully.

CHAPTER 49

Tuesday, September 27

Sol kept his eyes closed, enjoying Butch's warmth, the feel of his skin against Sol's, the smell of him, a mixture of soap that lingered from their shower, and underneath it Butch's raw, musky scent that had Sol burying his face in Butch's neck, breathing him in, stroking his chest, feeling the beat of his heart.

They'd talked for hours, Butch asking questions, Sol answering them, and by the time his eyelids had grown heavy, Sol had a better idea of what made Butch tick. He was obviously still figuring it all out, but one thing was clear—Butch was a submissive.

He has so much potential.

Except that wasn't what drew him to Butch and he knew it.

"Morning." Butch rolled over and snuggled against his chest, and Sol was blown away by the sweetness and intimacy of the embrace.

He feels so good in my arms.

"Morning."

"What you got planned for today?"

"Nothing so far. I think the other guests want to enjoy their surroundings. There was some talk about riding out with one of the hands to see where the cattle are grazing."

"You going with 'em?"

The idea came to him, and he knew he should dismiss it, but…

"Didn't you promise me a ride to Mirror Lake?"

Butch pulled back and beamed at him. "Seriously? You wanna do that?"

The light in his eyes and the unfettered joy in his voice unraveled all Sol's intentions. "Yeah, I would."

"I could have Matt make us up some lunch to take with us."

Sol had to smile at that. "A picnic?"

"Why not? I can't tell you the last time I did that. And it's a glorious spot for a swim too."

Sol stretched to grab his phone and peered at the forecast. "Hell no. There's a high of fifty-two degrees today. My balls'll shrink to the size of peas."

Butch chuckled. "I can always warm 'em up for ya."

"I'm sure you could." He put his phone down and cupped Butch's dick. "Ready for it to go back on? Or have you had enough?"

Butch went quiet for a moment, and Sol would have loved to know what was going on inside his head. Then he nodded.

"Yeah, put it back on. I liked it."

Sol pressed his lips to Butch's forehead. "I had a feeling you might." On impulse, he rolled Butch onto his back, then covered him with his body, pinning him to the mattress.

"Love it when you do this," Butch murmured before Sol claimed his mouth in a lingering, chaste kiss.

"That's good," he murmured back against Butch's lips. "Because I love doing it."

The trouble was, he could *so* get used to it.

They sat on bedrolls, and Butch debated grabbing one of the blankets he'd brought along and wrapping it around him. It was way too cold to swim, but the air up there was fresh and exhilarating, the sky dotted with clouds. A breeze ruffled the water, and the sound of it lapping against the rocks filled him with peace and contentment.

"I love it here," he said quietly. "This is where I come when I wanna think."

Sol sat beside him, arms resting on his knees. "I can see why. It's such a beautiful, tranquil place." He leaned into Butch. "What are you thinking about right now?"

Butch sighed. "Scott." He gazed out at the lake, listening to the light wind catching in the branches of the trees. "I still feel guilty for the way I treated him, but I'm glad I know the truth. But part of me wishes…"

Sol's strong arm was around his shoulders. "Wishes what?"

"That I'd had the courage to be honest with him. That we could've been friends. That he could've found enough courage to tell me what was going on, and then maybe I could've helped." His stomach churned. "All I did was make things worse."

"We all wish we'd done stuff differently when we were kids," Sol told him. "But as for being honest with him, you know what it was like back then. Can you name me one kid who was openly gay? Or bi?"

Butch shook his head.

"Exactly. No one wanted to stick their head above the parapet, and that included me." He went quiet, but it felt as though the silence had weight, even significance.

"My turn to ask." Butch looked him in the eye. "What are *you* thinking about?"

Sol gave a shrug. "We all have regrets, right? All of us can think of one or two moments in our lives when if we'd acted differently, *said* something, we might have changed the outcome." He stared at the sky over their heads.

"You thinking of something specific?"

Sol swallowed. "Maybe? But there's a possibility that if I'd acted differently, I might not be sitting here with you now."

Butch's breathing hitched. "That sounds like one serious outcome."

"And one I'm not going to talk about." Sol straightened, and it was as if he'd cast off the layer of sadness that had settled on him. He lay on his back, his arm outstretched. "How about you cover us with one of those blankets, and we lie here and gaze at the sky for a while, listening to the water?"

Butch couldn't think of anything he wanted to do more.

They lay together beneath the blanket, watching birds fly overhead, drinking in the sights and sounds surrounding them. Sol's body was warm against his, and Butch would've happily stayed like that for hours.

His mind drifted back to Sol's words.

What did he mean, he might not be sitting here?

In spite of all their conversations, there was so much he didn't know about Sol, and damn it, he *wanted* to know. Granted, he knew Sol was a good man, caring, supportive, generous, and skilled in areas Butch was only just beginning to learn about. But there was a yawning gap between high school and the present. Sure, he knew Sol had moved from Casper to Gillette, from Gillette to Cheyenne, and then San Francisco, but that was just geography.

What about his history?

Time was running out. The days between then and Saturday were being eaten up by a ravenous beast that cared little for Butch's hopes and dreams.

He wanted more moments like this. And maybe if he got them, then Sol would realize what he was holding in his arms, and would want to *keep* hold of Butch for longer.

Telling Sol how he felt was not an option.

Not yet, at any rate.

Not until he'd seen some indication that Sol felt something for him, until he was certain to avoid rejection.

Because that would break him.

Wednesday, September 28

Robert approached the barn door with caution. He wanted to make sure he wasn't about to walk into the middle of a scene. He couldn't hear anything, so he guessed he was safe.

One of the Doms—Darren, maybe?—sat on a chair, staring at his phone. He glanced up as Robert came closer. "Hey."

"I thought I'd stop by to check everything was okay," Robert said with a smile. "And also to see if there was any feedback you could give us to improve things in the future."

Darren returned his smile. "This is an awesome place you have here. And this week so far… I haven't been this relaxed in a long while."

"I'm happy to hear that." Robert gestured to the main room. "Did we miss anything?"

"God, no. You guys thought of everything. The accommodation's fantastic, the food is amazing, and your people are really helpful. Plus, I've learned a lot."

"Really?"

Darren nodded. "I haven't been a Dom all that long, and Luke and Wyatt are my first subs." His expression grew solemn. "Sol gave me a reminder of what's important."

"He did?"

"Yeah. He has so much more experience than I do, and he's a damn good teacher. You know where he is right now?" Darren pointed along the hallway to the private rooms. "He's with my boys, talking. He's so good with them, like he really knows how to get through to people."

"He's a counselor, among other things," Robert told him.

Darren's face brightened. "Yeah? That explains a lot. I think that's awesome, you having someone here to teach, guide, demonstrate... I had no idea you offered that too."

Up until that moment, Robert had had no idea either, but he was certainly thinking about it now.

"It's such a great balance," Darren continued. "A peaceful new environment to explore kink, and have time to chill as well. I tell you, it was exactly the breathing space we all needed."

"I'm glad."

One of the doors opened, and Luke, Wyatt, and Sol came out.

Sol smiled at Darren. "I think these two would like a little alone time with you."

"Can we go for a ride?" one of the subs asked.

"Sure." Darren pocketed his phone. "Let's go see Paul, and then we'll find a trail."

"Paul will find horses for you," Robert told him. "And there'll be a few ranch hands around if you want a guide. They know all the trails."

Darren beamed. "Sounds great." He glanced at Sol. "Thanks. And sorry about the other morning. You were right to call me out."

Sol's eyes were warm. "We all make mistakes, right? The important thing is we learn from them."

Darren nodded. "Come on, boys. Let's go for a ride." He grinned. "And then later on there might be more... riding."

Both subs flushed.

The three men walked out of the barn, and Robert smiled.

"I thought you were here to relax and give the odd demonstration."

Sol chuckled. "Hey, they wanted a chat. I wasn't going to say no. The main thing is, now they'll talk to Darren about their concerns, which is as it should be."

Robert tilted his head. "Toby says you've been spending a lot of time with Butch. Everything okay there?"

Sol nodded. "Everything is more than okay. We've done a lot of talking."

Robert coughed. He wasn't blind. And from the front porch, he had a perfect view of the new barn—and who was entering and leaving it on a regular basis.

Sol and Butch were doing a damn sight more than talking, he'd bet money on that. But Sol showed no sign of wanting to talk about that, so Robert said nothing.

It's their business.

"I'm glad I caught you. I was going to ask if you wanted to join me and Toby for a drink Friday night. Last night and all."

Sol smiled. "That would be great." His phone buzzed, and he peered at the screen. His face brightened. "I think I'm needed elsewhere."

"Then I'll let you go." Robert tipped his hat and headed out of the barn.

He had a feeling he knew exactly who had messaged Sol, and part of him was *so* freaking happy about that.

It's about time.

The few times he'd seen Butch since Sol's arrival, there was no mistaking the change in him. He seemed relaxed, except it was more than that.

He finally looks happy in his own skin.

That had been a long time coming.

CHAPTER 50

Thursday, September 29

Butch stared at the pile of chips in front of Zeeb. "Dude, cash 'em in. This lucky streak has gotta end sometime. Grab the cash while you still can."

A crowd had gathered around the roulette table, not that it was Zeeb's first run of good luck that night. He'd won a stack of chips playing craps, he'd had a couple of great hands at poker, and right then it didn't look like he could lose.

"Butch is right," Teague added.

"Remember what I told you about my uncle?" Walt chimed in. "He'd won thousands, and lost it all. Don't be a sap—take the money and run."

"What Walt said." Paul frowned. "Quit while you're ahead."

Matt chuckled. "Don't you guys know him by now? You tell Zeeb to do something, and it's a surefire way of getting him to do the complete opposite."

"I have to agree with Butch." Sol gestured to Zeeb's pile. "The odds of you keeping all that have to be astronomical. And no, I *don't* believe some higher power is looking out for you just because it's your birthday, though that *is* a nice theory."

"If you won't listen to all of us, listen to *him*, why don'tcha?" Butch pleaded. He hated the thought of Zeeb's birthday being ruined. "You can't keep this up all night."

Zeeb regarded him with a smile. "And what if I bet I can?"

Butch rolled his eyes. "You'd bet on that?"

"Sure, why not? This is my lucky night, right?" Zeeb grinned. "Okay then. If I get to the end of tonight and I've got less money than I started with, I'll have lost, and I'll pay you a forfeit."

"Dude, you've got nothing I want." Then he matched Zeeb's grin. "Now wait a sec. Maybe I do have an idea after all."

Sol laughed. "Zeeb, you see that gleam in his eyes? Be afraid. Be *very* afraid."

Zeeb folded his arms. "I can take whatever he dishes out. Let's hear it."

"If you lose, you have to find a guy willing to kiss you." He gave the others a mock glare. "And none of you count, y'hear?"

Walt cackled. "You are evil."

"Totally," Paul agreed with a grin.

Zeeb shrugged. "Fine. I accept. But if I have *more* money than I started with…" His eyes sparkled. "You owe *me* a forfeit."

Butch had a feeling Zeeb had already worked out what it was to be.

"I'm listening."

"You know those photos Sol took of our boys? The ones for the website?"

"Sure."

Zeeb smiled. "If you lose, you have to wear that black leather collar you wore in the photos for twenty-four hours."

Butch glanced at Sol, who didn't look happy about the idea.

Sol cleared his throat. "Zeeb, I'm sorry to spoil your fun, it being your birthday and all, but he won't be doing that."

"He wore it for the photo," Zeeb remonstrated. "What's the diff?"

"That was a photo shoot." Sol paused for a sec. "Look, all I'm going to say is, for some guys who are into BDSM, putting a collar on a guy is the equivalent of putting a ring on his finger." He stared at Zeeb. "It *means* something, okay?"

"And you'd be such a guy?" Zeeb asked.

Sol nodded. "I'm old school, all right? A collar is important."

Zeeb took a breath. "I'm sorry. I had no idea."

"It's okay," Sol assured him. "Just come up with something else."

Zeeb stroked his beard, then suddenly he gave a broad smile. "I got it." That twinkle was back. "Butch has to kiss you for a whole minute."

"Then you'd better ask Butch how he feels about that," Sol fired back.

As far as Butch was concerned, it was a pretty safe bet.

He gave a smug smile. "I'm not worried. Your luck won't hold out forever."

At least, he hoped it wouldn't. Not that he didn't love the idea of kissing Sol, far from it.

He just didn't want the others seeing how much he enjoyed it, because then that cat would be out of the bag again, and this time it might not wanna go back in.

The hotel lobby was quiet by the time they filed through the door. The woman on reception smiled at them.

"Was it a good night?"

Zeeb cackled. "It was for me." He headed over to the couch by the window, and delved into his pockets.

"What are you doing?" Teague asked.

Zeeb dropped a pile of bills onto the seat cushion. "I'd have thought that was obvious." He glanced at Butch. "Figuring out if it was a bad night for you." He grinned at the others. "Who's gonna count it all?"

"Wait a minute," Butch interjected. "How much did you start with?"

Zeeb frowned. "About a hundred dollars."

"'About'?" Sol chuckled.

"Give or take." Zeeb emptied his pockets of more of his winnings, and Teague started counting. Butch tried to gauge how much money there was, but Teague turned his back to them all.

Zeeb waggled his eyebrows. "Gettin' nervous, Butch?"

"You. Wish." Zeeb had lost a lot at the poker table before they'd called it a night, and he was feeling quietly confident.

While Teague got on with his task, Zeeb gave the others a speculative glance. "So… which of you organized a little female comp'ny for me tonight?" When everyone stared at him, mouths open, Zeeb rolled his eyes. "You're kidding, right? Not one of you fuckers found me someone to warm my bed? Fuck, I dropped enough hints."

Walt cackled. "You were serious? We couldn't tell."

Matt pulled his phone from his pocket. "Want me to look on Grindr for ya?"

Zeeb huffed. "Don't tempt me." When laughter broke out, he snorted. "Hey, I'm forty. I could be a late bloomer. And I might be up for a little experimentation."

Sol grinned. "I bet I could find you someone to experiment with."

Zeeb guffawed. "Yeah no."

Teague turned around to face them, laughing. "Well, what do you know about that?" He handed Zeeb a wad of bills. "Two hundred fifty-five dollars."

Zeeb's face glowed. "Wow. Seriously?"

Something fluttered in Butch's belly.

"Count it if you don't believe me."

"Oh, I believe you." Zeeb stuffed the money back into his pockets, strolled over to Butch and stood in front of him, hands on his hips. "Hey, mister. I think you owe me a forfeit. And seeing as I'm gonna be sleepin' alone tonight, don't disappoint me. I need cheering up." Butch looked at Sol, and Zeeb laughed. "Just close your eyes. It'll be over before you know it." He glanced at the others. "Who's gonna time it?"

"I will." Teague got his phone out.

Sol walked to where Butch stood, and smiled at Zeeb. "Excuse me, but you need to give me a little room."

Zeeb took a sidestep. "By all means." He chuckled. "I get a better view from over here anyway."

Sol locked gazes with Butch. "You okay with this?"

Butch knew he was asking for consent.

He smiled. "Better than okay." *Fuck it*. They'd find out sooner or later. At least this out it over with in one fell swoop.

"Then close your eyes, Butch."

He laughed. "Uh-uh. When I kiss you, I keep 'em open."

Sol took Butch in his arms, leaned in, and Butch lost himself in a slow, sensual kiss, not bothering to rein in his burgeoning desire. Sol slid his hands down Butch's back, grabbed hold of his ass, and squeezed, pressing their bodies together, making Butch more aware than usual of the cock cage that imprisoned his dick.

Sol was hard, and Butch prayed this was the night he got to come.

Then Sol moaned softly into the kiss, and Butch opened for him, their tongues dancing, while all around them he caught the sound of hitched breathing and gasps.

"Okay, your minute is up," Teague announced.

Butch had no intention of stopping, and it seemed Sol was of the same mind. He looped his arms around Sol's neck, his heart racing when Sol cradled his head in his usual intimate manner, each of them feeding the other soft, intense noises of passion.

"He said you can stop now," Zeeb said in a loud voice.

Sol broke the kiss and released him. "So how long was that?"

Teague chuckled. "One minute forty-five seconds. I was this close to asking if someone had a bucket of cold water handy."

Butch gave Zeeb his full attention, his heart still thumping. "Forfeit paid."

"That wasn't the first time you two have kissed, was it?" Zeeb narrowed his eyes. "You've been holding out on us."

Sol burst out laughing. "Yes, he has, but he's done doing that." His eyes met Butch's. "Haven't you?"

"Yup."

No more hiding.

Sol grabbed his hand. "And now I'm taking him to my room so we can finish what we started." And with that, he headed toward the elevator with Butch in tow, leaving behind them a group of five men laughing and whooping.

"Hey, *I'm* the one who should be getting' lucky tonight," Zeeb called out, which resulted in yet more laughter.

As the elevator doors slid open, Sol leaned in close.

"Just so you know?" His breath tickled Butch's ear. "The cage is coming off, and you get to come."

It might have been Zeeb's birthday, but Butch was getting the best gift of all.

"Sol," Butch moaned as Sol drove his cock all the way home. "I'm getting close." He dug his heels into the flesh of Sol's ass, arms locked around Sol's neck, his chest covered in a sheen of sweat.

Sol kissed him, a deep, lingering kiss that pushed him closer to the edge. "Hold on as long as you can, baby."

That last word almost broke him.

He'd expected their usual frenetic fucking, but *this*... Sol's unhurried thrusts set him alight, and he couldn't get enough of Sol's kisses. The long glides of his shaft into Butch's ass, the exquisite friction, the way Sol stared into his eyes as he moved in and out, the pace measured... All of it was fucking *perfect*.

Sol stilled, and then tremors wracked his body. That slow throbbing inside Butch made him want to weep, and he dug his fingers into Sol's back, clinging to him as Sol filled the latex, bearing down to squeeze around Sol's shaft, loving the groan of pleasure that tumbled from him.

"Sol," he begged, his body tingling, his dick smacking against his belly, jerking with each thrust, a pool of pre-cum trickling into his navel and leaving trails over his skin.

Sol shuddered, his back arched, and Butch couldn't tear his gaze away. Sol's body glistened, sweat dripping from him, and he bent lower to meet Butch's mouth in a leisurely kiss.

"Touch yourself," Sol whispered against his lips, and Butch let out another moan as he pulled on his cock, his balls tight, his stomach quivering as he shot so hard it made his head spin. And through it all Sol kissed him amid soft murmurs that fed Butch's soul.

"Beautiful man. So fucking beautiful when you come."

Sol held him, cradled him, and Butch's heart soared.

So this is what love feels like.

It was more than the joining of bodies—that connection he'd felt weeks ago had developed into something deeper, richer, more satisfying than he'd ever imagined possible. And when it was all over, once Sol had disposed of the condom and wiped them both down with a towel, he held Butch to him as though he were fragile, the sounds of their breathing filling the air.

"This just gets better and better," Sol murmured, stroking Butch's damp hair.

"Not sure how we can top that." Butch smiled. "But I'm sure we can think of something, although we might have to wait till your next visit." He kissed Sol's chest. "You know I'm gonna be counting the days, right?"

Sol's hand stilled on his head, his breathing erratic.

Butch nuzzled Sol's neck. "Fuck, you always smell so good. I might have to steal the pillowcase from your room back at the ranch, so I can sleep with the smell of you in my nostrils. And that tee you left with me… you're gonna need to use it as a cum-rag again before you leave, because the smell has faded."

Sol's breathing deepened, and Butch knew he'd fallen asleep. He didn't want to move for fear that would somehow shatter the moment, and he'd lose this glorious feeling that went bone-deep.

"Sol," he whispered.

Nothing.

"Sol, you awake?"

Nothing.

Butch sighed. "I never thought I'd be into all this—you know, BDSM—but I love the way it makes me feel," he whispered. "I love the way *you* make me feel too, like I can do anything. But I guess that's what it feels like when you love someone. I never had this before, this awesome, earth-shattering feeling." He swallowed. "It scares me a little too. I never realized it could be like this. I watched Toby and the boss, saw how they were together, growing toward each other, connecting, and I thought I'd never find anyone who'd fit me the way *they* fit." He smiled to himself. "And then you came along. I've loved everything we've done, all of it, and I can't wait to do more. I know your life is in San Francisco and mine is here, but that doesn't have to be permanent, does it?" He sighed. "I need to say all this when you're awake, don't I?" He glanced at the lotus flower on his right arm. "You nailed it, didn't you? New beginnings." Butch closed his eyes and breathed deeply, drinking in Sol's warmth, his strength, his scent.

Sleep came and took him, and he sank into its velvety arms.

Sol lay there, not daring to move.

Aw fuck.

Fuck.

Fuck.

CHAPTER 51

Friday, September 30

Butch switched off the engine and got out of the truck. He didn't mind running errands, but he wasn't sure why the boss had chosen him to take several packages to the post office. He knew why he'd been reluctant to go: the minutes of Sol's last full day were ticking away, and they were precious. He guessed Sol felt the same way. He'd been awful quiet that morning, ever since they'd woken. He hadn't even wanted to go find breakfast, so Butch had driven them back to Salvation.

Butch had a good explanation for Sol's lack of conversation and appetite.

He doesn't want to go.

The previous night's admissions had tumbled out of him, and the only reason he'd come out with all that was because he knew Sol couldn't hear him.

He must know how I feel about him.

After that kiss in the hotel lobby, *everyone* had to know how he felt about Sol. Butch was happy not to hide his feelings any longer. What was more, if Teague knew, then that meant Toby and the boss would also know.

Speak of the devil…

Toby was walking toward him, and one glance at his face sent ice trickling through Butch's veins. Toby wasn't smiling, and the light had gone from his eyes.

"What's happened?" he demanded. "Is it the boss? Is he okay?" His heartbeat quickened.

"Robert's fine," Toby assured him.

Butch gave his brow an exaggerated wipe. "Thank God. I thought for a minute something was wrong."

When Toby's expression didn't change, that trickle of ice swelled into a flood.

"Something *is* wrong, isn't it?"

"Let's go for a walk."

Butch frowned. "Now? Sorry, but can this wait? I need to get back to Sol." He flushed. "I don't know if you heard about last—"

"Butch." Toby looked miserable as fuck. "Sol's gone."

The words did not compute.

"Gone where?"

"To the airport, half an hour ago."

Butch's brain seemed to be stuck in neutral. "No, that can't be right. His flight's tomorrow."

"Something came up."

Toby's words finally sank in.

"But… he wouldn't have left without saying goodbye." Butch pulled his phone from his pocket and checked for messages.

Nothing.

Ice packed around Butch's heart and he struggled to breathe.

"Did… did he say when he'd be visiting Salvation again?"

Please tell me he's coming back. Throw me a lifeline here.

Toby swallowed, and the pain Butch saw in his eyes sent a spike of fear lancing through him, a shard of hot steel searing him.

"I don't think he'll be back," Toby said in a low voice.

Then it hit him.

He wasn't asleep, was he? He heard every word I said. Jesus. Me and my big mouth.

So much for thinking he and Sol were on the same page.

They weren't even in the same book.

"It's my fault," he murmured, his throat tight.

Toby frowned. "What makes you say that?"

Butch didn't answer. He was too busy trying to remember everything he'd said. One line stood out.

I guess that's what it feels like when you love someone.

There could only be one explanation. Butch had gotten it all so fucking wrong.

It was just sex, wasn't it? I read way too much into it.

But damn it, the way Sol had fucked him last night—

No. That wasn't right. The way they'd *made love* last night. That was what had given him the courage to speak the way he did.

How could I get it so wrong?

"Oh my God." Toby expelled a breath. "You're in love with him."

There seemed little point in hiding anymore.

"Yes."

"Does he know that?"

"I said something last night that might've given the game away. I didn't think he could hear me. Turns out I was wrong." His chest felt as if a boa constrictor had curled itself around his ribcage and was slowly tightening its coils.

I scared him off, didn't I?

"Fuck." Toby's face contorted.

"I shouldn't have said anything."

And Sol shouldn't have bolted, not like this. Not without one single fucking word.

That stopped him in his tracks.

"So much for communication," he said, unable to rein in his bitterness. "What the fuck does that say about the relationship between a Dom and his sub?"

"Wait—you and Sol—you're—"

Butch barely heard him. "I thought we were supposed to be open and honest with each other, or does that only go one way?" He snorted. "Great lesson you're teaching me here, Sol."

"Hey. *Hey!*" Toby's face tightened. "If he's your Dom, then don't doubt him, okay?"

Butch gaped at him. "Are you for real? He just walked away without a goddamn word."

"I know, but…" Toby took his hat off and scraped his fingers through his hair. "This isn't like Sol, all right? He doesn't back away without an explanation, not as a Dom at any rate. He always keeps things professional, just like I do."

"You call this professional?" Butch's heart pounded, his body was tense as fuck, and his stomach quivered.

Toby tried to take hold of Butch's arm, but he shrugged free. "Butch, come with me, please. We need to talk."

"I'm not talking to anyone but Sol. This has nothing to do with you."

Toby rolled out a heavy sigh. "But I think I'm the only one who can shed light on this."

Butch froze. "What?"

"Sol may be a Dom, but he's also someone with a past, and I guess it's hard to talk about that past, even if he does understand psychology and deals with people's problems all the time." Toby's eyes were warm. "He just has a hard time dealing with his own." He laid his hand on Butch's arm, only this time, Butch didn't shrug it off. "Come on up to the house. We can't talk here, and there's stuff I need to tell you."

"About Sol?"

Toby nodded. "There are things you need to know."

They walked toward the sloping path. Butch's head was spinning, and he wanted to throw up.

Am I ever gonna see him again?

By the time they reached the house, Butch was on the point of calling Sol to tell him to turn the fuck around and come back.

I don't want to lose him.

Toby led him into the living room and indicated the nearest couch. "Can I get you a drink?"

Butch's heart stuttered. "Am I gonna need one?"

"Frankly? Yeah."

"Bourbon. Make it a large one."

"Am I invited to this party?" The boss stood under the gallery, his glasses in his hand.

Toby sighed. "You need to hear this too." He went over to the liquor cabinet. "Sol didn't leave because he had an emergency, or whatever reason he gave you for leaving early. He was running away."

"From what?" The boss took the glass Toby offered him.

Toby inclined his head toward Butch. "From him. And before you say a word, this isn't Butch's fault, okay? This is all on Sol." He joined Butch on the couch, and the boss took the armchair facing them. Toby leaned back against the cushions. "I only know all this because four years ago, me and Sol, we got drunk at a party, and it just poured out of him. I think it was still pretty raw."

"*What* was raw?" Butch fired back.

"I was going to ask the same question," the boss added.

Toby took a long drink from his glass. "Losing Liam."

Liam? Who the fuck is Liam?

Butch listened as Toby spoke in a low voice, and as the minutes passed, his stomach churned and a flush of hot guilt rushed through him. Sol had listened while Butch had spoken about Scott's death, and not once had he shared his own history, his own hidden pain. When Toby finished speaking, Butch stared at him in horror. *Now* it all made sense: why Sol had backed away so viciously, why everything that had happened with Liam had forced Sol into silence and made him bolt.

"That's so fucking *awful*."

"I know."

"But…. Why didn't he tell me? Why did he leave the way he did? What does Liam have to do with me?" Butch fought to maintain his self-control.

I don't understand any of this. His initial rage bubbled up once more. *Why the fuck couldn't you talk to me, Sol?*

"You'll have to ask him that," Toby said.

"That's a little difficult when he isn't here, don'tcha think?" Butch glanced at the boss. "Did you know any of this?"

He shook his head, his eyes filled with compassion.

"Can I say something here?" Toby's voice was gentle. "I know you're angry—I'd probably feel the same way if I were in your shoes. But… This is the hardest lesson for anyone new coming into the lifestyle. You get to see the person behind the stereotype, how Doms and subs come in all shapes and sizes—and with all kinds of faults, flaws, and last but not least, a history. We all have the ability to fuck up and shut up when we shouldn't. And while you're learning about those faults and flaws, about who someone really is, they're doing the same about you." He sighed. "And sometimes—just sometimes—something comes along, like *you* came along, and throws them off course."

"So what do I do to get Sol back on course?"

Toby didn't answer.

Butch wasn't about to sit there and wallow in self-pity, not when he could do something to alleviate the ache in his chest.

He drained his glass. "Boss? I got a favor to ask. I'm gonna need the weekend off."

The boss expelled a breath. "Go pack a bag. I'll drive you to the airport myself."

Relief shuddered through him. His heart felt as if it was breaking, but tangled up with his sorrow was the burning need to discover what the fuck was going on.

And the only one who had the answer to that was Sol.

CHAPTER 52

Saturday, October 1

San Francisco

Sol removed the last rope from Tyler's body, and a ripple of applause came from the ten or so guys who'd been watching the Shibari demonstration.

"That was really good," someone said, and there was murmured agreement.

Except Sol knew the truth. It hadn't been *that* good, not really. He'd lacked focus, and it hadn't helped that every time he tied a knot or tightened a rope around Tyler, it wasn't Tyler he saw in his head, but a certain cowboy, his head bowed as Sol drew the rope over his nipple, teasing it, loving the shudder that ran through his body…

Enough. That chapter is over.

It didn't help that a still, small voice in his head kept suggesting it didn't have to be.

Tyler let out a contented sigh. "Thank you, Sir."

Sol patted his shoulder. "Thank you for helping." He smiled at Will who walked up behind Tyler and hugged him. "And thank *you* for loaning Tyler to me for the demonstration."

Will waved a hand. "Don't mention it. I know my boy's missed this since Toby left. I figured if I was going to give him what he needs, I'd better learn how to do this."

Sol took in Tyler's blissful expression. "You already give him what he needs—you."

Will beamed. "He's such a special boy." He kissed the top of Tyler's head. "I have a room for us, where we can be quiet for a while."

Tyler's face glowed. "I'd love that, Master." The two men walked off together, Will's arm around Tyler's waist, Tyler's head against Will's shoulder.

You could have what they have.

He wanted to shut out such thoughts. He didn't want to be

reminded of what he'd lost.

What he'd walked away from.

"Hey, Sol." Sean crossed the floor to join him at the stage. "You got a minute?"

"I have now. What's up?"

"We've got a new guy here today, checking out the club. A sub. Apparently he's heard of you."

Sol managed a smile. "Wow. I have a reputation?"

"So could you show him around, maybe answer any questions?"

"Sure." When Sean didn't move, Sol gave him an inquiring glance. "Was there something else?"

"Are you okay?"

Damn. He'd thought he'd done a better job of masking his emotions.

"Not really, but I will be. Time will take care of that."

And about a thousand miles.

"If you need to talk…"

Sol smiled again. "Thanks, but I'm fine. Now, where's this sub?"

"I left him in my office. You can talk in there. I've got an errand to run. Casey's around if you need him." Sean strode off in the direction of the main door.

Sol tidied his ropes and placed them neatly on the stage, ready to go back into their bag. He headed for Sean's office, grateful for the distraction.

It was going to take a whole lotta distraction to drive Butch from his thoughts.

He opened the door, and—

Fuck.

Butch stood by the window, gazing out at the street. He turned as Sol closed the door, and the first thing Sol noticed were his eyes.

The light he so loved to see there had died, and that had to be Sol's fault.

Butch said nothing, and Sol figured it was up to him to start the conversation.

"How did you know where I was?" He frowned. "Stupid question. Forget I asked. It was Toby, right?" He walked over to where Butch stood. "Why are you here?"

Butch's eyebrows shot up. "And you talk about stupid questions?" Sol opened his mouth to say something, *anything*, and Butch held his hand up. "Before you say another word, I know, okay? I heard the story from Toby—well, the bare details of it."

Sol's heart plummeted. "What story?" Except he already knew the answer.

Damn you, Toby.

Butch looked him in the eye. "Liam." Then he fell silent, as if he was waiting for Sol's explanation for being a complete bastard and running out on him like that without a word.

As if it were that easy. That was why Sol had walked away when he did.

Talking about Liam *hurt*.

When no words came, Butch gave a fraction of a nod as if in confirmation, and Sol's heart hammered.

Say something. Anything.

He swallowed. "Look, would you mind if we sat and talked, just… not about that?" *Before my legs start shaking.* Seeing Butch again messed with his head *and* his heart.

Butch went over to the two chairs in front of Sean's desk and sat in one of them. Sol joined him, his hands clammy, his heartbeat racing. He had no clue what to say, but that didn't matter—Butch got in first, his face tight.

"I'm so sorry. That was… just horrific. But what I don't get is why I had to hear about it from Toby, after all the stuff I shared with you—and what it has to do with why you left. That last part, especially."

Sol struggled to form his tumultuous thoughts into cohesive sentences.

"I had to go. I was getting in way too deep."

Butch stared at him, his face flushed. "If you mean you were falling for me, then for fuck's sake, *say* so. Don't dance around with words."

"Okay!" he blurted. "I realized I was falling in love with you. And I was pretty sure you felt the same way."

A sigh escaped Butch's lips. "Yeah, I'm in love with you, and that's something I've never felt before, or said to a living soul. Now tell me why two guys falling in love is such a bad idea that you turn tail and run. It's not like it was when we were growing up. Even Montana has moved with the times. You can say you're into guys and no one bats an eye, at least, not in public."

Sol clasped his hands, his pulse quickening. "I started imagining a life with you, not just as your Dom but as your lover… That's when I knew I had to pull the plug. Because I've *been* there, okay? It ended in disaster. It broke my fucking heart, and I will *not* put myself through that again."

Even as the words left him, he knew how pathetic they sounded.

Butch gaped at him. "Wait a sec. You hightailed it outta there because you were afraid you'd lose me like you lost Liam? Have you any idea how irrational that is?"

"Most fears *are* irrational," Sol countered.

"Yeah, but most fears are rooted in something else. You know what *I* think, Mr. Counselor? You need some counseling. And by the way, I got a news flash for ya." His eyes blazed. "I'm not Liam. And the chances of those exact circumstances happening again are pretty fucking remote." He paused to draw breath, his chest rising and falling. "You ever see that movie, *The Princess Bride?* Walt made us watch it one time. It was okay—all right, it was good, but I wasn't gonna tell him that. Anyway, there was this one line that stuck in my head. Wesley says something about life being pain, and that anyone who says different is selling something. That fucking *nailed* it." He grabbed Sol's hands and held them tight. "Life *is* pain, and we can't avoid it. Would I rather have gone through my life not being tortured by guilt? Hell yeah. But everything I went through, all the pain and emotion I suffered? That made me the man you see today." He squeezed Sol's hands tighter. "And that man wants you. Sol the Dom, Sol the lover… You talked about being a long-distance Dom, and you know what? I didn't want that. I wanted to share your life—both parts of it. Because you can't separate them. You said so yourself. They're you."

Sol's breathing caught. "You don't want to be my sub."

Butch blinked. "Oh really? Then what the fuck did we spend last week talking about? Was that just shooting the breeze? Why don't you come right out and ask me?"

Sol didn't move, didn't break eye contact, his lips parted.

Butch took a deep breath. "For the second time, I'm *not* Liam.

And I think we're a good fit. No—a *great* fit. So why don't you think about what it is you're throwing away." He let go of Sol's hands and stood.

"Butch, I—"

He let out another sigh, and it was as if a cloak of fatigue covered him.

"Like I said, I heard the bare bones of what happened to you from Toby. I came here in the hope of hearing it from you, because... communication, right? I needed to see if you could tell me, if you still trust me enough to share with me—that everything you said about communication wasn't just bullshit."

Sol's heart quaked, but the words wouldn't come.

Butch looked him in the eye. "When you decide to be as open with me as I was with you, you know where to find me." He paused to draw breath. "Because I think you need to tell someone. After all we've been through, I'd hoped that person—" He swallowed. "That *submissive*...would be me. So here are my last thoughts, for what they're worth. I'm here for you just like you were there for me, but I need to see that we're not gonna run into this... communication breakdown again, no matter how much it hurts. And like I said, you know where to find me. I'm not going anywhere." He touched Sol's face, his fingers so gentle that Sol had to fight the urge to weep, and bent down to kiss him, not on the lips but on the forehead. Then he straightened, walked toward the door, opened it, and left the office.

Shit, that hurt.

Why the fuck aren't you walking out there and telling him to come back?

That counselor barb had found its target. *How does the saying go? Physician, heal thyself? I told Toby, Alli, and my parents, didn't I? And I felt better.*

Except part of him knew that wasn't true.

Besides, if Butch already knows what happened, why the hell is it so important to hear it again, but from my lips? It had to be more than just communication, reestablishing trust...

Then it came to him. That kiss...

Butch had recognized he wasn't going to get resolution right then, so he'd done the first thing he could think of—a kiss full of promise, a pointer to set Sol on his own path of self-discovery and healing.

He's trying to get me to talk through my pain.

That new knowledge only served to heighten the worth of the man who'd just walked out of that door—and the path Sol had to follow if he was going to keep Butch in his life.

CHAPTER 53

Friday, October 14

Salvation

If Butch had to describe how he felt, the closest he could come to it was being thrown off a horse in the middle of nowhere, without a phone to call for backup, no gun either, and with a pack of wolves nipping at his heels.

Talk about being up shit creek without a paddle.

He'd been home for almost two weeks, and not a day went by when he didn't check his phone at regular intervals, hoping for a text, an email—hell, even one single goddamn emoji—to be confronted with nothing.

Nada.

Zilch.

Toby and the boss hadn't asked how the meet-up with Sol had gone, and that was probably because they knew the answer—it had to be written all over his face, in every trudging step he took, in the slump of his shoulders, and in the fact that talking about anything to anyone had become a chore.

They weren't the only ones not asking questions. His fellow ranch hands were treating him as though he were made of glass. Even Zeeb hadn't fired his mouth off like he always did, and that was enough to convince Butch the trumpet had sounded for the Second Coming, and he'd slept through it.

Why the fuck did I go there? Did I really think I could get Sol to change his mind?

Maybe not, but he'd *hoped*, that was for damn sure.

He'd walked out of that club and along the streets, not really seeing anything, until he'd found a bar. With a beer and a whiskey chaser in front of him, he'd gotten his phone out and booked himself on the next flight out of San Francisco, which had been five-fifteen the following morning, with a stop in Denver. He'd downed the beer and the whiskey, then bought another round. After the third beer he came to his senses and left the bar in search of food, moving on autopilot. He'd tried to sleep at the airport, curled up on a row of three seats, but his brain wouldn't shut down.

After seven hours of travel, he landed in Bozeman early Sunday afternoon, and caught the shuttle. Teague picked him up, and either Toby or the boss must've said something because he didn't ask a goddamn thing, for which Butch was profoundly grateful.

But here he was, almost two weeks later, and the ache in his heart hadn't diminished. He'd spent the day mucking out the stable with Paul, the smell of horses and hay surrounding him, a comforting scent that felt like home.

If home was where the heart was, then Butch's was a thousand miles away.

By the time supper was over, he was already dreading another night of little sleep. He went outside, itching for a smoke, but he'd finished his last pack three days ago and hadn't bought any more.

I guess I chose the wrong time to finally quit.

The bunkhouse door creaked behind him, but Butch didn't turn to see who'd come out. A moment later, Teague joined him at the paddock fence.

"Thought I might find you out here," he said quietly.

Butch didn't respond.

"There's a bottle of bourbon in my cabin, and I think it's got both our names on it. So why don't you join me for a drink in front of the fire, and then we can talk?"

"Who says I wanna talk?"

To his surprise, Teague put his arm around Butch's shoulders. "You don't have to say a goddamn word. I *know* you, remember? I've been meaning to say something these last few weeks, but I kept putting it off, thinking you'd come around."

"And tonight you got tired of waiting, is that it?" Lord knew, Butch was getting tired of waiting to hear from Sol.

"Something like that. I'm a good listener. And I think you need to get a helluva lot off your chest."

Butch debated telling him thanks but no thanks, when a wave of exhaustion washed over him, leaving him spent.

"You know what? You're probably right."

Teague patted him on the back. "Then let's get out of this cold night air."

They walked past the paddock, past the Leather barn, and arrived at Teague's cabin. Once inside, Teague pointed to the couch in front of the fire, then went in search of the bourbon. He poured two stiff drinks, set the glasses on the coffee table, then knelt in front of the fireplace and got to work assembling a fire.

"You need anything?" he asked as he set light to the paper under the kindling.

Butch sighed. "Only Sol, and I don't think you've got *him* hidden around here someplace."

Teague's sigh matched his. "Dear Lord, you *have* got it bad."

He joined Butch on the couch, leaning back against the cushions. The crackle of the logs was a pleasant intrusion, and Butch sipped his bourbon, relishing its warmth.

"I don't have to ask if it's serious, do I?"

Butch nursed his glass between his palms. "You wanna know how Sol first knew he was gay? He had the hots for someone in high school." He stared into the flames licking over the wood. "That someone was me, apparently."

Teague's breathing caught. "Holy fuck."

"Not that he was out back then. And me? I was a mess." Between sips, Butch told Teague about high school, Scott, his death, Butch's assumptions, leaving home, and learning the truth from Sol. He left nothing out because Teague had nailed it.

He knew Butch from balls to bones, so why hide the truth from him?

Teague's face tightened. "Your bad dreams... they were all about Scott, weren't they?"

He nodded. "What I didn't know was Sol was dealing with his own pain." He gave Teague the cut-down version Toby had given him, then told him about the trip to San Francisco. "And that's how I left it, with a kinda ultimatum. Except I'm starting to realize he isn't gonna open up to me. I mean, it's been two weeks."

Teague chuckled, and Butch bristled.

"What's so funny?"

He drank a little, then studied Butch. "Remind me again. How long did it take *you* to tell someone about Scott?" He shook his head. "Pot... meet kettle."

Butch frowned. "You sayin' I should wait? But the longer I

do that, the more I think he's not gonna talk to me."

"He'll be back." Teague's voice brimmed with confidence.

Butch stared at him. "But how do you *know* that?"

Teague arched his eyebrows. "He loves you, that's how I know." He cocked his head. "And you love him."

Yeah, Butch was past hiding.

"It shows, huh?"

He laughed. "Oh, just a tad." Then his expression sobered. "Have the dreams stopped?"

It took Butch a moment or two of mental reckoning. "Yeah," he said slowly.

"And what do you think of his… lifestyle? Could you cope with that?" He chuckled again. "Not unless you've suddenly discovered you're a submissive, and that would be—" His words died as Butch's cheeks heated up. "Oh. My. God. You dark horse. Seriously? Is *that* what you two were doing all that week?" He grinned. "So tell me more."

"I can't talk about this, okay? Not when everything is so up in the air, and I have no clue what's gonna happen." Not when it felt as though snakes were writhing in his belly.

Teague nodded. "You're right. And I shouldn't have asked. I wouldn't ask Toby what he does with the boss, right? It's none of my business." There was that head tilt again. "But you *do* like it, whatever it is you do—did—with him?"

Butch got where Teague was coming from. "I didn't go exploring this to please Sol, if that's what you're asking. I did it for me, because it felt… good."

"Then I hope he pulls his head outta his ass and realizes what a fine man he has in you." Teague's voice rang with warmth and sincerity, and tears pricked the corners of Butch's eyes.

"I don't deserve that, not from you. Not after how I treated you."

Teague took Butch's hand in his. "And I'm sorry about the way I spoke to you. I got it wrong. You weren't using him." He squeezed Butch's fingers. "I'm going to pray things turn out the way you want. Because you deserve that." He released Butch's hand.

Silence fell between them, but it was a comfortable silence, and Butch was grateful to have cleared the air. He glanced at

Teague. "Can I ask you something? Those nipple clamps Toby put on you for the photos… did they really feel that good?"

Teague laughed. "Hell no, they left good in their dust—they felt *amazing*."

"Something you might wanna try again someday?"

Teague's eyes sparkled in the firelight. "Maybe?" He smiled. "You seem a little better."

"Best I've felt since I got back from seeing Sol," Butch confessed.

"Then stay here tonight. You can sleep on the couch—or in my bed if you want." His eyes were kind. "I just thought you might need a bit of company."

Teague's words of so many weeks ago came back to him, and Butch knew what he had to do. He put down his glass, leaned across, and kissed Teague on the mouth, a fleeting, chaste brushing of lips. "Thank you," he murmured. "For everything."

Teague's eyes glistened. "Thank *you*, for that." He wiped them.

"And now I'm gonna go back to the bunkhouse," Butch told him. "'Bout time I got my act together around here. Tomorrow is a big day: old guests out, cleaning, new guests in…" He stood, and Teague rose too. He followed Butch to the door and stood there as Butch walked away.

"Hey, Butch?"

He stopped and turned. "Did I forget something?"

"No. Just wanted to say… I'm glad you're my older brother."

For the second time that night, Butch followed his instincts and seized Teague in a hug, not failing to catch Teague's gasp.

That hug had been long overdue.

Butch released him. "Me too. Now get some sleep, Mr. Foreman. You're way too sweet right now. You need to find your bossy head for the morning."

Teague laughed. "Goodnight." He closed the door.

Butch strolled toward the bunkhouse, his heart a little lighter. *Ball's in your court, Sol. I've done all I can do.*

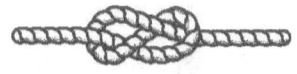

Sunday, October 16
San Francisco

Sol stared at his monitor and told himself for the third time that day to get a grip. Putting this site together had been the stereotypical blood-out-of-a-stone operation, and it had been like that for two weeks.

No one to blame for that but me.

He'd checked his phone almost every hour for the first three or four days after Butch's surprise visit to the club, until the message had gotten through—Butch wasn't going to be in touch.

If anything's going to happen, it'll have to be me who initiates it.

Which was fair enough. This was his mess, right? He had to be the one to clean it up.

His phone rang, and for one split second he ignored his last thought in the vain hope Butch had changed his mind. He peered at the screen.

Alli.

It would have been easy to put the phone on mute, but he'd hardly spoken with another person during the last two weeks, and the guy behind the deli counter at Publix didn't count. A lot of thinking and very little human interaction had left him craving the sound of another voice.

Preferably someone who wasn't going to give him a load of grief, and where Alli was concerned, the call could go either way.

Fuck it.

Sol clicked Answer. "Hey."

"I'm just calling to make sure you're still coming next month."

He frowned, the words not computing.

"November? Thanksgiving? Mom's turkey that will feed the five thousand?"

Aw shit.

He could still cancel—family was the last thing he needed—but the knowledge that Alli would be crushed kept his mouth shut.

Besides, I gave her my word.

After a moment of uncomfortable silence, Alli's voice came over the phone.

"Something's happened."

Despite his warring emotions, Sol smiled. "Never could hide anything from you."

"What can I say? It's a gift. So tell me… does the lack of calls from you have anything to do with High School Guy? Apologies, but you didn't give me a name. You had this dilemma, right?"

Had one. Still have one. And it's not going to be solved until I do something.

"Solomon Peter Davenport, why do I suddenly have goosebumps?"

He winced. "You know I hate it when you call me that."

"Did you go back to Montana? To that ranch?"

Maybe talking to Alli would be therapy.

If he could talk to her, then there was no reason why he couldn't talk to—

"Sol?"

He let out a sigh. "Yeah, I went back. And things were going well… until I ruined it all."

"Is it fixable?"

That was what he loved about Alli. She was solution-oriented.

"I don't know," he said. Which was a lie, because *absolutely* it was fixable.

He just had to bare his soul.

"Well, are you at least going to *try* and fix it?" Before Sol could answer, Alli plunged ahead. "This guy is important, isn't he?"

Butch was right there in his head, that hat shading those amazing eyes, the same ones that had captivated him back when Sol was seventeen. Butch smiled, and warm light made his face glow, the warmth of the setting sun as they stood beside a paddock, the air rich with birdsong.

"Yes, yes he is."

"Then ask him to come with you at Thanksgiving."

He blinked. "Seriously?"

"I said you could bring a guest, didn't I?"

His pulse raced. "I… I can't."

"Why not?" A heartbeat of silence. "Sol Davenport, you just told me he's important."

"I know."

"Then *do* something. How many chances at happiness do you think we get in this life? Not enough to let one pass you by, I'll tell you that much."

And there it was, the kernel of truth he'd been searching for.

I thought it had passed me by. I hadn't expected a second chance.

Liam stared at him from the photo, and Sol could hear his voice in his head.

Then grab it while you can, babe. Sub, lover, friend—he's the whole package. What are you waiting for?

It was a question Sol couldn't argue with any longer.

"Sis, I'll see you next month, okay? Gotta go." He hung up, his heartbeat rapid. He opened a window on his laptop and typed in United Airlines. His phone rang again, and he half-thought it was Alli, but the number showed up as unknown. He clicked on Answer, then loudspeaker. "Hi, Sol Davenport here."

The brief snatch of silence that followed had him thinking it was a wrong number, until a familiar voice filled the air.

"Good afternoon."

Sol's hands were suddenly clammy. "Hey, Robert. You were the last person I was expecting to hear from."

"Yeah, I can believe that. I was calling to give you feedback we received about your sessions."

Okay, that was surreal.

"I see."

"The other guests were extremely complimentary. At least one commented about the benefits of having a trained Dom on staff. And that kinda gave me an idea." A pause. "Well, it *did*—until the thing with Butch happened, and that had me reconsidering." Another pause. "You know what? I shouldn't have called. This is just awkward."

"Don't hang up!" Sol blurted.

Robert fell silent.

"I messed up, okay? I know that. And… well, I'm going to fix it. In fact, I was about to make a start on that when you called."

"Is that the truth?" Robert demanded bluntly. "Because I've been waiting to see how things panned out, only now, I can't wait any longer. The next guests arrive in a week, and I wanted to have things in place by then."

"Robert, *what* things?"

"Look, I was calling to tell you to either shit or get off the pot. Butch is here in some god-awful limbo, and making him wait like this is fucking cruel. To be honest, it's a real dick thing to do, and I didn't think you were a dick."

Sol loved the fact that Robert wasn't afraid to speak his mind.

"I like you, Sol, but Butch is family, so in the grand scheme of things, he comes first, even if that means my plans don't come off. And this whole situation is awkward. You need to repair the damage you've done, but not if the only reason you're doing that is because of my offer."

Sol saw the light—well, some of it, because Robert kept dancing around whatever idea he'd wanted to discuss. *What offer?*

"Robert… I was looking up flights to Bozeman when you called."

He caught the hitch in Robert's breathing. "No shit."

"Yeah. I'm staring at United's page as we speak. I'm coming back to Salvation to make things right."

"Hallelujah." The joy in Robert's voice was unmistakable.

"So why don't you tell me your idea, and we'll take it from there?"

Robert spoke rapidly for a couple of minutes, and Sol listened with a mix of growing incredulity and excitement. When he was done, Robert paused. "Well? What do you think? I know, it's a lot to take in, but—"

"Robert…" Sol took a breath. "You know this depends on Butch, don't you? Because this will only work if he's happy with it."

"Then book that flight and get your ass back here. There's a man waiting for you."

"I'll message Toby with the details." Sol paused. "Are you going to tell Butch?"

Robert chuckled. "Nope. I wanna be there when he lays eyes on you. I think he might explode with happiness on the spot. He's missed you. And no, he didn't tell me that—he didn't have to."

"I think we've got a lot of talking to do before we get to happiness."

But that was Sol's destination. He'd been there once, and he wanted to revisit, only this time he figured on staying.

Maybe for the rest of my life.

Everything rested on Butch, and Sol was praying like crazy.

CHAPTER 54

Saturday, October 22
Salvation

Three weeks sure had rolled around fast.

The second group of guests for the Leather barn were due to check in, and Butch had been in there since breakfast, making sure the rooms were ready, the benches and sling wiped down... If it wasn't nailed down, Butch cleaned it.

Saturday night supper for the hands had been moved first to the following Saturday, the twenty-ninth, and then to Monday, when the boss realized how close it was to Halloween. That would be Butch's baby too. He needed to collect the skeletons stored in the attic up at the house, complete with cowboy hats and holsters, ready to be hung at various locations around the ranch. The boss's dad had insisted on celebrating Halloween in a big way. Butch had an idea why. Keeping the hands on the ranch was way better than letting them loose in Bozeman. The boss was not going to let any of them forget about Lacey's bar in a hurry, especially Butch since he'd been the one to bust a pool cue over Vince Traynor's head.

Stupid bastard had it coming, not that such an argument cut any ice with the boss. Butch was still amazed he'd let them go into Livingston for Zeeb's birthday bash, but thankfully there'd been no shenanigans.

Only what Sol and I got up to in our room.

That ache in Butch's chest was back.

"Butch? You in here?" Zeeb called out from below.

"Yup," he hollered down. "Just finished cleaning the bathroom." He came down the stairs to find Zeeb standing in the main room, trailing a finger along the spanking bench's black vinyl covering.

The sight of it made Butch's balls tighten.

Wonder what that feels like? It wasn't the first time the thought had occurred to him.

Zeeb glanced at him and grinned. "Just checkin' for dust."

"Did you want something?"

Zeeb nodded. "Toby called."

"I thought he was out someplace. I didn't see his truck earlier."

"He went into Bozeman, I think, but he's back now. Said he wants you to go on up to the house."

"That'll be for the Halloween decorations." The boss obviously wanted to make sure everything would be ready. "Is Matt making that cake again?"

"The one that looked like body parts, all red inside? Lord, I hope so, it was delicious. Never did figure out how he got that red jelly to ooze out like blood." Zeeb studied him. "How you doing?"

Butch kept his expression neutral. "I'm just fine." And if at some point that day it had occurred to Butch to wonder how Sol would be spending Halloween, he'd dismissed it just as quickly.

He didn't need to torture himself any more than he already had done.

Zeeb was still watching him. "You sure about that?"

"No, but it's the only answer you're gonna get." Butch took a deep breath. "I know you're asking because you care, but—"

"We *all* care, okay? And I'm the only one askin' because I drew the short straw. Which I was kinda hoping for, by the way. Just so long as you know, we're here for ya. Anytime, Butch." Zeeb held a hand up. "And you don't have to say another word. You don't wanna talk about it, and that's okay. We're goin' nowhere."

Hearing his own words to Sol echoed only served to exacerbate the ache in his chest.

He forced a smile. "Thanks. And now I'd better get up to the house." He headed for the door. Zeeb meant well, but Butch wasn't ready to talk about Sol.

He wasn't sure if he ever would be.

Butch strolled up the path, wishing he'd worn his coat. The stiff breeze chilled him a little. He went into the house and straight into the living room. "Here to pick up the dead bodies," he called out, grinning.

The boss came out of the kitchen. "That can wait. I need you to check on the state of the cabin."

"Sure. Someone got a guest staying tonight?" That was weird. No one had mentioned such a thing.

And how would you know that, when no one is talking to you?

"Yes," Toby said as he followed the boss. "You do."

Butch frowned. "Then you know something I don't, because I ain't got a guest tonight."

The boss chuckled. "You do now."

There was movement behind Toby, and Butch's heart skipped a beat when Sol walked into the living room, dressed in jeans, boots, and a black sweater.

Holy fuck. He came. He's really here.

"Hey." Sol's grave expression sent a trickle of fear dancing down Butch's spine.

It was all he could do to manage a nod.

"And that's our cue." The boss patted Sol on the arm. "We'll give you some space."

"Hey, don't go on my account," Butch protested. "This is your house, after all."

"We're going into Bozeman. Again." Toby smiled. "*Someone* offered to buy me lunch, and I wasn't going to say no." He gazed at the boss with gleaming eyes. "About time he took me on a date. Of course, we're really there to pick up the first guests too." He threw Butch a warm glance, and then the pair headed out the door.

Butch couldn't move, couldn't speak, and Sol didn't close the gap between them.

This isn't going to be good, is it?

Fuck it, *one* of them had to get the ball rolling.

He cleared his throat. "Well, you got here." Butch narrowed his eyes. "Eventually."

"Yeah, about that." Sol took a step closer. "I'm sorry I made you wait. I'd have been here a week ago, but I had a lot of things to do before I could—"

"I missed you," Butch blurted. He swallowed. "I've been wandering around this place like some goddamn lost soul these past three weeks."

"I'm sorry," Sol repeated.

"I convinced myself you were never coming back."

"I'm sorry."

Butch rolled his eyes. "Will you quit apologizing, and get over here and kiss me?"

It was as if someone flipped a switch, electrifying Sol into action. He closed the gap, his arms wide, and Butch stepped into their welcoming circle, relishing the scratch of Sol's five o'clock shadow on his cheek, the smell of him, the taste of his lips.

"Missed you too," Sol murmured against his lips.

"Missed you more."

Sol chuckled. "Doubt that." Then all talk was forgotten when Sol cradled his head the way he'd done so many times before, claiming Butch's mouth in a lingering exploratory kiss that sent Butch's internal thermostat from warm to If-I-wasn't-standing-in-my-boss's-living-room-I'd-be-naked-right-about-now.

Sol broke the kiss, his hand gentle on Butch's cheek. "I believe I have something to tell you."

That was all it took to get Butch's heart pounding.

"Then let's sit down." He managed a chuckle. "Because right now the only thing holding me up is you." They sat on the large squashy leather couch, and Butch twisted to look at Sol. "Before you start... You sure about this? Because I know this is opening up an old wound." With a razor blade. A blunt one at that.

"Yes, it is, but you were right. I need to tell you everything." Sol took Butch's hand in his. "Just not sure where to start."

"Was Liam the first guy you ever loved?" He flushed. "I know you said I was your first crush."

Sol's smile reached his eyes. "First guy who ever showed me the ropes? Pun intended. I thought I loved him. Kris was older than me. I met him at a party in Gillette. Weren't any clubs or leather bars to speak of, not in Wyoming, but I worked with a couple of guys who were in the lifestyle. They invited me to a sex party, and there he was, this leather daddy with a full beard, a ring through his nose, the largest nipples I'd ever seen, 'cause *man* he loved to play with 'em, and a humongous dick."

Butch snorted. "Guys like that are thin on the ground in Bozeman. Least ways, *I've* never seen one. So... you thought you loved him."

Sol shrugged. "It was good while it lasted, but I soon realized he wasn't into me like that. He taught me a lot, I'll say that for him. Then I moved to Cheyenne, and in 2010 I met Liam." His face tightened. "BDSM was all new to him, and fuck, he just opened up like a flower. The guy was a natural submissive." Sol cupped Butch's cheek. "Not unlike you, actually."

"Me?"

Sol smiled. "Oh yeah."

"Tell me more about Liam." Now that he'd gotten Sol started on the subject, Butch didn't want to distract him from it.

"I fell for him, hard and fast. Even took him to meet my folks, and they fell under his spell too. They hadn't much liked the idea of me with an older guy, and Liam was about six years younger than me. We got a house together, and I thought, this is it, I've found my happy place." Sol's Adam's apple bobbed sharply. "And we *were* happy, right up till June 2017."

Butch's throat seized. "You don't have to tell me the next part if you don't want to." Hearing Toby's cut-down version had been bad enough.

Hearing about it from Sol's lips had the potential to break him.

"Yes, I do, and we both know it." Sol rested his head against the seat cushion and closed his eyes. "Liam was into music in a big way. I was kinda old school—"

"Yeah, I noticed that about you," Butch quipped.

Sol opened his eyes and gave him a mock glare. "I meant, I preferred classical, while he loved pop, country... So anyway, he asked if I'd go with him to a concert at the Cheyenne Civic Center. Layla Roberts and her band were playing there, and he'd bought two tickets. I swear, he had every one of her albums. Of course it wasn't my thing, so I said I didn't want to go."

Butch's skin prickled. The Cheyenne Civic Center. The Layla Roberts concert. It had been on the news for about three days, casting a pall over the whole ranch.

Liam was one of the nine.

He shivered.

"Liam must've asked me four or five times, and I kept saying no, so eventually he asked a coworker if they wanted my ticket, and they said yes. The night of the concert, he kissed me, said he'd be back around midnight, and off they went." His eyes glistened. "Last time I saw him, he was wearing a tee he'd had made for the occasion, with a photo of Layla surrounded by red hearts."

Butch's chest tightened. He remembered the news footage, the usual tweets abouts thoughts and prayers for the families of the nine dead concert-goers, the others who'd been injured, the stuff they'd turned up about Driscoll Gavin Delaney, the forty-seven-year-old man who'd apparently taken it into his head to buy an AR-15-style rifle, smuggle it into the arena, then fire into the crowd before a security guard took him down with a couple of body shots, including one to the leg.

Bastard had died from his injuries, and no one listened to his family who proclaimed him to be a good man. The shit the police found on his laptop made everything they said a goddamn lie.

He laid a hand on Sol's arm. "It's okay, you don't have to tell me any more. I remember."

Tears streaked Sol's cheeks. "I'd already heard the sirens when I got the call from the police. It was all over the news. I just couldn't believe Liam was one of the victims. I kept on thinking that until they asked me to identify his body. His coworker survived his injuries. And when I told my parents..." He shuddered out a sigh. "They loved him too, but they blamed me for his death."

"What the fuck?"

He nodded. "I know, right? They said if I'd gone with him, Liam would still be alive."

"They can't know that," Butch protested. "That's totally illogical. If you'd been there, Liam still might have died. You both might have lived... In the end, it's all guesswork. You could've done everything or nothing, and adding a whole heap of guilt to any of those scenarios wouldn't change a thing."

"I know!" Sol's voice rose, and Butch squeezed his arm. "That was when I decided I couldn't stay in Wyoming anymore. So I packed up everything, gave all Liam's stuff to Goodwill, except for a couple of things, and I moved to San Francisco." His eyes held such pain that Butch flinched. They glistened as his tears flowed once more, and Butch didn't hesitate. He held Sol close, not giving a damn for his soaked shirt, his own tears wetting Sol's cheeks.

Sol needed to be held.

At last, Sol's tears ebbed but Butch didn't move.

"Thank you for trusting me," he whispered. They sat in silence, Butch listening as Sol's breathing slowed to its usual speed, content to hold him, to comfort him. "I said I'd be here for you."

"And you were." Sol tilted his head, and their lips met in a sweet kiss. Sol laid his head upon Butch's shoulder. "Sorry it took me so long to tell you all this. And you were right. I needed to share this with you." Then he sat up and looked Butch in the eye. "There was something else I needed to ask you as well."

Butch's heart raced. "Yeah?"

"I imagined a life with you once, and I ran from it. But I'm not running anymore. I want to make this work—if you still want that too."

There was a drumming in Butch's chest, a rush of adrenaline, a grin he couldn't contain. "Yeah, I still want it. And we'll figure out a way to make it work. You visit here whenever you can. I don't mind waiting, as long as I know you'll be here."

Sol's eyes sparkled. "But that's what I came here to tell you. You won't have to wait. I got a new job, in Montana."

A wave of euphoria crashed over him. "Really? That's great. Where?"

"There's this ranch that just started something new, a place for guys into BDSM…" Sol didn't break eye contact.

No. Fucking. Way.

"Here?"

Sol nodded. "Robert asked me to work here full-time. It's one week out of every month, and the rest of the time I've got my website design. Plus, there's a clinic in Bozeman that has a vacancy for a counselor. *This* is what I spent last week doing—getting all my ducks in a row."

"But what will you do here?"

"Same thing I did the opening week. I'll do demonstrations, teach, talk…"

Butch frowned. "Will you have to live in the Leather barn?"

Sol laughed. "I don't know yet, I just got here, remember? We haven't sorted out the fine print yet."

A trickle of cold stole through him. "Which came first—the decision to accept the job offer, or to talk to me?"

Sol shifted closer to him, his hand on Butch's nape. "You come first. *Always.* Do you hear me? I'd already made up my mind to come back here when Robert called."

Relief surged throughout his body. "Okay."

"But that leads me to my next question." Sol cupped his bearded jaw and gazed into his eyes. "You still want to be my sub?"

Holy fuck.

Butch's heart danced. "Yes."

Sol beamed. "I am *so* happy you said that." He lurched up off the couch and across the room to where a bag sat under the window. He picked it up and came back to Butch. Sol reached into the bag and removed a square flat box, and a smaller one. He opened the first, and Butch's breathing caught when he saw its contents.

A metal chain nestled in white cotton batting, its two ends looped through a small padlock.

"The boss wears something like that sometimes," Butch said in a low voice. "I've seen it."

Sol nodded. "You remember the black leather collar you wore for the photo? This is a permanent version." He raised Butch's chin with his fingers. "This is for you if you'll accept it, only not yet, okay?" His mouth went down at the corners. "I know I did some damage—that whole non-communication thing—but I promise I'll be open and honest with you from now on. And if you think you're ready—no, *when* you're ready—then…" He straightened. "I'd like to put it on you. I'll have the key. Any Dom who sees this will know you're not available—you're spoken for." He closed the lid, and Butch breathed a little easier.

"You're right. I don't think I'm ready for that yet."

Sol's sigh came from someplace deep. "You say that, but you know what I see when I look into your eyes? How much I screwed up. So you're right to be cautious." He bit back a smile. "There's also the fact I know stuff like collars—visual links between a Dom and sub—can be overwhelming for a new sub." His eyes twinkled. "Especially one who's only recently come out about his own sexuality. But we'll get there. There are a few things we'll need to discuss before we do, however." He placed the box on the coffee table. "You were right about something else too. I have two parts to my life, and they both matter. Most of the time it will be just you and me—Sol and Butch—boyfriends. Partners." He smiled. "Lovers."

Butch's heartbeat quickened. "But there would be times when you'd be working with other guys—in scenes, right?—and that might involve… sex. You said as much."

Sol regarded him steadily. "Exactly." He cocked his head. "Scenes you might also want to be involved in. How do you feel about that?"

All those times he'd contemplated Sol in a scene with a sub, he hadn't once considered he might be a part of it.

But he was considering it now.

Butch swallowed. "You don't have to worry about my feelings toward you having sex in scenes or with your clients. Believe it or not, my head accepts that." He managed a smile. "I know all about sex not involving emotions. That was what I had with Race, after all, and every other guy I fucked. But as for how I'd feel about being in a scene with others… I guess I won't know until we get to that part."

"Sex in a scene is just that—sex." Sol leaned in and kissed him. "What we share is completely different. And you're right. We won't take a step in that direction until you really want it—if you ever get to that point."

Butch inhaled deeply. "Thank you."

"The one thing that matters more than anything else? Consent. I will never expect you to do something you don't want to do, okay? You're going to find things you like the sound of, and then at the last minute you'll change your mind and pull back, and that's fine, you hear me?"

"I hear you."

It was all good.

Sol picked up the smaller box. "This isn't related to BDSM, but it *is* important to me." He opened it, and Butch forgot to breathe.

Inside was a ring.

CHAPTER 55

Sol's heart thumped. "This isn't what you might think it is."

Butch tore his gaze away from it and gave him an amused glance. "Well, it *looks* like a ring made of green glass. And while I didn't suppose you were about to get down on one knee—" He clutched his chest over his heart. "—Because that would be *monumentally* fast work, not to mention a huge presumption—I *am* intrigued."

He removed the ring from its wadding. "This is agate, a gemstone, and I chose the color because it reminded me of your eyes."

Those same green eyes that were staring into Sol's, their pupils large, framed by long black lashes. The fact Butch didn't appear to be freaking out gave him the confidence to continue.

"I chose agate—something *else* I was researching this last week—because it's supposed to be a soothing, calming gemstone that heals anxiety and helps in the strengthening of relationships." He took Butch's left hand in his. "And if you wear it on your ring finger, that will tell anyone who sees it that you're spoken for. That you have someone who loves you." He couldn't resist the lure of Butch's mouth a second longer. Sol leaned in and kissed him, slow and sensual. "That you're mine," he murmured against Butch's lips.

"Lord knows I'm that," Butch whispered as their lips parted. He drew back with a happy little sigh. "I'll wear your ring, Sol. I think it's a beautiful idea. I just wish I had something to give you."

Sol smiled. "You already gave me something." Another sweet kiss as he slid the ring onto Butch's finger, thankful to have estimated its size reasonably well. It wasn't a perfect fit, but it would do its job until Sol replaced it with something more permanent.

"What was that?"

"Your heart. You also gave me the chance to think and come to my own conclusions. You put your cards on the table and respected me enough not to pressure me, even though that had to be difficult, not to mention heartbreaking at times."

Butch cleared his throat. "Um, that's more than one thing, y'know, but hey, feel free to keep going." His lips twitched. Then Butch locked his arms around Sol's neck and kissed him like it was about to be abolished.

Their foreheads touched. "Love you, Sol Davenport." Butch's fingers were gentle as he stroked Sol's head. "Never thought I'd say that to anyone."

Sol claimed his mouth again, with as much hunger as the previous kisses, his hands on Butch's back, his shoulders. "Love you too," he murmured between kisses. "And I thought I'd had my one and only chance to say those words."

Their foreheads touched, and they stood there, Butch seemingly as unwilling as he was to move from that spot.

"When do you have to head back to San Francisco?"

Sol cradled Butch's head, breathing him in, trying to burn the moment into his memory. "I'm working this week, so—"

Butch jerked his head back. "He's got you on the payroll already? *Man*, that dude works fast."

Sol laughed. "Guests were arriving. Robert wanted me on board by the time they got here. So yes, I'll start earning my keep right away. I won't be staying in the barn though. He suggested I could use the cabin down by the creek." He gave Butch a light kiss. "Wanna stay there with me? You won't have any guests in the bunkhouse to take care of, right? And whenever I'm not doing demos or scenes, I'll be with you."

"And when this week is over?"

Sol kissed his forehead. "I'll stay for Halloween, okay? Then I'll fly back to San Francisco and start packing. I'll be back here with my U-Haul before you know it."

Butch blinked. "You're gonna drive a thousand miles?"

He laughed, amazed at the lightness that flooded through him. "I'd drive across the entire country if I knew you were waiting for me at the end of my journey."

Butch smiled. "And then we start another journey."

He nodded. "Together." He released Butch, picked up the box containing the collar, and placed it back in his bag. "I'll keep this safe until it's needed." Then he slung the bag over his shoulder.

"I guess we'd better saddle up and ride to the cabin."

Butch chuckled. "Seeing as you're one of the staff now, I'll let you into a little secret. There's a back way through the forest, and all we need is a truck."

Sol grinned. "Then what are we waiting for?"

"I think I've found my happy place," Butch murmured.

Sol hooked his leg over Butch's and kissed his chest. "Oh?"

He sighed. "With you in a bed. Preferably after we've made love."

Sol nuzzled his neck, and Butch's cock reacted. Sol chuckled. "Uh-oh. Round two looks imminent."

Butch snorted. "In your dreams. We're in our fifties. Our days of going at it all night are long past. Not until we're gonna resort to the little blue pills."

"I already take little blue pills." Sol reached over him to the nightstand and grabbed a white bottle. He handed it to Butch who peered at the label.

"Descovy," he read aloud. "What's this?"

"It's my PrEP medication."

Butch rolled over to face him. "You mentioned that once. I didn't know what it was at the time, so I did a little research. You take it to prevent HIV?"

Sol nodded. "It's good at what it does, but it can't prevent stuff like STIs. That's what condoms are for."

"Are all the guys you do scenes with on this?"

"Most. It makes sense if you have a lot of different scene partners. But one thing doesn't change. Every guy I fuck has to show proof of his latest test."

"Test?"

"Yeah. If you're taking PrEP, you get an HIV test every three months. A blood test at that."

"I've never had one of those. Then again, I've never fucked without a condom, and my sex life before you was limited to one act, so I guess you could say I've always played it safe. I've never had a blood transfusion either, and the only drug I've ever taken? Beer." Butch studied the little bottle. "Can you get tested if you're not on PrEP?" His pulse quickened.

Sol took it from him and replaced it on the nightstand. "Of course. I tell everyone to get tested regularly. You have a regular check-up, don't you?"

"Sure. They check my weight, heart rate, blood pressure, the usual stuff. Then there's the prostate check, which feels nothing like when you put *your* fingers inside me." Butch grinned. "Maybe that's a good thing. Only, they're not doing that anymore—I have to have a blood test now."

"A PSA test. Yeah, that's because of your age. I have the same test."

"Seems like there are more tests now than there ever were before. I guess that's down to age too. Jesus, you hit fifty and it's all downhill from there. They screen for colon cancer, lung cancer, diabetes…" He paused. "I quit smoking, by the way."

Sol's soft kiss to his neck spoke of his approval. "Do they test for STIs?"

"Yup."

"Well, I share my HIV and STI results with all my partners and vice versa. It's good to know you're not about to share something… unwelcome."

"Don't suppose you know if there's a place around here where a guy could get tested?" He aimed for nonchalance, but knew he'd failed the second Sol cupped his cheek and locked gazes with him.

"As a matter of fact, I do. There's a clinic in Bozeman."

Butch chuckled. "Let me guess. Something else you were researching last week."

"Got it in one." Sol studied his face. "Is that something you want to do?"

There was a fluttery feeling in his chest. "Yeah, it is."

"Butch… you've always used condoms, right?"

He nodded again. "But… if it was safe… I…"

Sol rolled him onto his back and pinned him to the mattress. "You want us to go bare?"

Lord, his heart…

"Only if it was safe… and if you wanted that too."

Sol said nothing for a moment, and then he kissed Butch on

the lips.

"I do, but it's going to be a goal. Does that work?" Another kiss. "We still have a lot to talk about, but bareback is going to be on the list."

"Sounds good to me." Then he groaned when Sol undulated against him, making him aware of his own hardening dick.

Sol chuckled. "So much for being in our fifties." He snaked his hand between their bodies and curled his fingers around Butch's shaft. "I know exactly where I want this to go."

Butch smiled. "I think we're on the same page."

Finally.

Monday, October 31

Butch and Diana sat on one of the couches in the living room, the air filled with laughter as everyone gathered to watch Walt bobbing for apples. There was only one left, and he was the last to take his turn.

Diana chuckled. "I think that apple is proving to be a slippery little sucker."

On every table a pumpkin sat, eyes glowing, and candlesticks stood on the mantelpiece, fake cobwebs draped from their slender stems, the flames flickering. Logs crackled in the fireplace, and the smell of mulled wine lingered. The three guests for the week had joined in the festivities, and everyone seemed to be enjoying themselves.

Butch glanced across the room to where Sol, Toby, and the boss sat around the fire, deep in conversation. Sol would be leaving the following day, and Butch was already dreading it. He knew Sol would return as fast as time—and packing—allowed, but he also knew he'd be counting the days.

Minutes.

Seconds.

Diana's warm hand covered his. "Have I told you how happy I am for you?"

He chuckled. "You might have mentioned it once or twice."

She lifted his left hand and peered at the ring. "This is beautiful." She lowered his hand and laced her fingers through his. She'd made an excellent recovery, and Butch had a feeling it wouldn't be long before she'd be back riding Blackheart.

He sighed. "You know what occurred to me this past week?"

"No, but I think you're about to tell me."

"I was thinking about us."

She rolled her eyes. "Talk about ancient history."

"Hear me out," he remonstrated. "It was never supposed to be you and me. Newt's the right man for you. The good Lord had someone else in mind for me." He gazed at Sol, his heart light. "And he's standing right over there."

"The Lord clearly has good taste," she quipped.

Sol glanced at him, and beckoned him to join them.

"Looks like I'm wanted." Butch freed her hand and got up from the couch, accompanied by a roar of delight.

Walt had apparently gotten his prey.

The boss smiled as he approached. "We've been talking about you."

"Thought my ears were burning." Butch joined Sol on the small couch, and Sol automatically reached for his hand.

"Things have changed," Toby began. He glanced at their joined hands and smiled before continuing. "You're not single anymore."

"What gave it away?" Sol said with a chuckle, squeezing Butch's fingers.

"What Toby is *trying* to say is that you can't live in the bunkhouse anymore," the boss declared.

Butch frowned. "But… I'm in charge of the bunkhouse."

"That part won't change," Toby told him. "You just won't sleep there anymore."

He stared at them. "So where *am* I gonna sleep?"

"You know the land behind the Leather barn?" The boss grinned. "That *is* what you all call it, right? Well, I'm going to have a new cabin built, like the one Teague has. It won't be huge— there'll be space for one bed—but it'll be plenty big enough for the two of you."

Sol smiled. "It'll be close to the barn. Better still, it'll be private."

"And until it's built, you and Sol will share my mom's old cabin." The boss's face tightened. "I haven't told the boys yet that they're going to lose their guest space. I feel bad about that. They've only just been given it."

"You don't need to worry about that." Teague walked over, a bottle of beer in his hand. "I spoke to the boys after you told me your plan. They're happy with it." He grinned at Butch. "Zeeb said at least they'll know where you are now." He arched his eyebrows. "Just remember you still work here, okay? Don't you be sneaking off to do God knows what with your…" His eyes sparkled. "I don't know what to call Sol. A couple of labels come to mind."

"He's my boyfriend," Butch stated emphatically. Then his heartbeat raced, and his stomach quivered. "And sometimes he's my Sir."

Oh my God, the light in Sol's face…

Sol's breathing hitched. "Have I told you today that I love you?"

Butch beamed. "Only a few times. I stopped counting."

He would never tire of hearing those words, not if he lived to be a hundred.

Epilogue

Thursday, November 24, 2022
Casper, Wyoming

Alli came into the kitchen as Sol placed cups and saucers on a tray.

"Coffee's ready," he told her. From beyond the door came the sound of laughter, and he smiled. "Sounds as if they're getting on like a house on fire. Who's winning?" Alli's son Luke had brought the game of Articulate with him, and so far they'd been playing for over an hour.

Alli rolled her eyes. "Dad."

He shook his head. "Still can't believe you're a grandmother." Lucy was only six months old, and Sol had begged to hold his new grand-niece every chance he got. The sight of Butch cradling the baby, gazing at her with an awed expression, had sent warmth flooding through him.

He's going to make a really cool great-uncle.

Alli glared at him. "I am *way* too young to be a grandmother, do you hear me?" She glanced toward the door. "Dad likes Butch. So does Mom." She smiled. "So do I." Then she narrowed her gaze. "You might've warned me who you were bringing."

"Why? It was much more fun this way." Butch had walked up to her with a grin, and asked if she was still the same pain in the ass she'd been when she was thirteen. Her expression of shock had been worth it.

"Don't think I didn't notice."

He feigned innocence. "Notice what?"

"That ring on his finger? The one you haven't mentioned yet?" Alli folded her arms. "Something you want to tell me?"

He smiled. "That's between me and him. And before you ask, no, we're not engaged, there are no wedding bells about to start pealing, no announcements imminent, okay?"

"But it *is* serious, right?"

Sol looked her in the eyes. "As serious as it gets."

Alli gaped at him, and a second later, Sol had his arms full. She hugged him. "I think that's awesome. I am *so* freaking happy for you." Then she released him. "Nearly as happy as I was to learn you're living in Montana. At least you didn't have to travel far to get here."

Sol laughed. "I'd rather have seven hours in a car with Butch than fly from San Francisco." He grinned. "Even if I had to put up with his choice of music for half the trip," he added loudly.

"I heard that!" Butch hollered from the dining room where they were playing.

Sol cackled.

"Does this mean you'll visit more often? You know you're welcome to come stay with me and Hugh. Now all the kids have left the nest, we've finally got a guest room."

"I'd like that." Laughter broke out again, and he smiled. "It *is* good to be back home again." It hadn't been that since Liam died.

The door opened, and Alli's son Jem came in. "Anything I can do to help?"

Alli smiled. "And that's my cue to go see if anyone wants a turkey, stuffing and cranberry sandwich." She left the room, giving Jem's arm a squeeze as she passed him.

"You can help me take the coffee through when it's done brewing." Sol glanced at the delicate chain around Jem's slender neck, with its little padlock. "I like Taylor, by the way." Jem's boyfriend—Dom—was maybe thirty, with a refreshing habit of looking people in the eye when he spoke to them, and Sol's parents clearly liked him.

Jem's face glowed. "He's cool, isn't he?"

"Does he make you happy?"

"About as happy as Butch makes you, I reckon." Jem smiled. "He's pretty cool too." His expression grew solemn. "I'm so glad you found each other. I've been hoping for that ever since…" He swallowed. "I know I was only ten when it happened, but I'll never forget that day."

"I stopped hoping long ago," Sol confided. He glanced toward the door. "I didn't see him coming." Sol smiled. "And now I couldn't imagine life without him."

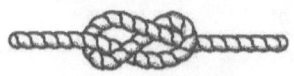

Saturday, November 26

"You're very quiet."

Sol's words pierced the rolling cascade of thoughts that had tumbled around his head ever since they'd left his parents' place. "Sorry. Got stuff on my mind."

"That much is obvious."

To Butch's surprise, Sol pulled off I-25 and into the parking lot of the Loaf 'N Jug.

"We stopping for coffee?" Butch asked. "We haven't been on the road a half hour yet."

"If you want coffee, sure, we can get some." Sol switched the engine off. "But what *I* want is for you to be honest with me. Because I'll be damned if I'm going to sit here worrying about what's going through your head all the way back to Salvation."

Butch's stomach roiled. "There's something I need to do… and I want your help, because I don't think I can do it alone."

Sol squeezed his shoulder. "Would it have anything to do with visiting your folks?" Butch jerked his head to stare at him, and Sol nodded. "Yeah, I thought so. I didn't bring it up because it was your decision. But I hoped while we were in Casper that you might want—"

"Closure? Or build some bridges?" He gave a hard swallow. "In my worst moments, I have this nightmare where I turn up and they don't even recognize me. I mean, it's been *thirty-four years*, for God's sake. And while I think seeing them again will help close this chapter in their lives—and mine—I also think any therapist worth their salt would say that sometimes it's best to just… move on."

"Have you considered contacting them? Maybe finding out if they've ever tried looking for you? It can be scarily easy to just disappear, and living on Salvation all these years wouldn't have made it easy for them to locate you. If they haven't, *then* let it go."

He'd had the same idea, but being back in Casper, so close that he could have driven there from Sol's parents' home…

Butch took a deep breath. "I have to see them, even if it's for the last time."

Sol's hand was a welcome weight on his shoulder. "Okay then. I'll turn the car around. And if it goes belly up, I'll get you outta there." He leaned across and kissed Butch's cheek. "I've got your back."

Butch gave him a grateful smile, then straightened. "Let's do this."

Before I change my mind.

Sol switched the engine on, and pulled back onto I-25, heading south toward I-26, Butch giving directions, amazed at how readily they came to mind. When they turned right on 33 Mile Road, Butch's heart skipped a beat. The last time he'd seen it was the night he walked away from Casper Creek Ranch.

"How many acres are there on your dad's ranch?"

Butch knew Sol was trying to distract him, and he welcomed the question. "I forgot. You never saw where I lived, did you? About six hundred sixty, give or take." He paused. "You know what I missed most about the ranch? There was always something to look at. I used to walk along South Casper Creek when I was a teenager, and from my bedroom I could see the Casper Mountains. There's a wetland where I used to sit and watch so many different types of birds. And there were always antelope, mule deer, and whitetail deer moving through and around the creek bottom. The water was so clear. I'd paddle in it in the summertime."

Then he caught his breath at the sight of the two-story, white-painted house that hadn't changed in thirty-four years, the barn still standing behind it.

Sol turned right into the dirt track that led to the house, and Butch's heart slipped into a higher gear. As they drove closer, he spied two cars and a pickup truck parked beside the house.

"I guess someone's home," he murmured. Then he froze. "You know what's just occurred to me? They might not still be living here. They could've moved."

"They're here. I checked." Sol pulled up behind the truck and switched off the engine. "You ready?"

Butch managed a chuckle. "Not really, but I'm doin' it anyway." They got out, and he was disconcerted to find his legs shaking a little. He walked slowly to the front door and paused, his finger hovering over the doorbell. "I used to hate the sound of this bell when I was a kid."

"Why? How bad could it sound?"

Butch pressed it, and it was as if someone had crossed a bell with a buzz saw, a long continuous ring as grating as nails on a chalkboard.

Sol winced. "You grew up with that? You have my sympathies."

The door opened, and Butch's chest constricted.

Mom got old.

She'd lost a couple of inches somewhere since the last time he'd seen her, and the few wisps of gray visible at her temples back then were now submerged in white hair, cut short and swept back off her face. She wore large round glasses that kinda gave her the appearance of a wise owl, and her plain blue dress wasn't long enough to hide…

Despite his nervous state, Butch burst out laughing.

"Still wearing bunny slippers, huh, Mom?"

Her mouth fell open. "Oh dear Lord. Brian?" Then all the breath was knocked out of him when she threw her arms around him and hugged him, the top of her head barely reaching his shoulder. She buried her face in his chest, her shoulders twitching, and he knew she was crying. "Can't believe you're really here." His shirt muffled her words.

Butch kissed her soft hair, thinner than he remembered, his heart quaking.

Whatever he'd been expecting, this wasn't it.

"'M trying not to step on the bunnies," he teased, going with humor.

She snorted into his shirt, then glanced up at him. "Your father says I'm too old for bunny slippers. I told him where to go." At last she released him, wiping her eyes. She took a step back and gazed at Sol, her brow furrowed. "Aren't you Clare Davenport's boy? Sol, isn't it?"

Butch chuckled. "He hasn't been a boy for a long time, Mom."

"Yes, ma'am, that's me." Sol smiled.

"I see your photo every time the quilting circle meets at her house." Her eyes widened. "*Now* I know why she called me about ten minutes ago. She said it was to check if I was home."

"We just came from there," Sol told her. He frowned. "She couldn't have told you we were coming. We didn't know ourselves when we left the house."

It seemed to Butch that *someone* was determined to give him a push in the right direction.

I was supposed to be here, wasn't I?

Mom tut-tutted. "What am I thinking of, standing here on the doorstep? Come inside." She stood aside for them and they crossed the threshold, following her along the hallway into the kitchen. Butch breathed in the sight and smells of the familiar room. It was as if he'd stepped back in time. The cabinets he remembered were still there, painted sage green, and the walls and blind were the same shade of pale lemon. Even the countertops were the same, thick layers of oak Butch recalled his dad varnishing when Butch was just tall enough to see over them. The air was filled with familiar aromas, and on the table was a plate containing the remains of a turkey, a loaf of homemade bread, a bowl half-filled with stuffing, a similarly filled bowl of cranberries, and a jar of mayo.

Butch smiled. "Dad still likes his leftover sandwiches, then."

She returned his smile. "No change there."

"You stayed on the ranch." It didn't seem possible, not after all these years. "I thought you'd have moved long ago."

She chuckled. "Your father gave the ranch to your brother and he runs the place, but all of us still live here."

He glanced toward the door to the living room. "Is he in there? Dad, I mean."

She shook her head. "Deke, Kathleen and the boys went for a walk down by the creek and your father went with them." She indicated the food on the table. "Can I get you something to eat?"

"No thank you. We had a late breakfast."

She chuckled. "I know all about Claire's breakfasts." Her eyes twinkled behind her glasses. "Why'd you think the quilting circle meets there so often?" Then she stood still, and Butch was dismayed to see tears trickle down her wrinkled cheeks. "I can't believe it. We had no idea if you were even alive."

"Mom, sit down, please." He pulled a chair out for her, and she dropped into it, tugging a tissue from her dress pocket. She wiped her eyes, then looked from Butch to Sol and back to Butch. "How come you're here together?"

Butch was way past hiding. "Sol's my boyfriend, Mom."

She blinked. Blinked again. "Well, shoot."

"Mom?" His heartbeat quickened.

"You just won me fifty bucks, but if I'd known I'd have to wait this *long* to collect, I'd have told him I wanted it with interest too."

"I don't understand."

She sighed. "The week after you left, I told your father you'd run away to be with some boy. He bet me fifty dollars I was wrong." Then her face tightened. "When you ran away, all I could think was that your father was right when he said you were responsible for Scott's death. Why else would you have left the way you did?" She swallowed. "Can't tell you how angry I was with you, but I still wanted to find you, because you had to be really hurting to do that." Sol sat first, then Butch, and she stretched out her hand to cover his. "Do you have kids?"

He shook his head.

"Then you can't know."

"Know what?"

"*Nothing* stops you loving your child, no matter what they do."

"Mom…" Butch's chest ached. "I wasn't responsible. For the longest time, I thought Dad was right, that Scott killed himself because of me, but—"

"I know."

He froze. "What? You know about Scott's uncle? What he did?"

"You think something like that would stay hidden? Melissa called the cops, her brother tried to make a run for it, but they finally caught up with him when he tried to cross the state line into Utah. The story made front page news of the *Casper Star-Tribune*." Her eyes grew flinty. "And then I got angry all over again, with your father for believing that of you in the first place, with Melissa for coming over here that night and laying the blame on you, and yes, with you too, for not sticking around." Her eyes glistened. "I was kicking myself too, because you running off like that could only mean you didn't feel you could tell me what had been going on." She stared at Butch. "I tried to find you when I didn't know whether you were guilty or not, but if I'd known back then what I know now? I'd have tried even harder. But by the time the story broke, you'd been gone twenty years. For all I knew, you could've taken the same route out of this world that Scott did."

His heart quaked to hear the pain in her voice.

Then she squeezed his hand, her gaze drifting to the ring on his finger, and her eyes widened. "Oh my."

"It's not what you think," Butch began. Then he reconsidered. "Okay, it *is*, but—"

The door opened, and a gruff voice said, "I left them at the creek. Too damn cold for me out there. Whose car is that, May?"

Panic bubbled up from someplace deep, and Butch wanted to turn tail and skedaddle out of there.

Mom squeezed his arm. *It'll be okay,* she mouthed.

Then his dad walked into the kitchen and came to a halt when he saw Butch.

"Christ Almighty."

Dad's hair was still wavy, except now it was white like Mom's, his beard too. He stooped a little, and that was a shocker, because Butch remembered when this man had towered over him.

He rose, his right hand outstretched and trembling a little. "Hello, sir."

Dad stared at his hand, then closed the gap between them in two strides. He grabbed Butch and hugged him, his cheek pressed to Butch's.

"You're alive, boy. Holy crap, you're alive."

Tears pricked Butch's eyes. "Yes, sir," he whispered.

"I swore if I ever got my hands on you again, I'd whup your ass for putting us through this, but now that I see you?"

Then Butch realized his cheek was wet.

He caught Sol's croak as he tried to speak, and his mom was crying again, but all he could think of was that he was standing in his mom's kitchen and his dad was hugging him.

Crying.

He could even believe his dad loved him.

Then Dad let go of him, wiping his eyes with the back of his hand. "We've got so much to talk about, son."

Talk about an understatement. They had thirty-four years of catching up to do.

Mom cleared her throat. "Brian isn't alone, sweetheart."

Dad frowned. "He isn't?" Then he stared at Sol. "Who're you?"

Sol held his hand out. "Sol Davenport, sir. I went to Natrona County High School with your son."

They shook. Dad gazed at him, perplexed. "And why are you here?"

Before Butch could get a word out, Mom said with a smile, "He's Brian's boyfriend."

Dad gaped at her. "You've got to be kidding."

Mom grinned, her hand held out, palm facing up. "Now pay up."

He ignored her, and took Sol's hand once more. "The two of you aren't planning on going anywhere right now, are you?"

Sol glanced at Butch, who smiled.

"No sir, there's nowhere else we need to be. We're gonna stay a while."

THE END

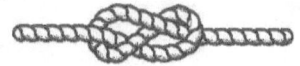

THANK YOU

As always, I have some special people to thank.

Kevin R Davis and Furious Fotog for that awesome photo – Kevin, you were exactly the Butch I was looking for.

Jason Mitchell, who continues to be the best alpha.

Miski Harris, for her medical knowledge.

Daniel Parry, for his *cough* technical expertise.

Trio Reviews, for catching all those pesky typos.

Alexander Cheves, for his advice.

Jack L Pyke and Blake Lockheart for their BDSM-related expertise.

And last but definitely not least, Legrand Wolf and the wonderful men of Carnal Media, for providing me with so many sources of inspiration. ☺

ALSO BY K.C. WELLS

<u>Learning to Love</u>
Michael & Sean
Evan & Daniel
Josh & Chris
Final Exam

<u>Sensual Bonds</u>
A Bond of Three
A Bond of Truth

<u>Merrychurch Mysteries</u>
Truth Will Out
Roots of Evil
A Novel Murder

<u>Love, Unexpected</u>
Debt
Burden

<u>Dreamspun Desires</u>
The Senator's Secret
Out of the Shadows
My Fair Brady
Under the Covers

<u>Lions & Tigers & Bears</u>
A Growl, a Roar, and a Purr
A Snarl, a Splash, and a Shock

Love Lessons Learned
First
Waiting for You
Step by Step
Bromantically Yours
BFF

Collars & Cuffs
An Unlocked Heart
Trusting Thomas
Someone to Keep Me (K.C. Wells & Parker Williams)
A Dance with Domination
Damian's Discipline (K.C. Wells & Parker Williams)
Make Me Soar
Dom of Ages (K.C. Wells & Parker Williams)
Endings and Beginnings (K.C. Wells & Parker Williams)

Secrets – with Parker Williams
Before You Break
An Unlocked Mind
Threepeat
On the Same Page

Personal
Making it Personal
Personal Changes
More than Personal
Personal Secrets
Strictly Personal
Personal Challenges
Personal – The complete series

Confetti, Cake & Confessions
(FREE)

Christmas
Connections
Saving Jason
A Christmas Promise
The Law of Miracles
My Christmas Spirit
A Guy for Christmas
Dear Santa
Santa's Secrets

Island Tales
Waiting for a Prince
September's Tide
Submitting to the Darkness
Island Tales Vol 1 (Books #1 & #2)

Lightning Tales
Teach Me
Trust Me
See Me
Love Me

A Material World
Lace
Satin
Silk
Denim

Southern Boys
Truth & Betrayal
Pride & Protection
Desire & Denial
The Southern Boys Trilogy

Maine Men
Finn's Fantasy
Ben's Boss
Seb's Summer
Dylan's Dilemma
Shaun's Salvation
Aaron's Awakening
Levi's Love
Maine Men – the Complete Series

Salvation
Wrangled

Second Sight

In His Sights
In Plain Sight

CrossBow Protection (with Parker Williams)
Broken Warrior

Standalones
Kel's Keeper
Here For You
Sexting The Boss
Gay on a Train
Sunshine & Shadows
Double or Nothing
Back from the Edge
Switching it up
Out for You (FREE)
State of Mind (FREE)
No More Waiting (FREE)
Watch and Learn
My Best Friend's Brother
Princely Submission
Bears in the Woods
Holy Hell – with Parker Williams
Teasing Tim
Str8 B8

Anthologies

Fifty Gays of Shade
Winning Will's Heart

Come, Play
Watch and Learn

Writing as Tantalus
Damon & Pete: Playing with Fire
.

ABOUT THE AUTHOR

K.C. Wells lives on an island off the south coast of the UK, surrounded by natural beauty. She writes about men who love men, and can't even contemplate a life that doesn't include writing.

The rainbow rose tattoo on her back with the words 'Love is Love' and 'Love Wins' is her way of hoisting a flag. She plans to be writing about men in love - be it sweet or slow, hot or kinky - for a long while to come.

www.ingramcontent.com/pod-product-compliance
Lightning Source LLC
Chambersburg PA
CBHW020920020726
47495CB00002B/272